Ceae

D1104238

WHITE MYTHOLOGY

Two Novellas
By W.D. Clarke

WHITE

MYTHOLOGY

—SKINNER BOXED—

—LOVE'S ALCHEMY—

Two Novellas by W.D. Clarke

Copyright 2016 W.D. Clarke

ALL THAT IS SOLID PRESS

Ontario, Canada

Cover design & book typography by Dave Bricker

ISBN: 978-0-9917100-3-4

This is a work of fiction. Names, characters, places and incidents either are the product of the author's imagination or are used fictitiously, and any resemblance to actual persons, living or dead, events or locales is purely coincidental.

For my father, W.A. Clarke III

It began when Weissmann brought him to Europe: a discovery that love, among these men, once past the simple feel and orgasming of it, had to do with masculine technologies, with contracts, with winning and losing.

—Thomas Pynchon, *Gravity's Rainbow*

This tune goes manly.

—William Shakespeare, *Macbeth*

CONTENTS

SKINNER BOXED

Love's Alchemy

SKINNER
BOXED

WEDNESDAY

— XMAS PAST —

In the struggle, if that can be called a struggle in which the Ghost with no visible resistance on its own part was undisturbed by any effort of its adversary, Scrooge observed that its light was burning high and bright; and dimly connecting that with its influence over him, he seized the extinguisher-cap, and by a sudden action pressed it down upon its head. The Spirit dropped beneath it, so that the extinguisher covered its whole form; but though Scrooge pressed it down with all his force, he could not hide the light, which streamed from under it, in an unbroken flood upon the ground.

—Charles Dickens, *A Christmas Carol*

1

PURE BULL***T

D R. ED WOKE UP sweating and breathing heavily, and sat bolt upright, with an instant-on alertness that he had not experienced in years. His heart 'felt' dangerously fast, and he immediately 'thought' of his computer, which had recently been tampered with by his 'son' and whose CPU was now running 'overclocked'. There followed hard upon this naggingly recurrent worry a rumbling in Dr. Ed's lower abdomen, and he made an anxious dash for the master bedroom's en suite toilet.

The upshot of what disappeared into the downspout hardly deserved the appellation 'stool', and was not at all what Dr. Ed was accustomed to (firm, long, and in terms of odour, sweetly horse-like). Rather, today's effluent was a curious (and, as it would turn out, portentous) mixture of gas and, not quite metaphorically speaking, what his more nautically inclined colleagues termed 'black water'.

Naturally, Dr. Ed was not at all content to greet the dawn in such a disquieting manner as this. His wife, thankfully, had not been roused by his helpless bleating, honking and groaning. She also failed to be stirred by the subsequent, more quotidian noises of Dr. Ed completing the trinity of his morning ablutions with a shower and a shave. And she snored right through the sliding and banging of various dresser drawers and kitchen cupboards, through the dentist-drill-whine of the coffee grinder, and through the banal enthusiasms of the SNOOZE YOU LOSE morning show on 1040 CRUZ. She was a self-medicating sleep-walker and an enthusiast of the narcotic action of (both over-the-counter and prescription) nighttime cold and headache medications, and would not regain consciousness until she was good and ready.

After his coffee (psychotropic Honduran beans that came in smallish, cheap cellophane packs, which Dr. Ed's wife poured by the dozen into a large *Chock Full O' Nuts* tin and kept, erroneously, in the freezer—a continual replenishment of which was couriered to him on a regular basis by an ophthalmologist colleague who performed charity work in that Central American hot spot), Dr. Ed found that he had to go *again*. His subsequent visit was as unusual, as discomfiting and as murkily unfathomable as the first, but this second passing left him feeling temporarily less ill-at-ease, in relative terms, than before. But … relative … to what, exactly?

Oh, he calculated, he figured, as was his wont, that this nascent little 'situation' of his was somewhat analogous to the manner in which nicotine works its own small-scale 'wonders' on the central nervous systems of those habituated to its charms. That is, there is a momentary release of and relief from 'pressure', relief which is always accompanied by and predicated upon the knowledge, the *foreknowledge*, statistically speaking, that *more of the same* is assuredly *on its way*.

Like many of us, Dr. Ed was accustomed to spending more time in the washroom than was strictly necessary to the performance of the various bodily functions to which that part of every modern house is dedicated. And like many of us, Dr. Ed filled those 5-10 'extra minutes' a day with some unchallenging, often demulcent reading material. *Unlike* many of us, however, Dr. Ed had done the math, had crunched and digested the numbers involved, and had assimilated their significance: those 5-10 minutes of lavatorial seclusion equalled approximately 150-300 minutes a month, which worked out to about 30-60 hours per year, time literally wasted, sitting down, reading, to be honest, crap. Stool softeners for the constipated 'mind'. Unguents for those haemorrhoids of the soul. It made him shudder to 'think' of the number of *New England Journal of Medicine* and *Psychiatry Today* articles he had neglected to wrestle with over the years, favouring in their stead such frothily diverting and easily catabolised tales from the likes of the ubiquitous *John Bull* and its (somewhat less popular) sequel, *Commodore Commode*.

Today, however, Dr. Ed uncharacteristically if understandably eschewed these rough-but-ready, populist certitudes, in favour of several minutes of quiet reflection, reflection upon the arresting, rather unusual dream from which he had, not quite 30 minutes previously, so abruptly awoken.

Now, Dr. Ed was 'certainly not' the kind of 'frivolous charlatan' to get his patients wrapped up in the interpretation of the endless winding sheet of their dreams. For Dr. Ed, the entire field of psychotherapy was suspect, replete as it was with, as Dr. Ed put it, 'the frippery and quackery of feather-bedding timewasters'. Freudian, Jungian and other, more contemporary and trendy variants of depth psychology were 'beyond the pale'. They were relics from a pre-scientific pre-history, the almost-unrecognizable ancestral kin of 'proper psychiatry', of which he was a professor at the university and the department head at UNIVERSITY HOSPITAL. Truth be told, a small but statistically significant number of his patients had reported having considerable success with a ten-session course of Cognitive Therapy (which taught them the pragmatics of recognizing and refraining from acting upon pernicious, self-injurious 'thought' patterns), but then again a number of patients had reported having had success with a ten-session course of Rolfing too for G-dsake, so, well, go figure.

So Dr. Ed maintained no active professional interest in dreams, neither in the diagnostic fruits which are allegedly borne of their interpretation, nor in the therapeutic efficacy that supposedly arises from bringing them from the 'unconscious' to the 'conscious' 'mind'. Nor, it must be added, was he the least bit interested in either the form or the content of his *own* nocturnal narratives. Indeed, it was something of a personal joke of Dr. Ed's that Freud, that 'great' dream-reader (*Traumdeuter*), that puffed-up old spinner of yarns, had 'discovered' or rather imagined there was a connection between an adult individual's dream-states and the 'repressed' but psychically active traumas of childhood, and that the patient's dream was therefore the 'royal road to the unconscious'. And this *imagined* connection, as Dr. Ed saw it, was based upon some rather spurious etymologizing on Freud's part, or to use Freud's own terminology against him, upon some unconscious 'wish-fulfilment' of the late, great Viennese witch-doctor's. Freud may have considered himself a scientist, but Dr. Ed's pin had him wriggling in an entirely different collection of exotic specimens: amongst the family of august, Germanic theoreticians, the species of the 'professional' philologist. Like his forerunners Hegel and Nietzsche, Freud's reputation rested not so

much upon empirical research as upon the 'creative' misinterpre-
tation (the *Kleinamen*) of, and the invention of novel terminology
for, previously extant phenomena. Thus: the significance of the
dream (*das Traum*, a word of Old High German origin, a variant
of which is also found in Old Norse), in terms of both theory and
praxis, is for Dr. Ed's Freud inextricably linked to an etymological
consanguinity with the Ancient Greek *traumatikos*, or 'wound',
from which both the modern German *das Trauma* and the English
'trauma' are derived. In short, Freud was, or rather 'thought' he
was, lifting from the ancients again, and dreams are old traumas
that present themselves in disguised or displaced form, so as to
prevent injury to their dreamer.

This was all just pure bull***t, of course.

Dr. Ed had only taken two courses in which Freud had even
been *mentioned*: he had had one-half of a lecture on Freud in
an undergraduate arts elective course (A History of Western
Thought: From Plato to Nato); and 'The Case of Anna O.' was
the subject of a two-hour seminar in History of Psychiatry I
in med school, but Dr. (then just plain) Ed hadn't read the text, and
the presenter had succeeded in inducing much needed sleep, and
etc. etc. But any fool knew that dreams are randomly produced by
the pons or primitive part of the brain as a by-product of the initiation of REM sleep, and ... and, for G-dsakes, that was, G-dammit,
that: that was all the hell there was to it.

But today, this lumbering dream of his own held him in what was for Dr. Ed a kind of Gothic thrall, held him in that mixture of credulity, scepticism and involuntary awe experienced by a child viewing, back to back, *Godzilla* and *Godzilla vs. Megalon*, a double bill on the small screen for a grey, late autumn Saturday afternoon. There, giddiness tag-teamed with dread, and brute freedom was, if endangered, always dangerous. And yet it was still to be prized, prized above all else. And what if an entire city of concrete and tarmac had to be destroyed in the process? The human world, revealed as a prison-house of bureaucratic unreason (intuitively understood as such even by the pubescent, nascent Dr. Ed), deserved to be razed to the ground, didn't it, after all? But after all, after all the bullets, mortars and missiles (greedily consumed by young Ed as so much tea, so many cakes and ices), after all the name calling and cursing, it was discovered that the beast was our servant—nay—our ally and protector! Godzilla would defend to the death—he would!—the very human civilization which had sought to destroy him! He *was* our friend, he was our friend *indeed*, but no, he could not be tamed!

For the first time in years, Dr. Ed remembered having dreamt; he had forgotten the details, but, significantly, he remembered the '*feeling*': the sensation of a peculiar kind of presence, the presence of a kind of absence, in the thoracic region of his anterior body, slightly to the left of midline. And although it was definitely an *absence* that he sensed, it was not as if he was lacking anything that he had had the night before. Rather, it was as if the dream had been a sea creature that had briefly come ashore, and had laid an egg—a hollow egg—in his chest, and had then departed, leaving him to be the incubator of a (parasitic?) nullity. What's more, he found himself 'thinking' about this Leviathan and imagining its shape, its proportions and features, from time to time throughout the morning. He'd admired it, had stared semi-consciously at its jagged outline for those couple of minutes on the can, but then it crouched away, back to the anterior regions of his 'mind' as he brushed his teeth, where it lingered, teasingly, while he searched for and eventually located the diaspora of items he required for his journey to work—his hospital security pass, his wallet, his keys, his gloves, his galoshes, his hat.

The dream's tail-end boldly surfaced three more times, indeed: the first was when he took a brush to his shoes for a quick spiffing-up at the front door; the second was shortly thereafter, when he remembered that he had forgotten his DAY-TIMER upstairs and dashed up to retrieve it (the DAY-TIMER was lying on his bed-side table, and there he once more encountered his still-sleeping and evidently faithful wife, and proceeded to give her his usual, casual valedictory kiss on the forehead); the third occurred in his car, a (for North America) rare PEUGEOT 405 sedan. Dr. Ed was driving along Highway 2 to the hospital, and once more, and for a few teraseconds only, it flashed its serpentine luminosity towards him as he sipped coffee from a wide-bottomed travel mug and returned to the morning show with DJ Carl di Souze on AM1040. By the time he became aware of the dream's sudden reappearance it had already departed, already retreated to its unfathomable lair, where it hibernated all day, awaiting the night.

2

RUN-OF-THE-MILL

BUT THEN AGAIN: that morning, from 08:00 until noon, Dr. Ed, very much the active choleric and not at all the contemplative melancholic, saw 15½ patients, each of whom was granted 0.25 hours of his time. 8 of these were run-of-the-mill exogenous depressives, female, all on tricyclics, all now relatively stable, and all fat. 2 were bipolar endogenous males, both in their early 40s, one of whom was setting sales records at the ailing firm of UNDERWOOD OLIVETTI, while the other was driven to his appointment by his mother, with whom he lived.

One of the low-lights of the forenoon was a patience-trying but admittedly intriguing pair of pre-pubescent male twins, whose parents were both psychologists and, he guessed, both completely insane. Dr. Ed wisely insisted upon interviewing the progeny separately from the progenitors. The parents elected to go first, and were all business. They instructed Dr. Ed upon the overdetermined hornet's nest of reasons why the twins had set fire to the middle school cafeteria the day before. What it all boiled down to, however, Dr. Ed learned, was that the twins had simply over-reacted to a commission of grave injustice against them: they had been 'caught' by their English teacher 'plagiarizing' each other's work, and the teacher had made matters worse for herself by drawing the class's attention to the brothers' symbiotic learning partnership, and by insisting upon giving them a '0' for the assignment in question. It was all very plain and clear, as the parents then informed Dr. Ed of their intention to sue the local school board for creating a learning environment that was injurious to their sons' self-esteem, and wanted Dr. Ed to issue a statement in support of their claims.

Upon interviewing the twins, Dr. Ed discovered that the boys harbored a number of grievances, all of which departed quite significantly from the outline described by their sperm-and egg-donors. First of all, there was a woeful lack of choice of dessert items in the cafeteria, which was run by 'dog-faced old cows' who spoke like the poor people who, in fact, they were. Second, the school was 'friggin' old and grimy', and, although there was indeed a nice shiny new one not far from where the boys lived, it was (by bureaucratic edict, this much was true) in a different school catchment area *entirely*. The third reason was related to the second, but Dr. Ed put it down to proleptic sexual posturing on the boys' (who were not yet twelve) part: apparently, the 'bitches' at their school were 'poor, butt-ugly pancakes', while the ones at the new school were 'juicin' and 'ripe for breakin'-in', and the boys wanted to get to the new school as quickly as could be.

Dr. Ed then showed the boys to the waiting room, entered the nurse's station via another door, wrote in their files a quick preliminary diagnosis of attention deficit disorder and *possible* severe personality disorder (for further study, thrice weekly), scribbled a prescription for *Haldol* and *Ritalin*, and told his nurse to inform the parents that the boys should take the medication until further notice, that he would pull as many strings as he could to get their sons into a special clinic for 'Gifted-At-Risk' children in the City, and that he would indeed be sending a letter both to the Principal and to the school board.

Dr. Ed then returned to his office (with no immediate intention to follow through on any of the above), closed his door, and took a couple of deep breaths. 2½ more appointments until lunch, 2 of which were heartbreaking, because they involved medication-resistant teenage-onset schizophrenics. Dr. Ed made a mental note to have Nurse Sloggett schedule all future appointments with them for earlier in the day, if possible. The appointment with the ½, on the other hand, was always a good way to round out a morning, for she was a pleasant patient of some years standing, a privately paying queue-jumper. She was also a pharmaceutical tourist and (for the last six months, anyhow) a self-diagnosed multiple personality disorder whose other half consistently failed to show. She and Dr. Ed would usually revert to discussing such matters as current and forthcoming FDA trials and recent drug patents until their time ran out. She was an eccentric, assuredly, but a consistently harmless, harmlessly consistent one. She listened 'thoughtfully' to what he had to say, was polite in her manner of questioning, and showed due deference to the profession. And so he was thankful for her, for his ½. Ah, *if only* (he had often said to her at the close of a congenially fruitless session), if only there were more patients like her, the world would be a far, far saner place!

Dr. Ed smiled that sad smile, the one that meant 'I'm sorry, but our time is up for this week', and, as this last patient quitted his chambers, he allowed himself a little sigh. He was not big on sighs, as a rule, and did not enjoy placing himself in too-close proximity to those who were. Sighing connoted, amongst other things, inertia, and Dr. Ed was *not* big on inertia. Now, there were a number of things that Dr. Ed was not big on, and one day around Xmas two years ago, after an unpleasant row concerning his wife's enthusiasm for Daytime Drama, his wife made up a list of these dislikes, and wrote them, without title or heading, upon the dry-erase grocery list board in the kitchen, with a blue permanent marker:

CATS MUSHROOMS PHYSICAL DISABILITY
SMALL TOWNS   LOUD MUSIC   TEARS (ESP. HERS)
    DANDELIONS   AGGRESSIVE FEMALES

  CHRYSLER CARS   UNIONS   SPORTS

CONTROVERSY, ARGUMENT, 'EMOTIONAL' DISPLAYS OF
  ANY KIND WHATSOEVER

IMITATION LEATHER GERMAN OPERA
  EVANGELICAL MINISTERS

ANYTHING **SHE** WATCHES ON TV

TELEMARKETERS   POLITICIANS   CIVIL SERVANTS

SPIRITUAL PEOPLE, STREET PEOPLE, FAT PEOPLE,
  LOUD PEOPLE, BALD PEOPLE, MESSY PEOPLE,
  IMMIGRANT PEOPLE, FOREIGN PEOPLE, OLD PEOPLE,
  YOUNG PEOPLE, LITTLE PEOPLE, SICK PEOPLE,
  WEAK PEOPLE, OTHER PEOPLE

PEOPLE!!

 HIM

  HER

    THEM

        US

        THIS

Dr. Ed was not too keen on *that*, either, but said nothing to his wife (or to anyone else) about it. It was probably the Seven Year Itch, if one could believe in such a thing. Whatever it was, he knew that it, too, like so much else in life, would pass.

He was right, of course (he always was). It did.

3

DISPASSIONATE

NOW, DR. ED WAS NOT a particularly bigoted man. And he did have his sensitive side. He would never confess to it openly, but that list of his wife's did in fact hurt him, and deeply—but, of course, only briefly. He was not the type to carry grudges long, and he would never, ever have done, or do, anything like that, to her. It was both bitter and vindictive, what she did, and it bore the tell-tale mark of *Schadenfreude*—a word he liked the sound of, denoting a 'feeling' he never, ever allowed himself to feel. However, knowing Dr. Ed and his legendarily even temper, his wife's mendacious little act could not have given her very much pleasure at all. Perhaps, he considered, it was all a result of those new diet pills....

But no, Dr. Ed was not a particularly bigoted man. And as for that list of hers: as a chronicle of dislikes, it was more or less accurate, give or take a few items, and leaving out the maudlin attempt at character assassination at the end. But dislike is a broad kind of word, capable of embracing a good many gradations and levels, and if Dr. Ed disliked anything, it was the sloppy kind of 'thinking' that his wife had employed when she grouped all of those things together like that, as if they were all equal, as if they all had the same *valence*.

Take street people. Just as there are a great many kinds of people who live on the street, all with their own reasons for living there, so too would one have a great variety of reactions to them, if one had taken the opportunity to acquaint oneself with, say, John-by-the-liquor-store, or Joe-outside-the-bank, or Jane-with-dog-and-kid.

Now, one might happen to get to know, and to like *or* to dislike, any or all or none of them *qua* individuals. But in the abstract, as part of the seething mass of humanity, one would be obliged — one *is* obliged — to enter into an entirely different kind of relationship. It would be exceedingly difficult for anyone to 'like' street people, in this sense. One would either dislike *them*, generally (for their shiftlessness, for getting in one's way, for not pulling themselves up by bootstraps both personal and various, etc., etc.), or one would dislike the abstract *situation* (bad luck, personal crises, the free-market political economy, blahblahblah….) that brought them to their … station … in life. One *might* even be inclined toward compassion, but suffer from an initial sense of aversion which is — Dr. Ed would of course refrain from using the term 'instinctual', but he would readily admit that one's character is complex, and not always identical with what one would *like* to 'think' of oneself. And then there is *biology* to contend with—ahh, biology! And so the truth, Dr. Ed would maintain, is always a little darker, always a few shades more opaque, than one would prefer to admit....

But that list of his wife's *was* a cruel, low blow, wasn't it? If his wife 'felt' all warm and fuzzy about the homeless, well, that was just swell—& super, terrific, well done. But a more honest person would admit that one didn't always feel that way. Or take 'aggressive females', which was also on the list: *that* was supposed to signify that Dr. Ed was a misogynist, but nothing could be further from the truth. For truth is borne out by behaviour, not by inclination, and Dr. Ed had always behaved most professionally towards any female, aggressive or not, and had treated with dignity and respect all of his patients and colleagues, be they male or female (and, for that matter, Chinese or Hindoo). No, Dr. Ed's behaviour was impeccably gender- (as well as race-) 'blind'.

The truth is that a great many people in this dark, unreasonable world behave unreasonably, and Dr. Ed knew that it was his job to act, rather, as a beacon of light. One must tolerate people, give them the space to perform their irrational antics, allow them their moments of perverse insistence on this/that/the other, and, so long as no harm is done and such demands do not prove to conflict with one's own rationally considered priorities, one should allow such people to get their way, and to *let them see what good it does them*. For nothing is to be gained from forcing a showdown over an issue in which one does not really have a ... *personal* stake.

Dr. Ed was proud of the fact that he had, at the hospital at least, a reputation of dispassionate fair-mindedness. Once, when the female residents had exerted a not-insignificant amount of pressure upon him, with the aim of the establishment of a quota system for gender equity as regards the department's hiring practices, he gently reminded them that professional expertise would be the *sole* criterion employed by the search committee, of which he was chairman. The complainants were, of course, quite angry with this, but when it turned out that the next two vacancies were filled with extremely capable females, their resentment was replaced with a renewed and deepened respect for their department head. Everyone thus grew to understand that Dr. Ed was the kind of man who listened, who assessed each situation based upon what he considered to be its merits, and who acted accordingly. No politicking, no favouritism, no guff.

And the department had been rolling smoothly along ever since.

Take this more recent example: just the other day, a longstanding patient, a particularly shrill woman whom Nurse Sloggett had named 'The Emu', had walked right through Reception and into his office—without an appointment, of course. She'd slammed the door on her way in, and it was most fortunate that Dr. Ed was in-between patients at the time, for he had a number of quite withdrawn and disturbed individuals on his card that particular morning, all of whom he had just started treating with an experimental new drug *Alba* (which targets the brain receptors for 'feelings' of overwhelming guilt, burden or loss) as part of a Phase Ib clinical trial for the pharmaceutical giant EUMETA PLC. Anyhow, the Emu was herself evidently deep into a manic phase, and she shouted that she had stopped taking her lithium because it had made her gain weight. Unfazed by her melodramatic entrance, Dr. Ed calmly explained to her that while it was *possible* that lithium was the culprit, it was more likely the Imipramine. She listened, he elucidated, she nodded, he proposed, she agreed, he explained, soothed, reassured. It was all over in less than 5 minutes, and when he genially sent her on her way, she thanked him, and held in her hand a EUMETA exercise and diet plan, as well as prescriptions for *Alba* and lithium, both of which she would get, as a newly-minted participant in the clinical trial, free of charge.

4

SANTA CLAUSTROPHOBIA

D R. ED'S SIGH was a relatively shallow one, shallow at both ends of the respiratory cycle. It just barely agitated the 'egg' in Dr. Ed's chest, and would most likely have gone unnoticed by anyone else in the room, if anyone else had been in the room. But Dr. Ed was alone. It was quite nearly noon.

Dr. Ed made a quick call home to see if his wife had yet hoisted herself towards the vertical. Getting no answer, he left no message on the answering machine, hung up the phone, swivelled his chair 90 degrees to face his computer, and logged on to UNIVERSITY HOSPITAL's Unix server.

```
USERNAME: EDWARD_B@UGH.ORG
PASSWORD: PAVLOV
```

His e-mail in-box was full of quotidian effluvia: hospital safety bulletins, university staff postings, calls for papers, drug company propaganda. He typed ctrl-s for 'select all', and was about to type ctrl-d when he spotted a sender who was not one of the usual suspects: fraser@hoteldieu.org. Hôtel Dieu was the Catholic hospital on the other side of town, and Dr. Ed didn't know anyone named Fraser personally, there or anywhere else. He knew *of* a Fraser Keith, a local oncologist, and of course there was Fraser Arnott, who headed up OB/GYN at his own hospital, but neither of them could want to speak to him for any imaginable reason. Who could it be?

He opened up the file, whose Subject line contained only:

RE:

The message read:

SEE YOU AT THE HOLISTIC EXPO?

Holistic bolistic, Dr. Ed 'thought', and then wrote an equally terse reply:

DO I KNOW YOU?

And sent the message on its way. Wasting no more time on the lamentable contraption, Dr. Ed logged off, shut the computer down, pushed the palms of his hands into his thighs, levered himself upright, removed his white smock, hung it upon the coat tree by the door, retrieved his waist-length *Barbour* oil-cloth coat and his tweed hat, put on his galoshes, and stuck his head through the door that led to the nurse's station.

—Back at 13:00, he needlessly reminded Nurse Sloggett, who was a *particularly* aggressive female in her mid-forties, and who had proven herself to be as admirably intractable as a Tiger Tank in her capacity of Gatekeeper for the 9 years that Dr. Ed had been Senior Consultant here, something which he had commemorated without fail every birthday (May 12) and Xmas, with suitably expensive tokens of his professional esteem. He even kept a list in his filing cabinet of these presents, to make sure that he did not erroneously repeat himself, as used to be his wont, for Dr. Ed knew that he was not a man of too very much spontaneity, and would likely commit just such a *faux pas* again if he did not organize himself into behaving otherwise.

The list was at that very moment languishing at the bottom of Dr. Ed's teakwood 'To-Do Box' (itself a gift of an Xmas Past—ca. 1991—from his wife), and this was because we were now into the second week of Advent, and Dr. Ed's P.I.M. or Personal Information Manager program, *Orgtastic!!* (which was—perversely, given what Dr. Ed 'thought' of the Church—still, out of habit, programmed to display the feasts of the Roman Catholic liturgical year) had reminded him of this fact. And Dr. Ed needed reminding, for he had made it a practice—ca. 1967—of limiting his 'thinking' about his lack of church-going to twice-yearly, at Xmas and Easter, and limiting his actual attendance to precisely never. His wife's own attendance at her Pentecostal Fellowship Centre was sporadic, but, all-in-all, less virtual.

Dr. Ed's master list read:

	NURSE		**WIFE**	
Year	Birthday	Xmas	Birthday	Xmas
1985	Flowers	Hickory Farms Basket	Emerald Ring	Longines Watch
1986	Chocolates	Fruit Basket	Charm Bracelet	Fur Coat
1987	Parker Pen Set	Picture Frame	Dishwasher	Washer/Dryer
1988	Movie Passes (4)	Bath Gift Basket	Gas Stove	Microwave/ Convection Oven
1989	Car Wash Passes (10)	Dinner for 2	VCR	TV (27")
1990	Dinner for 2	Dinner for 2	Mobile Phone	Radar Detector
1991	$100 Gift Certificate	$200 Gift Certificate	TV (bedroom)	$100 Gift Certificate
1992	Gold Necklace	Chanel Dress	Gold Necklace	Chanel Dress
1993	Sapphire Broach	t.b.a.	Sapphire Broach	t.b.a.

It was ca. 1991, when he was *particularly* busy—finishing a
PhD in Behavioural Psychology (to beef up the federal research
grant potential of his MD (FRSC) in Psychiatry), establishing his
corporate Operations Research consultancy firm, SYNOMICS, as
well as negotiating with the hospital for sufficient office space
to facilitate the integration of his research, his private practice
and the training of his numerous residents & post-doc fellows,
all of whom also required more-than-merely-adequate research
facilities—that Dr. Ed had first had the brainwave of conserving
his gift-hunting ideas and energies by giving his wife and nurse
identical presents. At the time it had just made sense; he knew
that he and his wife were stuck in some kind of mysterious rut,
and needed out of it—somehow, anyhow. A little voice in Dr. Ed's
head told him it was necessary to send *her* the message that *she*
was important in *his* life, regardless of what had apparently transpired between them, whatever it was. That little voice told him
to move past recrimination, toward reconciliation; the question
was, though, the obvious one: how?

Whenever he 'thought' of his wife, he 'thought' only of their
apparently many, unfathomable problems, not of any solution to
them. His marriage was a vast splotchy blackness, both a stultify-
ingly opaque Rorschach test and a regrettable (yet perhaps inevitable) stain on the otherwise impeccable white linen suit that was
his professional life—that is, his life.

This was when Dr. Ed had his brainwave. It was so simple, he wondered why he hadn't 'thought' of it before: whenever he wanted to 'think' of his wife, he would 'think' of Nurse Sloggett instead. He would then *transfer* any warm, thankful, unconfused (yet Platonic) 'feelings' that he had for Nurse Sloggett onto his wife, and thus succeed in behaving *at home* the way he behaved at work: that is, calmly, rationally—and fairly. The plan was simple, and brilliantly conceived. And, whenever so deployed, thus far, it had worked.

Dr. Ed paused in his doorway for a moment to consider Nurse Sloggett. Unlike his wife, she was a bit homely, neither beautiful nor ugly. Unlike his wife, she was stout, solid, neither fat nor thin, and that ravager, time, had taken very little away from her looks, such as they were. And, again, unlike his wife, she was an efficient bundle of energy, a real facilitator, someone who ironed out the wrinkles in that impeccable white linen suit of his. Dr. Ed was thankful for Nurse Sloggett. What would he ever do without her?

5

WHOSE DISEMBODIED HEAD

NURSE SLOGGETT NODDED a wordless of course/goodbye at Dr. Ed, whose disembodied head then retreated as suddenly through the door's narrow opening as it had arrived. Dr. Ed then left his office the back way, towards the service elevator.

The physical plant of UNIVERSITY HOSPITAL was, for a Canadian institution of this sort, a relatively handsome one — from the outside. It had been completed in the late 1960s, when the infrastructural enthusiasm of the post-war boom (having collided with the twin evils of increasingly bear-minded markets and parsimonious — and usurious — central banks everywhere) was just beginning to draw to a close. The dour limestone of the original building, a building that could be numbered among the country's oldest, was at that time dwarfed by (rather than supplemented with) a new addition, which was conceived by the very same architects who were charged with updating the central post office. Its confident, modernist façade was a collage of granite, aluminum and glass that emphasised rather than diminished its essential boxiness, with prominent rectangular panels and bold vertical lines.

The hospital addition had not aged too well, however. To be honest, even when new it had suited the conceptual aspirations of its architect somewhat more fully than the workaday needs of its subsequent inhabitants; but now, in 1993, it was just plain old. You would not know it if you were somehow spirited directly into Dr. Ed's dominion ('Old Building', 4th floor, F-wing, avoiding the crumbling plaster in E-wing, climbing past outmoded Radiology and dank (with 'non-functional' air-conditioning) Geriatrics on level 2, circumspectly skirting the horror that was nominally the Cafeteria on level 3 — whose state of repair was so very much 'temporarily inoperative' (its steam generating plant was now essentially shot, and the kitchen! Well, all meals were trucked in from the City, over 150 km away, weren't they?)) that, had you taken a wrong turn and somehow ended up surrounded by a bank of microwaves that filled three walls in a U-shaped alcove, all of which were re-reheating melamine bowlfuls of re-reconstituted dehydrated mashed potato flakes, well, let's just say that you would have been glad you were, like the lucky game-piece landing on the first corner of the Monopoly board, 'just visiting'.

But if you somehow bypassed all of that and found yourself, again, somehow, inside Dr. Ed's private fiefdom, you would see something altogether different. The sallow tiling of the past had been replaced with a pleasing, padded blue carpet throughout. Painted-shut windows had given way to tinted Argon-filled double-glazing. Back-breaking wooden chairs from 1945 had been sold off to the local school board, and staff and clients alike now perched contentedly atop lumbar, thorax and cervical spine-sparing ergonomic wonders. Green X-ray death machine CRT terminals had finally met their maker, and no-glare, low-EMF monitors now stood in their stead, switching themselves on and off and notifying maintenance as needed, as did the HEPA-quality air filtering/conditioning system and the full-spectrum overhead lighting. The entire floor had been treated to a retrofitting with fibre-optic cable, and every computer was linked to the university's Unix-based network. Dr. Ed's department was a hospital within a hospital, the wealth and refinement of civilised Rome at the centre of an increasingly neglected and therefore chaotic Empire.

A few other departments had followed Dr. Ed's lead in courting private sector monies. The Fertility Clinic was a good example, as was Physiotherapy. Ophthalmology was a contender, and though the Biotechnology lab in the basement was only just now catching on, it was said to be 'making great strides'. But the vast bulk of the facility remained neglected, and the hospital was, in turn (so Dr. Ed 'felt') thereby neglecting its patients.

Shooting out of the service elevator at ground zero, Dr. Ed moved rapidly through the Los Alamos post-blast landscape of Emerg. Acoustic ceiling tiles were missing; wires were hanging down; the walls on the north side had been given one coat of a purplish gray two years ago, while the south facing wall retained its original ear-wax beige. The corridor was littered with gurneys, and as he rounded the corner into Admissions, he encountered the usual congestion. Dozens of mothers and fathers, all with children in tow, were packed into the waiting room, all low-priority no-family-doctor influenza broken bone, etc., etc. cases. Dozens more milled about in the foyer, waiting their turn to be seen by the triage nurse before they could be allowed to wait their turn for a randomly multiple number of Medicare hours. Dr. Ed wove his way through them all with the speed, grace, and inexorability of an Yvan Cournoyer or a Guy Lafleur skating across the opposing team's blue line.

Dr. Ed paused before entering the revolving door to the outside to look back, having noticed his psychiatric colleague and golfing partner, Bernie Berenstein, looking at a file. Dr. Ed remembered that he had promised, and had forgotten, to take Bernie's on-call on Monday. That wasn't like him, forgetting like that.

Luckily, nothing had come of it, and today, today was, well, today was another day.

Today was Wednesday. Wednesday, December 8th, 1993. It was both the anniversary of the Buddha's enlightenment and a Roman Catholic feast day, the Feast of the Immaculate Conception. *Orgtastic!!* had reminded him of these facts with a sound file of his own choosing, sampled and programmed by his 'son' several months ago, not long after they had first made contact. The piece was from Pergolesi's *Stabat Mater* (*not* Christopher Hogwood's commendable, all-digital 1989 release, recorded on period instruments with The Academy of Ancient Music, but the miraculous 1981 recording by Lamberto Gardelli, with the Ladies of The Hungarian Radio and Television Chorus — Dr. Ed knew his music, alright). But ah, ah yes, 'Inflammatus':

Inflammatus et accensus	Be to me, O virgin, nigh
per te, Virgo, sim defensus	lest in flames I burn and die
in die judicii.	in his awful judgement day.

In the old days, in the *very* old days, a long, long, long time before he was *Dr.* Ed, Dr. Ed used to fast on Fridays (to mark Our Lord's Passion) as well as on major feast days such as this. But that was in the old days. These days, he (most certainly) did not.

6

FREE WILL

D R. ED WORKED so close to the downtown core that he didn't
need to drive his car to go out for lunch. He didn't need
to—he liked to. And he often did. But who wouldn't, if they too
owned a (red) 1993 MAZDA RX-7? The MAZDA RX-7 is arguably
the best production sports car in the world. After all, if you can't
hear it screaming 'Drive Me! Now!' at you, brother, then you
should just go get yourself a G-ddamn hearing aid, or go in for
some voluntary euthanasia. Cos' the RX-7 *rocks*.

So why wasn't Dr. Ed driving to lunch?

6a.) Voluntary Internal Combustion

(i.) *Carpe Diem*. These early December days were just *too*
beautiful: sunshine, blue skies, temperatures in the low
single digits. Not exactly Indian summer, but pretty well
the next best thing, given that November had been unusually Novemberish, with rain on 22 or so of its 30 days. And

while today was just like yesterday, which was pretty much like the day before, who knew how long it would last? *Carpe Diem*. And as Dr. Ed walked briskly eastward along Bagot St., which neatly bisected City Park and led him past some charming red brick century homes, resident blue jays scrapped with non-migrating grackles at the birdfeeders. Both were ignored by the chickadees, who jumped around the branches of the leafless maple, oak and chestnut trees and chirped their optimistic little dittie-dee-dee-dees while gray and black squirrels darted hither & thither, rushing to build up their stores for the long winter ahead. Little meteorological receptors in their brains told them there would be major storms in everyone's future, while Dr. Ed's 'thoughts' tended to the present (and, to the extent that that ol' egg-in-his-chest could force itself upon his pragmatic attention, to the past). As he walked east along Bagot St., there was also almost no wind to speak of; what little there was was content just to nuzzle up against the left side of Dr. Ed's neck, gently, as a lover might.

(ii.) That awesome RX-7 was being prepared for winter hibernation by Dr. Ed's handyman, Perry. The wheels were being taken off, the oil changed, the gas tank filled, and then the whole thing was to be put up on blocks, and covered in a white sheet. He could've gotten away with driving it a few more weeks with weather like this, but why chance it? Dr. Ed was reduced to driving his clunker, his winter beater, a 1989 PEUGEOT 405, whose electrics (in particular the heated seats) were always going up the spout. As for Dr. Ed's wife, she, for the record, drove a '92 GMC Suburban, year-round.

(iii.) That dream, that dream.

6b.) The Enigma of the Unfinished Bowl of Soup

Dr. Ed was observed arriving at his customary haunt, BUDDY'S LITE BITE (EST'D. 1973), at his usual time, 12:15, and sat alone at his usual table, where the east-facing wall met the south-facing window. He then duly received, without having to place an order, his usual meal, the Soup'r Sandwich special, which, for him, always featured a toasted (not grilled) Reuben-esque, with horseradish and mustard, no butter. Buddy (his real name) always used genuine (that is, live, not canned or bottled, but sold in litre-sized milk cartons) sauerkraut flown in especially from Tancook Island, Nova Scotia. For Dr. Ed, and Dr. Ed alone, Buddy kept a stash of real Emmenthal cheese, from Basel via LOBLAWS grocers, with which to smother the hot corned beef of his *best* customer— Dr. Ed. Buddy did so not because Dr. Ed could tell the difference (he couldn't), but because of their shared history: they had known each other since that best time of their lives (according to Buddy), Kindergarten and Elementary school. From nap-time on brightly coloured towels to their first double-date, going to the grade six church hockey league sock-hop with the seventh-grader Quigley twins, Bud-n-Ed had been famously, intricately intermeshed, like *Velcro*. And if their interests and activities had largely separated these two-halves-of-a-whole ever since, oh, about grade eight (Buddy's path had taken him, at nineteen, to the east coast and into the Navy and onto the frigate HMCS YUKON, where he had earned his chops as short order cook, bon-vivant and lady-killer), they still maintained great affection for one another, as both would—with great jocularity—attest.

But Buddy would really mean it.

Buddy was too good-natured, too authentically *happy* to ever compare himself to his friends. Even when he was down, Buddy was (comparatively speaking) up, and his moments of introspection only descended to 'wistful', never towards 'plaintive', and certainly never approaching 'morbid'. As Dr. Ed saw it, however, Buddy needed clinical help, and fast. By Dr. Ed's estimation, Buddy was by this point in his life aging at twice the rate of his pals. He was alarmingly rotund, nearly spherical—and it did not help matters that he wore his short-sleeve perma-press shirts untucked, so that it looked like he was wearing a tent. He was completely bald on top, but his hair was all shag-carpetty on the sides, with lamb-chop sideburns to boot, and his skin was, well, funny, full of splotches and unevennesses, cliffs, crags, scree & craters.

But ask anyone, Digger over there, anyone. Buddy was one funny guy, should've been on TV, a real character, so many stories.... Take nine years ago for instance. Now *that* was a knee-slapper, man-o-man. See, Ed comes into the LITE BITE, babe in tow; Buddy hasn't seen him in what, fifteen, sixteen years? Not since '67, when the whole gang had piled into Buddy's van and they'd all flown, as high as Sputnik they was, down the highway to Expo, in Montreal.

What times, eh? Who was that fox Ed was with then? Agnes or somebody, from the island or something. But anyway, now, presto! It's 19-eighty-*whatever* and here Ed is again, appearing out of Nowheresville, unannounced, announcing to Buddy that he's going to marry this new babe he's got hanging — and I mean *hanging* — offa-his-arm, and she's *real class*, you know what I mean? From the City, and who'da thunk it but would Buddy like to be Ed's Best Man?

—Are you, Buddy had said, are you kidding? I mean, Jesus! Darling, did you know that I've known Eddy Haskell here since....

—It's Dr. Ed now, Dr. Ed's fiancée had said.

—How's his bedside manner these days, anyway?

—I wouldn't know. I'm his fiancée.

—Pleased ta meetcha, I'm Chef Boiardi.

Chef Boiardi, can you believe that? That Buddy's a riot, a regular riot, what a maroon.

When the Phase 1b trials for *Alba* had been awarded to his department, Dr. Ed had immediately 'thought' of Buddy. He would be perfect, Dr. Ed figured, for this drug, for part of its 'mandate' was aimed at just such sub-clinical, functional patients as his friend: those who 'get by' from day to day, those who experience no major, incapacitating crises, but whose diagnostic profile placed them significantly outside the first standard deviation.

Dr. Ed's wife, with that list of hers, was spot on about his 'feelings' as regards fat people, though. Dr. Ed couldn't help the physical revulsion that he 'felt'; it came from ... well, wherever those kinds of things come from. Of course, he never let it show in public, but fat people also moved him to a profound state of pity, for they could be counted among what he considered to be 'the truly helpless'. They could exercise all they wanted; they could diet, stomach staple and liposuction themselves until they were eviscerated versions of their former beings, but none of that mattered. None of it mattered because it was all so very much short-term; long term change, though, was fundamentally a question of will-power, and—it must be said—fat people (like most people, actually) just did not have any. They did not possess any such magical power because will-power is largely a function of—an epiphenomenon of—brain chemistry. And that's where *Alba* came in.

Dr. Ed's hypothesis/hunch went further, and one sunny day, when the café was pretty much empty, he had explained it all to Buddy, with that famous tone of voice that he had, that stealthily reassuring, calm-yet-resolute, indefatigable voice, the voice that convinced you that dispassionate reason must be your buckler and shield, your one refuge and your only shepherd in life. *Listen up*, that voice said: *reason* must appear to you as a *guide star*.

Like most funny men, and like many fat-but-functional people (Dr. Ed had gently said, in a tone as placid as a bowl of evaporated skim milk set down before an eight-week-old kitten), Buddy concealed a deep sadness, sadness hidden somewhere below the surface of those roiling high spirits, sadness concealed beneath all of that excessively pronounced adipose tissue—and, surely, Buddy being a man's man after all, would agree that no amount of ... of *therapy* (that is, undignified whining and peevish whingeing, as well as the subsequent, expensive and infinite analysis of previous sessions of whingeing & whining) would ever uproot it. It would never be uprooted because, fundamentally, there was nothing to uproot. Buddy's sadness, as complex and overdetermined as it might seem at first glance, was at least two removes away from its first cause. At one remove away were all of those experiences (storms, floods, heat waves, drought) which had accompanied Buddy's transition from acorn into massive oak. The important thing, however, was to look at the structure of the oak itself, and to thereby discover what the original acorn had most likely been lacking, what nature had given it a surfeit of, and what lay within the normal range....

Anyhow, that deep sadness was hindering Buddy from being the Buddy that only Buddy could be. Sure, Buddy had a good little business going with the LITE BITE, but there was something lacking, wasn't there? *There was*, and Buddy had tearfully but briefly confessed that which he had always dreamed of, but of which had proved himself forever incapable: of sharing his life with someone, with ... his very own *Special Lady*. And Buddy had always, since he had first gone to sea, longed for a real family to be part of, to be the benevolent patriarch of and breadwinner for. His dreams were populated with the tantalizing images and sounds of an elusive, warmly bustling hearth and home. Oh, how he wanted to be surrounded by children, by cats, by dogs, by laundry and chores, by school projects and report cards, by bruised knees and 'feelings', by the first dates and first loves of his first born! Oh, he had wanted it so, *so* badly—but of course, in the course of time he had given up, knowing that it would or could never come. Whereas in the past his motto (taken from a pop song by the band Trooper—'I'm here for a good time, not a long time') had made women come-and-go into-and-out-of his life to the diurnal rhythm of sunset-to-sunrise, now he seemed to have entered a long winter-seem-ing summer's night of passively just-being, of emptiness and loneliness, and of all manner of other words, all ending in -esses.

It hadn't taken much, in the end, for Dr. Ed to convince Buddy to take part in the *Alba* clinical trial; Buddy's personal motivation aside, Buddy was also easily led by those he held in high esteem, and Buddy's esteem for his old pal Dr. Ed was stratospheric. Buddy had booked an appointment with Nurse Sloggett the very next day; Dr. Ed had instructed her to place Buddy in the 'third quartile'. And Buddy? He was 'fan-tastic, just-super, never-happier'. *Alba* was, he was sure, 'a for-sure, frigging bloody miracle'. He'd even dropped a few pounds.

The Reuben sandwich always came with a cup of the daily soup, of course, whichever it happened to be, and while a full bowl was only 95¢ extra, Dr. Ed had never, in the nine years that he had been coming to Buddy's for lunch, availed himself of this upgrade. Nor had he added a hot or cold beverage for

$1.25, a side salad for $1.50, or a home-baked dessert item for
$1.75. The reasons for this are straightforward:

(i.) After his morning coffee(s), it was plain ol' water the rest
of the day for Dr. Ed.

(ii.) He hated salads of all kinds — well, other than his Irish
Catholic mother's 'special salad', the recipe for which was
to place a slice or two of tomato on top of a bed of iceberg
lettuce, and smother the works in French (or Thousand
Island) dressing.

(iii.) Dr. Ed, whose maternal grandfather was Scottish
Presbyterian, had always been keen on thrift and averse to
unnecessary self-indulgence.

But he liked his soup, Dr. Ed did. Boy, did he ever — that is,
as much as Dr. Ed liked food, really, at all. Bodily appetites
generally just weren't, he maintained, his thing. He ate sparely,
eschewed strong drink, disapproved of his own 2-or-so cup-a-
day coffee habit, played no sports, and indulged in marital relations with his wife, when she proved willing, no more than
twice per month. He had never smoked. Dr. Ed's only avowed
weakness was the occasional indulgence of his sweet tooth, a
regrettable characteristic acquired in childhood, at the knee of
his overly-indulgent (and deceitful: the honourably strict *pater
familias* had always been conveniently absent when sweets were
distributed) mother.

Today's soup was beef barley, one of Dr. Ed's favourites. As
previously stated, Dr. Ed claimed to like the Soup'r Sandwich
special at least partly for its inherent variety. But the truth was,
the soups never varied all that much. Monday was chicken rice;
Tuesday, split pea with ham; Wednesday, beef barley; Thursday
(slotted appropriately into the working week, Dr. Ed 'felt'),
comforting french onion; and Friday was fish (for the many
Roman Catholics, retirees mostly, who stopped in after the 11:30
mass in the chapel attached to the Cathedral, just up Johnson
street, at Clergy) chowder. Although Dr. Ed couldn't stomach the Church much these days, he still appreciated, to the
extent that his attenuated taste buds were capable of appreciating anything, a good fish chowder. A good fish chowder
couldn't be too thick (as New England clam chowder was), too
thin (pseudo-British pubs, springing up like purple loosestrife,
tended to use powdered milk, margarine instead of butter, and
skimp on both the fish *and* the potatoes), or too weird (forget
curried fish chowder, chilli-dilly fish chowder, or fish chowder
molé — he'd seen such flagrant blasphemies, and worse, at the
chichi kinds of places that his wife liked to frequent on her regular 'CHARGE IT!' credit-fuelled excursions to the City). No, a
good fish chowder was like *Buddy's* fish chowder, milky rather
than creamy, but with plenty of body, on account of the copious
quantities of haddock and potatoes therein. Simple as pie, Q.E.D.

The only soup that Dr. Ed did not like was *corn* chowder, which was Saturday's. But Dr. Ed never went to Buddy's on Saturday—never, as in, i.e., *ever*—and anyway this wasn't Saturday, or (unfortunately) Friday. Or Thursday (thank G-d, the afternoons of which were devoted to his 'no-hoper' patients, mostly residentials from the Psych. Hospital, all of whom were 4th quartile *Alba* recipients). This was Wednesday. Wednesday, December 8th, 1993. And Wednesday was beef barley, Catholic feast day or not, and beef barley suited Dr. Ed just fine.

'Just fine', customarily speaking, that is. But not today. Today, his face sporting a crimson hue, Dr. Ed left the Lite Bite abruptly, a full 15 minutes earlier than his punctilious usual, after an extended trip to the 'Heads' (as the nautical sign in the Lite Bite called the men's and ladies' rooms), leaving an embarrassingly extravagant tip on the table, along with an untouched sandwich and a half-eaten bowl of soup.

6c.) An Emerging Pattern of Deviance

Outside, in the fresh air, Dr. Ed paused, uncertain of his (the wind had since changed directions, and was now blowing fresh from the east) destination. He *could* return directly to the hospital, but did he want to? Was there any point in arriving early for what promised to be an uneventful afternoon of predictably routine appointments? Before he was aware of having made up his 'mind', he found his feet taking him towards Union Street, past the county courthouse, towards the Physical Education centre and the hockey arena. After he had walked about 600m he realized that he was returning to work via this unorthodox, eccentric, and altogether circumferential route (if his habitual, to&fro lunchtime journey described a predictably straight-forward 'L', this peculiar re-routing could only be described as resembling the jagged outline of an eggshell, broken length-wise by some supernaturally gifted chef), but upon awakening to this reality Dr. Ed decided (uncharacteristically) to 'go with the flow'. He made a choice; he chose not to wilfully override whatever it was that was taking him on this journey. It was as if he was following a hunch, but someone else's, and if the hunch was to be followed, then it was to be followed on *his* terms, and his terms *alone*. He might 'take advice' from this 'subordin-ate', this post-lunch-hunch, but he remained in the executive position: *this* was not to be something that happened *to* him. This was Dr. Ed, free agent, forging his own path, choosing to behave in a manner which was altogether contrary to his customary inclination. He was choosing to *veer*.

And so it came to pass that a certain departure from the norm, a distinct willful swerving led Dr. Ed to the hockey arena. Dr. Ed then imposed his will on the afternoon one more time: he chose to pause outside the arena, momentarily, so that he might peruse the Coming Events display. *Caduceus Wholistic Fayre!* [*sic*] it said. *Thu-Sun Dec 9-11!* Only 1 day away. Huh, but that, of course, left at least 3 questions unanswered:

(i.) Why would he care about the Caduceus, er, Fair, or 'Expo' anyhow? And:

(ii.) Who the hell was Fraser? And:

(iii.)What did he want with Dr. Ed?

7

2.5 Things About Her

THE AFTERNOON passed predictably in all other respects, just as Dr. Ed would have predicted. Everyone, he noticed, had performed exactly according to script. Nurse Sloggett, for one, had been her predictably efficient, invisible self. As regards his patients, those who seemed to be on an improving track had improved to a predictable extent; those who had been previously stagnant had remained predictably so; and those who bore the misfortune of a steadily worsening condition had indeed worsened, just as one would have, in fact, predicted. He *did* feel for this last group, really he did, but if pharmacology had not yet isolated the particular biological mechanism that was the mainspring of their disorder, what could be done for them? One simply offered an empathetic ear; an empathetic ear was all that they could count on. They endured, or tried to, beyond the horizon of science. Sadly (but predictably), however, human endurance had its all-too-human limits.

As he left the office for the day, Nurse Sloggett reminded him that she would be absent on Thursday to attend a memorial for her late husband, who had died in 1991. She would be replaced, she said, by the same, capable temp whose services she always retained on such (thankfully rare) occasions. She would be replaced by Vicky, Vicky Verky.

Dr. Ed's wife was (again, predictably) out when he got home (he was on time; it was 5:15). Out shopping, most likely, Dr. Ed presumed, what with the stores now staying open late for Xmas. But she was always out shopping, Xmas or no. Shopping was one of her 2.5 essential, predictable things, her defining traits, the *sine quibus non* of her existence.

Now, when Dr. Ed had first met his wife, her behaviour had been wildly *un*-predictable. She had been all over the place, doing all kinds of things, whereas he'd only been in a couple of (very similar) places, doing one particular thing. Her unpredictability had been the only stable thing about her, it had seemed to him back then. In this respect, she had resembled, and had surpassed, the two great loves of Dr. Ed's life:

(i.) His mother, Mary, from whom he had been 'emotionally' estranged for 27 years but with whom he communicated, in a superficial way, regularly.

(ii.) Dark, dark-eyed Agnes Hume, a girl he had fallen for in high school and whose heart he had broken, when the going got tough, by … by going.

Back in 1983, when Dr. Ed's wife had first appeared to him (a mystical apparition for a medical *apparatchik*) she had come across as almost, well—crazy—but this had seemed to be the 'good' kind of crazy. It was the kind of crazy that a man in need of a little craziness likes. It was 'creative' crazy rather than 'destructive' or 'harmless' crazy (both of which were just another way of saying plain-old-crazy). She'd been an *electric* crazy, a crazy with *energy*. When he met her, her kind of crazy had been as unfathomable as simultaneous knowledge of both the position *and* momentum of an electron. Oh, she was an electron alright, an erratic, perturbed energized electron, captured from another, far less attractive orbit by the infinitely greater valence that Dr. Ed had to offer.

She'd been a commercially unsuccessful sculptress, involved in a relationship with a surly, equally obscure Czech print-maker named Erazhim. For eight years they had lived and worked together, she and Erazhim, and for eight years the worlds of art and commerce had passed the two of them by. And the more workaday reality neglected them, the more their art rejected the sublunary world. They retreated into geometry. His wood-cuts, which at the outset of his career had had the draughtsman-like precision and intricacy (but not the love of paradox) of Escher, ended up looking like Etch-a-Sketches, black on gray, like a Miro without colour, form or composition. Her work, which had at first been a relatively pleasing plagiarism of Henry Moore, eventually settled on Archimedean (and then Platonic) solids. Her

-53-

very last piece, created not long after meeting Dr. Ed, had been
an acrylic cube.

She and Erazhim had been living with this neglect, and living
in relative penury, for eight long years when Dr. Ed first met
her at the wake of his mentor (and her uncle), Simon Sainsbury.
Simon Sainsbury was a Professor Emeritus at the university and
had been a past director of the Eastern Psychiatric Hospital, where
Dr. Ed was working at the time. For his part, when Dr. Ed first met
his future wife he had been celibate for sixteen long years. Not
since 1967 had he had anything at all to do with women, excepting, of course, the requisite relationships of a strictly professional
nature that are inseparable from the quotidian life of the psychiatrist. All during that period his one and only focus, his overrid-
ing obsession, had been his work. His work, his life.

Dr. Ed's wife had changed all that, for a while at least. She'd
brought to his world something that it had lacked, something that
(he would never have admitted) he'd missed; it was something
that, in the past (long-lost in the long-past past, in the petrified
forest of the heart, where ghostly, romantic ideals clutch on to
mute yearnings and forever perform their static waltz, frozen
in the tar sands of human time) Agnes and his mother had once
provided: a bit of drama, a sense of danger, the knowledge of
never knowing where one stands, the necessity of risk-taking,
the primacy of continual courtship. When he met her, Dr. Ed's

wife had as many faces as a dodecahedron. By the time of their marriage, he'd learned to woo them all. First came the quickly traversed 'front nine': the Little-girl-lost, the Siren, the Wicked Step-sister, the Pandora-finds-Hope, the High Priestess, the Empress, the Courtesan, the Madonna, the Moll. Only much later, and much more slowly, did she reveal her Holy Trinity, her consubstantial three-in-one of haughty Hera, disdainful Daphne, and above all, moody Medusa.

Around this time, a few years after they were married, Dr. Ed's wife had ceased her sculpturizing and commenced her shopping—which promptly became, as Dr. Ed called it, her thing #1. Then her unpredictability began to level out, to flatten, to move from three into two dimensions, from dodecahedron into dodeca-gon. But it wasn't her *shopping*, her thing #1, that caused it, this loss of dimensionality. No indeed! For it was only in her shop-ping that she kept a residual portion of this former self alive. As her life (following the lead of her body, following the lead of her 'mind') steadily lost its elasticity, it was only her shopping that persisted in giving it form and meaning. It was shopping, in fact, that saved her. Her shopping *had* to become as mercurial, as ener-getic, as her former life had been; it just had to. For she *had* to express herself, and failing that she *absolutely* had to find a surro-gate, to locate some other outlet for 'realization'. And shopping was it.

It had taken Dr. Ed almost a year to discover, at the bottom of her seemingly random mercantile manoeuvres, a habitual *pattern* of procuration, a distinct *method*, and one that he eventually worked up into a handy algorithm: She would EITHER shop in town on three (or four) *consecutive* days OR she would go to the City for three (or four) *successive* days of shopping. In either case, she would buy three (or four) different colours of the same outfit, and EITHER return all of them OR return none of them, the very same day: IFF [IF AND *ONLY* IF] ALL of them, THEN she would buy three (or four) different outfits at three (or four) different merchants on the three (or four) succeeding days, AND all of these would be in the same colour. However, in every case, whether she returned ALL OR NONE of the *original* selections, she would nevertheless return to the Mall the same day to purchase three (or four) appropriate accessories *for each item purchased on that day.* That made nine (or twelve, or sixteen) accessories in all, with each group of three (or four) subject to the same deliberations regarding the possibility of return or exchange as the initial three (or four) outfits!

That was his wife's thing number 1.

Thing number 2 had to do with her family tree. Dr. Ed's wife came from a long line of daughters who, somehow, had borne only daughters. Dr. Ed's wife had 4 sisters, but no brothers. On her mother's side she had three aunts (but no uncles), all of whom had given birth to varying quantities of daughters (but no sons). The maternal narrative pointing back to the families of her grandmother and great-grandmother and beyond told much the same tale.

Dr. Ed's wife's family were evangelical Christians, and they spoke of it as a 'blessing' from the Lord, but it proved to be much more like a curse for the sisters of Dr. Ed's wife, each of whom had 'felt' compelled to thwart, each in her separate way, what appeared to be their biological and spiritual destiny. In the late 1960s the eldest daughter had become a Maoist, and had had herself sterilized. The second daughter had converted to Roman Catholicism and had joined a convent. The third daughter had married a missionary, and had adopted twelve children, all boys, when she and her husband lived and taught in the Ivory Coast. The fourth had become a hard-headed-and-hearted economist, rarely leaving her office atop the tallest of the phallic bank towers in the City. As for Dr. Ed's wife, she had herself embraced the sexual revolution wholeheartedly, and had been on the pill since her last year of high school.

At first, Dr. Ed had accepted his wife's outright refusal to discuss, let alone to have, children. He had accepted it when they were newlyweds because their sex life was so good (3x/week, *without fail*), and he would have been loath to 'interrupt' it. He had accepted it from year 3 to year 5 because he had been monumentally busy with his career. He had continued accepting it in years 6 & 7 because … because … he honestly couldn't remember why because. By year 8 his acceptance had become second nature, and he no longer wanted children at all—and had developed, in fact, a particular *aversion* even to the idea of having them. Ironically, however, just this past September he had been rooting about in his wife's closet, busily confirming that his wife was taking her birth control pills, when he spotted a bottle of *Clomid*, a commonly prescribed fertility drug. He emptied the contents into the toilet and tossed the empty container into the waste basket. And the incident passed without comment on either side.

It was around this time that a young man had appeared on his doorstep and had rung his doorbell. The purple dye on the boy's face testified to the fact that it was 'Frosh' or initiation week on campus, and that he was most likely one of the first year engineering students, who were always out canvassing for one charity or another at that time of year. Dr. Ed was quite prepared to give a little something to the cause, whatever it was, and he adopted an expression of good-natured neighbourliness as he made greetings. Dr. Ed was not at all prepared, however, for what the boy then said. He asked Dr. Ed if he was Dr. Ed, and when Dr. Ed informed him that he was indeed himself, the young man said, looking at the ground:

—Sir I ... I think I'm your son.

Thing #3 about Dr. Ed's wife counted, in Dr. Ed's estimation, as only ½ a thing. It *used* to count as a whole thing, back when they'd first met, but now it didn't. It didn't count anymore because it was, in Dr. Ed's eyes, the most supremely boring, the most ultra-boring, the boring-est-est, most predictable thing of all about his wife. That thing, that ½-a-thing, was that she was the baby in her family.

Now, everyone knows that babies like to be babied, and that the baby of the family, of pretty well every family, does in fact usually get what is coming to him or her: lots and lots (and lots) of baby-ing—of baby-abying, in fact, from their first coochy-coochy-coos right on up to their Sweet 16 convertible. And everyone knows that it is pretty much an inevitable and unavoidable fact that this would be, would always be so. After all, families are families, and babies are ... well, babies.

It is also inevitable that the *non*-babies in a family get treated to a significantly less amount of babying themselves, and resent their babied baby siblings—that is, to a certain extent. That certain extent is proportional to both the *total amount* of babying energy (and financial resources) available to a given set of parents, as well as to the *perceived babying differential*, i.e. the *perceived* percentage difference in babying, relative to a given *normative standard*. And in a family of 5 children, for example (such as in Dr. Ed's wife's family), the normative standard would be ⅕, which would mean that each of the 5 children would be entitled to ⅕ of a family's love, attention, Xmas gifts, etc. Now, in a family of only 2 children, the normative standard would be ½, so that the perceived differential could be much higher.

Sibling resentment was thus the mathematical *product* of these three great factors: (i.) the Total Energy (or Carrying Capacity), E_t of the family; (ii.) the Perceived Sibling Differential, D_p; and (iii.) the Normative Standard, S_n, which as a fraction turns the resulting formula into a quotient:

$$R_s = E_t \frac{D_p}{S_n}$$

According to Dr. Ed's calculations, then, Sibling Resentment (R_s) would be greatest in small, wealthy families, and smallest in large, poor families. It all added up. However, there was something else, something as yet unaccounted for by Dr. Ed's model. Dr. Ed knew at a visceral level that sibling resentment was most likely to be 'felt' and/or expressed by first-born children, who in terms of age are located at a further remove from the baby than are younger siblings, and who must always feel that they were the 'Error' in the parental 'Trial-and-Error' approach to child-rearing. Dr. Ed was cognizant of this complicating factor, but to this date had proven unable to establish an imaginatively satisfying pseudo-mathematical model for it.

Now, Dr. Ed was himself a first-born. Verymuchso. And in the average first-born's eyes, the babied baby of the family is a *BIGlittlebaby*, a *CRYbaby*, a spoiled-rotten-little-*BRATbaby*. In this, Dr. Ed was no exception; his attitude towards the baby-like qualities of his wife's behaviour was not exactly a supportive one. But this had not always been the case.

When he had first met his future wife, he had courted her, as both he and she had seen it, with exhaustive rigour. In the first weeks there were flowers every day (something that struck his future wife as a delightful anachronism, a holdover from the dark suit/skinny tie days of young men borrowing their father-knows-best-mobiles and driving their dates through Eisenhowerville and McCarthyton to the Nuclear Sock Hop at deTocqueville High, with perhaps a chaste and wholesome fully clothed stopover on the way home in the parking lot atop Big Rock Candy Mountain). There were also all manner of little presents, from boxes upon boxes of MOIRS *Black Magic* chocolates, to books (*The Love Poetry of Rod McKuen, Come Be With Me* by

Leonard Nimoy), long-playing records (Max Bygraves: *Sing Along With Max*, Ray Conniff: *The Love That Loves To Love*), and jewelry (two silver hearts on a silver chain on St. Valentine's Day, a Star Sign charm bracelet on her birthday, a golden tennis anklet for Xmas). And Dr. Ed's future wife took all of these, and more, in her stride, seeing it all as part of the natural order of things. After all, she knew the drill. She'd had male admirers before her dour and parsimonious painter Erazhim had come along, and she knew what to expect from the courtly courtier. So, naturally, she enjoyed being the focus of her future husband's attention, and foresaw no reason why it must ever stop.

But stop it did, and it did so just as they were both getting comfortable with each other, too, just 24 months or so into their connubial adventure! The manner in which its surcease came to pass is full of complications in the medical sense of the word—replete with secondary eruptions and related, consequent paroxysms, but despite the rather convoluted trajectory of their relationship (marked by any number of fits and starts, by progressions and regressions, by bitter tantrums and sour recriminations here, and by sweet, tearful reconciliations and subsequent, pungent lovemaking there) its underlying pathology was in no way occult.

Aside from her refusal to have children, it had all boiled down to this: Dr. Ed had found himself in the discomfiting yet familiar role of becoming intimate with a beguiling, yet profoundly disturbed patient: he had stumbled, despite his best intentions, into a relationship with a person whose catalogue of needs and wants could never be assuaged, but which were destined to continue metastasizing. Dr. Ed's wife was, he eventually realized, someone who could never be satisfied with the tangible but finite rewards of the mating ritual of the human species. There *just had to be more*, always, always always. How had Dr. Ed ended up on this degenerate, embolic artery of life?

It was sometime around 24 months into his marriage that Dr. Ed had come to feel, with increasing acuity, that his problem had been self-inflicted, that in courting his wife he had participated in a kind of self-willed delusion borne of an entirely irrational and heretofore undiagnosed neediness of his own. His wife had thus appeared on his personal horizon in the classically delusional manner, much as fertile, green fields commonly appeared to sailors afflicted with the delirium known as calenture, sailors who had wearied of and who had been worn down by their ship's continual, aimless drifting in the doldrums of the tropics. The hot, sticky, airless tropics. The unending unreason, the sinister sensuality and the pointless passions of the tropics.

It was time, he'd eventually realized, for a return to the north! After the sauna, first a good birch-switching and then a roll in the snow! Out of the hot tub and into a bracing cold shower! Lassitude, be gone! Dr. Ed was not a man to tire easily, but 'tired' had not begun to describe how Dr. Ed had come to feel about his wife's unceasing quest to be nurtured and coddled. They both needed this, this limbeck or medicinal, this emetic, this purgative drug, this rhubarb and senna. And so henceforth—and so hence! No more mollycoddling!

—No More Mollycoddling! he had pronounced one night, around about the time of his dissertation defence, when his wife had characteristically simpered that they were all out of Margarita mix and that there was no money in her allowance account (however could she expect to be allowed to go shopping, to go to town, if her allowance account was always empty?), and would he mind ever so much to pick her up some more?

—Hand-Holding Stops Here! he said. Newsflash: Coddling, Cosseting Condemned! Pampering Proscribed! Read All About It In Saturday's *Loyalist Ledger*! Babying Babies Banned!!

Perhaps it was more complicated than that, their hymeneal negotiations, their bickering and dickering, their bartering and chaffering. Perhaps we fail to give Dr. Ed and his wife their due, perhaps just as Dr. Ed himself did. Perhaps, at some level, they have nurtured an intergrafting of hands, of eyes, of hearts, an 'interassurance', as the Poet says, 'of the mind'. Perhaps they have cultured, in their own idiosyncratic fashion, a variety of love, and the appropriate metaphor might be:

> *Not transaction, but translation, a forever-*
> *ferrying across the border*
> *of duty-free goods.*

Perhaps, perhaps.

Perhaps, too, we should not sketch her, as Dr. Ed has, in such broad strokes; perhaps there is simply more to her than is being suggested. Perhaps it is just not true that 'there's no there there'. Hmm, perhaps. But again: her *behaviour* suggests otherwise....

And perhaps Dr. Ed, moreover, shouldn't be made out to be some kind of simpleton, some kind of *caricature*, some archetypal derivative, some mutant species of egghead/caveman. Perhaps. But he did *say* the things recorded here, he did in fact utter them. And since we can never *really* get inside the 'minds' of Other People, since we can only *pretend* to know what drives them—to discover what causes, explains, and, ultimately, excuses their actions—all we have to go on, to quote the Man himself, is their behaviour.

Everything else is, well, fiction.

Isn't it?

8

... ALONG WITH MAX

WE REPEAT: Dr. Ed's wife was (again, again, again, predictably) out when he got home. He was on time; it was 17:15.
Out shopping most likely, Dr. Ed presumed, what with the Mall
now staying open late for Xmas. He'd already said as much, to
himself, but he'd say it again, and *again* if need be: She was out
(and *would* be out, pretty much every night now, at least until the
24th) shopping, single-handedly buoying-up the local economy,
and eating up, thereby, what remained of Dr. Ed's line of credit.
But this was something that Dr. Ed did not 'mind', something
that he was almost happy to witness, for not only was it a regular occurrence (and regularity of all kinds was always prized by
Dr. Ed), one that should be a seasonal fixture of any honest calen-
dar, secular or liturgical, it also got Dr. Ed's wife out of Dr. Ed's
hair even more regularly than during the other eleven months of
the year. So December was Dr. Ed's favourite month of the year.

The very word 'December' *meant* being bloody well left alone; it meant blissful, utter private privation, the peace & quiet of sequestral downtime. The adjective 'sequestral' *was* in fact the word that popped into his head whenever the month of December was mentioned, and a fine adjective it was, too. Dr. Ed liked how the word brought to 'mind' a sequestered, passionately rational, impartially deliberating jury, even as its medical sense denoted the presence of dead bone or other matter, cut off from surrounding, healthy tissue. For that's what the life of the 'mind' demanded of you, that you die to yourself and others, that you embrace the many privations of desert life, that you remain amongst your fellows but not of them. The scholar's world was an incorporeal, eremitical one, to be sure, as arid but also as surprisingly full of surprising life forms (and other surprises) as a real desert — as the desert of the Desert Fathers of the early Christian church, who left the teeming world of the Many behind to commune in solitude with the One.

Dr. Ed did have one *close* friend, however, and that was Max. He and Max went back, oh, more than ten years now, going on eleven, actually. Their friendship had endured even longer, by some months, than Dr. Ed's relationship with his wife. They had been through a lot together, he and Max, Max and he.

And so it was with some surprise that Dr. Ed, having returned home on time, discovered Max's name on a note (an actual note, actually pinned to the kitchen notice board, and seemingly in his wife's very own handwriting!). *Something* had to be up. One of his wife's many rules was to *never leave notes* describing her activities or whereabouts. This rule dated back a half-dozen years or so, to a bright summer evening when Dr. Ed, 'feeling' on top of his game after securing yet another well-funded research project for his department, had dared to call into open question the domain, range and periodicity of his wife's peregrinations. He shocked her still further, not only by talking back to her firm and final dismissal, but also by insisting that he had the right to 'at least the vaguest inkling of her whereabouts'. She turned on her heels and immediately went out to *Herland* at the mall, where she purchased a little device which might give her husband his due: the vaguest inkling of her whereabouts. The device resembled an overlarge board-game spinner:

Today, however, his wife had unpredictably forgone the use of the spinner and had left a note. Something *was* up. The note read:

> OUT & ABOUT...
>
> MAX AVEC MOI—MEME...
>
> BACK PLUS, PLUS TARD...

Something was *up*. Dr. Ed's wife had never, ever, in the nine years of their marriage, gone *any*where with Max. She hated Max. Max was disgusting. Max stank, Max was obese, Max was constantly passing wind, Max was surly and anti-social. What's more, Max's mere presence made Dr. Ed's wife (who was naturally *very* social) feel like *she* was anti-social and behave in a most unbecoming, anti-social manner. Max was not exactly a misanthrope *himself*, but somehow he caused other people to act misanthropically whenever he was around. But that was what Dr. Ed liked about Max: Max encouraged — no, *induced* solitude. Dr. Ed never 'felt' as so-blissfully-alone as when he and Max were together.

When Dr. Ed had first made Max's acquaintance, he 'felt' sorely in need of a friend. Not the kind of friend who was poking his nose into your business, mind you: his nurse (Nurse Sloggett) and (of course) his wife provided him with more than a surfeit of *that*. No, Dr. Ed had needed somebody just like Max, someone who would just uncomplainingly *be* there, someone who made no *demands* on one's time and patience. And Max had fit the bill nicely; together, they formed a 2-member live-and-let-live-society, a tiny syndical-ist collective, of sorts. Their undemanding friendship had easily weathered the demands of Dr. Ed's burgeoning career, and had managed to survive (and even thrive) throughout the term of Dr. Ed's 9-year marriage. Dr. Ed would sometimes shake his head, as in disbelief, at the 'thought' of it: 9 years, huh? Now that's not nothing, no sir, it is indeed not. But then Max and me, I mean Max and *I*, we go back *11*. Now that's *something*.

Normally (and while, strictly speaking, only those who fall within 1 standard deviation from the norm would qualify as such, in this case we may judiciously include those who lie 2 or even 3 standard deviations away), when friends heed nature's siren call to marry themselves off before it is 'too late' to do so, when they begin to prostrate themselves before the seemingly ineluc-table goddess of fecundity and to commence vigorous and seri-ous procreation, we begin to see much less of them than previ-ously. Much less. *So* much less, in fact (as, walleyed, sallow-faced, slack-jawed, pork-chopped and dough-balled, they persevere—*oh, how they persevere!*—as they must, with all that '*parenting*'—such a horrid neologism—to attend to), that they may as well have signed on as conflict resolution experts and have themselves flown off to Belfast, Jerusalem or Cyprus for a decade or 2.

But Dr. Ed and Max were not 'normal' friends. If a statistician were attempting a curve-fitting of any or all of the many parameters of friendship, Dr. Ed's and Max's data would certainly be termed 'outliers'—falling well beyond the normal range. They were both as content to be with each other as they were otherwise solitary and aloof from their fellows. They each required regular, extensive amounts of time together, but when they were apart each seldom, if ever, 'thought' of the other; it was just *assumed* that each would be there, *for* the other, *when* called for—and, of course, they both always had been.

Dr. Ed saw their 11 years together as a kind of summer camp canoe trip: a safe, controlled and predictable journey when viewed in retrospect, but punctuated by useful, pulse-quickening surprises when experienced en-route. When Dr. Ed had endured his way through the nerve-numbing rapids of his engagement and the subsequent, unavoidable eddies of his marriage, Max had calmly paddled at Dr. Ed's bow, and had provided a welcome, steady assistance through the narrows and over the rocks that came their way, never once complaining or sulking, as Dr. Ed became more and more (if that is at all possible) engrossed in his work as the years passed.

Wisely, Max had always let Dr. Ed chart his own course, and had kept his own counsel as Dr. Ed was forced to perform all manner of requisite, delicate maneuverings as they entered the serpentine switchbacks of Dr. Ed's acquisition of a department headship. Otherwise, however, it had otherwise all been pretty much smooth sailing thereafter, as Dr. Ed had expertly J-stroked his way down the organizational river. There had been that recent, unforeseen portage (during which Max had, of course, shouldered his-share-and-thensome of the burden) when, out of the blue, Dr. Ed was suddenly and genuinely (albeit somewhat unsuccessfully) reunited with his now-adult 'son', Ted, but Max wasn't complaining. Life was good.

Lest, however, the impression be made that theirs was more of a parasitical than symbiotic relationship, it must be noted that Dr. Ed had also been there for Max (when necessary) as well. Not only had (i.) Dr. Ed indeed sympathised-like-hell with Max over that to-do surrounding Max's vasectomy, as well as (ii.) provided much-needed mediation during the flap that Max had had with that bitch next door—it had been Dr. Ed, after all, who had initiated their relationship in the first place. And it had been Dr. Ed, *after all*, who had given Max a hand-up when he had most needed it, when Max's future prospects appeared to be at the nadir of their bleakness.

In fact, if such a one as the great Jeremy Bentham had plotted Max's eudaemonic prospects (in *hedon*-units, **h**, against time, **t**) just prior to the commencement of their friendship, the resulting graph could only have suggested that the short term did *not* 'look good' (to put it euphemistically) for poor ol' Max. The short term appeared to be *so*-not-good that his long-term prospects were unchartable. The short-term chart was so *very* contra-positive that even the notion, even the *suggestion* of a 'long' term, as far as Max was concerned, was a dream originating in an opium pipe stocked with extraordinary psychotropic powers indeed:

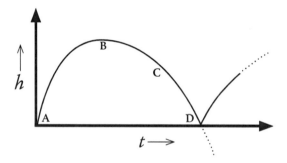

Now, a savvy analyst would have spotted latent problems during the period when things actually looked pretty good for Max, which corresponds to the interval between points A and B on the short-term chart. At this time in his life Max had a family, was eating well and was getting regular exercise. Life seemed pretty good to Max, and he had no complaints worth mentioning. However, although his prospects for a well-lived life were improving with respect to time here, they were improving *less and less rapidly* as time passed; that is, Max's prospects were experiencing *negative acceleration*, until, at point B, they *stopped improving altogether*.

At point B, Max's prospects were hovering, momentarily, as it were, in mid-air; but from here on in they took a long, relentless and remorseless tumble. Point B marks the occurrence of Max having embarrassed himself and his family for the, shall we say, n+1th time. The event was not in and of itself all that significant, but the n+1th time proved to be just one time too many. But it was not really poor Max's fault: Max had digestive problems, and was thus much less well-equipped to handle the vegetarian diet that he and the rest of his family had recently and rigorously adopted. One by-product of his newly-chronic dyspepsia was a copious quantity of intestinal gas, gas which contained a remark-able concentration of various signature sulphur compounds, gas that had to be released, gas that would *not* be refused, gas that, despite his family's frequent and vociferous protestations, was visited upon them at 2-4 minute intervals for 2-3 hours thrice daily, subsequent to meals.

The trajectory of the curve in between points B & C indi-cates an inexorable decline in prospects precipitated by a steady withdrawal of affection, which was itself occasioned by the very decline in prospects which *that* in turn consequently occasioned. Invariably, such negative feedback loops act in a much more protracted, almost stealthy manner than the positive loops which produce the kind of sudden *rise* in prospects illustrated by the curve from A to B. These negative loops work almost, as it were, invisibly, steadily eroding the subject's quality of life and thereby nearly always ensuring that the subject enters one of a limited number of endgame scenarios which inevitably result in fatality—be it via individual choice, by misadventure or by 'natural causes'.

Finally, that the change which the above curve undergoes from points C to D is characteristic of such scenarios is easily confirmed by performing a second derivative on the curve at point D, which indicates that Max's prospects were negatively accelerating at a near-infinite rate—as the slope of a tangent to the curve at this point would be, mathematically speaking, 'undefined'.

It was at point D, as the curve was just crossing the horizontal axis (indicating that Max's prospects were 'poor'—meaning, of course, that Max now possessed *no* prospects to speak of, *what*soever) that Dr. Ed had chosen to intervene on his behalf. He had seen a short Xmas-related feature on Max's plight on the local evening news—the season for goodwill, aiding the needy and less fortunate and all that—and had called the station, which put him in contact with the charitable organization that wished to help Max (and many others in the same predicament), but which lacked the sufficient funds to do so. Then, moved not so much by empathy as sympathy, Dr. Ed then took Max under his wing, providing him with a roof over his head and three square meals (none vegetarian) a day.

But what was going on here? Something was up, to be sure. Dr. Ed's brain calculated quickly, running through the various possible permutations and combinations—many of which were possible, but relatively few *probable*—until it settled upon the one, the only one, that his wife could have actualized, the only *do-able* one.

'Do-able' was a word that held special meaning for Dr. Ed. This was because he considered himself an 'expert amateur' lexicographer (expert because his vault of knowledge was a self-confessedly vast one indeed; amateur because it was something he did in his spare time, that is, whenever he had any time, which is to say, since he was a professional scientist and all-around serious person, never really very often—hardly, in fact, hardly ever, at all).

As a neologism 'do-able' fascinated him in a way that other neologisms did not. Take, for instance, the alleged verb 'to impact', e.g.

'our increasingly negative revenue stream impacts our quarterly earnings big time'. Now, 'to impact' was roughly contemporaneous, in Dr. Ed's estimation, with 'do-able': Dr. Ed clearly remembered first hearing 'impact' used as a verb at a conference on bulimia back in 1988, in Anaheim California, at the KNUTTS BERRY FARM conference centre and theme park. The drug company SIRRIUS was handing out rollerball pen/lights at the *end* of the LogJam fun ride; to obtain a pen/light one was obliged to take the ride, which wound its way past Tayberry Thicket to Gooseberry Gulch, etc. This Dr. Ed had grimly yet determinedly done, in order that he might then have something to bring home to his wife. After 5 patience-trying minutes he and the 3 others in his 'log' were floating in the tepid, overly-chlorinated waters of Loch Loganberry, having been 'swallowed' down a 'throat' from the 'delicious' height of 40 feet or so atop Blueberry Thrill. While drifting briefly and unproductively in the lagoon and waiting to be—well, disgorged—he heard a fellow passenger seated behind him remark to his companion: 'On the one hand, exhuming Iran-Contra is a definite non-starter; on the other, neutralising Iraq would impact positively on the President's foreign policy credibility gap.'

'To impact' had even slipped (if this admission is not too too much of a strain on credibility) into Dr. Ed's own usage. At meetings with the heads of other, less well-endowed departments, he would hear himself employing the verb as part of a strategy of empathetic truth-evasion, uttering such harmless little fibs as: 'Make no mistake: these funding claw-backs have impacted the functionality of everyone in this room; we're all in this together, here'. Similarly, 'Your dosage has been ratcheted skywards in the past two months—how has this impacted your self-esteem?' was something he might slip into standard doctor/patient chitchat, just to keep things up-close & 'personal'. And just the other day in the staff lunchroom, he had tried 'the Bengalis really impacted the Bears big-time, eh?' (followed by 'What was the final score? I had to dash to the can….'), albeit unsuccessfully, on 'the Guys' from Emerg.

'Do-able' (or—naturalizing it by dropping the hyphenation—'doable'), however, was different. Whereas to his discriminating ears 'to impact' sounded 'classy', 'do-able' sounded … well, 'brassy'. While 'to impact' communicated a certain, no-bull***t intelligence, 'do-able' smacked of philistinism = bad taste + new money, a nasal, leather-look arrogance, & etc. However, so far as Dr. Ed knew (which, admittedly, was not all that far, and extended only to a few members of his social circle, which was admittedly a small one) he was one of the first Canadians to document this neologism's infestation of the continent.

Like so many other pesky nuisances (e.g. fire ants, killer bees, the career of George W. Bush), it had first arisen in Texas. He had first spotted it, again, at a conference, this one on the psychopharmacology of erectile dysfunction at TEXAS CHRISTIAN UNIVERSITY (home of the Horned Frogs). He'd linked up with a colleague from Med School days, who'd suggested a quick side-trip east to Tyler in his rented CADILLAC *Eldorado*. The colleague was a running fanatic, and was entering the annual Tyler Rose Festival 10 kilometre footrace. He advised Dr. Ed to position himself at about ¼ mile from the finish line, so as to be ideally situated for the final sprint. This Dr. Ed did. The winner, from Kenya, took quite a bit less than half an hour to complete the course and claim his prizes ($5000 cash and a year's supply of chicken-fried steak at FAT MAN & LITTLE BOY restaurants state-wide). His colleague had told Dr. Ed to look out for him 'on or before the 40-minute mark', which would be for him a 'PB', or a 'Personal Best'. He made good on this prediction, and went by Dr. Ed at 38:12 by Dr. Ed's watch, looking, in Dr. Ed's estimation, fairly strong. Moments later, however, a tall, spindly-looking Texan in a headband and a 1970s ADIDAS t-shirt (next to a bubba in a t-shirt that sported a marijuana leaf above a slogan which read: 'Your TexAss is Grass') struggled apoplectically by, and someone in the crowd shouted out at him: '40 minutes, Hal! Do-able, bud, *do-able*!' One year later,

Dr. Ed first heard its use back home, at UNIVERSITY HOSPITAL, in an elevator. It was sprinkled into a conversation between two gastroenterologists regarding a breakfast cereal company-sponsored study on the development of colo-rectal polyps. The plague had arrived.

Damnitall, something was *surely* up. Max, out with his wife, back later? The only do-able hypothesis was that his wife had taken Max with her out of some kind of sense of duty, on some kind of charity mission; and that Max had gone along for the ride, had gone along with *her* because he'd *had* to. The only possible reason for his Max and his wife to spend *any* time together was … an emergency! Something had to be wrong with Max! G-ddammit, his wife had taken Max to the vet's, he knew it, he just knew it! Jesus *Christ*, why didn't she *call* and *tell* him?

9

2 Chocolate Freak-outs

T HE CLICHÉS hit him hard, where it counted — below the belt like a ton of bricks. Insult super-positioned itself atop, as it were, injury, leaving Dr. Ed in a state: leaving him in such a state that, he now realized, he was quite *beside* himself. And though it had been years since he had 'felt' that any such stock phrases could possibly apply to him, by his own admission he had to admit that any and/or all of them did, now, tonight. And how. And more. He was, he recognized in a bad way. The long and the short of it was that in the process of falling apart, he had gone to the dogs. If he'd seen it once in his practice, he'd seen it a thousand times. But not as regards himself, no, of course not, at least not since … why, since 1967.

First of all, he'd gotten all hot under the collar, had worked himself up into a sweat until he was in quite a substantial lather. He'd then ran his motor, flipped his lid and blown his cool, subsequently blowing several fuses and at least one gasket, which in turn induced him to blow his stack as well as his top. Finally, he cracked, came apart, went to pieces and just plain blew up. He hit the ceiling. He hit the roof.

At this point, his nerves were so bad, he was unnerved. Unnerved, unmanned, unstrung; unstuck, unglued, undone — something, some *thing* had got a tenacious *hold* on his nerves and twanged, frayed, frazzled, jangled them. It had shattered them. But then came the jarring, shaking, stretching and rending, which continued unabated — relentless, unappeasable — until he was fairly stricken, shaken even, his hopes both dashed and crushed. In the end, he found that he was completely shot, shot to pieces actually, yet somehow still very much perturbed, and continued to boil over into a flustered swivet of a tizzy. He was in a state, a state of being quite, *quite* beside himself.

He and Max had been through a lot together, by gosh and by golly, and to lose him now, after only 11 years was … it was un-'think'-able. Maybe he was wrong, maybe his wife had some *other* reason for taking Max with her. There could *surely* have been some other destination than *that* one?

No, no, no. No, the vet's was the only doable possibility. His wife had suffered to take Max in the car exactly *twice* in the past nine years, and both times it had been to the vet's. Both times Dr. Ed had been away, attending some conference or other, and on both occasions a depressed and lonely Max had tunnelled his way out from under their backyard fence, situations whose very nearly disastrous outcomes had forced his wife to act decisively on Max's behalf.

The first time, Max had run across the road and collided side-long with the Dickie Dee ice cream boy, who was pedalling his wares down the sidewalk opposite their house. Max had succeeded in catapulting the lad over his handlebars and into a telephone pole, giving him a severe concussion and 3 broken ribs, one of which came perilously close to puncturing his left lung. Max had himself been knocked out cold, leaving Dr. Ed's wife to suspect and hope that the collision had been fatal. However, Max had subsequently regained consciousness at the vet's a half-hour later, coming through the trauma like a trooper, completely uninjured.

The second incident had involved an intimate encounter with a porcupine. Max was in no immediate danger, the vet had told her over the phone, but he advised her against waiting until her husband's return to deal with nearly two-dozen barbed quills lodged in the poor dog's nose. The dog was, he said, most likely in a considerable amount of pain, and the wounds could easily become infected.

Accordingly as well as somewhat reluctantly, Dr. Ed's wife had put Max in the rear of her Suburban, and had proceeded to drive him the mile or so to the animal hospital. Just before the parking lot, Max, who had been staring intently out of the left side rear window, spotted a Yorkshire Terrier being led to the vet's front door from its owner's car on one of those retractable 20-foot leashes. Max had then abruptly jumped into the front seat and onto Dr. Ed's wife's lap, causing her to veer off the road, over the curb and onto the vet's front lawn.

Afterwards, a plethora of orthopaedic specialists had each, in succession, given Dr. Ed's wife a clean bill of health. She insisted, however (and continued to insist, to the present day), on unspecific, shifting, intermittent and yet very real neck pain, and stepped up her number of weekly chiropractic visits from one to three. The Yorkshire Terrier was quite a bit less fortunate, having been killed instantly by the Suburban's oversized 17″ right front tire. Upon his return, Dr. Ed hastened to offer its owner a replacement Yorkshire puppy as well as $5,000 for her 'emotional trauma'. He paid for the replacement of the vet's lawn sign and for his wife's front bumper and left front fender out of pocket, to avoid the inevitable hit to his insurance premiums.

But something was up, something was wrong, wrong with Max; Dr. Ed could 'feel' it in his bones. Of course that was just a metaphor, but that's just what it 'felt' like: he could 'feel' it in his bones, and as a consequence he could 'feel' the adrenaline entering into his blood, doing its thing to both body and 'mind'. He knew, intellectually, the pathways and reactions involved, but intellectual awareness was of little use here, just now.

Dr. Ed panicked. And then Dr. Ed did what he always did whenever panic had him (which was hardly ever) in its ratcheted grip: he went on a doughnut run.

It was still early evening, and he had at least a couple of hours to kill; he knew that his wife—and Max, of course—would not be back until well after nine, until well after the mall's doors had been locked behind her. She'd have taken Max to that new VETPLEX out by the AUTO RANCH on her way to the TOWN CENTRE (which was neither in the town, proper, nor at the *centre* of anything, at all), he was sure. She would've gotten Max in&out of the vet's, and would have left him in the *Suburban* so that—he knew her routine—she could maximise the time available to do her thing, with Dr. Ed's money. To save time she'd have eaten in the food court, he predicted, at WOK FO YU, perhaps, at GIT 'R' INDIA, or at THE MEATING PLACE—or, if she was back on her diet, at FRUMPY'S (*'in motion with fresh food notions'*). Not that he cared, not that he was missing dinner: Dr. Ed made all his own meals, anyhow.

Dr. Ed pulled into THE DONUT HOLE, ordered a milk (extra-large, plain) and a half-dozen doughnuts: 1 Double Chocolate Iced, 1 Chocolate Sour Creme, 1 Chocolate Filled, 1 Chocolate Glazed, and 2 Chocolate Freak-Outs (a limited-time-only premium item, costing 10¢ extra apiece, it was a Chocolate Sour Creme Cruller that was Filled, Iced, and then Glazed). He ordered it all 'to go', but sat down and ate them in the store, shrewdly leaving the 2 Chocolate Freak-Outs, as well as most of the milk, for last.

He was just about to tuck into the first of these when the call came through on his pager. Table-talk in his vicinity (to his right, a boyfriend/girlfriend spat concerning whose body was more juicin'—today's *Sun's* page 3 girl or page 63 boy; to his left, a pensioner performing a dramatic monologue concerning his late wife's manifold shortcomings; to his front, 3 teenaged males exchanging the derisory snorts and valedictory grunts of cave-man sportspeak; to his rear, a mute husband-and-wife pair, staring with complacent inertia into their double-doubles) stopped abruptly, all eyes turning toward Dr. Ed.

Historically, doctors used to be able to rely on their pagers to successfully broadcast their privileged social stature to the world, for, not so very long ago, it was only doctors who carried them. No More. Nowadays, the presence of a pager suggested that a man like Dr. Ed could easily be taken for any number of things: a plumber, a drug pusher, a real estate agent, a delivery boy....

This drizzle of mildly curious attention hardly fazed Dr. Ed, who lifted up his pager to squint at its tiny liquid crystal display. It read:

CALL DR. PETE LA FRAMBOISE EMER G 776-2323

—Huh, Dr. Ed 'thought' with mild surprise, for this had happened before, though not frequently. One of my patients.

10

RE: MRS. MISSY PLUMTREE

Background
   Missy Plumtree (née Watt), D.O.B. 06-06-68, had been first admitted into care on 08 December 1992. At that time she was a doctoral candidate in English Literature at the university, and had no prior history of clinical depression—or of any other psychiatric disorder. Her husband of six months, Mark Plumtree, an electrical engineer and major in the ROYAL CANADIAN SIGNALS REGIMENT, currently describes her as 'bright, mercurial, vivacious'. Her mother, Mrs. Harriet Watt, recounts that Missy, an only child, had been 'cheery and outgoing' as a young girl, but became 'bookish and introverted' and 'given to moods' in her teens. These periods of emotional volatility usually persisted from 12 to 24 (and, occasionally, to 36) hours 'or so'. Mrs. Watt's term for these episodes was 'the Grumps', an affliction apparently shared by her father, the late Francis Watt. Mrs. Watt maintains that Missy had been (and currently remains) unaware of

the circumstances surrounding her father's death, and that her daughter believes that her father died of heart failure.

Francis Watt had been deceased for 6 years when Missy was first referred to UNIVERSITY HOSPITAL by her family physician. Mrs. Watt described her late husband as a 'strict but loving' father, and his relationship with his daughter as 'normal'. Mr. Watt had been a high school science teacher, and encouraged his daughter's precocity, facilitating the acceleration of her studies to the extent that she graduated from secondary school at 16 years of age. Missy enrolled in computer science at the UNIVERSITY OF WATERLOO, but upon the death of her father in the fall of 1986, abruptly terminated her studies. After a 6 month hiatus she transferred to English Literature, in which she received an honours degree with first class standing. She moved to her present address in 1989 in order to commence graduate studies in that subject, was awarded an MA in 1990, and continued on with her doctorate on a SSHRC federal research grant.

She had celebrated her marriage to Major Plumtree in May of 1990, just prior to completing her comprehensive exams. Thereafter, she was commencing work on her dissertation when, according to her husband, her alternating periods of depression and elation began to become somewhat exacerbated. She was admitted to the psychiatric unit at UNIVERSITY HOSPITAL in December of 1992 by Major Plumtree, who had found her at the municipal airport attempting to book a ticket to northern Ontario. When Major Plumtree suggested that Missy accompany him to the hospital Missy replied that she would kill herself if she were forced to do so, but eventually relented.

The admitting physician, Dr. Michael Tannenbaum, described her in his notes as 'uncommunicative but clearly agitated', and that her only statement during the initial interview was a muttered complaint of 'being controlled and manipulated by her husband'. Dr. Tannenbaum suggested a 72-hour stay in the hospital, to which Missy assented, and she was immediately prescribed 900 mg of lithium daily (note: creatinine satisfactory as serum concentrations reached 0.9-1.1 mmol/L in subsequent blood work) as well as given a course of lorazapam—8mg (2mg BDS + 4mg HS) for manifest agitation and anxiety. Missy continued with Dr. Tannenbaum for 9 months thereafter as an outpatient, during which time she had ceased all work on her dissertation and had clearly slipped into a state of clinical depression. Dr. Tannenbaum then referred her to the *Alba* Phase 1B trial.

Preliminary Interview 27-09-93
Missy Plumtree is briefed on the randomized, blind dosage allotment process [Missy = 3rd quartile], as well as on the anticipated therapeutic benefits and possible side effects of *Alba*. She agrees to the terms and conditions of this study, and certifies that she is not

currently taking any other medications. She agrees to a weekly monitoring of blood levels as well as a bi-weekly interview with a member of the clinical trial team. She is not currently pursuing any form of psychotherapy or counselling outside of the clinical trial and agrees to refrain from doing so until the completion of the trial. She signs the patient contract and waiver stating that the terms and conditions have been explained to her in full and that she agrees to abide by them. She is then given appointment dates for 27 blood level tests and 13 interviews for the following 27 weeks, to end on March 31, 1994. She is taciturn and somewhat distrustful in manner, but complies with requests readily, and appears somewhat optimistic that *Alba* will produce a salutary effect on her mood. Prescription is written for 30mg 1x/day, renewable bi-weekly.

Clinical Interview #1 12-10-93
Missy's blood levels appear to have stabilized at 58 and 60 μg/ml, within estimated normal range. She does not appear to be suffering from any side effects at this time, nor has she experienced any improvement in perceived outlook. She is informed that while side effects usually appear within 48 hours, improvements in mood are to be expected within 2–4 weeks. She is encouraged to discuss her situation whenever it feels appropriate to her. She assents to this suggestion, but does not engage in dialogue.

Clinical Interview #2 27-10-93

Blood levels remain stable, at 58 and 61 μg/ml. Still no change in perceived outlook, but Missy is reminded that this is statistically normal, and that there is a projected 70% probability that she will see an improvement inside of 6–8 weeks. Missy relates that she has been fighting with her husband, but declines to elaborate. Mildly probing questions receive no response.

Clinical Interview #3 09-11-93

Blood levels again stable, 59 and 60 μg/ml. No perceived change in outlook. Missy appears resigned to pessimism regarding the drug's efficacy. When asked if she feels she is pessimistic by nature, she smiles —wryly— and says to ask her husband. When asked why, she does not respond. She then adds that her husband wonders if a higher dosage might bring about an improvement in patients who prove unresponsive to lower dosages. She is informed that while higher dosages may prove to be more efficacious in some cases at reducing serotonin re-uptake, *Alba* also appears to produce elevated dopamine levels, levels that are contra-positive to some patients. The kinetics of dopamine and its role as a precursor to adrenaline are then explained to her in layman's terms. She is reassured that as a *possible* participant of one of the higher dosage quartiles, her dopamine levels, while presumably increased over baseline, should not prove a hindrance. However, she is also reminded that she must report any feelings of anxiety or panic to the trial's administrative nurse. She is then reassured that, if she has been selected to receive an above-median dosage, she should see some improvement by the end of the eighth week.

Clinical Interview #4 23-11-93

Blood levels increased: 72 and 76 µg/ml. Missy is quiet but agitated, and taps her left foot repeatedly and rapidly on the floor. When queried as to how she has been feeling, she adopts a 'thinking' posture, then looks up blankly and does not respond. Upon the mention of her husband, she breaks down, sobbing heavily. Missy confesses that he and she have been fighting continuously since their honeymoon, and that her husband is convinced that she is a pathological liar. She refuses to say more, except that her husband is waiting in reception, and wishes to have a minute or two of the doctor's time.

Major Mark Plumtree is calm, considerate, concerned. Missy has been agitated lately, he says, and he wonders if she is suffering from an adverse reaction. He is informed that her blood levels are up considerably, but that this, in-and-of-itself, is not necessarily causally related to Missy's current mental state. When Major Plumtree is asked if there is something else that might be upsetting her, he relates that they 'did indeed have a bit of a blow-up' the previous night, regarding Missy's sexual conduct. Major Plumtree had been unhappy to discover a letter from a lover that Missy had taken just prior to the beginning of their relationship, whom Missy had abruptly and secretly abandoned upon meeting her future husband. Apparently, Missy had then confessed to a further string of casual lovers that she had taken in the period immediately following her father's death. She had then run outside in her nightgown, clutching a large, boxed Xmas present that she had bought for Major Plumtree. Major Plumtree had no idea where she might have been heading, adding that he had intercepted her before she reached the end of the street.

Missy is subsequently directed to have her blood levels tested on a twice-weekly basis, as well as to monitor her agitation level and to contact the administrative nurse if she experiences any further anxiety.

Clinical Interview #5 07-12-93
Missy called in sick, rescheduling for Fri. 10-12-93. Her blood tests read 78, 81, and 80 μg/ml. A fourth test has been rescheduled for Fri. 10-12-93.

11

HER DIAGNOSIS

DR. ED ARRIVED at Emerg just before 20:00. Upon seeing him, the doctor who had examined Missy pulled him aside.

—Pete Laframboise. Dr. Ed stuck his hand out.

—Ed.

—How's Emerg tonight?

—Hopping. Full moon time.

—How is she?

—Physically there's just a minor contusion to the forehead, above the right eye socket. But, obviously, she's very … upset.

—Where is she?

—103. Anyhow, this is just the hunch of a non specialist of course, but I think there's more going on here than endogenous depression, Ed.

—How so? What are her blood levels?

—94. But check out the husband; he's in the waiting area.

—Did you speak with her?

— She's not overly communicative.

— No, she's not.

— See, I knew her before all of this. She was a friend and a classmate of my wife's, always a bit shy, but she had these ... bright ... eyes.

— Eyes.

— She had a *mind*, a personality. There was always a lot going on upstairs.

— Did she tell you anything?

— She described what happened, if that's what you mean. The husband apparently called her a 'slut' and a 'liar', and said that she was 'slime'. She repeated the word 'slime' several times, in fact. Things progressed from there. He left for the day, she called him repeatedly at work, alternatively begging forgiveness and accusing him of being unfair. Eventually he had his secretary intercept her calls.

— But he met up with her after work?

— He called home and said that he was going out for dinner and a movie with friends from the base, and would not be home until late. So she went looking for him....

— And?

— And accosted him outside of the movie theatre, distraught. When he turned away she proceeded to hit her head against a telephone pole, 'to get his attention', she said.

—To get his attention?

—I guess she felt there was no other way.

—You believe her?

—The way she described it, it was as if she were merely an observer or bystander. She wouldn't answer questions, but … well, talk to her yourself, you tell me. I'd say her attempts at self-injury aren't *simply* reducible to a … to a mood disorder.

Dr. Ed frowned, said nothing, put his thumb beneath his chin and his index finger beside his mouth so that they formed an 'L', to indicate that he was reflecting seriously upon this last statement.

—You tell me, Ed, Pete continued, you're the Man here. I'm just a bone-setter, but I'd say she needs, *they* need, marriage counselling more than anything. More than just putting her on anti-depressants, anyway.

—Hmmm.

—I realize I'm overstepping the boundaries here.

—Not at all, not at all, Dr. Ed lied. Tell me, what gives you this impression?

—Talk to the husband, suss him out. I'd say he's manipulative, like she says. Controlling, but suave. He's shocked, has *'no idea'* why she did what she did. No idea, Ed. Like it has *nothing to do* with him.

—Are you being objective here, Pete? You're not speaking like a doctor, you're….

—Getting emotional, yeah, I know. Like I say, Missy was my wife's friend, before she got married. Listen, don't take my word for it, just talk to Missy, then the husband. I'd bet that if you listen closely, you'll find there's a whole subtextual thing going on between them. He's getting her to act out a lot of his ... negative energy for him.

—Pete. '*Negative*'? '*Energy*'?

—That's my wife talking.

—I'll keep her diagnosis in mind.

—But then she's not usually far off the mark on these things.

—Have her come in for an interview; we could use a clairvoyant on staff.

—I'm serious, Ed.

—So am I, so am I. Now where is Mrs. Plumtree?

—Out in the hall. The husband is in the waiting room.

—Cheers, Pete.

—Yeah, cheers ... Um, Ed?

—Hmmm?

—Don't let anything happen to her, OK?

—Of course. I mean, of course not.

As expected, Missy was uncommunicative. By the time Dr. Ed found her, her gurney had been moved from the overflow hallway into an examination room. She was in 103, sitting on the examination table, hugging her knees. She was short, 5′1″, and in this position she resembled a sulking child. As Dr. Ed approached, she turned her back toward him, turned onto her left side, and curled up into a ball. He spoke to her gently, but she began humming to herself. He posed several questions, but each went unanswered. When he mentioned that he would be speaking to her husband, the humming grew louder. He patted her tensed shoulder, then took his leave.

Major Mark Plumtree sat waiting in the decrepit waiting room. He sat with an energetic, erect attitude (with *rect*itude) reading a near-decade-old edition of *Popular Mechanics*. Dr. Ed cleared his throat as he approached, and the Major looked up. They exchanged pleasantries. The Major was a bit of a cold fish, but try as he might, Dr. Ed could not read any of Pete Laframboise's speculations into anything that the Major told him. The Major had been at the movies with a couple of friends from the base, like Pete had said. He hadn't seen Missy since earlier that morning. They had certainly had an argument at breakfast, he admitted, during which he had questioned her honesty and integrity over a personal matter regarding which she had kept him in the dark, as it were. But you know how it is, the first year of marriage?

Dr. Ed did indeed know.

Yes, the Major had ignored Missy's calls, but she was making it impossible for him to do his job. He had also ignored her at first when he came out of the movie theatre, but only out of embarrassment—she had made quite a scene. He regretted that this might have pushed her towards hurting herself in any way, but she obviously needed more help than he alone could give her.

Dr. Ed concurred.

Dr. Ed wrote out a prescription for lorazapam and gave it to the Major, asking him to take Missy home and put her to bed. He reminded the Major of Missy's rescheduled appointment for the following morning, and asked him to bring Missy in himself if she proved too reluctant or agitated. The Major agreed readily.

—We can sort this out, said Dr. Ed. We may need to take her out of the *Alba* trial and try something else.

—I see, the Major said.

—By the way, tell me, what, exactly, did she say?

—You're referring to … ?

—As she struck her head against the telephone pole?

—Right.

—She *did* say—or rather yell something, didn't she?

—She did. She yelled one thing, over and over.

—Yes?

—'Feel my heart. Feel my heart,' she said. 'Feel my heart.'

12

THIS JUST IN

D R. ED SIGHED. He was at a stoplight, almost home. He was weary, and he was hungry. No, he wasn't—yes, he was, no, yes. The short-term energy of the doughnuts had evaporated into the ether, leaving him 'feeling' simultaneously full & tired, empty & wired: flemty, twired. His digital watch had just chimed only moments ago; it was now well past 22:00.

'Feel my heart.' Unfunnily enough, that was just what Agnes had said when he'd finally summoned the courage—after she'd come back (empty-handed, so to speak, from her involuntary stint at the convent)—to up and leave her, after much indecisive gnashing of teeth, after plenty of guilt-ridden hemming & hawing, oh, what?—27 years ago now. But: 'Feel my heart', wow. Spooky. *That's* for sure.

—Ahh, there she be.

His wife's Suburban was docked asymmetrically in the driveway, which should mean that Max would be back, too. Time for our bedtime walk, Maxxy, our l'il constitutional, eh boy? Just Max & he, he & Max. The wife would stay at home. Gladly. And watch TV.

She'll be deep into a manic microcycle, he 'thought'. Always happens after a shopping expedition. Not after *every* shopping expedition (of course—just after the successful ones—which worked out to about 7 out of every 8 trips, or 87.5%), but shopping's always the trigger (of course). She'll be like this for at least 36 hours. Then she'll be helpless for 48–72. Christ. It was to be expected, he supposed. But if it was to be expected, at least it was also fairly predictable, both quantitatively and qualitatively speaking.

Her periodicity was far too compressed to qualify her as bipolar, or manic-depressive. The classic bipolar cycle is measured in terms of weeks, not days, and, when graphically displayed, appears something like:

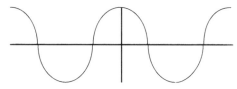

Her oscillations, on the other hand, looked more like:

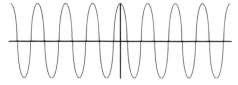

So, while (needless to say) *that* particular label was a definite no-go, as far as his wife was concerned, there *were* other exciting new developments on the pharmacological front. The identification of psychiatric disorders sometimes spurs pharmacological research, but sometimes it also happens the other way round.

And so it goes: just last month, he'd gotten wind of a new drug (code-named *Equinox*) being developed at NEXCEUTICA LABORATORIES (one of the NEXUS family of companies— NEXCHEM, NEXGEN, NEXCOM, etc.— 'Where Mother Nature Meets the Mother of Invention') down in Boston. NEXCEUTICA were concurrently sponsoring SUNY WATERTOWN's push to verify a potential new mood disorder that matched his wife perfectly, and for which *Equinox* was the answer. And if *Equinox* survived the FDA gauntlet (after which a HEALTH CANADA rubber stamp of approval was a for-sure *gimme*) it would answer the prayers of them all—i.e., NEXCEUTICA, Dr. Ed, and, quite possibly, even his wife. Dr. Ed had purchased 1000 shares of NEXUS (which trades on the NASDAQ, symbol: NXS) the previous April at 39½; it had recently closed at 62¾.

For the record, Dr. Ed did not currently hold any shares in EUMETA PLC., the makers of *Alba*. EUMETA trades out of the U.K. on the FTSE. Its symbol is EU.

She wasn't home. Max wasn't home. The lights were off. He didn't bother to look for a note: there wouldn't be one. As he made his way next door instead, to see his wife's best friend (and fellow TV addict) Margaret, to pump her for information, he was momentarily aware that, in his haste to locate Max, he was forgetting something of considerable practical import. But any knowledge of such forgetting was well forgotten by the time he rang his neighbour Margaret's doorbell. He didn't like Margaret, and did not like the fact that his wife *did*.

For her part, Margaret Murphy, a 55-year-old 33-year-old (or was that the other way around?), looked considerably displeased to be called to the front door in her fluorescent pink track suit at such a primetime hour as this. Dr. Ed had interrupted a particularly engrossing made-for-TV docudrama (*The Price Is Right Models: Their Tragedies and Their Triumphs*) and his wife wasn't there, and was there anything else he wanted?

—Do you have a moment? he asked.

—Nuh-yeahhhhh. Uhhh, Ray's n't here, if's him yer after. Ray, her invisible husband, was a lawyer.

—Working?

—Sort of. Whatever. *Pop-Tart?*

Saying this, she peeled open the heavy gauge plastic/foil composite wrapper off of a pair of dewberry frosted pastries, and moved one of them half-heartedly through the air, in his direction.

—No thanks. Uh, Margaret … ?

Only Dr. Ed addressed her using her proper name. Everyone else used one of 2 nicknames that she had picked up at the Cruelty Masterclass otherwise known as high school. Her first nickname, 'The Midge' dated from 11th grade biology, and owed itself both to the skeletal, gnatlike appearance (replete with piercing mouth parts) of the family *Ceratopogonidae*, as well as to their insatiable appetite. The second came later, in Grade 13: her older brother's friends, the O'Gallivan boys, had come from university for a weekend visit, and by Sunday dinner 'Smurphetella' (a portmanteau word which combined 2 of her obsessions: a certain gooey, chocolate spread from Holland, and her impressively vast collection of plush toys) had been engraved upon her forever.

—Hwa? she said, her mouth already full.

—Margaret, do you know anything about Max, did anything happen?

—Bax, she said.

—Yessss….

—Bax's Bozrate, she said, simultaneously swallowing.

—Pros*tate*, Dr. Ed corrected.

—Knees Tess.

—Needs Tests.

Smurphetella took another gobble from the pop tart, finishing the first one off, then morphed into The Midge, screwing up her eyes in a cataclysmic effort to remember something that Dr. Ed's wife may or may not have told her.

—Or ripes day, she said hopefully, putting a good half of the second pop tart in her mouth.

—Overnight stay, yes yes, go on.

—Top we pee to bee, she whined, sputtering moistened poptart crumbs in his direction.

—Stop re—Uh, Margaret, is it serious?

She swallowed, with gusto, a shockingly large mouthful, while raising her index finger as if to say 'One moment please, due to an increased volume of calls all of our lines are busy; you have been placed in queue and a customer relations associate will be happy to serve you shortly.' She then clutched at an English pint glassful of coffee and poured two-thirds of it down her throat (a trick that she had taught, much to Dr. Ed's embarrassment, Dr. Ed's wife to perform with beer) and let out a tremendous belch. She then gave him the look that always scared him the most (because it telegraphed the message that she was entirely at home in her body, and could easily take on three times a man as Dr. Ed was): a gee-shucks, gosh-golly, isn't-life-just-the-best-thing-ever, shit-eating grin.

—Is what serious, lover-boy? You know I'm not the serious type.

—Max, Max. I was asking about Max. Is it serious, whatever it is he's got?

—Oh, him. *He'll* be fine, she said, showing so many mercury amalgam dental fillings that he was temporarily blinded. She then waved her hand in emphasis, like she was jus' one-a-tha-fellahs. Her hand waved 'G'won. C'mon. Re-lax, g'way, gedd*outta*here.'

—Where's your husband, Margaret? Dr. Ed asked, feigning interest. He looked toward the door.

—Yeah, he *was*, like, *help*ing at Lions Club Euchre—or was that Kinsmen Tv Bingo? Anyway, by *now*, what time is it, oh he'd probably be at the Oddfellows Hall or the Legion for a couple of beers. Unless….

—Unless?

—Unless, what day is it?

—Wednesday.

—Which Wednesday?

—Which? What do you mean, which? he said, backing away from her slightly.

—Of the month: first, second, which?

—The second, he said, moving towards the front door.

—Well, then, Sam's at the Lodge.

—The Lodge?

—You, know, the *Lodge*, she said in a stage whisper. The *Masons*.

—But he's, but you're ... you're both Catholic! said Dr. Ed, opening the front door and putting his hand on the cold aluminum latch of the screen door.

—So? That don't matter none. It's a business thing. Sides, you know Sam, he likes everyone, and vice the verse it appears, vicky verky.

—Well I best be off, he said, then, turning back to face her: but, um, did she by any chance, did my wife say ... where she was going, or when she was coming back?

—No.

—She didn't say.

—No.

—Oh, OK, goodnight then.

—But you know me. *I* wouldn't say even if she did say.

—But she didn't say.

—You got it, Pontiac.

Dr. Ed went across her lawn to his own front porch.

—Hey Eddy boy, she called out, good luck eh, bust a gut!

He didn't look back, and couldn't summon the conviction to utter a 'Huh?' to this last remark, his supply of snappy questions and tolerance for stupid responses having simply *run out*. Closing his own front door behind him and re-entering the near-polar conditions (his wife not being home to frustrate his thermostat-programmed settings of 14°C/57°F daytime/evenings, 8°C/47°F nights) of his dark, empty, Max-less house, he did not hear The Midge/Smurphetella call after him one last time.

—Your Ex says Max'll be fine!

Dr. Ed slipped into his flannel pyjamas and put a mug of milk into the microwave. When it was done he stirred in some *Horlicks* malted milk powder, went up to his bedroom, found the remote control under a pile of his wife's 'things', got into bed and tuned in the local news station. He took one sip of his *Horlicks*, and placed it on the night table beside him, lying back into a pair of hyper-stuffed goose down pillows (one of his wife's many 'little finds'). He 'thought' once more of what Missy Plumtree had said to her husband, internally hmm'ed, ha'ed and huh'ed into putting it at the back of his 'mind', and promptly fell asleep, not giving another 'thought' to the matter. Nor did he give another 'thought' to 'that dream' he'd awoken from that morning, or to the whereabouts of his wife. As he nodded off (with the TV still on, something which was, it must be said, more to be commonly associated with his wife), he had only one image in his 'mind', that of Max, his most trusted friend and companion. Thus, as Dr. Ed fell asleep, worried by but also somehow strangely reassured by the presence of Max's absence—which floated through the room of Dr. Ed's 'mind' like a Ghost of Christmas Past—Dr. Ed missed the night's top news story: tomorrow's weather.

Tomorrow's weather, the weatherman said, promises a *defi*nite turn for the worse: it is going to get *warmer*, but *boy*, is it going *to snow*! A *mon*strously large, *warm* gulf *air* mass has col-*lid*-ed with an '*Al*berta *Clip*per', *ow*ing to a pro*nounced* southerly dip in the *jet* stream down as far *south* as *San Antonio*!

The *up*shot? Well, this little *doozy* of a system has started out *nas*ty and is only going to get *nas*tier as *time* wears *on*! *This* morning, residents of North *Tex*as woke up to *light*ning and *racquet*-ball-sized *hail*! *Pound*ing on their *roofs*! By afternoon, the *storm* had moved *on,* into *Ar*kansas and Tennes*see*! *Ham*mering *both Little* Rock *and Memphis*! With a *one-two punch*. Of *hail*! *And Ice*! Pro*vok*ing *Gov*ernors in *both states* to de*clare* a *State* of E*mer*gency. The *storm* then proceeded to *cover Jack*son, with up *to 3 centime*-tres! Of *freez*ing *rain* by rush hour com*mute time*! And by *early eve*ning *strong* winds had *driv*en a *dump*ing *of over 30* ceee-emmm *of snow* into 1 metre-*high*! *Drifts*! In *southern and central* Ken*tuc*ky!

It is snowing *hard* at the *pres*ent moment *in* Louisville, and the *storm — is* pro*ject*ed — to pum-mel the O*hi*o Val*l*ey during the *dead* of *night*. And! It's *track*ing north-north*east* incre*di*bly *quick*ly, and *will* cross the Detroit River and begin to blanket Windsor! By *sun*rise.

*East*ern parts of the province *should* ex*pect* to be hit to*mor*row in the early *after*noon. What's that, *John*? Wait ... reports *state* that it is *al-ready snow*-wing in Bowling *Green* ... is that Kentucky or Ohio?

We'll get a *fix* on that, but tonight's *Weath*-er *Word is*, that by the *drive home* tomorrow *even*ing, we should be *absolute*ly *plas*-tered—by the *white* stuff!

Coming up in other news: leash laws for *cats* proposed at City *Coun*cil; re*sults* from the Houseproud Club's *an*nual Hometown Town*home* competition; *cov*erage of the pre-*qual*ifying rounds of (one of De*cem*ber's highlights!) the Celebrity Pro-*Am cur*ling bonspiel; *and*: local *lamb* makes *mince*meat of the competition at the *Royal Winter Fair*....

This just in: an al*leg*ed discovery of unaccounted-for, unidenti-fied human re*mains* at the Logan Crema*tor*ium. Municipal police *spokes*person Polly Purfoy de*clined* to comment on the discovery, as it is '*cur*rently under investigation' ... *Details after this:*

THURSDAY

– PUTREFACTION –

In the first Decoction *(which is called* Putrefaction*) our stone is made
all black, to wit, a black earth, by the drawing out of its humidity; and
in that blackness, the whiteness is hidden.*

—Khalid ibn Yazid, *Secreta Alchimiæ 44:16*

13

NEVER WONDER

HIS PRE-SET ALARM had gone off at 06:50, and then again at 07:00, at increased volume. It went off a third and final time at 07:10, and did not stop ringing until its DIE HARDER batteries gave out, at 07:36. Dr. Ed awoke at 07:58, 'feeling', as the Scots say, 'absolutely guttered', as if he'd had a dozen pints of *90 Shilling* ale. But he hadn't, of course. Instead (and Dr. Ed knew this, was aware of it with the kind of clarity that only prophets and demagogues ordinarily lay claim to), he had merely dreamed. Oh, the doughnuts certainly hadn't helped matters, matters which, hard upon waking, forced him into yet another lengthy sojourn on the toilet. But the doughnuts were just the fall guys, pasty patsies that were mere accessories to a crime perpetrated inside his own 'mind'—that is, his brain. The real criminal was 'that dream', the exact same one which had troubled him the day before, and the details of which were now receding faster than a steroid-user's

hairline. As the panic of diarrhoeal (aptly taken from the Greek
-*rhoia*, from -*rhein*, 'to flow') convulsions (in the midst of which
the conviction now presented itself to Dr. Ed's 'mind' that he
had an inkling of what epileptics went through) gave way to the
mere cacophony of flatus, all knowledge of the contents of the
dream passed from his consciousness. What remained was only
the vague sense that it had something to do with a woman. The
question was, though: which?

His wife had not come home overnight, either. *Christ.* He got
dressed quickly, taking his customary two coffees in a thermos
on account of already being late (it was 08:00, and the first of his
patients would, with increasing impatience, already be waiting
for him, in the waiting room. *Christ.* Jesus *Christ.* Christ *Jesus.*

He put his galoshes on and stepped outside. It was 08:09. The
sun poked its timid nose through the branches of dormant trees;
the sky was light blue and getting bluer by the minute. Nice day,
anyway, he 'thought', unaware that the approaching storm (of
which he remained unaware) had become stalled, and that it
seemed to be more interested in wreaking havoc upon southern
Ohio than in taking it out on Ontario. It was now moving north-
eastward much more slowly, and its anticipated arrival had been
pushed off until late Thursday evening.

The air was bracingly cold, and dry. An agitated little breeze
was stirring sand out of discrete little piles on the roadway, getting

everything moving. The morning was still young, but it was sending a signal: this was no time to be standing idly by while the world swept past you.

A few in-breaths reminded Dr. Ed of what it was he had forgotten the night before, of what he had forgotten to *do*—to plug in the block heater for his Peugeot. There was *no way* it would start in *this*, he 'thought', meaning the temperature, which was -16°c or just above 0°f. In fact, the Peugeot needed a block heater for anything under -3°c/25°f, which meant that the drive to work was scuppered. He tried starting the car anyway, but it was as he had predicted: the car would not turn over. When he turned the key in the ignition, nothing—a great *big* nothing—happened. For a few moments he sat there (while his bum froze on the black leather seat) wondering what to do. This was not like him. It was not like him to wonder.

The Suburban *would* start, of course, but there was no question of taking it. He daren't. To say that his wife never let him drive it would be like—it would be like saying that all triangles had three sides, or that all bachelors were unmarried men. It would be, it would be tautological, that's what it would be. It would also be tautological to say, because it was fucking true by definition (there, he said the f-word, something else that was not at all like him), to say that he was freezing his ass off, not his bum or butt or buttocks, his *ass*, sitting in this idle—no: dead—car, 'thinking'—no: idly wondering—wondering just what his friggin' options were, on this cold friggin' morning, in this friggin' cold world.

Lessee: first off, he couldn't hoof it. He lived in the suburbs, where the taxi service was significantly worse than in the city proper, where it was reckoned by those few who had ever managed to hail a cab to be several million rungs below the level of frequency provided by the notoriously underfunded public transit system. Cars. Cars were the thing. You had to have one, at least one, and although Dr. Ed *owned* three cars, he did not, not at least for the moment, *have* even one. The trouble was, Dr. Ed needed to have one, to operate one, to use one, not at some other, later moment, but at *this* moment. Now. Now, G-d Damn It. Now.

He called the answering machine at the office, left a message for Nurse Sloggett's Temp explaining his situation, and resigned himself to trudging to the bus stop, to freeze and to wait in the gritty suburban winter landscape. And: 'feeling' a caffeine withdrawal headache coming on, 'feeling' the breeze coming on, 'feeling' the breeze mature into a wind. The bus was late. The breeze was climbing, from Force 4, past Force 5 on its way to Force 6 (which it would reach, later in the day) on the Beaufort scale. The bus was 15 minutes late.

Correction: the bus *was* 15 minutes late, but 15 became 20 as the bus driver picked Dr. Ed up, shifted the transmission into Park

and let the diesel engine idle. 5 minutes later, an OUT OF SERVICE
… SORRY! bus pulled up behind the one Dr. Ed was on, and the
two drivers exchanged places.

—Cutbacks, said a student, seated across from Dr. Ed, to his
companion.

—Unions, said the other.

—Ruling class toadie!

—Prole wannabee!

—GATT fatcat!

—AFL/CIO simpleton!

—CIO?? CIA you idiot, CIA!!

—No way, moron, no way. N-double-a, NAACP!!

—Fascist bastard.

—Pinko Commie Faggot.

—'Pinko'? Whaddyou mean, 'Pinko', what the, what in the
hell's that?

—Beats me. Pink. Not quite red. Fucked if I know, don't ask me.

—Don't ask *me?* Bluesuit/Blackshirt, pink/red/what*ever*, right?

—Pink, then, fuck-face, pink. Not *quite* G-ddamn red. Almost
fuckin' there, but *not* fuckin' quite.

—So let me get this straight, I'm a not-quite-red commie faggot?

—If you like.

—I'm a not-quite-red *Red?*

—If you wish.

—I don't wish anything, buster, I'm only repeating *your* words back to you.

—Words? Words. Words! Them's not *my* words, pal.

—Mine neither. Then whose are they then?

—No one's, fuck. Fucked if I know, just fuck the fuck off with that. Words. Just words, got it?

The one then looked on in mock consternation as the other commenced in song, quite near the top of his lungs:

> *Words, words, words, oh!*
> *S'all pooh and pee and turds!*
> *Chew'em, Spew'em*
> *Piss-n-Shit'em out*
> *Cover your eyes, close your ears*
> *Shut your mouth, they's still appears*
> *Ya just can't stop those words*
> *From gettin' out....*
>
> *Your mind is in the gutt-er*
> *Your brain is in the sew-er*
> *Tho' yer livin' high up on the hog up on the hill*
> *You can screw the lid on tight*
> *Keep your daughters home at night*
> *But you just can't stop your mouth from spewing swill!*

An old man who was sitting near Dr. Ed and who noticed the look of disgusted incomprehension on his face, leaned over and whispered:

—They go through this every day, they do.

—This?

—Or some such thing.

—Who are they?

—Boys. From my neighbourhood.

—They should be removed from the bus.

—We've all gotten used to them. They're a bit daft, but they're harmless.

—They're young. Young and brainless.

—Well we've all been that.

—Not me, pal.

—Not I.

Dr. Ed stood corrected. —Not I, Not I, he conceded, slumping, uncharacteristically, into his seat.

Suddenly the bus pulled into the central terminal and lurched to a halt, not at its designated loading bay, but in the middle of the parking lot.

—This bus is no longer in service, a digitized voice said. The next vehicle is due at ... Bay ... 11 ... in ... 7 ... minutes ... Please disembark at this time....

Dr. Ed decided to walk the rest of the way to the hospital. This took 20 minutes more, but further lateness seemed a small price to pay for sanity's sake. But he did not *just* walk; he *never* 'just' walked, or 'just' did anything. No! Dr. Ed made his way along the tidy sidewalks and streets with the unrestrainable vigour of a man in the full rudeness of health. He *strode* along determinedly, *swinging* his arms *purposefully*, in satisfaction of having the possession of the full knowledge concerning a certain undeniable fact: the undeniable fact that it took more than a few minor nuisances or chance inconveniences to put Dr. Ed off of *his* stride!

As he strode along, then, Dr. Ed made mental notes to himself, which he then sorted, arranged and stored in the orderly, legal-sized filing cabinet of his 'mind', as was always, on walks such as this, his wont. He made a highlighted, boldfaced and exclamation-marked mental note to cut to the chase in getting to the bottom of Max's whereabouts. He made a sober but liberally italicized sans-serif mental note to give his wife a stern but compassionate talking-to, regarding Max of course but *all the rest of it* as well. And he made a tertiary but no less significant, Times New Roman mental note to immolate the PEUGEOT as soon as was humanly feasible. This *was* urgent, and could not wait until spring, until his RX-7 was back in action.

No. The previous year's mild winter had lulled him into complacency, but he was now fully roused. This was urgent, and reasonably so. He needed something, and what he needed was something *trustworthy*. Something Japanese. Luxury and style, to a certain extent, yes, but on his own terms. As he matured, reliability was becoming more and more important to him, in *so* many ways. Individuality and flair were good, were all well and fine, but did one have to sacrifice reliability to obtain them? Dr. Ed wanted something *bulletproof.* And he'd get it, too. And soon! — after which that damned PEUGEOT would thus be … *no* more!

When he arrived at the hospital, and had followed a newly-erected detour route around the cafeteria (in which there had been an electrical fire overnight, due, presumably — or so one of the many females scurrying about had said — to 'some rodent or other making a picnic out of the wiring'), he lurched headlong into F-Wing and up to the 4th floor. As he did so, Dr. Ed began to 'feel' — that is to say, began to imagine — a 'force field' pushing him back, away from his departmental offices. This was both odd and disconcerting, in part because Dr. Ed did not believe in force fields, but also because he did not believe in the imagination.

Dr. Ed was, when it suited him — which was almost always — an *ontological materialist.* He believed that all reality was erected from the building blocks of matter. Psychological reality, then, was constructed by the building blocks of the brain, brain cells which in turn could be reduced, broadly speaking, to chemistry. Psychology depended upon biology, which amounted, in the end, to chemistry. There is no 'soul', there is no 'mind', or at least one which is not epiphenomenal, i.e. the mere *by-product* of the chemical processes of the brain. Dr. Ed was happy with this position, and it put paid to all manner of silly, mystical notions, the very kind of notions that misguided patients tended, more often than not, to have.

There was only one problem with this position, however: free will. If material causality was a fact, then it ruled out free will completely. Free will, which Dr. Ed very much believed in, was a bit of a spanner in the works, as far as materialism went, because free will was not 'free' if it was materially caused. How could you get perfectly sane, competent people to accept responsibility for their actions if they knew that all their behaviour, indeed everything about them, was a mere by-product of chemical interactions? You couldn't.

Dr. Ed was no philosopher, and had never heard of the half-way house called 'soft determinism', whose adherents had attempted to map out and negotiate a passage around the Wandering Rocks of scepticism and between the Scylla of nose-to-the-ground materialist determinism and the Charybdis of pie-in-the-sky libertarianism. Nevertheless, Dr. Ed found his own trap-door: it was simple, yet ingeniously effective, and it sorted the world out quite nicely indeed. It involved paying attention to the practical, lived experience of normal, everyday people, people making normal, everyday decisions, and it ignored the conundrums of the wider philosophical debate altogether.

It went like this: people with a normal psychological makeup certainly *experience* life as if their choices matter. Most have a '*felt*' *conviction* that they can freely choose between two widely divergent possibilities, and that the consequences of these choices are real and meaningful. Certain genetic predispositions might tip the balance in one direction slightly more than in another, but on the whole, people with *normal* psychological makeup do not feel compelled to behave in any manner other than how they would *choose* to behave. *Abnormal* psychology, on the other hand, begins with abnormal brain chemistry; abnormal patients experience the world quite differently from their normal counterparts. They '*feel*' that they *lack* choices, that they are *driven* to behave in ways that they would never choose, if given the choice. But that was just it: they do not '*feel*' that they are *given* a choice.

Modern psychiatry, on the other hand, was attempting to give them that 'feeling', that 'feeling' of possessing the capacity to make choices. Drugs such as *Alba, Solara, Bicamera, Assuage and Prolepsin* (as well as, perhaps, hopefully, this newcomer, *Equinox*) were doing for those whom nature had deprived of normal neurotransmitter levels what public health and education had done for generations of the economically disadvantaged—giving them a fighting chance on a more level playing field. They really were. And these drugs were only giving these unfortunates something that everyone else already enjoyed: the *experience* of willpower, the very *possibility* of choice, the potentiality and actuality of 'feeling' that, regardless of external contingencies, one is always '*choosing*' to 'choose'.

Dr. Ed did not 'feel' that this '*Weltanschauung*' of his was simplistic or reductionist. On the contrary, for those who would persist, for those who would insist upon continuing to smuggle in such tired, metaphysical shibboleths as 'the soul', fairy tales belonging to a more innocent, naive and credulous time, he had only pity and contempt. G-d was long-dead, and the soul had died with Him. All else was at best sentimentality; at worst, cynical (but, as the New Age was proving, profitable) deceit.

To say, then, that Dr. Ed 'felt' a 'force' that was pushing him back, away from his office, is to say that he 'felt' a 'presence' in his lower abdomen, the cause of which was most certainly adrenaline, the fight-or-flight hormone whose precursor is dopamine. It was obvious to Dr. Ed why this might be happening: he had just had a very stressful last 16-or-so hours, and (understandably enough) did not 'feel' entirely up to the demands of meeting his Thursday morning patients, all of whom were part of the *Alba* trial. What he was 'feeling' (he told himself, to talk himself down from this quite reasonable 'emotional' response) was a quite reasonable 'emotional' response, and there was nothing to be alarmed about. Max was fine. His wife was fine. Everything, all manner of things were, and would continue to be, fine. He just needed a couple of deep breaths, a belated morning coffee from his thermos, and a few minutes' peace in order that he might collect wayward 'thoughts' such as these, before seeing his patients. Dr. Ed took a deep breath in, exhaled still more deeply, and opened the door to the clinic. It was 09:27.

14

A 'Switch' To 'Flick'

IT WAS 09:27. Sitting at Nurse Sloggett's desk was *not* the usual, capable Temp whose services were always engaged on those (thankfully rare) occasions when Nurse Sloggett was unavoidably absent. Sitting at Nurse Sloggett's desk was his 'son', Ted. Dr. Ed went around the glassed-in nursing station, up to the desk, placed both his palms down upon its edge, and leaned over it. Numerous 'emotions' had arisen within him, among them: anger (of course), embarrassment (that his 'son' might have told someone, anyone, about their … 'relationship'), fear (ditto, but additionally, the fear that Ted might have screwed something—anything—up, as far as the job was concerned), and, again, anger (obviously).

—Hi, 'Dad'.

—Don't call me that, Ted. Especially not here.

—What's the matter?

—Nothing.

—You're late, later than your message said you'd be.

—I don't want to talk about it.

—4 of your first 6 patients have already left. I told them to call back tomorrow to re-schedule.

—Fine. I'll need a couple of minutes.

—Uh, could we have a talk, at some point, 'dad'?

—I told you not to call me that. Not here, certainly.

—But you are my dad, you know.

—Only theoretically.

—No, not theoretically, dad. *Tech*nically. You did, in fact, *sire* a son.

—Technically, then. OK, technically speaking, I'm your father. Now, could you tell me just what the hell you're doing here?

—Uh, I think I'm working here. I work for the Temp agency, LaborValu. You know what their motto is?

Dr. Ed did not respond. He tried to look as coolly at this young man as he could, but the *sang-froid* had all leaked out of his corroded radiator, and his temperature light had just come on.

—'We're all work and no play.'

Dr. Ed looked at him for a lengthy-seeming 4–5 seconds, and then said, with as much composure as he could muster:

—We'll talk later, I promise. I need a few minutes, then I'll let you know when to call the first patient in.

His 'son' nodded wordlessly, and then Dr. Ed went into his office. He composed himself, then placed a phone call to LaborValu. In a polite, 'emotion'-less tone of voice he spoke to a Customer Relations Associate named Eustasia Sculpin, who explained that his usual temp had not called to confirm, and so they had been forced to send Theodore. Dr. Ed made it clear to Ms. Sculpin that he appreciated their efforts on his behalf, and assured her that 'Theodore' was both hard working and courteous. He had, however, one request to make: could the agency somehow flag his file, so that, in future, only *female* Temps be sent to his office? A large number of the clinic's patients were women, who were, or had been … victims … of sexual and/or 'emotional' abuse, and they would 'feel' much less threatened by, that is, 'feel' more, more at ease in, you understand, in a … clinical environment which was….

Etcetera.

Now Dr. Ed had what he liked to call a 'switch'. And he had the ability to 'flick' this 'switch', which was 'located' somewhere in his 'mind'. If he ever overreacted, if something ever got him upset, worked up, '*emotional*', then, when he realized what was happening, he simply 'flicked' this 'switch', and the 'emotions' were 'diverted', through a 'gate'. The 'gate' did not lead to a 'filter', where they would be made to simply disappear, no; nor did they lead to an 'attenuator'. Rather, the 'switch' diverted them into a kind of 'capacitor' or CCD (charge coupled device), where they could be temporarily 'stored', until there was sufficient time & energy to process them, later on.

He'd initially realized that he had a 'switch' to 'flick' back in his last year of high school, when he'd first met Agnes, Ted's mother. He didn't know, at the time, how useful it would soon prove to be, but the idea of it resonated strongly within him, the idea that you could 'compartmentalize' certain potentially troublesome aspects of your 'self', so as to more effectively deal with the storms and stresses of life. The original idea had come from a Dr. Matthews, his Grade 13 History teacher at St. Aloysius College, an all-male Roman Catholic day school which was 'semi-private' in the sense that there was a tuition fee, but it was much less than the private schools—and the fee was waived for families who lacked the means to pay. It was Dr. Matthews who had planted the seed, but it was Dr. Ed himself who had changed the physical basis of the metaphor, from Dr. Matthews' explanation of the various rooms in a house, to the one that Dr. Ed still employed—that of the *switchable electrical circuit*.

It was mid-winter. The class was what would now be called an 'enriched' one, in that all but the best-and-brightest students had been diverted into their own 'stream'. Dr. Matthews was pushing them hard, expecting from the class the maturity, curiosity, perseverance and quality of work which one would normally associate with the 2nd year of university. They were studying Modern British History, from the Hanoverian Succession to the present day, and had reached the second half of the 19th century, deep into the reign of Queen Victoria, and marked by the many pitched battles in Parliament between the Whig leader, William Gladstone, and his Tory counterpart, Benjamin Disraeli. Of the two, Disraeli was clearly Dr. Matthew's (as well as Queen Victoria's) favourite, and the class had been able to kill several periods getting Dr. Matthews to regale them with anecdotes about Disraeli's life and times.

First off, Disraeli's father was a Jew, and for a Jew — even one who had converted to Christianity — to become Prime Minister of Europe's leading colonial power was simply unheard of. He was also a writer, and his novels *Coningsby* and *Sybil* had become the catalyst for a movement known as Young England. 'Conservatism, yes', went his rallying cry, 'but what shall we conserve?' The Disraeli anecdote that impressed young Eddy the most, however, was not delivered in class. Rather, Dr. Matthews bequeathed it to him when they met after school one day, to discuss Eddy's falling grades and overdue assignments. Dr. Matthews wished to know what had happened to cause this sudden turn for the worse, and moreover, what had happened to that essay that Eddy was writing on 'Victorian Ideas of Poverty and the Poor'?

Eddy came clean with his teacher, at least partly because the older man was kind in a grandfatherly way towards his students, helping them out whenever he could, without trying to be 'pals' with them, as some teachers are wont to do. Eddy told Dr. Matthews about how his girlfriend, Agnes, had become pregnant, and how, when her parents finally noticed, they had conspired with Eddy's parents and the parish priest to send her to the Mother House of the Sisters of St. Joseph, where she would have the baby and give it up for adoption. She hadn't left yet, but things were a bit difficult all around at the moment, and, Eddy wondered, while it was certainly not excusable, could he still possibly hand that assignment in?

Dr. Matthews graciously granted Eddy an open deadline on his essay, adding that he could hand work in over the summer to get the credit, if necessary, and that Eddy should take care *not to worry* overmuch, that things have their own way of working out, that life must take its own course. That was not a prescription for passivity, or for giving up, however; rather one must always, as Machiavelli once said, know what lies within one's proper sphere of influence, and what must be left to Fortune, and so act accordingly. Or, as the soldiers' maxim went, one must 'trust in G-d, but keep one's powder dry'. By 'powder', Eddy eventually came to understand that Dr. Matthews had meant 'gunpowder', by which he had really meant 'one's own devices'. Well, Eddy was certainly going to place his trust in those, and not in some 'G-d' who never showed his face and who allowed all manner of bad things to happen to not-so-bad people!

Dr. Matthews then let Eddy in on the story that was going to change his life forever. Eddy was aware, was he not, that Disraeli had been a great admirer of Charles Dickens? Eddy was. Dr. Matthews had mentioned this to the class, and had reminded them of it on several occasions. Well, there is a character in Dickens' novel, *Great Expectations*, named Wemmick, whom Disraeli would certainly have appreciated very much, Dr. Matthews went on. If you visited Wemmick at the strange, miniature castle that was his home, if you crossed over the moat that he had constructed to separate himself from the modern world, and had proceeded from his drawbridge into his parlour, he would have appeared to you to be the most generous and hospitable man you had ever met, and one full of colour, full of life. However, if you had the misfortune of visiting him at work, at the office of the ultracompetitive and successful lawyer Jaggers, for whom he toiled ceaselessly, you would have encountered an entirely different being. For here was a man who worked in black and white, in a world of instrumental reason, of *intellectus*, rather than *ratio*, in the 2-dimensional, parcelled-out world of Utility. It was a world that could be depicted only in terms of the axes of a grid, a world whose Rules of Engagement could be defined only by an algorithm of debits and credits, the outcome of which could be understood only in terms of winners and losers. It was the 'Real World', and Wemmick had to at least work, if not live, within its constraints.

At work, Wemmick had what Dickens called a 'post office' box opening or slit for a mouth, and all the colour and humanity of the man was entirely absent. If the post office mouth 'smiled' it was only the mechanical appearance of a smile and nothing more. Wemmick acted thus because it allowed him to survive the rigours of working for Jaggers. Disraeli, reading Dickens, could only have seen this for what it was—an indictment of, again, what capitalist businessmen call 'The Real World', of what 'The Real World' does to people, of how people have to deform their humanity in order to survive it. Yet, Disraeli would also have taken another lesson from Dickens as well: while 'The Real World' may be nothing more than the collective insanity of a nascent industrial age, it does not just disappear because one can raise one's drawbridge and shut one's curtains upon it. Collective or communal insanities can impose themselves upon the individual with very real consequences. Just look at fascism in Germany, or at Cold War paranoia in the U.S. Other people's madness can unleash havoc upon one's entire world, and one has to *compartmentalize* one's life to survive, just like Wemmick.

And it's not just society at large that one has to worry about. On a much smaller scale, one's friends and family can often successfully impede one from accomplishing what one must (if one is to remain true to oneself) accomplish. To take a trivial example, one's friends might be playing a game of hockey outside one's window, while one attempts to practice at the piano. If one allows their enthusiasm (or even one's own desire to be distracted) to become a real distraction, then what will one ever *accomplish?* Or again, take Disraeli, for instance, who went through terrible agony over his wife's ill health at one point. When he went in to work, however, by G-d, he went in to work!—and left his troubles at the door.

It wasn't that he learned to *forget* his troubles, Eddy, it was that he found a way to put them into … into storage for the time being. He learned to *separate* his two lives, so that they did not *bleed* into one another, and I am telling you this now because these troubles that you are trying to endure at the moment, make no mistake, they *are* a test of your character. How you come through in the end, Eddy, well it's up to you. But I suspect that you will overcome them. Perhaps you and Agnes will one day marry, perhaps not. Who's to say? And while I'm not sure that the right decision is being made by your parents on your behalf, well, what can you do? You've got to soldier on.

And so soldier on he did. The very night that Agnes was parcelled off on the train to Petropolis, young Eddy made the crucial discovery; he found the 'switch'. He was lying on his bed reading *The Fountainhead* when he discovered it, when he discovered that he could 'flick' it. Then he 'flicked' it 'off', and it pretty much stayed 'off'. And from that night on, whenever he 'thought' of Agnes on the cinema screen of his 'mind', where the image of her beatific face used to be he would now draw a blank, by just 'flicking' the 'switch'. Moreover, her name, which had heretofore borne such unbearable, almost-mystical, lexical weight, now resumed its proper station, and revealed itself for what it truly was: a mere word, two syllables, Ag-nes.

And so thereafter Agnes gradually became no more than a part of his past, and he, well, he looked forward, forward, forward into the future — into his *own* future. It's not that he *never* looked back. He did. Just not all that often. And never very far.

15

JUMPING TO CONCLUSIONS

Dr. Ed 'flicked' his 'switch'. It worked. It usually did. True, the 'switch' *had* malfunctioned the previous evening, when Dr. Ed had become aware of Max's and his wife's ... unexplained absence. Yet (though he was still at a loss to explain precisely *why* this had happened), he was happy to report to himself that it had been merely a temporary glitch, and that his ability to 'flick' the 'switch' had *definitely* returned to him. He 'flicked' the 'switch', put the telephone handset back into its cradle, and, engaging the intercom, directed his 'son' to send the first patient in. It was 09:42.

That morning, Dr. Ed attended to the hardy 2 who had stuck it out in the waiting room, plus a further 10, all in a record 1 hour and 2 minutes, all before breaking early for lunch at 11:00, as he always did on Thursdays. He averaged just under 6 minutes per patient instead of the usual 12.5, getting them out of the office by giving each exactly what they wanted—what each said they wanted, at any rate, or what they *would* say that they wanted, Dr. Ed was certain, if they could ever just get around to getting around to saying it. And if he couldn't give each&every one of them *exactly* what they asked for — if that lay beyond his scope and ken — well, then Dr. Ed made sure they got the next best thing.

09:44 got more Imipramine, as did 09:49, while 09:54 coaxed out of him a doctor's note to cover 4 half-credit final exams at the university. 10:01 got switched from lorazapam to diazepam, and 10:06 got the promise of a letter to the CANADA PENSION PLAN's Disability Appeal Tribunal. 10:14 proved a bit sticky, for a minute or 2, but was eventually guided to the door with vague but reassuring assurances. 10:22 was also mollified by the (eventual and abrupt) bestowal of a promise, a promise instantly regretted by its bestower, to interview 10:22's husband, whose antics were the 'actual' source of 10:22's 'issues' — as 10:22 termed her numerous recent persecutory delusions. 10:29's ill-defined symptoms of neurasthenia were to be taken seriously from here on in, as were 10:35's, with whom, Dr. Ed suspected, 10:29 was becoming intimately involved. Going against the grain of Dr. Ed's preliminary diagnosis of acute connubial infarction, 10:40's wife's artful, disingenuous portrayal of ingenuousness got 10:40 into the *Alba* trial. 10:48 came and went without saying a word, this for the 3rd time in a row. Finally, in came 10:52, Dr. Ed's final patient before lunch, which was very much a relief for Dr. Ed, for the last patient before lunch on Thursday's had always been, since the beginning of the *Alba* trials anyway, Buddy. And this is how it always went with him: the nurse would take some blood, they'd shoot the breeze a bit about his 'feelings', and then they'd walk over to the LITE BITE together, Thursday being the day Buddy sagaciously kept himself out of the kitchen and let his apprentice take over. Today, however, Dr. Ed 'felt' like keeping to himself, and 'felt' he had to break it to Buddy right off the top, to clear the air.

—Don't have the time today, sorry, he said as Buddy's bulk plunged with a 'Woof!' a full eight inches into the disarming plushness of the oversized patient's chair.

—That's OK, Eddy, Buddy said, smiling a capacious, toothy smile and rocking side-to-side on his haunches by way of settling in.

Buddy was the only person (besides the Midge) who would, or could, conceivably call Dr. Ed 'Eddy'. And it was something of a stretch even for Buddy, although Buddy himself was quite unaware of just how much of a stretch it was. Buddy's forward momentum through his own life was fuelled by a strongly-willed innocence, by a stubborn refusal to see anything but The Good in others, particularly in those he counted, rightly or wrongly, as his friends. And so Buddy's version of Dr. Ed *had* to be called Eddy, for Buddy rightly or wrongly saw a different man seated across the desk from him than most everyone else, the man across the desk included. For better or worse, the Dr. Ed who Buddy saw was a still-17-year-old boy, an Eddy who even Dr. Ed himself could hardly remember (and certainly had no interest in), an Eddy who still hadn't even really encountered, let alone fathomed, words like 'loss', 'despair' or 'betrayal'.

—That's OK, really, he repeated, when Dr. Ed remained in awkward silence. Really.

Dr. Ed opened up Buddy's manila medical file, a clear signal that he had 'flicked' his 'switch', and that the session had begun.

—How has your exercise program been coming along? he said.

—Still swimming 3 times a week, well, 2 to 3 times anyhow, but you know me.

—You're still….

—Still the same ol' Buddy.

—That you are. And you're watching what you eat?

—I'm watching alright, I'm watching myself *eat*. Both men laughed briefly.

—It's not a pretty sight, either, Buddy added. As well you know!

Dr. Ed smiled wanly, but said nothing.

—Seriously now, Eddy, I have something to confess to you.

—Yes? said Dr. Ed, noticeably straightening his already Royal Military College-esque posture.

—You're not going to like this.

—Buddy, speaking as your doctor now, of course, it's not my *position* to 'like' or 'dislike'. I'm here to observe, assess, diagnose, treat, and, to a certain extent, advise you. 'Like' is not a part of my ... *function* here; 'like' doesn't enter into it—ever, at all.

Buddy had sat in this chair oh, 6 or 7 times since he started on the *Alba* trial, and was quite used to his friend 'speaking like a doctor', but today Dr. Ed appeared to be, if that were at all possible, even more doctor-like.

—Ok, anyway, you know what I mean, I mean, in your terms, that you are going to *analyse* what I'm about to reveal to you, and you will 'thoughtfully' *conclude* that my decision was rather ... *unwise*.

—Reveal what, which decision, Buddy?

—The one I'm trying to tell you about.

—Just tell me.

—It's not that easy.

—C'mon, it's just me: Dr. Ed.

—I'm a bit ... scared to, Eddy.

Dr. Ed frowned, just a little. Normally, Dr. Ed did not mind at all if patients expressed their 'emotions', so long as they kept it short & sweet and didn't *wallow* around in them for minutes on end. But Buddy was different, a bit of a special case; Buddy was a 'friend'.

—You're afraid to tell *me*? he said. Or you're just afraid, period?

—No, well, yes, that is, a little. But I mean I'm afraid of the decision, of my decision, itself.

—Of its consequences?

—Yes.

—Tell me about the decision, Buddy.

—Well, it's a 2-part decision. The one flows from the other, or both flow into each other, I'm not sure exactly, it's a bit of a chicken-and-egg thing.

—Then start with the chicken.

—I'll start with the how do you say … clinical aspect first. No, I won't, I'll start with the personal, the personal side of it.

—Fair enough.

—We've been friends for a long time, Eddy.

—That's right, yes.

—And I want you to know that I appreciate everything you've done for me, which is a lot. And we both know that part of my … 'problem', for want of a better….

—I prefer 'condition', actually.

—Right, yes, 'condition' is better, definitely. Well, part of it is, was due to my lack of, um, success, that is with the ladies, currently I mean.

—You would 'feel' more fulfilled in a long-term relationship.

—In any relationship.

—Yes.

—But yes, long-term, I hope.

—You hope.

—Eddy, I ... I, I'm going to ask Nurse Sloggett to marry me.

—Yes? I.

—I?

—I didn't know that you ... two ... were, were involved.

—We're not.

—I *see* ... now, don't you 'think', perhaps....

—I know what you're going to say, Eddy, first things first, I know, I know, Lord knows I know.

—But still. You.

—Everything's interrelated just now. Inter-, inter-*twined* is the word I'm looking for. I've always been ready, no, *set* to share my life with someone, Eddy, but, and you've got to hear me out here, but I've never quite gotten around to getting out of the starting blocks, and right now, right now I'm fairly certain, certain as I ever get at any rate, certain that that someone who I've been always ready for, well, that they, I mean she, is ready, ready to share her life with me.

—But, but what makes you so, so *certain*, Buddy, that it's Nurse Sloggett, that she's the one?

—Do you know her first name, Eddy?

—Of course. It's, wait a minute, it's....

—It's Agnes.

—Of course.

—The same as.

—Yes.

—Agnes, your Agnes.

—I don't have an Agnes, Buddy. I have a wife. You know my wife, don't you?

—Don't get so touchy. You're s'posed to be helping *me*, remember? By your Agnes I mean Agnes from way back when.

—Back when. What's that got to do with Nurse Sloggett and you?

—Well, she was at the restaurant last Saturday.

—And?

—And we got to talking.

—Yes?

—And she said to call her by her first name, Agnes.

—And that's all?

—No, well, she also talked about her late husband.

—Frank. Ran a chip truck down by the lake.

—That's right. Well, she said Frank's been gone 2 years now, and she still hasn't been out on a date.

—Which is common, of course.

—Yes, well, she's going out on a date with me, Eddy!

—A date, OK, but a proposal of marriage? Aren't you just … ?

—Jumping to conclusions? Aren't you?

—Explain it to me, then.

—Then listen. We were talking, we were talking about her husband, and I was saying how much the whole team missed him, and what a great skater he was—untouchable, when he wanted to be—when just like that, she, how else can I put this, she fell into my arms.

—Wha … ?

—No, *lis*-ten. It just happened. When I said what a great man he was, she said she wished she'd gone in his place, or at least with him, and that she wanted, when the time came, to be buried in the same grave.

—What did you say?

—I said I understood how she could love someone *that* much, but that I hoped that 'that time' was not coming anytime soon.

—And you asked her out?

—No, she asked me out—as a friend.

—I don't….

—We saw a movie Saturday Night, something called *Steel My Heart*.

—How was it? said Dr. Ed, by way of wondering what to say next.

—Good. Solidly entertaining. She said she'd like to do it again sometime, and kissed me on the cheek, and I said how about next Friday.

—Tomorrow.

—Right, and she said why don't I cook you dinner, and I said I'd love to be cooked for. And….

—And.

—And she said, it's a date. It's a date, Eddy!

Buddy got up, slapped Dr. Ed on the back, looked at his watch, moved toward the door. Dr. Ed, taking Buddy's lead, stole a glance at his own watch as well.

—Yes, time is pressing in on us a bit, he said.

—Well, I haefta go do a few errands....

—Hold on, I want to get this one thing clear. Did I hear right, or did you not say that on the basis of her suggesting cooking you dinner tomorrow, that you're going to ask her to marry you?

Buddy took two steps back toward Dr. Ed's desk, his broad smile vanishing momentarily as he did so. He became suddenly as earnest as a temperance crusader.

—Oh, no, he said. I'm not going to ask her *tomorrow*. I'm just telling you all this, in confidence I might add, because I want you to know, that's all.

—You want me to know because....

—Because you're my friend, Edward, I want you to know. I want you to know that *I* know, that I just *know*, that, that she's the one, that's all. Do you know what I mean?

—I do, Dr. Ed said, realising as he did so that while 'Eddy' might know what Buddy meant, *he* most certainly did not. I do, he said. Really.

—I better go, said Buddy.

—Wait a minute. You said that you had 2 things to say, didn't you?

—Oh, yeah, I wanted to talk to you about the *Alba*.

—How's the past week been?

—Really good, actually, except—

—Except?

—Well, I've never felt more confident or on top of things, since I've been on it. But, um, Ed, how long does it stay in your system?

—After you've stopped taking it, you mean?

—Yes.

—It's half-life is about two weeks, and generally speaking, that's how long it's expected that you'll experience an effect, after taking your last dosage. Why? You haven't interrupted the treatment plan, have you?

—Well that's about right then.

—Buddy?

—I want to pop the question to Agnes a week Saturday.

—What's going on, Buddy?

Buddy began backing once more towards the door to the waiting room. —I'm off it, Ed. I know I'm better on it, but it makes me different, and I want to be *me*. For her. I want her to know the *real* me. With all the blemishes and bruises, but all the trimmings too. Sorry about this. He put his hand on the doorknob.

—I think we should discuss this fur—

—Time's up, doc, gotta go. Don't worry. We'll talk. Wish me luck. Tomorrow. Bye!

16

UNUSUAL LEVELS OF ACTIVITY

As REQUESTED, Dr. Ed's 'son', the Temp receptionist, brought him the local paper, as well as an egg salad sandwich on whole wheat from the 'side out' vending truck, whose prices were lower and whose egg salad contained, the rumour went, the promise of slightly more egg (and correspondingly less mayo) than that of the 'out front' vending truck. But the egg salad actually turned out to be 'faked' (must have meant flaked) 'white tuna' (or a few grammes thereof), slathered in white goo, on bread so white it could have been considered Aryan. Well, at least the boy had gotten him a chocolate bar. But no, it was not a chocolate bar, but a candy bar. The wrapper promised more than it (or any other candy bar) could possibly deliver: sumptuous, scrumptiously rich, fudgy nougat surrounding a sinful, caramelly centre, which, after being rolled in golden, peanutty nuggets, all got slathered in a thick, chocolatey coating that would tempt your taste buds into outright concupiscence. The confection was called *Infidelity* (the bar that dares speak its name). Dr. Ed tossed it onto his desk, unwrapped his sandwich, sat down, flipped on the computer, and scanned the front page of the paper.

Huh?

A ball of starch-clad mayonnaise, caught in mid swallow, bolted back up to the top of Dr. Ed's throat. **BODY FOUND** was the main headline. Unidentified female discovered at Logan cemetery. Huh. Jesus. But no, it couldn't be. 10 to 1 she'd gone Xmas shopping, to the City. 10 to 1, I betcha. He called home again, and again the answering machine picked up the call. Dr. Ed left his second message of the day:

—Uh, dear, it's, it's your husband. Just wondering where you are, if everything's all right. It's … 11:20. I'll be home at … I'll call before I leave, later this afternoon.

Then, once more, Dr. Ed successfully 'flicked' his 'switch', and promptly forgot, or sent into cold storage, his irrational extrapolation from the scant facts of the newspaper article. There was, admittedly, a good chance that she was already home, but not lifting up the receiver: his wife would usually have returned his messages on the same day, but she never answered the phone when there was a good show on. A 'good' show' could be defined as either a soap opera, a talk show, or (even better, and perhaps marking television's leap into the so-called postmodern era, in which everything is a copy of an imitation of nothing more than a shadow) a talk show about soap operas, or talk shows.

Back when she'd been with Erazhim, the print-maker, he had always chided her about the self-referentiality of her art, how by merely re-presenting (for example) the feminine form *sans* destabilizing ironic commentary, she was indulging in a *de facto* capitulation to hegemonic, bourgeois, patriarchal culture — to its fetishistic celebration of the voluntarist subjectivity of the utility-maximising *individual*, and by extension to the entire phallogo-centric military-industrial complex.

The phallo-what? She didn't have a clue what he was going on about (and, she guessed correctly, neither did he). So she ignored it. But she liked the sound of that term 'self-referential'; it stuck with her. And, she realized later, she had *always* liked things that somehow referred back to themselves. Pictures of women linger-ing tellingly in front of mirrors, idly gazing into the looking-glasses of their own saucer-sized pupils. Escher's portrait of those eponymising, self-inscribing, symmetrical hands. Silly love songs about silly love songs. Poems about the poet's obsession with the poem's lack of obsession with the poet. Even the self-help fad of re-birthing, and the subsequent re-parenting of the inner child, even that had something to be said for it, something life-affirm-ing, something that 'life' with Erazhim did *not* have. When she finally left him, when she started seeing Dr. Ed, she gave up trying to create order 'out there', in bronze, marble or whatever, sens-ing the obvious superiority of taking care of her 'inner' life for the first time. Art was merely the expression of a kind of failure in life, and, if you sat and 'thought' it over for a second or two, who needed that?

Dr. Ed put down the receiver, moved his keyboard closer to the edge of his desk, typed MAIL at the Unix command prompt (his terminal was part of a small network built and maintained expressly for his department by their corporate partners, EUMETA, and which included both GOPHER AND WAIS servers), which brought up the PINE mailer. His mail account listed 32 new messages, 27 of which were from the PSYCHED listserv@usc.edu. One of the remaining 4 was a CFP (call for papers) for the 2nd annual Personality Architectonics Conference, which was to be held in Helsinki. In February. Not too bloody likely! Dr. Ed 'thought'.

There was also an email from his mother, addressing him, as Buddy did, as Eddy, and reminding him that he had forgotten, yet again, his father's birthday, on the 6th, Monday. He should call, she went on; his father wasn't upset or anything, he'd just like to hear from his 'Number 1 Son', that's all. It was always nice to hear from him, why couldn't it just be a bit more often, so please do call sometime. Etc., etc....

Dr. Ed shot her a typically terse note back, indicating (tangentially) that he was sorry, promising (without actually promising) that he would call, soon if not precisely tonight, and hurriedly explaining that he had a lot on his plate, on his 'mind', just now, and that Max was 'poorly'. He signed off simply, 'ED', in block capitals.

The penultimate message was from Major Mark Plumtree CSR, plummy@csr.dnd.ca. It was from yesterday afternoon, 21:00 GMT. 16:00 EST, hmm? How Major Mark Plumtree CSR had gotten Dr. Ed's email address was a mystery to Dr. Ed, but what Major Mark Plumtree CSR wanted was *not*. It was as plain as day: he wanted, nay, demanded **A MEETING** with Dr. Ed **THAT VERY AFTERNOON**! He had been trying to reach Dr. Ed **ALL MORNING**, but Dr. Ed's **INCOMPETANT** [*sic*] **RECEPTIONIST** had kept **PUTTING HIM OFF**! Missy was **OBVIOUSLY, TERRIBLY ERRATIC**, not to mention **MUCH WORSE THAN BEFORE**. And **SOMETING** [*sic*], obviously, *MUST BE* **DONE ABOUT IT.**

Dr. Ed was about to call his 'son' the 'receptionist' on the intercom, to make sure that *in no way* was Major Mark Plumtree to be given an appointment *that* afternoon (Missy had a rescheduled appointment for the following morning, after all), when his 'son' called him.

—Yes?

—Uh, dad?

—Uhhh, that's Dr. Ed, *Theodore.*

—OK, sir, but I'm Ted.

—I know Theodore, I know. Now what do you want?

—Not all that much, sir, I mean not personally, myself I mean.

—But *you* rang *me*.

—Yes, uh, there's someone on line 1 for you.

—Deal with them. No, wait, tell me: who?

—A Rick something, from Colonial Credit.

—I'll take it … that's Rick?

—Or Dick. Dick, I think.

—Got it. Dr. Ed pressed the button for line 1. Dick, this is Dr. W. Edward Blanchette speaking.

—That's Cee Aich Eee Tee Tee Eee?

—That's it.

—And your mother's maiden name is?

—Malloy, Dick.

—Thank you, sir. My name is Rich, by the way.

—Sorry, Rich.

—That's OK, sir.

—What can I do for you?

—Sir, Colonial Credit has the policy of contacting its customers in the event of any significant deviation in spending patterns, that is, whenever there are … unusual levels of activity in their accounts, for the purposes of fraud prevention, you understand.

—I understand. Ah, are you inferring that I fall into that pattern, Rich?

—Do you mean implying, sir? Sir, over the past 24 hours your account shows a 20-fold increase above the daily average for the past 12 months.

—It's a joint account, said Dr. Ed.

—Yes sir. Is there any way the card could have been recently stolen or lost, sir?

—The wife, the wife's out buying up the town, Dr. Ed explained, engaging in pure, nervous speculation.

—Yes sir. We just wanted to make sure, sir, that you....

—Yes.

— ... were aware of this, for fraud prevention purposes.

—I'm aware of it, Dr. Ed lied. I'm all too aware of it. Which town is she buying up, by the way? he added, by way of an attempt to appear gregarious. I've lost track.

—I'll check for the most recent transaction, sir, bear with me just a minute. Sir, I have the transaction. SAKS FIFTH AVENUE, New York City, 10:30 a.m. today, Thursday December 09.

—Well, then. Would you mind telling me how much it was for?

—Of course, sir. It was for 2,495 dollars in U.S. funds.

—Fine, no problem. That's the wife all right. Thanks.

—You're most welcome. Is there anything else I can do for you today, sir?

—No, no thanks, thanks for calling, thanks.

— Good-day, sir.

Dr. Ed put down the receiver, frowning at the reflection he cast in the computer's CRT screen. There was one last email in his account. It was dated yesterday afternoon, and it was another one from fraser@hoteldieu.org.

17

AN ORPHAN

CANCEL ALL of my afternoon appointments, please.
—But....

—I said cancel them, Ted. I have to ... I'm going out.

—What shall I do with them, sir? Reschedule?

—No. They're part of the *Alba* trial. I'll have Nurse Sloggett deal
with them in the morning. Oh, better send each of them down
to the lab for blood workups, though.

—What about Major Plumtree?

—Has he been calling?

—You know he has.

—How do *you* know that I know? Have you been reading my
e-mail?

—I *told* you, sir, when you arrived this morning.

—I don't recall discussing that. Nevermind. You never told me
and I haven't checked my e-mail, OK?

—He's called 6 times at least, sir. Says his wife has 'pretty much lost it'. Ted invoked quotation marks with a movement of his fingers.

—What a *prick*, said Dr. Ed, shocking them both with the unaccustomed severity and aggression in his voice. Resuming a more moderate tone, as if he were giving dictation, he continued: Strike that. If, that is, *when* he calls back, tell him to have her taken directly to Emerg.

—That would be impossible, sir.

—Why's that?

—He said Missy disappeared last night, on the way home from Emerg. She got out at a stoplight and just ran off.

—Oh.

—I'd call him as soon as possible if I were you. He's hopping mad, said he was holding you personally responsible for her condition.

—That's preposterous.

—He hasn't seen her since. She either took all of the drugs, or took them with her, cos she left an empty bottle on the car floor.

—I see. Anything else?

—Uh, when can I take my lunch hour?

—Nurse Sloggett usually pencils that into the daily schedule.

—She hasn't.

—Unusual, hmh. Well, is there a block of time that's unfilled?

—Yes, several. Not a full hour anywhere mind you, bu….

—Just string a couple of short breaks together.

—Um.

—I'll pay you time & ½.

—Sure.

—Splendid.

—Super. Um, I….

—Just be sure to hang the little sign by the photocopier on the front door to the clinic, plus a notice for any patients you might miss detailing what I've just told you.

—Aye Aye, Cap'n. You OK, if you don't mind me asking?

—I suggest you get yourself a newspaper, Ted; you're going to have a slack afternoon ahead of you.

—I've got a book thanks.

—Oh. Fine. Well then, I'm off.

—You want to know what book it is?

—No, not really.

—*Great Expectations*. It's about….

—Bye, then, said Dr. Ed, retreating back through the reception room door.

— … an orphan.

18

THE PYNCHON METHOD

O UT ON THE PAVEMENT, walking northwards toward the campus centre, Dr. Ed 'felt' a mixture of relief and anxiety: relief because he had just ditched—for the first time ever—his afternoon responsibilities, anxiety because he knew his feet had a destination in 'mind', but unsure as yet where they were planning to take him. He soon found out: they turned right on University and made their way up the gentle incline past Alumni Hall, the Registrar's and the library, and then crossed Union St. at the lights, turning right again at the Student Union building. Then there was just the Physical Education & Recreation Centre, a building he had never been in, not even during his student days, and to which the hockey arena was attached. His feet kept on, towards the long line of doors that made up the arena's front entrance.

The doors were all locked. Paper signs, which were scotch-taped onto every other door, advised him as to what his feet's next course of action would be:

Caduceus Holistic Fayre

Thur 12–5 • Fri 12–8 • Sat 9–5

Please follow your bliss!

(through the Phys. Ed. Centre entrance)

Admission:

Adults $5.00 • Children 12-18 & Unwaged $2.00

Children under 12 Free**

(**with coupon one child/adult please**)

Dr. Ed ruminated about he knew not what for some minutes, and then glanced at his watch. It was 11:47. This will have spoiled the better part of a week's worth of somebody's hockey, he 'thought', with malice occasioned by the ingrown defensiveness and scornful haughtiness of one who natural selection has forced out of the life of the body and into the life of the 'mind'.

Dr. Ed passed wind, and then burped. He had 'thought' (erroneously, it was now made manifest to him) that those particular issues at least were, if only temporarily, behind him. He retraced his steps the 40 or 50m or so back to the Phys. Ed. building, went down a long corridor back to the arena, and found that the doors there, too, were locked.

Realising that he was obliged to wait 12 minutes before the doors opened, he unbuttoned his greatcoat, loosened his tie, and slumped against the textured concrete wall. By dribs and drabs, he was joined by quite an eclectic assortment of hominids. First came an aging hippie couple. The woman was sporting a pan-African OXFAM fair-trade multi-layer ensemble, and was marsupially encumbered with a genderless infant via a homemade *Snuggli*. The man held onto a superannuated border collie with one hand and a 1970s pile jacket with the other. He wore a neon orange sweatshirt with black letters that screamed:

I Made A Mint In Herbal Tea …
ASK ME HOW ! ! !

Soon a tall, pretty but housewifely, fleshy woman in her mid-thirties queued up, with her son in tow. The son, who was about 8 or 9, sported the kind of crew cut that boys get when fathers yank them from their tearful mothers (usually age 2 or 3) and cart them to their barbers, to get rid of those long, girlish curls. The boy was also roughly as wide as he was tall, and while he busied himself with digging with a spoon made of candy into a package of *Fun Dips!* (a metalloplastic pouch filled with a pucker-inducing, 'frooty' powder), the mother stood, with one knee bent, reading a book—*The Recovery Discovery*[1]—her long, wavy brown hair falling repeatedly across her face, obliging her to intermittently shoo it back behind her ear.

Dr. Ed could not, for some reason that was currently opaque to him, take his eyes off of her. *Her face said it all*, but Dr. Ed's eyes were looking, not listening:

1. Lost Intimacies

i.) The blinking, consubstantial infant, now geargreedy boysboy, grimly eager to find a fitting role for himself in the grim rituals of his tribe. Mornings find him wolfing down bowlfuls of *Frankenberry* cereal, followed by (before school, if it is springtime) a peculiarly Hobbesian, State-Of-Nature form of scrub baseball—nasty, brutish and short. The war-of-all-against-all continues, rain or shine, each&every mid-to-late afternoon—replete with varying monikers and differing guises, but subsumes, always, under one consistent archetype: Cops & Indians, Cowboys & Robbers, Coppers & Paupers, you name it....

---

1. *The Recovery Discovery* (1991) by Jasmine Heartsong. Other books in her Wellness Wisdom series (a chronicle of one remarkable woman's spiritual odyssey through the 1980s and beyond) include, in order of publication: *A Light In The Night, Heartsong Daybreak, Time For Me!, Past Lives/Present Loves, I'm Every Woman,* as well as the omnibus edition, *The Road To Eden Reader.* Available from HERA PUBLICATIONS.

ii.) Seemingly benign neglect at the hands of the Moneyman husband, and accruing evidence that his eyes (if not—as of yet—his hands) have strayed elsewhere: tattletale corporate credit card receipts found crumpled in the laundry, a SuperSex here, a Babes & Toyland there, all part & parcel of the cost-of-doing-business, he would explain, if she pressed him.

She knows not to press. Every so often, he gets an unconscious signal to make it all up to her anyway, and they go off alone to Cellphone Laptop Conference Call Spreadsheet Meet & Greet 2nd Honeymoons at Whistler, Palm Springs—or, even, once, Hawaii. All of which of course is extremely diverting and such-and-so-forth, but which ultimately serves only to remind her that her plight is similar to:

2. **The Similar Plights of Similar Friends**
   —of Jennifer Kilpatrick and Christina Buryman, *bien sûr*. But don't forget: Marjorie Maples, Stephanie Stillwater, even Heather Hippodrome (she for whom absolutely *every*thing is always, maddeningly, 'super'). Sheer ubiquity makes it all easier to talk about if not to take. She and her friends have thereby been brought '*much* closer' together, and furthermore manage to cope with a familiar brand of contentment extracted from unending cycles of Powershopping, tennis

makeovers at varying locations, group discounts on hospitality lessons, Gardening by Raoul, and the:

3. **Wednesday Book Club**

   —which, in reality, functions as a round-robin Mendacity Slowpitch and Four-handed Insinuation Tournament, masquerading as an inebriated cookoff disguised as a 'Merv's Moms Reading Group'. Somehow, however, they *have* managed to 'discuss' such recent bestsellers as: *The Kitchen Witch,* by Clarissa Hopes, *The Pot Luck Club,* by Toni Grievesend, Patrice Fouré's *Seduced By Bordeaux* (sequel to *Adrift In Tuscany,* prequel to *Obsessed With Alsace*), and Abby Dawn Ersatz's *A Laundry List For Stormchasers.* As uniformly excellent as these reads have been, however, they have given her not even the tiniest bit of insight into her:

4. **Real (if often pre-conscious) Sorrow**

i.) A father recently lost to a mother's recent loss to cancer.

ii.) A brother she can't talk to anymore, a sister who refuses to speak with her, and a husband who has nothing to say.

iii.) The memory of a long-lost first love making comet-like re-entries into the troposphere of her dreams: gentle Michael Fury, whom she and her girlfriends had teased throughout their childhood together, had courageously declared his love for her during their senior year at high school. She found herself nurturing a growing attachment to him, but he was a socially awkward fellow, and more than a bit of a dreamer. Moreover, it was clear that he had no prospects (and on this she found that she was in agreement with her father)—no prospects whatsoever, and accordingly she forced herself to break both of their hearts when she went off to university in Vancouver. She got over it, studied psychology, made the kind of friends that one in her circumstances makes. Poor Michael took a job in a book store back home, waited for letters that she did not have the heart to write. Inevitably she met Richard, a Commerce student from a good family in Delta, BC, and came back east with him when opportunity knocked, first at P&G, subsequently at J&J, and finally, a couple of years ago, at DuPont, in, wouldn't you just know it, her old hometown, just after the birth of her third child. Someone eventually told her: during her long absence Michael had finally married someone else, someone a number of years his senior. But then, not so long ago, he'd contracted Acute Lymphoma, or Viral Leukemia, or some such awful disease. You wouldn't believe how many people turned out for the service. Everyone just adored him, that Michael....

The doors opened. Dr. Ed turned his head, 'felt' a surge of pressure from behind and went with the flow. The little beachball of a boy brushed by his leg and rolled past him down the hall. The mother called after him in a distracted voice,

—Michael! Stick close, hon, stick close!

His attention focussed firmly on whatever it was that lay before him and which led him onwards, Dr. Ed did not really notice that he shivered noticeably. He kept moving ever forward into the arena with unconscious purposefulness, passing with obvious scorn the predictable parade of hucksters and wing-nuts. It was some minutes before he came to a full appreciation of a 'feeling' of a distinct loss of his centre of gravity. He halted in the middle of the BodyWork section of the fair, and realized that *something* had been eating away at him for—for how long? It didn't matter. What did matter was that he now fully *comprehended* the seriousness of this ... evaporation ... of his accustomed powers, and that he was determined to get to the bottom of it. He *would* get to, and yank out the entire *root* of it, he determined, and started forward again, reflecting as he did so that it had *something* to do with that G-ddamn 'Fraser'. And he was hot on Fraser's tail, he was sure, here in the G-dforsaken 'BodyWork' zone, amongst the Chiropractors and Chiropodists, the Reflexologists, Rolfers and Reiki Masters. And ... would you look at that? Jesus.

Not that any of this *shocked* him (it was all a bit of old hat, the hat covering the ever-greying & thinning top of the Age of Aquarius, surely) in the slightest. No, it *galled* him. It galled him to 'think' that human beings insisted on continuing to be as irrational as this. It was almost 1994, for Christ's sake, and here we are, still doing this touchy-feely-thing-with-the-hands gimmick: *'Healing Hands', 'Healing Touch', 'Hands of Light', 'Therapeutic Touch', 'The Midas Touch'* (now there's a good one), *'Soul Touch'* and (my G-d!) *'InSoul'*! Keey-reist!

There were indeed, however, some … phenomena that Dr. Ed had *not* encountered before; systems, methods and techniques that were still far beyond the horizon of conceivability the last time he had checked into the workings of all this lunacy were now … why, they were at this very minute relentlessly *proliferating* — in this very arena. He walked past one man who was giving a microlecture on something called *'Metallurgical Frequency Resonance Therapy'*. Another entreated potential customers to don what appeared to be gimmicked-up stereo headphones so that they might sample the aqueous benefits of *'Hydrophonic Neuro-Somatic Integration'*. And — get this — there was even someone (unbelievable, in this day and age) actually giving a live demonstration of *'The Pynchon Method'*, which was no more, really, than a shameless & debased repackaging, Dr. Ed observed, of the thoroughly discredited practice of *'Psychodonture'*, which had itself enjoyed a *very* brief flowering in certain fashionable circles in postwar New York before being driven quickly underground by threats from the relevant regulatory bodies.

Dr. Ed moved on into virgin territory, into the 'Miscellany' section. He passed quickly by the discounted (not 10, not 20, but a whopping 30%!), discontinued home-use colonic irrigators, refused a free sample of *Soynk!* (a vegetarian pork rind, or pork scratching), and unsuccessfully avoided the gaze of the roving eye in a 6-foot-tall holographic ROSICRUCIAN pyramid. Twisting his neck around to continue to watch it watching him, he forgot where he was going and crashed into a display table for *ChocLite* (a fat-free carob-flavoured candy bar, sweetened with sorbitol and stevia extract, and approved by the national governing council of the COCOA-NUTS FOUNDATION), sending its contents, the surprised sales representative and Dr. Ed himself hurtling to the ground.

—I'm very, really I'm, I'm terribly … sorry, said Dr. Ed, after the upending had been re-righted, and he had hurriedly helped the fellow re-box the 12 gross or so of *Choclite* bars.

—That's OK, no worries, no worries at all, the *Choclite* man said. Happens all the time.

—It was that damned eye's fault.

—I?

—The eye in the pyramid, said Dr. Ed, pointing to the looming hologram.

—Oh, yes, it's … hypnotic, isn't it?

—Yeah. And … spooky, a bit.

—I'll say. But you, you don't look like a man who's easily spooked, the sales rep said, turning on what was obviously his 'selling voice'.

—Not usually, no, but this has been a … a bit of a weird day.

—Tell me about it. One of those days when you're on the road, and every other car seems to be driven by a psychopath.

—No kidding.

—Yeah, I came down from the City this morning, and the 401, lemme tell ya, the sales rep said, making a strange back-and-forth motion with one hand near each of his ears.

—What's that? said Dr. Ed.

—What's what?

—That thing with your hands.

—I'm telling ya', the man said, repeating the strange motion with his hands, people today, drivers 'specially, they all need a big cleanout upstairs, know what I mean? They need the *mental* floss, you see? *Mental* (and, Dr. Ed got it now, his hands were going horizontally back-and-forth beside his ears) … *Floss!* I'm Dan Chiddle by the way. You got a booth here?

—Uh, oh, no, I'm, just a bit of a tourist, I guess.

—You're not from the area?

—Yes, no, I mean, a tourist at the fair itself.

—I figured as much. When I dusted myself up off the floor, I said to myself for some reason, 'that guy's too normal to be an inmate here.'

—Inmate?

—You know, 'the inmates have taken over the asylum'?

—Oh.

—Yeah, I thought, who else would come crashing into me like an out-of-control lunatic, except someone completely, manifestly *sane*—you catch my drift?

—Um?

—Never mind. Hey, would you like a free sample? We'd just need to get your e-mail address, for....

—Uh, no, I.

—... for our new electronic newsletter.

—No, thanks, said Dr. Ed, leaning, and glancing, backwards.

—One for the wife, maybe? This little doozey's got *aphro-des-i-acal herbs*.

—My wife, uh. I.

—Here, take two. She'll go crazy, trust me.

—No, thanks, rea—

—Here, *please*, the sales rep said, simultaneously thrusting *three* of the candy heart-encrusted silver-foil-wrapped confections into the palm of Dr. Ed's hand and grasping him in a two-fisted handshake.

—Thanks, uh.

—Dan. Dan's face froze into a Cheshire-cat smile.

—Thanks, Dan, said Dr. Ed, stumbling backwards and sideways with considerable but now-careful haste. He nevertheless collided with another table, but reached out a hand to steady himself before upending anything.

—Sorry. Don't know where my head's at today I guess, he said without looking around.

—A bit ironic that, isn't it? a female voice said.

—Excuse me? said Dr. Ed, genuinely shocked, wheeling around, to come face to face with....

Feel My Heart.

—It's, he said.

—Hi Ed, the woman said. It's been a while.

—Uh? How...?

—I'm a veterinarian now. I moved back to Enterprise a few months ago.

—That's good, uh....

—I've been wondering when we'd bump into one another. Anyhow, I'm at the fair here to build up my client base. There's a surplus of vets right now, but I also have this homeopathy background, hence all this stuff here.

She gestured with her hand over the table that Dr. Ed had just bumped against. There was an assortment of bottles and vials, a number of books on the subject of veterinary homeopathy, two visual charts, not much else. He looked at her. Unlike him, she did not evince the slightest trace of being disconcerted to have had him bump into her like this.

—It's kind of Spartan, she said.

—Better to say 'low-key'.

—You know me, she said.

Both fell silent. Unsure of what else to do, she cast her eyes to the ground. Dr. Ed scrutinized her. Unlike himself, she hadn't changed all that much. She was still quite slim, still in possession of that same remarkable musculature (all the more remarkable as she had always been a relatively sedentary person)—thin alabaster skin displaying a tonus which called to 'mind' a considerable, heels-dug-in breed of determination, determination which was also evident in her firm, not-quite-clenched jawline. Determination was apparent too in those almost-black eyes which she now raised back up to meet his, eyes which testified to deep emotional resources—and to a deep emotional complexity, he remembered. If not for her hair, which was still long but whose reddish-black now bore significant veins of silver, she would pass for 30. He was 44; that made her 42. They had not seen each other for 27 years.

Feel … Feel My Heart.

—How are you, Agnes? he said finally.

—I've been well, thanks.

—You look….

—Life's treated me gently, for the most part. And you?

He answered in kind. He told the truth, or a version of it, that being, that he really … couldn't really complain, for the most part. Yessiree. But then all of that seemed rather meaningless just then. He 'felt' overwhelmed; he 'felt' like he was 17 again and he remembered, suddenly and most distinctly what 17 years-old was like, how love had taken him hostage then, had possessed him the way it possessed medieval knights like Chaucer's Palamon and Troilus. He remembered how simple and pure it had felt, and how complex and hostile the rest of the world had been—and was still, by comparison. What's more, seeing Agnes here, after such a lengthy interval, shocked him into the partial realisation that he had traded the one world for the other. He was now, in 1993, entirely at ease in that very world which, 27 years earlier, had seemed to threaten him (or so he had then 'felt') with extinction. As for the world of love, well….

—About Max, she said.

Dr. Ed was floored at the mention of the name of his friend, his dog.

—Uh? he said.

—Your wife dropped him off yesterday. I called and left a message this morning, but….

—She? Dr. Ed interrupted.

—He's fine. I removed a kidney stone yesterday … He's resting well. You can come pick him up in the evening, if you like.

—Sure, uh, I better be, I have to….

—6 o'clock, say?

—Yes, um. Do you, have you met….?

—Yes?

—Never mind, it's complicated, we'll, I'll, see you later.

—But you were going to say?

—No, I'll, at 6, see you then.

Dr. Ed backed away, looking around this time, and avoided—just—bumping into Dan Chiddle (who had been looking on and listening to their conversation with interest) a second time. He then turned and walked rapidly away, ignoring the imprecations of the INSTANT KARMA soft drink company sales rep to try their 'Buddha Betel BlastOff', 'Dharma Kola Cola' and 'Sangha Sarsaparilla'. He wove his way through the remainder of this Purgatorial landscape, successfully avoiding eye contact with an Iridologist, side-stepping around an aging Hempster (with his petition to save 'heritage varieties' of marijuana from, his sandwich board said, near-certain extinction at the hands of corporatised, GMO hydroponic monoculture), and gamely aimed for the exit. Once he hit the door to the street, he fell first into a trot and then into a semi-canter, unsure of quite where he was going, certain only of what he was running away from.

19

WESTERN HEMISPHERE, THE EARTH

O
UT OF BREATH after 500m or so of exertion, Dr. Ed reached
the end of Union St., where the street forms a T-junction
with Barrie St., at City Park. Here he had to make a decision: to
cross the park and head towards downtown (and then what—go
shopping? catch a bus or taxi [to where?]? get drunk/buy stamps/
get a haircut/have a heat-to-heart with his stockbroker about
potential risks in the Latin American 'emerging market'?), or to
turn right and rectangle it back to....

Beaufort #	MPH	Description	Effect at Sea	Effect Ashore
0	≤1	Calm	Sea like a mirror	Smoke rises vertically
1	1-3	Light air	Ripples formed w/o foam crests	Wind direction shown by smoke drift
2	4-7	Light Breeze	Small Wavelets, crests don't break	Wind felt on face, leaves rustle
3	8-12	Gentle Breeze	Large wavelets, crests begin breaking	Leaves, twigs in constant motion

Beaufort #	MPH	Description	Effect at Sea	Effect Ashore
4	13-18	Moderate Breeze	Small waves, with frequent white horses	Dust and loose paper are raised
5	19-24	Fresh Breeze	Moderate waves, chance of spray	Small trees in leaf begin to sway
6	25-31	Strong Breeze	Large waves, extensive foam crests, spray	Branches move, whistling telegraph wires
7	32-38	Moderate Gale	Sea heaps up, foam blown along direction of wind; spindrift begins	Whole trees in motion Inconvenience is felt walking against the wind
8	39-46	Fresh Gale	Moderately high waves of greater length; edges of crests break into spindrift. Foam blown in streaks along direction of wind	Twigs broken off trees. Wind generally impedes progress.
9	47-54	Strong Gale	High waves appear Dense streaks of foam arise along direction of wind. Sea begins to roll. Spray may affect visibility.	Slight structural damage occurs (chimney pots and slate removed).

He went a very abrupt right. South on Barrie for a block and then east on Penforth for another, into the hospital through

Emerg, then up, over and in, his stride rate and anger level increasing the closer he got to the….

—Listen you little pecker-head, he said.

There was no one in the office save Ted, who was leaning back in the receptionist's chair and reading his book.

—Yes?

—Are you Fraser, G-ddammit?

—Who?

—Don't be coy with me. I'm on to you.

—Huh?

—fraser@hoteldieu.org. *You* know.

—Don't have the least effin' clue what yer on about, uh, 'dad'.

—Did you or did you not send me those e-mails?

—Excuse me?

—Did you *send* me those *e-mails*? said Dr. Ed, raising his voice significantly.

—It's not getting any clearer, 'dad'. You know what? I'd actually like to suggest that, when in doubt, if you're having problems with the locals—with making yourself understood that is   by all means, go ahead, yell. That's my motto anyway.

—What are you trying to do to me?

—A good question, and one I've asked myself many, ah, many times. It deserves a good answer, I'll give you that.

—So it *was* you!

—No. Not yet.

—Not *yet*? What!?

—I *want* to try, to do something, to you I mean, but I haven't tried yet. See, I'm not sure if what I want is right for me, at this stage.

—At what stage?

—At this stage in our relationship.

—I don't 'think' we have one, Ted.

—Oh, we do, we do.

—You.

—Anyhow, when I decide what exactly I want to do to you, I'll be sure to let you know.

—I.

—One way or another. 'Scuse me, sir, if you please. Smoke break. Union rules.

—The.

—Oh, about Major Plumtree's wife?

Dr. Ed said nothing, but stared at his son from behind white-hot eyes.

—The Major called again. Twice more.

—Yes?

—Just wanted to keep you informed, said Ted, leaving through the front door, cigarette pack and lighter in hand. Dr. Ed picked up the novel Ted had been reading, which had been left splayed open on the desk. It wasn't a novel at all, in fact. It was a book of poetry: *Donne—The Complete English Poems*. He opened it to the poem Ted had evidently been reading, 'Love's Alchemy', and scanned it. It was all Greek to him, save the closing couplet, which he repeated to himself:

> *Hope not for mind in women; at their best*
> *Sweetness and wit, they are but mummy, possessed*

—Huh, Dr. Ed grunted, flipping next to the inscription on the frontispiece.

Teddy boy,

Now THIS is the business, the full meal deal. Chew well and slowly. And good luck on your little Genealogical expedition eh? —Just remember... be prepared!
Scouts honour,

Mondo-man,
Vancouver, August '93

He tossed the book down onto the desk, and went into his office, whereupon he sat, inert, stupefied, ergonomically crumpled, down-but-not-quite-yet-out, his pinball brain tilting atop his multi-swivel executive leather chair.

—Let's get straight on this, Edward, he said to himself, his chin cupped in the splayed delta of his pensive fingers. First, your wife takes off on you, without notice. *Without notice* she drops off your dog at your long-lost girlfriend's farm. Unlike you, she somehow knows about the farm, and you've never even told her about the girl. OK. Next, someone named Fraser wants to meet you, or at any rate wants you to meet up with that long-lost girlfriend of yours at the so-called holistic fair, and that Fraser Somebody is, allegedly, *not* your so-called 'son' Ted. This Ted himself vigorously maintains. Which means … which means … hell, *fucked* if I know, he said, shocking himself with the obscenity.

—Meanwhile, he continued, after a considerable pause. Meanwhile, meanwhile your best friend is scheming to implement a snap proposal of marriage to your best—no—to your only—nurse. You are forced to conclude that he is, in short and to employ, ahh, layman's terms, at least temporarily *insane*.

The phone rang. Ted was still out. Dr. Ed knew, somehow, that it would be that monkey on his back, Major Mutation, the one with the wife who's acting bonkers…. He hesitated, but answered it himself on the 4th ring.

—Is Dr. Blanchette available? a woman's voice said. This is Major Plumtree's office calling.

—He's out all day, said Dr. Ed, about to immediately put the receiver down.

—Does he have a pager?

—He most certainly does not.

—Can I leave a message then?

—You neither can nor may, he said, remembering one of his mother's many little lessons.

He put the phone down and said:

—Right.

He left via the back doorway and took an eccentric routing through the hospital to ensure that he would have to confront neither Ted nor anyone else that he knew. He immediately climbed to the ICU on the 5th floor, and then proceeded to slipslide his way to the backside of the building, to a service elevator, dropping down to the boiler room in the basement without pausing at any of the intermediate floors. The elevator released him into a dark, cacophonic environment that was devoid of any discernible human presence, and while there was light sufficient enough for Dr. Ed to navigate his way across the short distance separating the elevator from the south (rear) 'emergency' exit, it was not sufficient to prevent him, in his haste, from missing a 'Wet Floor—Slippery!' sign. Thus, after his first few impatient steps he was sent hurtling backwards into the air, and found himself landing—*Whaa?!*—left elbow and then hip-first, on the concrete floor.

—Christ! was his 1st 'thought'; the ass of my trousers is ripped his 2nd; I—I don't think I can walk his 3rd.

He struggled to his feet, lurched toward the weakly glowing exit sign, realised that his shoe had come off in the tumble, and agonized his way back to it. He found his wallet there as well.

—Wouldn't want them finding *this* down here, he said, becoming aware that he was quite unaware of who, precisely (or was that whom?) he'd meant just now by 'them'. Deep breath now old boy, almost there....

Emergency Exit Only !
Alarm Will Sound If Opened !

—Yeah, right, whatever, he said, and pushed on the aluminum bar that opened the door. It opened, sounding, as promised, the alarm. And as if opening the door any wider would make the alarm ring more loudly, making the situation just generally worse, he slipped through the barely open crack and breathed in the cold chill of the afternoon.

—Smoke? he 'thought', turning around to face....

—Hey, hi 'dad', said Ted, grinding the butt of a cigarette into the cement.

—What the... ?

—You look awful, that's the what.

 Dr. Ed stared at him mutely.

—Well I better be headin' back inside, don't want security to finger me for that alarm. And if I were you I'd....

—Yeah, said Dr. Ed.

—Yeah. You take care now.

—Mmh, said Dr. Ed, who then walked 'thought'-lessly off, to the south.

To the south of the hospital ran King St, on the opposite side of which lay John A. Macdonald Park, across from which lay the Great Lake, on the opposite shore of which lurked the United States of America. Dr. Ed heard himself saying as much as he walked over the road, across the park and up to the pebbly edge of the lakeshore. It reminded him of a rather childish 'game' in which one declared one's residency status in a progressive manner, from the narrowest to the widest possible sense, beginning with the street on which one lived and ending with the universe *in toto*. It was a childish kind of 'game' because (he knew) only a child could believe that one's place in the universe could possibly *mean* anything, even to oneself.

His uncle Joey Nicholls always got him to recite it at family get-togethers. At first, when he was merely 5, the attention of the entire household had excited him, but as the years passed and he came to understand that Joey and the other adults were, in a way, purchasing his boyish sense of wonder, extracting from it 'cuteness' and 'nostalgia' and turning the entire scene into a weird kind of fetish object. That was when he had begun to despise this ritual, and began a process which ultimately led him to distrust anything even remotely related to what might be called 'The Sublime'.

—William Edward Theodore Blanchette, 17 North St., Noman's Island, Frontenac County, Ontario, Canada, North America, Western Hemisphere, The Earth..., he heard something inside him saying as he stared out across the water and up into the sky.

The sun was shining; the sky was blue; the southeasterly wind predictably strong, forming large whitecaps on the open water which were beaching themselves with not insignificant force. Near to where Dr. Ed was standing, the lake funnelled down into the river, making, it was said, for some of the most consistently strong winds, and for some of the best freshwater sailing in all of North America. Wind speed rarely dropped below 15 mph here; today it was more like 30. The temperature had to be 20°F/-7°C. He couldn't guess what that made the wind-chill effect, but he didn't really care. The wind cut through his woolen greatcoat, made his face burn and his ears prickle. For the second time that day, Dr. Ed 'felt' curiously ... what, curiously *what*, exactly?

20

Cloud Illusions

Or, The Message In The Wind

Wind comes about primarily because of motions in the upper air, about which we can have no or little knowledge.
—Alan Watts, *The Weather Handbook*

Dr. Ed stood on the beach for quite some time. He stood there until he 'realized' something, until he 'understood', until he had done some substantive 'thinking' about just what it was that he was 'feeling'. He stood there until he came to the quite-nearly-epiphanic conclusion that he was in a very bad way, indeed. It transpired, approximately, as follows:

Well then, he said quietly, although he could hardly have 'thought' anyone could be around to hear it. There was only the wind-driven lake and the cirrus-striped sky to hear him. He stood facing the wind, which was coming from the south-east, and he looked toward the Martello tower in the near distance. It was ringed by ancient cannon, and was situated at the tip of a peninsula that jutted out into the lake and which was occupied by the Royal Military College.

—I, I'm … I'm really, I really am, he said.

> *While we are usually told to look to windward for the weather, it is a fact that most often the winds on which the bulk of clouds come are not in the same direction as those at the surface.* **This is particularly so when the weather is on the change.** *Then the winds in which the cirrus clouds ride are often moving at right angles to the wind in which the cumulus clouds ride.*

He became distracted by the sun. Both by the lower-case sun, and, not supernally but supersubstantially, the capital-S Sun as well, the insuperable Sun. The sun was just past vertical, he 'thought', after he had fallen to 'thinking', after he had shielded his eyes and turned his windblown face up, to face up to it. He was, he knew, *descending* into 'thought', mere milliseconds (if that) after the act of sensation. The moment of pure, untainted experience had passed, if indeed it had ever been there, and, from the little sun g-d's-eye-view in his 'mind', he saw himself begin to 'think' etymologically, to try to examine what he 'thought' he saw beyond the matrix of his own peculiar, contingent sensibility. He examined it, classified it, and, to the limit of his powers, comprehended and understood it. *Verstanden, compréhension, savoir,* he 'thought'. I 'see'.

—I see, he said aloud to the wind. I see I really am. I see it now. T-trying. Trying to see.

This is the classic 'windy sky' which has spawned all the lore about mares'
tails and in more modern times a song that speaks of 'rows and flows of
angel hair'.

The son disappeared. The sun disappeared behind a cirrus
cloud, momentarily giving the swells on the lake much
more ... contrast.

—Sunflower, he 'thought', *tournesol*. Heliotrope, sun-turner,
enslaved to the sun-god, to my father's son, my son's father. And
here I am, turning tropes, imagineering, screwing it all up, 'till,
'till I'm burnt by the Sun, no not the sun, the merely metaphori-
cal *Sun*. Fuck, *I* see it.

> *This sky obeys the principle of linearity to a remarkable degree and in*
> *effect says 'Look at me and do not ignore what I say'.*

—I see, his voice rising to a shout, heedless of the muffling action
of the disdainful wind. I see that I don't fucking see, that I don't

fucking *get it*, at all. (And where was *this* coming from? He didn't know, or 'thought' he didn't know, and that amounted to pretty much the same fucking thing, right? Whatever, but, perversely somehow, he liked it, he liked how it 'felt', how it still shocked him, but more: he just plain *liked* it, doing it, saying whatever the fuck he 'felt' like saying. Fuck it all. It's all fucked, anyway, isn't it?

> *So here we are ignoring the fussy little details along the edges of the banners and concentrating on the linear form of the whole upper sky. Just occasionally, when the coming weather is likely to be of the most violent kind, the density of these jet stream cirrus banners becomes such that they can cut out the sunlight and so show some shading of their bases. But such banners are rare, thank goodness.*

He turned around, his back to the wind, gazed back at the hospital across the road. Two young people walked by on the paved path just in front of him, arm-in-arm, with eyes only, he saw, only for each other.

—You there! he said, quite loudly but unsure of what he was calling out to them for. They did not seem to notice, however, that he was addressing them, that he was calling out to *them*. He turned around once more. So that was it, he 'thought'. That's what it was all allegedly about, is it, life, life lived with a small 'l'?

> *However, if you concentrate on a cirrus element or two and can unaided see them moving against the background of the sky, you are certainly looking at clouds carried in winds of a hundred knots or more.*

—Fuckers, he said to the wind. Brainless, mindless young *fuckers*. They'll learn a thing or two, they will. After a pause, he added: it's all fucked, anyway, really.

The wind did not respond.

That is when you begin searching the airwaves for a forecast.

—And anyhow, what could it all possibly have to do with me? What in the name of *Fuck* am *I* supposed to do about it? Huh?

Silence—of course. But it almost surprised him—almost, that there wasn't something more. Of *course*, how could it be otherwise, how could his... (he hated the word, it was *so* effeminate, but there it was, anyway) his ... *yearnings* be answered otherwise? Hadn't he learned, learned not to yearn, learned a G-ddamned lifetime ago now, learned that the universe was cold, forever indifferent to frail, contingent human needs and desires? He had; it was the kind of obvious insight of which an otherwise-blind 17-year-old is capable: the *kosmos* was unfathomably expanding, flying apart, shredding, each moment that much closer to certain, inevitable heat death. Of course. It wasn't exactly rocket science, now, was it? And it had thus been a no-brainer to adapt his life accordingly. The question was, though: if he'd dealt with all this in a satisfactory manner 27 years ago (and he *had*, he had been *certain* that he had), what was he doing here, now, in 1993, shouting at the wind again? Did he 'think' there would be any answer this time?

Of course not. But the fact that there would be (that there could be) no answer forthcoming—this nevertheless almost surprised him, still, even now, almost gave him pause, gave him reason to wonder—almost. And (because he could, or would, never have predicted it) he wondered why this was so.

> *However, there is a psychological factor in forecasts of snow. Rain goes down the drains but snow lays about for all to see. So forecasters, who are very aware of the disruption which is caused by snowfall, will tend to 'over-forecast' so that often threatened snow does not materialise. Or if it does, it may well have come later than forecast.*

He turned to go, finally, but something stopped him (or, more accurately, he saw himself stopping himself) momentarily. He turned back to face the wind, to face up to it, for a moment longer. He had one last thing to get off his chest, one last message to send.

—Well, fuck you, then, he shouted. Fuck *you*! A movement occurred in his lower abdomen, and he let out a loud, lasting, luxurious, numinous, cumulus fart.

> *Nevertheless, we can now say—and I have proved this time and time again by experience over many years and in many different situations—that the best statement of the [northern hemisphere's] Crossed Winds Rules for the man-in-the-street are as follows:*
>
> **Crossed Winds rule for deterioration**
> *Stand back to the lower wind and if high clouds come from the left the weather will usually deteriorate.*

Crossed Winds rule for improvement
  Stand back to the lower wind and if high clouds come from the right
  the weather will usually improve.

Crossed Winds rule for no immediate change
  If the upper and lower winds are more or less parallel then there will
  be no marked tendency to deteriorate or improve.

He turned away from the shore, away from the wind, and started walking, still painfully, back towards the hospital, towards the north. Beautiful, high white cirrus clouds snaked perceptibly past, on their way east. Despite the aching hip and elbow he 'felt' better now; that bit of primal screaming had done him a world of good, he had to admit. He hadn't said — he hadn't used language like *that* since — well, other than earlier today, of course — since, why, since he was 17 or 18, at least.

21

SOME DETERIORATION

It is particularly when some deterioration in the weather has been forecast and you are waiting for it to arrive that the Crossed Winds Rules come into their own. We have now, I hope, convinced many would-be forecasters that here is a method of foretelling coming change which will work wherever they may be, so long as they do not stray out of the temperate latitudes.

— The Weather Handbook

AND THAT'S QUITE enough foul language — quite enough, Dr. Ed 'thought', for a lifetime. Suddenly 'feeling' very much *himself* again, very much in terribly fine fettle, Dr. Ed crossed back to the west side of the road, 'thinking', verily, that he was very much ready to get on with things.

But what was there to get on with? Ted had already phoned and cancelled all of his afternoon appointments. Well, he could always just go back in anyway, and see if someone might turn up. But that would mean sitting around, wasting precious time, and this newly minted, cleaned-and-polished-up Dr. Ed 'felt' like being, yes, *active*. He wasn't due to have ward rounds with the residents and interns until tomorrow, so he struck that particular possibility off his mental list. Ahhhhh—he suddenly knew what he would do. He'd call the *Alba* team together for an impromptu meeting, to see how progress was progressing. Yessir, there was nothing like the 'thought' of a good meeting to get his juices flowing again. It made him 'feel' ready for anything, and he *already* 'felt' ready for anything. He could take on the world now, yes, and even that pesky Major Plumtree, no problemo. He'd ring the poor fellow up, straightaway.

Dr. Ed tickety-booed his way back into the building, humming a jazzy version of 'When The Saints Go Marching In'. The 'voice' he heard in his head was to his 'mind' Louis Prima, but in fact the singer was none other than Fred Flintstone, who had literally stumbled upon a career in Jazz while penniless-and-supposedly-on-vacation in Rock Vegas. None of this was material to our pro/ant-agonist, who himself ignored the pain in his knee and marched with a jaunty step to this jaunty little tune, nodding, smiling, saluting and sometimes even winking at all & sundry as he traversed a more traditionally kosher route back towards his department. He was a perambulating automaton of good old-fashioned bonhomie: he smiled, with just the right amount of quasi-shyness, at sexy admissions nurse Doone (remembering as he did so the interrogative graffiti in the 2nd floor men's washroom, middle stall—'WHOSE [*sic*] DONE DOONE (WHERE/WHEN/HOW)?'— as well as the various, predictable, and yet intriguingly appalling responses); he bumped into and exchanged manly sweet nothings with OB/GYN man and card shark Buster Stubble, parting from him with hastily made and vague plans to 'round up the boys' for an evening of some *serious* poker; he even found himself stopping to ask the cadaverous forensic pathologist Byrna Starnes how she was 'feeling'—apparently, not all that well—some military cadet jock hero type leaving quite the mess behind in a rollover out by Champlain Locks the night before, and she was still heavily into the secobarbital over it, albeit very much in a stiff-upper-lip kind of way. Tragic of course, but then life is for the living, and, why, here he was, himself again, popping into the F-Wing elevator & popping out again onto the 4th floor, 'thinking' that he first just might see if….

—Why, it's Dr. Blanchette, a pleasant surprise, a man said in a Sten gun staccato.

—Hello, Major Plumtree. I, I was expecting you, please come, in.

—I wasn't expecting *you*, the Major said. Your note here says….

—I was called out. Family emergency.

—Ah yes, of course.

—However, it, it resolved itself, much more quickly….

—Yes.

—Than I had foreseen.

—In my experience, doctor, and I realize that our professions differ in some respects, situations, ah, emergencies, do not, ah, resolve them*selves*.

—What can I do for—?

—She's gone missing, Doctor.

—I see.

—The hell you do, and that's just the point. I'm holding you and your drug responsible for this travesty. You've taken her natural....

—Natural?

—Don't interrupt me. Her natural mood swings and, and *amplified* them, beyond all recognition. She was never like this before. You've, you've created a different person, Dr. Frankenstein.

No Problem. Dr. Ed 'felt' up to this. He'd been down this particular path before, more than once. He just had to be patient, and wait this fellow out.

—Please, come sit down, Major. Let's discuss this like the professionals that we are.

—You can fuck right off with *that* bullshit, Blanchette. She could be almost anywhere right now, she could be dead for all you know or care, and I'm here to impress upon you, believe me, just how much you and your drugs have *fucked her up*.

—Please, Major. I have to remind you that *Alba* is still very much in an experimental phase, Phase 1b, to be precise. Do you remember what that means?

—Listen pal, I don't give a rat's ass's flying fuck if, hey you know what, I'm gonna sue and screw you 'till you fuckin' damn well *plead* for my forgiveness, and I've only got one more thing to....

—It means, Major—and if you don't drop your aggressive posturing this instant I'm going to have to call security—it means that treatment-resistant patients like your wife participate on a *volunteer* basis, and they are all made explicitly aware that the medication may indeed involve heretofore unforeseen contraindications....

—Like I said, I've got just one more thing to say.

And with that the Major landed a massive fist squarely on Dr. Ed's delicate, if already not-quite-straight, aquiline nose. With a *whhumppp* Dr. Ed (whose grade 5 nickname had been—on account of said proboscis having, it was erroneously assumed, noble pedigree—'The Eagle') suddenly crash-landed, right-side-up, onto the carpet.

— HOLY FUCK —

Many a time I got a smart clout on the lug and
was told to take that for a dirty little dogan.
— P. Slater, Yellow Briar: A Story of the Irish
in the Canadian Countryside (1934)

When he came to, a latex rubber glove was tugging on his nose. 'Feeling' no pain and yet in full possession of all of his other faculties, Dr. Ed had no trouble finding the fallacy in his earlier argument: the conclusion that he had previously reached (i.e., that his dramatic episode down by the lake had been cathartic, indeed epiphanic; and that *things*—supposedly numerous and yet elaborated upon with only a pathetic amount of detail—that things would be just fine, thank you, from here on in)—*that* conclusion was not supported by premises of—and this was shocking to be admitting to oneself—*of any kind.*

No, not at all. In fact, he had succumbed—and this was embarrassing to admit to oneself—to circular reasoning: he had used his conclusion as evidence *in support of* (such was the shabbily deported state of his 'mind', lately) his premises! Yes, the conclusion was used to shore up the very premises which were themselves supposed to support his conclusion! He was begging the question, yes, he was, something he had not caught himself doing since, oh, since 1984 at least.

And this was how he had done it: Dr. Ed *realized* he had been enduring a number of shall we call them 'frustrations', 'frustrations' surrounding events of, say, the past 24 hours or so. Dr. Ed realized this *because* he observed himself expressing 'feelings' concerning said 'frustrations', expressing them in a single, potent burst, in something one might classify as an alleged *catharsis*, and all because there *appeared* to be a certain logic at work:

Premise 1: All moments of catharsis involve the spontaneous, sometimes violent release of pent-up 'emotions'.

Premise 2: All frustrations produce pent-up 'emotions'

Premise 3: Dr. Ed had just spontaneously released pent-up 'emotions'

Conclusion 1: Dr. Ed had experienced numerous frustrations

Conclusion 2: Therefore, Dr. Ed had had a moment of catharsis

Hmmm.... Dr. Ed was just considering this argument, wondering whether it was truly 'Begging the Question' or if it were actually 'Affirming the Consequent', and connecting *that* conundrum to the question of whether all moments of catharsis produce experiences of epiphany (or whether, alternatively, the pathway of causation ran in quite the other direction), when the hand that had been tugging at his anaesthetised nose stopped tugging and a female voice, which seemed to be situated somewhere behind him, said:

—He's coming around, Doctor.

—Well then, what have we here? a male voice said, apparently from above. He certainly seems familiar....

Dr. Ed then opened, with some difficulty, one of his eyes, and tried to focus, with somewhat greater difficulty, upon the current situation, but his field of vision was restricted to the vicinity of the E.R.'s collection of antique ceiling tiles.

—Isn't it Dr. Blanchette? the female voice then said. From Psychiatry?

—Affirmative. Well then, he's definitely slumming it today, isn't he Nurse Turkington?

—Yes, Doctor. It does appear so.

—Uh, I, said Dr. Ed.

—Excellent diagnosis, nurse; he certainly is.

—Uhhhhhhhhhhhhhhhhhh, said Dr. Ed.

—Hello there, Ed, the doctor said. It's me, Pete the Raspberry.

—You … said Dr. Ed.

—And this is Nurse Turkington.

—Hello, Dr. Blanchette, she said.

—How are you feeling, Ed? said Dr. Pete.

—Where, wait a, said Dr. Ed.

—You're in Emerg, old buddy.

—A dashing young man in an army uniform brought you here, added Nurse Turkington.

—Said you needed your head examined, said Dr. Pete. But I suppose he meant your face.

—He said you fainted and fell face-first onto the floor, said Nurse Turkington.

—He hit me, said Dr. Ed, still unable to move his head and struggling to try to get his 2 interlocutors peripherally into focus.

—In any event, said Dr. Pete, it appears as though your nose may be broken, Ed. It's already fairly swollen, and it will most likely swell up a fair bit more over the next few hours. Try to keep some ice on it, we won't be able to say for sure if there's a fracture until the swelling subsides.

—How long will … ? said Dr. Ed, gingerly mapping the tumescent nasal region with his fingers.

—Give'r 4 days at least, said Dr. Pete. No more than a week. We'll be better able to determine if you'll require a splint at that time.

—Dr. Ed nodded sheepishly as he levered himself up into a semi-reclining position, then swung himself painfully around in an arc of 90 degrees, so that his legs now dangled over the right side of the gurney. He held his painkiller-addled head in one hand while the other supported him from behind. Christ, this took him back to Grade 5, when class bullies Billie 'Nasty' Roach and Danny Fautz had lifted Eddy and his soon-to-be best friend Andy O'Gallivan onto the horns of a rather nasty little version of the 'Prisoners' Dilemma': either fight each other after school out by the baseball backstop, until only one of them was left standing, or they both 'might' suffer a much more thoroughly brutal thrashing at the hands (and boots) of Roach, Fautz and assorted, otherwise-timid Grade 6 hangers-on—and if only one of them showed up while the other bawk-bawk-bawked his way back to the chicken coop, well, then watch out!

The short-lived 'fight' was over with one blow, as Andy had succeeded, with a deft right hook, both in knocking young Eddy off his feet and in breaking his jaw. After much caterwauling and threatening to sue Andy's dad for all he was worth, precocious Eddy then suddenly realized that the incident had somehow made he and Andy blood-brothers: in the end it had been a mortified Andy who had ran home and retrieved his mother, who in turn had driven Eddy to the hospital, where his feet had dangled in mid-air from a gurney much as they did now, swinging back-and-forth in an embarrassed, nervous rhythm all their own.

When Nurse Turkington had finished applying a sturdy gauze-and-tape bandage to the offended region, Pete Laframboise came back and kindly (if somewhat inappropriately) wrote Dr. Ed a prescription for a week's worth of *Tylenol* 4 with codeine phosphate.

> One tablet every 4 hrs.
> Not to exceed 6 tablets total in 24hrs.
> Not to be taken with alcohol or sedatives.
> Consult your doctor if you are taking anti-depressant medication.

—This should do you for a while, he said. Mind you, after the first 48, the pain shouldn't be quite so bad.

Dr. Ed swallowed 2 tablets on his way out of the doors of the hospital pharmacy, 2 more in the cab on the way home, and a 5th and 6th after rummaging through his wife's nightmarishly messy bedside table for clues to he didn't consciously know what, unearthing only an empty bottle of lorazapam, a nearly empty bottle of *Nocturne*, a half-empty bottle of herbal *BeCalm*, and an unopened package of *Slendereyes* topical cream.

—Holy Fuck, he said to himself for no empirically verifiable or falsifiable reason. Though he was flying now, approaching escape velocity, he was still semi-capable of appreciating the gravity of a situation which was, his normally quietist gut-level instincts told him, becoming somehow, somewhat desperate. His gut-level then informed him of something else, something of an altogether more immediate, metabolic urgency: as he passed wind, and passed as quickly as he could into his wife's private bathroom, undoing his belt buckle and zipper as he dove past her bidet and towards her toilet, one comforting 'thought' branched across his panicking neural synapses: whatever else may transpire, come what come may, the nitrogenous alkaloids of these codeine tablets [from the Greek *kōedeia*, for poppy head] would manage to do for him what laughable quantities of over-the-counter preparations of oil of bismuth had failed to provide: they would put paid to these compunctious visitings of nature; they would block and stop up all access to the passage of a certain varietal of remorse.

As yet another taxi cab sped him on his way back downtown Dr. Ed repeatedly added 2&2 together, his deductions arriving

9 times out of 10 (on admittedly speculative premises) to within $^+/-$4% of the same obsession-inducing answer. And 2&2&2 codeine tablets, plus 2 more, made 8, and Dr. Ed made a heroic attempt to 'think': yes, Buddy and Missy Plumtree had both been placed on above-median dosages of *Alba*, and both (now that he laboriously turned it over&over&over in his 'mind') appeared to have been suffering from acute hypomania — to say the least. He had no real proof that his wife had managed to get her hands on any, but he was intending just now to do a sweep of Nurse Sloggett's station and desk, for a little voice told him that she, too (for G-d knows what reason) may have been availing herself of the little white-and-off-white caplets.

Admittedly, he had no real evidence for any of this. Nevertheless, he 'felt' a compulsion to know, a compulsion to get to the bottom of at least something, a compulsion, funnily enough, that ventured (if only slightly) beyond the anxiety he 'felt' over the future of his own career, over his personal role as the director of this particular (heretofore uncontroversial) clinical trial. He glanced at his watch. It was 16:00.

16:00? That rang a bell, though he couldn't say why. He was generally finished with patients for the day by 15:00 or 15:30, so it couldn't be that. Oh, there were the ward rounds with the interns, and they were always at differing times of day, but no, they were always on Mon., Wed., Fri., never Thu. What, then?

—You a doctor? the cabby said, knocking Dr. Ed out of his increasingly eccentric personal orbit.

—That I am, said Dr. Ed. How did you know?

—I dunno. Just thought so I guess.

Something about the driver—obviously not his manner of speaking—communicated to Dr. Ed that this young man was highly educated. The name on his municipal licence, which was laminated and hanging from the rear-view mirror on a string, was Shboom, Daniel.

—Why do you ask? Are you a medical student yourself? asked Dr. Ed.

—Nah. Just curious if you knew anything 'bout that body.

—What body? Dr. Ed's 'switch' was suddenly 'overridden' by the 'tripping' of a 'breaker'.

—The one they found at the crematorium. They still haven't identified it yet, but now they're saying it was a probable over-dose. She's pretty average, otherwise, apparently.

—Average? How? Dr. Ed was somewhat more than mildly curi-ous. The newspaper article that had previously induced the disgorgement of his tuna-on-white had provided no physical details whatsoever, and he'd forgotten all about it.

—Well, the cabby said, turning partly around to look at his passenger, Caucasian female, unspecified age, brown eyes & hair, 5-foot-5. None of this is official mind you, but bits & pieces have leaked out to the press. Didn't you hear? It's been on the radio all day.

Dr. Ed was speechless.

—You alright, mister? Getting no answer, the cabby turned back, turned his tape player on, turned the volume up to an audible level, and then increased the volume on his 2-way radio as well, so that he would not miss out on any calls from Dispatch.

—*1-2-1 Base CanEx*, the dispatcher then said. *1-4-4 Oomen's Auctions, 0-8-1 MilCol.*

—All perfect squares, the cabby said. What you think'd be the odds of that? Well, here we are.

The cab pulled up into the covered semi-circular hospital entrance.

—*You know I love the Lord of Hosts*, went the voice on the tape player. *The Father, Son and the Holy Ghost. Through the darkness They will guide me. In my time of trouble He will hide me.*

—That'll be … said Dan Shboom the cabbie. Dr. Ed handed him a 20.

—*I dig the black girls*, went the tape player.

—*0-0-9 the Forum*, the dispatcher said.

—Keep the meter running, said Dr. Ed, handing Dan Shboom another 10 as he leapt out of the car.

—We're not on a metered system, actually, said Dan Shboom, but Dr. Ed had already started toward the hospital's automatic doors.

22

THE ICEBERG

Randy Van der Griff, former Team Canada rugby full-back and now Eumeta's Project Manager for its 'flagship' anti-psychotic drug *Differanz* as well as for its 'legacy' tricyclic anti-depressant, *Paradigm*, stood waiting near the empty nurse's station with a generic-looking piece of whitebread in a cheap-looking royal blue windbreaker, which bore the gold-embroidered logo of the well-known advertising firm of Happer, Baitman, Pancras & Kiln.

—What the hell happened to you? was the first thing to come out of Randy Van der Griff's mouth.

—Crazy patient's crazy husband, said Dr. Ed with a shrug.

—Jesus, Ed, that's nuts, said Randy. Dr. Ed shrugged. I was beginning to worry, Randy continued, that you'd left us standing at the altar. He now held his handshaking hand manfully out. When Dr. Ed took it but did not reply, Randy said: you know Stu Baitman, of course.

—Of course, Dr. Ed lied. He had had a hard enough time getting Randy, whom he had known for years, into focus—such were the kinetics of the 480 mg's worth of narcotic that he had swallowed.

—Well this is Stu's son, Stu II.

—Nice to meet you, said Stu II. Just call me Stu for short.

—Uh, how are you keeping Stu, said Dr. Ed, summoning each&every last dram of his willpower in an attempt to affect as conventional a demeanor as his chemically circumscribed circumstances would allow.

—Can't complain, Ed, can't complain, said familiar, friendly Stu.

—Good to know, said Dr. Ed.

—My old man has landed the EUMETA worldwide account, and he's promised me *Alba* when the flight deck's all-clear and the usual tedious hoops've been given the old in&out (and here Stu II made a circle with the thumb and forefinger of his right hand and a rude gesture with the index finger of his left). Randy here's pipelined for it as well, seeing how *Paradigm* is flatlining and Randy's the obvious Best Man at the Wedding.

—Great, said Dr. Ed.

—*Alba* will be a compkiller, Ed, said Stu.

—No kidding, said Dr. Ed.

—How far out are we, you figure? said Randy.

—That's a bit tough to gauge at the moment, said Dr. Ed, trying to be as unevasively evasive as possible. Ummm....

—Our appointment, as you'll no doubt recall, Ed, Randy said, a vulpine rapacity in his eyes belying the mock-seriousness in his voice, was initially to discuss the possibility of your authorship of an in-service pamphlet for the prophylactic application of *Differanz*, timelined for distribution from our booth at February's CAP-PHARMA[2] shindig.

—Where was that again? asked Stu.

—Virgin Islands, said Randy.

—British?

—American.

—Stupid fucks, said Stu. Um, pardon my French.

—Tell me about it. Anyway Ed, as regards the pamphlet, can we conference call that? I'd really like to give Stu II here a peekaboo at how *Albu*'s shaping up. Our man in DC is really pulling out all the stops with his man at the FDA, and *he's* ballparking a March/April '95 greenlight, providing there's no 2-minute-warning fuck-over from BAPTIST U.

—Who's in charge of that trial? asked Stu.

—Brian Johns, interjected Dr. Ed, recovering, in his own 'mind' at least, a decent sense of professional decorum. I don't 'think' *he'll* be digging up any skeletons at this stage of the game, he added.

Randy laughed. —No, not Brian, he said. He gave Stu a sideways eyeball.

2. CANADIAN ASSOCIATION OF PSYCHIATRIC PHARMACOLOGISTS.

—So how about it, Ed, said Stu, could we have ourselves a little sneak preview?

—Of the Math? Oh, um, our Biostats man hasn't crunched anything yet.

—Fuck the numbers, Ed, said Randy. Lessee the *anecdotals*.

—You see, Ed, said Stu, what Randy is alluding to, albeit somewhat, er, opaquely, is that we, as you probably already know, but here I go anyway, that we….

—Stu II loves this subject, Ed, let him roll with it….

—What we are talking about here, Ed, is nothing less than a revolution, we're talking….

—Postmodern psychopharmacology, said Randy.

—I've heard of it, said Dr. Ed. It's big at BERKELEY.

—Correct, said Stu. Then there's the work of 2 colleagues of yours, I'm sure you've heard of them, at the UNIVERSITY OF THE AMERICAS, Cadmon & Fallas.

—Of course.

—No doubt. They've co-authored a truly seminal paper that's to be published in *BodyMind* next quarter.

—Stu I's telling us at EUMETA to bet the farm on it, Ed, said Randy, with a smiling nod in Stu II's direction.

—And Randy here's getting his marketing cabal in bed with the R&D types on his end, said Stu.

—Without the Trads catching wind of it, said Randy.

—'Till it's a done deal, anyhow, said Stu.

—Trads? asked Dr. Ed.

—You know, Ed, said Randy, the dead wood. Prepostmodernists, if you will. Yesterday's men.

—Uhhh.....

—The paper's called, said Randy, 'The Linguistic Re-Turn: Dialogic Neuro-pharmacology and Social Reconstruction'.

—And given your pristine track record, Ed, said Stu.

—We knew you'd be keen to be groundfloored on this, said Randy.

—As Cadmon & Fallas see it, DSM-vi[3] will require a near-gutting....

—A total re-think....

—Of next year's DSM-iv. If I can run the abstract of what they say by you, we're beginning to see 'personality' as a kind of neuro-chemical *dialogue*, one which shapes....

—And in turn can be shaped by....

—The narrative pathways of the so-called 'self'....

—The interanimation of past experiences, said Randy, of present hopes and fears—and of course, of future possibilities. All of which is umbrellaed....

---

3. *Diagnostic and Statistical Manual, 6th Edition. DSM-IV and V* were published by the AMERICAN PSYCHIATRIC ASSOCIATION in 1994 and 2013, respectively.

— Or interpellated by, rather, the social meta-narrative, said Stu.

— Which in this case is, as Fukuyama's work on Hegel and Kojeve leave absolutely no room for doubt.

— The liberal democratic state.

— Of which America, being both progenitor and progeny....

— Shall place its *imprimatur*, said Stu, on the 'End of History' — uh, at any rate, in the Macro-sense of that phrase.

— While on the micro-level, the revolution continues....

— In an evolutionary kind of way....

— As all of the above perpetually co-determines the emergent Subject.

— Which nevertheless has a role to play.

— In an economic sense.

— In seeing itself as a consciously utility-maximising individual.

— In 'making choices'.

— 'Rationally informed decisions'.

— 'Choosing' which of the neuro-chemical modifiers.

— Supplied by us, of course.

— Will suit his or her currently perceived goals and values.

— So the conventional, subjective experience of 'freedom'.

— By which Cadmon & Fallas mean the *perceived* freedom of the 'Will'.

— Shall be *supplemented* by, not supplanted by.

— Shall be strengthened even.

—By all of this.

—Which, in turn (Randy's increasing tendentiousness now reaching its climax), shall serve to bind the subject ever closer to the bosom, er, to the meta-narrative of the post-national state.

—That is, to the transnational neo-liberal meta-narrative.

—And by that Stu means the emerging, nascent, permanent 'New Economy'.

—Don't confuse this with 'globalization'.

—That's a pre-postmodernist, mechanistic, dinosaurist paradigm.

—Yeah. 'Globalization' is so 1848.

—This marks a complete break with all that, said Randy.

—Yeah, a complete break.

—But, as I said, an incremental break.

—Incremental, almost imperceptible steps.

—Baby steps, this hardly being some Soviet or Maoist, Randy said, chuckling, *utopian* enterprise.

—Hardly, said Stu.

—But the next step is already underway.

—Stateside, the FDA and the FCC have co-authored a White Paper which the Clinton administration is, in its timid way, by dribs & drabs, implementing.

—'Consumer Rights & Pharmaco-Marketing', said Randy.

—They're way ahead of us, said Stu.

—They're ratcheting up while we're caught in a circle-jerk.

—A circle-jerk of hand-wringing.

—More & more, and whether the few remaining antediluvian interventionists at HEALTH CANADA like it or not, said Randy, prescription drugs *will* be pitched to end-users, not to doctors.

—The gate-keeping role of pharmacists and doctors, said Stu, will increasingly be seen as a trade barrier, no offence intended.

—Anyhow, the market will mushroom, said Randy.

—A total paradigm shift.

—And *Alba* will be, no, *is*, the ... tip....

—Of the iceberg, Ed.

—And you're standing on it.

—And we know you'd want a piece of it.

—Cos' Stu II here is gonna tow it to the Persian Gulf if he has to.

—And sell it to the Saudis.

—So to speak.

The dynamic duo here paused, caught their breath, and the three men triangulated one another for a second-and-a-half or so.

—So, Ed, where do we stand on this? asked Stu, finally.

—Oh, Ed's your man alright, said Randy. Aren't you, Ed?

—I am, said Dr. Ed, with chemically-induced ingenuousness, what I am.

—Heh, said Stu.

—Ha, ha, said Randy.

—Uh, Ed ... , said Stu.

—We really need, said Randy, to eyeball, those anecdotals.

—Either that or we haefta interrogate the Residents, said Stu.

—We're, heh, only semi-unserious, Ed, said Randy.

—Ha, said Stu. Only semi.

—Well I'll tell you what, said Dr. Ed, enjoying what at the moment 'felt' like a brainwave, can you come back tomorrow?

—Tomorrow's not workable Ed, said Stu, with suddenly increasing impatience.

—It's a non-starter, said Randy.

—We'll be in Quebec-ville, up to our tomahawks....

—Up to our trousersnakes in red tape.

—Fucking frogs got their jurisdictional vicegrips out, said Stu, shaking his head with some vehemence.

—Ratchet drivers, said Randy.

—Socialist nightmare.

—Commie bastards.

—Well ... said Dr. Ed coolly, sensing he had them over the proverbial barrel, and having heard all of this, and thensome, before, ... well, my administrative nurse is off sick and she has the—

—Password? said Stu.

—To the files? said Randy. C'mon, Ed, level with us.

—Don't dick us around, pal, said Stu, with sudden violence.

—We're on your side, Ed, said Randy, attempting to sound a reassuring note.

—Er … yeah, said Stu.

—OK, OK, said Dr. Ed with a pretense of anxiety, for he was by now 'feeling' *very* calm indeed. OK. I'll be straight with you.

—Like a fucking arrow, said Stu.

—Attaboy, said Randy, and then, to Stu: No arrow straighter.

—Straight's fine, but, said Stu. But who's the archer?

—You see, said Dr. Ed with not-too-easily feigned *gravitas*, I'm on my way out to, I just stepped in to, there's been a, someone's, now just how do I put this? He paused and looked each quadrilaterally in the eye before continuing, as if (and *only* as if, for Dr. Ed really & truly 'felt' absolutely *nothing* whatsoever just now, was wholly & completely discarnate, disembodied, a floating, comfy, pillowy, cumulus cloud of quasi-semi-consciousness), as if he were a judge assessing the character of 2 recidivist pot growers, or the Lord Almighty extracting what remained of their eternal souls from the quicksand of their bodies and weighing them up on His empyrean balance beam.…

—Can I, may I be candid? he said.

—Hell, shit yeah, said Randy.

—Go boy, git, giddyap, said Stu.

—Someone… , said Dr. Ed, has *died*.

Dan Shboom's cab moved westward along one-way Brock St. at a pace that was timed just right to make the synced lights as, one after another, they turned green, green, green. Dan's fare had dozed off in the back seat, but he knew where to take him.

—Aeh, Mister, we're aeh, there. Mister....

Dan reached back and gave Dr. Ed a gentle shaking at the knee. When that failed to rouse the dishevelled gentleman in the rumpled blue suit, Dan's second attempt shook him with considerable force, as if the matter were of some immediate urgency.

—Hwa? said Dr. Ed.

—We're there, said Dan. That'll be $8.50.

— Buh, uh... ?

—That's 8 dollars and 50 cents, sir.

—Yuh, I, uh, here, kip, kipit, said Dr. Ed, handing Dan a 50 dollar bill.

—That's far too much, sir.

— Kip it.

—Aeh, I better, um, let me help you.

Dan got out of the cab, opened the left rear door, reached in, took hold of his fare by the right wrist and left lapel, grunted Dr. Ed's feet out the door and heaved the rest of him upright, and then half-guided, half-carried him up the drive to the front walkway.

—Keyth, Dr. Ed mumbled, and as he fumbled iteratively but without haste through his pockets, Dan took in a 360 degree panorama of, of....

—Some place you've got here, Dan said with polite understate-ment—in a manner which was, if not innate, certainly essential and not accidental to his character, for he really didn't think it was 'some' place at all: he knew that it was, in fact, one of those houses that broadcast its superlative qualities down the street, up the avenue, and then out, up & over the entire subdivision with such clarity and singularity of purpose that it became the paragon & prototype of the style that eventually would become known as, variously, the Monster Home, the Contemporary Suburban Nightmare, or the EgoBox, truly a beacon to ticky-tacky elephan-tiasis if ever there was one, shining its powerful beam of bad taste out into the countryside and across the Great Lake. Try as they may, lesser lights could never succeed at appropriating to themselves the bravoura of this most singular of mansions, with its mismatched mishmash of styles, its Mock Tudor meets grey vinyl clad Cape Cod exterior, and its serene, Apollonian Greek columns—which guarded an imperial Roman entranceway that led to a vaulted, Gothic Cathedral-ceilinged foyer. Just to the right of (and strikingly proportioned to ³/₄ the size of) the main house there was a 3 car garage/granny cottage (currently unoccupied), which was connected to the main house by a glassed-in sun room, and in front of one of whose sporty wood-grained aluminum doors was parked Dr. Ed's wife's capital-T Truck.

The exterior was lit up, quite literally, like an Xmas tree, although there were no trees on what remained of the property *per se*. There were, rather, quite a large number of small topiary shrubs centre-justified to the east-west boundary of the lot, clustering around a pair of leering cherubs, which in turn hovered over and mimed (for it was coming on winter) urination into a 4-stage quartz/resin composite waterfall, which fed a small, currently-drained fishpond, which was itself connected to the stolid poured concrete of the front porch via a primrose-lined pathway of crushed quartz interspersed with composite flagstones and lit by motion-sensing black plastic pot-lights.

—Keyth, here, Dr. Ed ejaculated, handing the EUMETA-sponsored key ring to Dan Shboom, who opened a kind of porter's gate and led his charge inside.

Inside, the aspiring *cauchemar des banlieus* motif continued, although betraying the kind of bicameral, split personality that results from an uneasy truce in the everlasting marital tug-of-war: a step to the right of the foyer took one into the usual (if admittedly 'high concept') Living Room that no one had ever, or could have ever, lived in. In the centre, an X-tra wide hallway was lined on one side with newfangled giclée reproductions of Miro's and Kandinsky's greatest hits, on the other with hyper-realistic paintings of ducks & geese, and a wood-veneered balustrade spiralled up and away from this contested terrain to the 2nd floor. A jump to the left dropped one into a sunken, *Whopper* or *Big Mac* of a 'Family' Room, done up with The Works — red shag carpeting, a granite-fasciaed gas fireplace, black 'pleather' furniture, a 1970s, pleather-wrapped bar complete with a mirrored backdrop and chrome-legged, black pleather-topped stools, and a TV that had (G-d knows how) only just managed to fit through the front door.

Dan was going to deposit Dr. Ed on the recently re-covered Victorian love seat in the Living Room when the latter shook his head, uttered the word 'bencil' and pointed straight ahead into the belly of the house, and owing to the obscene amount of money he had just pocketed, Dan felt duty-bound to allow himself to be led onward, into the (frankly pornographic) kitchen. On the solid ebony Bauhaus-inspired kitchen table Dan saw a pencil clipped onto an Edvard Munch 'The Scream' notepad holder (one of Dr. Ed's wife's touches).

He picked it up and handed it to Dr. Ed.

— I will nid you litter, Dr. Ed slurred at him. Yor carrh mumb, mumber, phone, tanks. Dan wrote: AMY'S TAXIS, 541-1111, Car 36, Dan, and then he helped Dr. Ed into a cushioned ebony kitchen chair. He was going to thank him for the tip (one that was large enough to enable him to buy groceries for the week), but his fare had already fallen fast, fast asleep, his head resting upon a

Pre-Raphaelite placemat, which bore a reproduction of a painting by Dante Gabriel Rossetti.

It was a depiction of a pomegranate-eating Persephone, the model for which was one of the painter's lovers, a certain Mrs. William Morris. Dr. Ed could not see this, but Persephone not only resembled his wife, she also bore more than a passing resemblance to the mother of his 'son'.

FRIDAY

— SECOND WIND OF THE OPSIMATH —

The spirit who bideth by himself
In the land of mist and snow,
He loved the bird that loved the man
Who shot him with his bow.

— Samuel Taylor Coleridge,
The Rime of the Ancient Mariner

23

BABYFRESH ATOM BOMB

D R. ED AWOKE to what he 'thought' was thunder, but it was
only the sound of his own anxious and shallow, gulping
breaths that filled his now all-too-conscious ears. He'd had *that*
G-ddamned dream again. His heart was racing, his blood pressure was through the roof, his entire head was crammed up inside
his most-likely-broken nose, and his nose 'felt' like a fucking war
zone, like G-ddamned ground zero. He was still in his clothes,
still at the kitchen table. The 'Starry, Starry Night' kitchen wall
clock read 00:17. He was in a world of hurt.

— Fuuucckkk meee, he groaned as he searched the pockets of his
slacks and greatcoat in vain for the bottle of painkillers, having
similar luck with his briefcase. He must have dropped them —
where? In the back of the cab? He wasted no time speculating on
such matters, but climbed (with some difficulty) the stairs to the
2nd floor, went into his wife's cavernous bathroom and encountered

therein the pre-historically hideous, repellantly tumescent creature that was his own schnoz.

—Jee. Zuss. Jesusmaryjoseph.

He would re-bandage it momentarily, but the fact of his resemblance to a hypertrophied, genetically modified, morbidly alco-
holic Mr. Potato Head definitely took a back seat to the much
more compelling fact that Mr. Potato Head's uranium-yellow
nose had gone nuclear on him, the heat blast radiating outwards
at the speed of, well, heat?

— Owwwwww, fuhh, sweetmotherof *G-d*.

He frantically searched, but with a forgivable (considering the
circumstances) lack of systematic thoroughness through his wife's
medicine cabinet. At the front was an assortment of herbal shit:
ma huang, Valerian Combo, *dong quai*, St. John's Wort, etc., etc.
The real deal was most likely towards the back, and he impatiently swept the entire contents of the cabinet out onto the
floor to get at it. Lessee, lorazapam, *Paxil*, lithium, diazepam,
Curtol PM, *Stomach-It*, *Vivra-Pep!*, *Less-On*, *Diet Rite*—damn
it, none of this would do, but he swallowed a couple of *Midol*
anyway as he lurched out of the bathroom and over to the bedside
table. In his haste he yanked open both the drawer and the cabi-
net-style door at the same time and, lying as covert as daylight
beside the bestselling *Making The Most Of It* (the sequel to last

year's sleeper hit, *Having It All*), why, lordy lordy look who's 40, there, there they were by G-d, his wife's migraine pills. He clumsily hurried off the childproof cap and, as they were somewhat less potent than what he'd gotten at Emerg, dry-swallowed 4 of them.

Then, before he knew what he was doing, his sinister left hand was dialling the number, 544-1111, on the portable phone as he stumped back into the bathroom and swallowed a gulp of mouthwash.

—Car 36 bease, it's a … a sbecial … delivery. 1216, Boutelliers Boint. I bant to hire him espressly … excellent serbice … nid him right, right abay.

Soon Dan Shboom was speeding Dr. Ed back downtown in his tank-like '88 CHEVROLET *Caprice 'Classic'*. Dr. Ed was freshly bandaged-up and his hair was combed, but he was still wearing the severely-wrinkled suit—and he had left his greatcoat behind. While he had slept, the temperature had risen precipitously for some reason, and it could not now be more than a degree or 2 below freezing.

Dr. Ed handed Dan Shboom another 50 from the back seat. —I nid a drink, he said. Sebaral, in fact. Where do you rec….

—Last call's at 1 A.M. You've only got 25 minutes, said Dan.

—Is dere a, where would one, what you'd call a?

—An after-hours club?

—Yes. Becisely.

—Hmm, yeah. But it's a student-run thing. Off-off-campus, obviously. Problem is, it's a bunch of friggin'….

—Berfect, dake me.

—… engineers.

A few minutes later, Dan Shboom pulled up at the rear of an uncared-for limestone building in the downtown core, and, pointing at the metal fire escape, said:

—Street level's a PHARMATOPIA, and there's an artists' co-op on the second floor; the 'boys' are up in the friggin' rafters, which is accessible only from back here. S'not a proper attic or anything, s'all under the table. Landlord's actually an English prof, owns half of the student ghetto, who knows where he got the money for it.

—Bhat's his name? Dr. Ed asked, genuinely interested.

—He's gotta couple. Lord Slum Chum's one, but you might know him as Perfesser Fraser, said Dan. The mentioning of this name sent Dr. Ed's stomach into the floor of the cab. I've never had him, Dan continued, but the undergrads call him Monty Hall.

—Bh-bhy? was all Dr. Ed could say.

—Cos he's always willing to make a deal.

—Bhat kind of deal?

—Depends what you've got to offer, I guess. Like I said, I've never had him, but some Grad students I know have T-Aed for him, and they hate his guts.

—Why?

—Don't know exactly, but they do have names of their own for him.

—Such as?

—Some call him 'BulletProf', others, particularly the women, just call him 'The Penis'.

This information only served to confuse Dr. Ed further. He said:

—You don't habben to know of a Fraser who works at HÔTEL DIEU?

—The hospital? No, but this guy's no doctor, though; from what they say, he's barely a PhD. Anyways, to get into the club you'll haefta go up these stairs, and…. Dan paused, wrapping his knuckles on the dashboard.

—Just knock, knocka-knocka, knock-knock on the door, like that. And only do it once, or they won't open the door.

Dr. Ed nodded, and then repeated after him, knock, knocka-knocka-knock, but not too loudly, on the hood of the Chevy.

—That's it, said Dan. You got it, ace.

—Bait here, said Dr. Ed, backing away towards the fire escape. As long as it dakes.

— Oh, just a sec', said Dan in a stage whisper, gesturing through his window for Dr. Ed to come back towards the car. I almost forgot. The password. I'll haefta warn ya, though, they do make 'guests' run quite the gauntlet here.…

Dr. Ed, setting aside the nervousness that the name 'Fraser' had provoked, and 'feeling' conspiratorial now, bent over the car, resting his arms on the roof. — I'm game, he whispered back. What is it?

Dr. Ed wrapped on the door, as per instructions, but there was no answer for some time. The stairs had led him up to an exterior door, which he passed through into a short hallway, at the end of which was another door. There was nowhere else, no other door he could have gone to, so this had to be *it*. The hallway was lit by a single, bare bulb, which could have been no more (if that were possible) than a 20 watt-er. Something, probably the shit-brown indoor/outdoor carpeting, smelled to highest high heaven, emitting a combination of odours so vile that Dr. Ed had to get a willful grip on his gag reflex as he waited, waited, waited for someone to answer the door. He wanted a drink badly all right, but *this* badly?

Now, Dr. Ed had a good nose on him, nay, a great nose. At the moment, due to circumstances (the contusion, to be sure, but also the opiates, the opiates) beyond its control, it was operating on 50 or 60% capacity, but that still made it a very good nose. And so, as he stood there in the hallway, he performed an intuitive kind of spectral analysis on the location's several, stratified olfactory layers. There was (obviously) urine at the 'base' or 'foundation', but also beer of course, at a slightly 'higher', er, 'level'. And, yes, or he 'thought' so anyway, there was, sitting (as it were) on 'top' of these 2 smells, several different ... vintages ... of vomit. Then (and he could not decide whether 'circumscribed' or 'circumfused' was the most precise term here) came the residual fumes of a commercial-strength, lemon-scented cleaner, naturally.

And while none of this effluvial data was particularly earth-shattering, Dr. Ed's nose remained troubled by 1 final, teasing smell, something lying *beyond* these others, in another—what, exactly?—dimension? *Something Other*, at any rate, trying not to so much 'cover up' these baser smells, for that particular metaphor could never successfully *work* in this most peculiar case for the truly first-rate nose (something which Dr. Ed had never claimed to possess, but which, he was certain, was a reality somewhere out in the greater gene pool). No, even the adjectives 'mask' and 'cloak' were insufficient here, for Dr. Ed smelled a smell of truly audacious ambition, but whose osphretic reach so far exceeded its aromatic grasp that any nosebled numbskull or nasal naif, any dainty Dorothy lately arrived from cornpone Kansas could see that it was just not happening — that *anyone's* anyhow nose would know, if it paused for more than a second or two, that this attempt at olfactory invisibility had in fact achieved its *opposite*. For, while it might momentarily deceive this the most primal of senses in the shortest of short terms, anyone prone to giving pause for 'thought' would 'think', would bloody well *take notice*, that this scented *Wizard*, like that of Oz, was nothing more than a failed fake, a complicated, incompetently fraudulent ... façade!

Dr. Ed knew. He knew what it was. He'd smelled that smell before, but he had to *name it to tame it*. And it was on the tip of his tongue. It was just a few notes to the 'left' of the smell of Max's flea mousse. — *Wizard*, he said to himself. *Wizard*....

— *Babyfresh*, he said to the previously-empty hallway, just as the door upon which he'd knocked was jerked open, about 4 inches or so. A nose and a mouth poked through the crack.

— Huh? the nose&mouth said.

— Babyfresh, Dr. Ed repeated reflexively, not quite catching himself here, but still comprehending the gravity of the mistake he'd just made, and trying desperately to not let his nose distort the sound of his words.

— Sorry, Pal, the nose&mouth said, wrong password, wrong place. The nose&mouth backed away from the opening like a tortoise retreating into its shell, and made to close the door.

—No, baid, please, I didn't beally mean id, I, as the bassword
I mean....

This intrigued the nose&mouth, and brought it back out of its
shell. —Oh?

—No, I was jusd dalking to myself, oud loud I, I mean I was
beflecting, bondering, aboud dhe smell in dhe hallway.

—Ahhh.

A pause.

—There's a smell? said the nose&mouth.

—Yes, said Dr. Ed.

—Bad smell izzit?

—Yes.

—Go on.

—Well it's seberal bad smells, actually, bud I was 'dhinking'
aboud dhe air freshener....

—That's freshening the place up.

—Yes.

—Hence your usage of the term 'babyfresh'.

—Yes, um.

—We don't either approve or condone such ... vulgar language
here, sir.

—I realize dhad, Dr. Ed lied, wondering what the hell was going
on here.

—But context is everything, is it not, sir?

—Uh, I subboze zo.

—And just how *do* you have cognizance of this alleged 'baby-fresh', sir?

—Um, I.

—If I may be so bold as to ask.

—Iz dhis, said Dr. Ed, bill dhis … inderbiew … ged me indo dhis … club?

—One cannot say, sir, one can just never tell, can one? It all—why it all *depends*.

—Debends on what?

—One is not at liberty to discuss that with you, sir. Now if you would be so kind….

—Whad?

—The question, *sir*.

—Oh. 'Babyfresh' is a smell, I mean a scend, a commercial not a consumer broduck. Dhey use id ad dhe car bash.

—Which car wash?

—The 'Soff Cloff' one. And … you know … they sbray id in, afder dhe car's clean.

—Go on.

—Id's one of seberal choices.

—They just spray it in.

—Yes, widh a gun.

—A gun!

—You know, a sbraygun, addached do a long hose.

—How long?

—Whad? Dhis is absurd, how in dhe hell would I know? Lissen, bal.

—This is all part of the … *process*, sir, of gaining entrance, I assure you. Please continue: how long is the hose?

—Jebus, *I* don'd know. Kide long.

—Oh dear oh dear.

—What?

—Nothing, nothing. Now, about you, you like this, this 'babyfresh'?

—You kibbing? Id's dhe wife, she uses id ad home.

—I see. 'The', *ahem*, 'Wife'.

—Yes.

—But sir, you have perjured yourself. You have uttered 2 entirely contradictory statements. First, you say it is a commercial grade product, then….

—No, you don'd umbersdand, she doesn'd ged id from dhe sdore, she buys id off of dhe car wash beoble, im bulk.

—In bulk?

—Yes.

—Good.

—*Good*? Can I come im mnow?

—I'm sorry. I have to go, I'm being … summoned … from within.

—Go? Can'd I come mnin?

—In, oh … *Sir*, you'll have to forgive me, you'll have to ask to speak to the door-man. And I—I am not he.

—Dhen whad are you?

—Oh, nobody, 'specially.

—Bud.

Suddenly, Dr. Ed had the distinct 'feeling' that he had seen this nose and that mouth before, but he could not place either of them.

—Listen, pal, the voice then said, its tone suddenly shifting from '*noblesse oblige*' to 'You Talkin' To Me?' Here's how it's gonna be: you start from scratch. Knock as loud as *fuck* or buddy won't hear you. Now sai-yo-*fuckin'*-nara. Oᴋ?

The door slammed shut. Dr. Ed then waited a few seconds and then knocked, as he had been told. When it eventually re-opened, Dr. Ed wasted no time in getting to the point, and tried *even harder* to talk normally:

—I'm here to see a man about a dog, he said with mechanical precision to a gormless-looking, gold-on-purple rugby-shirted lug who wore a gold '95' leather engineering faculty jacket that had been Rorshached with purple dye. The lad also sported a purple face (the sure-as-shooting sign that he had been unable to relinquish the manifold splendours of 'Frosh' or initiation week) and a purple Mohawk haircut.

—What's your quest? the youth queried with all-too-real *gravitas*.

—The hair of the dog that bit me, said Dr. Ed, who 'thought': so far, so good, talking almost unlike a lunatic, just what in the hell do I 'think' I'm doing here?

—Who's the biggest dick, Tracy?

—Wilt the Stilt Chamberlain, Fuck.

—How many in the bag?

Christ, Dr. Ed 'thought'. As if.

—20,000, he said.

—Do the Math, said the gorilla.

—800 a year for 25 years….

—25 *glorious* years, said the apprentice engineer.

—Almost 3 women…, said Dr. Ed.

—Cunts.

This came academically, and without rancour. Dr. Ed stood corrected. —Er, yes, c-cunts … a day.

—Un-fuckin-believable, said this most laddish of lads.

—Impossible, said Dr. Ed, unable to stick to the script.

—Believe it, old man. 'S doable, *ab*-so-*fuckin*-lutely. Then he paused for a moment and stared at Dr. Ed impatiently with a look that said '*Well?*'

—Um, how's the weather up there? said Dr. Ed.

—Friggin' cold, old man. You know how cold?

Dr. Ed cleared his throat, and proceeded to recite, like a truculent, coerced schoolboy with his rhythmically inept, memorized Shakespeare:

As cold as a frog on an ice-bound pool,
As cold as the end of an Eskimo's tool,
As cold as a polar bear's frozen shit,
As cold as a witch's wrinkled tit…. (& etc.)

The door swung open wide to receive him. With Kantian aesthetic disinterestedness, with the cool, clinical, impersonal rationality that every medical and applied science student gets vaccinated with, the purpled engineer said:

— Congrat-u-fuckin'-*lations.*

— Fuck you very mush, said Dr. Ed automatically, and slipping finally, into broken nose speak.

He was thence propelled toward the after-hours club's copious stores of alcohol, along the venturi effect of a sigh.

24

HOLY SHIT

Holy shit, the boy said. But this was another boy, unpurpled, sporting not a Mohawk but the complete depilatory 'do' known as the cue-ball, and whose rugby shirt was coloured in reversi, purple-on-gold and partially hidden under a set of purple coveralls with '94' and 'RugRat' painted in gold on the back. That's some weird dream, he said.

Dr. Ed said nothing, and gulped down the last of the beer. While he was off looking for a urinal the beer had appeared out of nowhere, a squadron of 6-ounce glasses, 24 of them, making, what? 144 ounces, which was 8 pints, or 4 quarts, or a full, Imperial Gallon of ale between them. And now it was gone.

—What was this? he said, eventually, tipping his empty glass back and forth. He heard himself speak in his normal voice again now, or more-or-less, which meant that the drugs must be wearing off just as the alcohol was coming on, right?

—'*Wisconsin's Best*'. Worst is more like it, though. It's cost-effective, but it's skunkspiss, really.

—You only rent it, anyhow, said Dr. Ed, surprising himself by reaching back to a standard, jocular cliché he'd been taught years ago, and to which, including just now, he'd never once considered giving utterance.

—You said it, Man, said the boy, who then proffered his right hand in the air for a *de rigueur* 'high five'. You wait right here, and I'll go lease us a few more litres.

Dr. Ed had struck up a conversation with him a ½ an hour, or 2 bottles of Molson Stock Ale (what his father used to drink, probably still drank, back on the Island) into a solitary sojourn at the bar. *That* was an hour-and-a-½ ago, and he had been flanked by empty barstools, the jovially bellicose throng instinctively sensing that the occluded cumulo-nimbus formation above his comparatively ancient head portended stormy weather, and had duly wide-berthed him.

But then the boy, who introduced himself as Doug and who had his own reasons for seeking idiosyncratic company that evening, sat down on the stool to his immediate left, and was in no time telling Dr. Ed his own sorry little tale of woe: his girlfriend, of 4+ years running—since their senior year of high school, Mary was her name, a nursing student of course—had just 'dumped' him, that very evening. Worse, she had been 2-timing him with some cadet from the ROYAL MILITARY COLLEGE—since, it was still hard for him to believe, the fucking second week of term.

They'd even gotten engaged, she and the cadet—Mary had sent Doug a note—and were to be married the following May.

—A union of souls? Dr. Ed asked rhetorically.

—A 'Scarlet Wedding' more like.

—For a scarlet woman, Dr. Ed added.

Doug laughed ruefully.

—But what's a 'Scarlet Wedding'? asked Dr. Ed.

—It's a MilCol thing, apparently, said Doug. Getting married before graduation so they can do it in their red uniforms, the historical ones that make them look like Dudley Do-Right—or bell-boys. I guess if they waited 'til after grad, when they're actually in the forces instead of *jus' pretendin'*, they'd have to wear the standard, even uglier, modern military get-ups. 'Spoils the Picture', he added, his hands drawing the inverted commas in the air.

—Jesus, said Dr. Ed.

—Jesus doesn't have a whole helluva lot to do with it, said Doug.

—Never did, son, never did.

—Maybe. But maybe not.

—You religious? asked Dr. Ed.

—Not really. I was raised Lutheran, but I guess I'm a sceptic now. And you?

—I don't really 'think' about it.

—Why not?

—It's too long a story to get into, said Dr. Ed, surprised but not alarmed or offended by Doug's asking, with the ingenuousness of youth, questions such as this, questions of a most personal nature. It's just a long, boring story, he repeated.

—I've got nowhere to go, 'specially, said Doug. Shoot.

—Um, I … Ok, sure, why the hell not.

—Hey, let's grab that table, and another tray?

—Tray?

—Of beer. In front of you, what you've been drinking?

But the actual tray was leaning against the table leg. Doug picked it up and waved it in the air. —That's how it works here. Cheapest way to consume mass quantities.

And so they did. But before discussing Dr. Ed's ancient history, and the recent, recurrent dream that kept returning him to that rediscovered country, Dr. Ed wanted Doug to tell *him* something.

—Uh, Doug, he said, shouldn't you be more, I don't know, bitter, or angry, all things considered? You don't seem all that….

—That's what my housemates say. They've got this whole 'guys' list of things that have to be done in these kind of situations.

—Such as?

—Oh, I dunno, cut off his prick, for starters. Just meathead bullshit really, like having a blanket party?

—Which is…?

—The bunch of us throwing a sheet over the bastard's head and beating the crap out of him.

—Charming, but effective.

—Yeah, tell me about it. Anyway, yeah, 'course I'm pissed, but it's more than just that, you know?

—You're talking of sadness, loss, Dr. Ed offered automatically, if somewhat uncomfortably.

—Stuff like that, yeah, stuff you just don't talk about.

—But you're talking about it. Dr. Ed raised a glass to him.

—I'm drunk, said Doug, clinking glasses. And getting drunker, and so are you.

—Getting there, said Dr. Ed. But still, even drunk, you're not like the rest of these….

—Knobs? I sure as hell am, Ed, most of the time. Tonight's different, though. Tonight's—

He looked shyly, yet piercingly, into Dr. Ed's eyes. There's a *there* there, Dr. Ed thought, a something which spoke to, which broke, which smashed its way *past*, if that could possibly be possible, what was left of his….

—*Singalong! Two minutes to Singalong!* an amplified voice boomed over a potent P.A. system.

—Singalong? asked Dr. Ed.

—Yeah, 'Thursday Night Singalong' as they call it, said Doug. They do it every week, though it's not really, usually anyway, an actual *sing*-along. More of a group, um, recital I guess.

—I don't follow, said Dr. Ed.

—Well the hosts, they're called Fat&Pill, but their real names are Pat and Phil, they play, you know, a classic sketch or routine or whatever on the P.A., and everyone joins in.

—You mean *comedy*?

—Usually. Songs, too, supposedly funny ones, and, well, it's OK. Funny if you're drunk I guess.

—Oh.

—Usually it's things like Monty Python bits, or parts of the *Animal House* movie, Second City—the usual.

—And tonight?

—Tonight? They call it 'The Cablenet Swearing Guy'. Have you heard it before?

—No.

—It's been making the rounds for a couple of years. Some people call it 'Angry Cable Customer'.

—What is it?

—It's taken from the K-TOWN CABLENET company answering machine, apparently. This guy's bummed about his service getting called off and keeps calling the machine back, swearing more&more and louder&faster each time.

—Huh. And this is true, I mean, it's not made up?

—Seems it's legit, but you be the judge. Here, they're coming on.

Two young men, both in purple clown's wigs and purple coveralls identical to Doug's, came to the small raised stage at the front of the room, each grabbing a microphone. One of them, Dr. Ed instantly realized, had the same nose and mouth that had mocked him earlier, at the door. And then he realized who they were: the two young men that morning, on the bus, the pair who had been boorishly, heedlessly singing at the top of their lungs.

—I'm Fat, said the one.

—And I'm Pill, said the other.

—And *you're...* , they both said simultaneously, to the crowd.

—*Biggus Dickus!* the crowd roared in unison.

—I've got a wery gweat fwiend in Wome named Biggus Dickus, said Fat, or Pill, in an aside to his counterpart.

—And why are we here tonight, Fat?

—To get... , said Fat.

—Screwed, blued and tattooed! went the audience.

—Later! the pair said together. First, though, we'se gonna....

—*Singalong!* the crowd affirmed.

—*Course* we are! said, apparently, Fat.

—Hey, you know what, Fat, said Pill, suddenly 'serious'.

—What, Pill?

—I just called, to say, I love you, Pill sang.

—Oh?

—I just called, to say howww, much I, caaaarred.

—Really?!

—Yes I just called, to sayyy, I luhh—uhh—uhhvve yoo—oo—ouu....

—Wow.

—And I mean it, from the bott—tomm of my, harr—arr—arrt.

—Huh? Dr. Ed said to Doug.

—Stevie Wonder song, said Doug.

—Oh, said Dr. Ed.

—Ohhhh *yes* I do, said Pill.

—How sweet, said Fat.

—In fact, said Pill, now much more matter-of-factly, and pointing his index finger square in the middle of Fat's fat forehead, his thumb pointing upwards into the air. In fact, I've just sent you a lovely, loving love letter.

—*Love letter!* yelled a large-ish proportion of the audience.

—And you know what a love letter is? Pill asked, with menace in his voice.

—*It's a bullet from a gun!* the entire audience roared.

—*Blue Velvet*, weird cult film, Doug referenced before Dr. Ed could express his all-too-real confusion.

—Daddy Wants To Fuck! Pill screeched, pretending now to hyperventilate through an oxygen mask.

—And that's a good point, said Fat, stepping smartly forward now and adopting a Queen's English accent and a hyper-rational manner. An ad-*mir*-able concep-tion, which oft was thought, and ne'er so well express'd, and which, conveniently enough, segg-uh-ways most han-dee-lee into tonight's (and changing his voice into that of the echoing boom of a hockey arena announcer) Fee-churrrrr Prez-ennn-tayyyyyyyy-shunn!!

—It's back by popular demand! said Pill in an aw-shucks/gee-wizz/Gomer Pyle voice.

—Actually, it's snot, Pill (very much mock-serious and quietly shifty now). You just decided it was, all by your lonesome, as if, as if, as if you, *voted yourself king* or something!

—You don't vote for kings! went the audience.

—I thought we were an autonomous collective, Pill said.

—An anarcho-syndicalist commune, said Fat.

—Whatever, said Pill.

A look of hyperbolic shock and hurt came over Fat's fat face. —I really am surprised at you, Pill, he said in a highly effeminate voice, his arms now crossed in front of his chest and his general posture suggesting the attitude of a lover spurned. Not only do you mock my loony left-wing politics in a most cavalier fashion, you also take me, *moi*, for granted. Why....

—Can I have a hug? Pill suddenly interrupted.

—Not in front of the children.

—We can't keep it a secret forever.

—No, I.

Pill embraced him hard, to catcalls, whoo-whoos, beer glass-and-bottle poundings and deafening applause. Fat continued:

—And now for our feature. Some of you know it as.

—The Cable Guy! someone shouted.

—*We* like to call it, well what *do* we call it, Pill?

—We call it, Pill said, *basso profundo*, 'The Fuckin' Fucker's Fucked'.

—Yeah.

—Or 'Fuck This Fuckin' Shit'.

—Yep.

—Or whatever the fuck we call it.

—Eggs-ackly.

—And so, Pill said, here yas go. And he waved his right arm towards some unseen soundman, who started a very crackly, hiss-filled tape recording of a tape recording taken from a tape recording of a 1st generation copy of a tape-recorder style answering machine:

[Beeeep.] Where's the fuckin' service you cocksuckers? I paid for the fuckin' shit why don't you fuckin' *bring* it *onnnn?* Sick a' you bunchoffucking *baaaastards.*

[Click-thump.] Where's the fuckin' cable? I've been payin' you sluttin', fuckin' *ass*holes all along an' I got no *fuckin'* TV! Jeeee-sus fuckin' *Christ* what in fuck do you *want* for fuck-*all? [Click-thump.]*

[Beep-click.] I've been phonin' all these God-damn, cocksuckin' fuckin' numbers you got in this *fuckin'* phone book, *and they're all busy.* Well my cable's *fucked* and you're gonna hear from me ANY*WAY. [Pause.]* You bunch of Goddamn cocksuckin' fuckin baaastards. *[Click-thump, click.]*

[Beep.] I don't wanna *sell* fuck-all, I wanna watch fuckin' TV. You cocksuckin' fuckin' whores you got all these *fuckin'* numbers in the Goddamn cocksuckin' *fuckin* phone book, and they're *all* fuckin' busy. *I'm* a workin' man, I pay your cock-suckin' *fuckin'* bill, why in the name a' JESUS GODDAMN COCKSUCKIN' FUCKIN' CHRIST can you not SUPPLY me the GODDAMN MOTHERFUCKIN' WHORE'N'SLUTTIN' FUCKIN' GODDAMN COCKSUCKIN' FUCKIN' *SERVICE? [Click-thump-thump.]*

[Beep-thump, long pause, thump, beep, click, beep.] Hell-o you *Dogan*-faced, mother-fuckin', cock-suckin', whore-n-sluttin', God-damn, by-the-Jesus, fuckin' God-Damn, sluttin', fuckin' *Baaa*stards. *Where's* the *fuckin'* cable? PAYIN' for the fuckin' shit

and *I* ain't fuckin' *GETTIN'* it. ***GET IT ON THERE!*** you buncha fuckin' *baaastards. [Scraping click.]*

[Beep-thump, pause, beep, click click beep.] I can't watch AUTO-Mag without fuckin' TEE-VEE. Where's the service you bunch of Goddamn cock-suckin' fuckin' baaa-stards? [Thump-ump.]

[Beepclick.][Despondent.] I hate payin' for sumpin' I don't have. I cannot watch your Auto-Mag magazine if I do not have the service. I've been phoning all the other numbers that's been ring-ing busy; this is the *only* number I've been able to get a ring-from. *So* where's the COCK-*suckin God-DAMN* whore'n'sluttin' by-the-Jesus fuckin' ***SERVICE****? [Thump-click.]*

[Beepclick.] It's *me* again Mother-*fuck*ers. I have no fuckin' cable. You bunch of God-damn, whore-n-sluttin' *fuckin'* overpaid *cock*-suckers are doin' *FUCK*-ALL, for what *I'm* PAYING *YOU…JEEE*-SUS CHRIST you oughta try do what *I* do for a *fuckin'* livin'. *[Thump-ump click-click.]*

[Beep.] Hell-o mother-*fuck*-ers … My cable's back on, thank you very much.

— Um, wow, said Dr. Ed.

— Yeah, said Doug.

— He's got rhythm, I'll give him that, said Dr. Ed. Where's he from, exactly?

—We're pretty confident he's a local, said Doug. Fat's friend Steve, well his brother Brian's girlfriend works at CABLENET, and he said she said she got it off the after-hours answering machine there.

—Wherever it's from, said Dr. Ed casually, yet with an unmistakable air of authority in such matters, they'd have to have a sizable Orange community.

—Orange? said Doug, quite puzzled.

—Irish Protestant, after William of Orange. Glorious Revolution, 1688, Dutchman made England safe from Catholicism forever. You know.

Doug did not know. —Huh, he said?

—The guy on the tape said 'Dogan-faced bastard', which means 'Irish Catholic bastard', like me.

It crossed Doug's 'mind', though not in so many words, that his drinking companion was speaking somewhat *ex cathedra*-lly here.

—Oh, he said, not really cottoning on.

—Where I come from, he said, pointing in the direction of the far east end of the Lake, from Noman's Island….

—Where? said Doug, who was from the City and not at all interested in local geography.

—Just east of town, where the end of the lake funnels down into the river. Anyway, we have a long history of Protestants versus Catholics. Every July the Orange Proddy Dogs as we called them would parade through town to lord over us

Dogan-faced bastards their King Willy's thrashing of us at the Battle of the Boyne, and we'd always have a bit of a scrap with them.

This was a lie, for Dr. Ed had never willingly fought anyone in his life.

—Oh yeah?

Dr. Ed then uncharacteristically noticed that Doug was not in the least interested in any of this, but, somewhat pre-occupied perhaps with that thing concerning his by-now-ex-girlfriend, was only pretending to listen, out of what seemed to be natural politeness, so he said:

—Where is *your* family from, Doug?

—You mean originally? The Ukraine. My grandparents settled in Thunder Bay, and most of my family is still there, but my dad went to the City. Um, Ed, I'm kinda curious about what you said earlier, about your 'alleged son' as you call him. You said that at first you thought I was him, when, you know, you knocked over my buddies' table of beers back there.

Dr. Ed's face reddened. —Jesus, wasn't *that* embarrassing, he said. I didn't mean to make your friends up & leave on you.

—Fugg-gedd-aboud-it, said Doug, who had been speaking seriously, but who became jovial once more at Dr. Ed's super-seriousness. They were leaving anyway. They'd accomplished their goal of getting me here and getting some serious brewskies into me, so I could drown my sorrows etc., but they haddta go do a last-minute concrete cram.

—Concrete cram?

—For tomorrow's test.

—We're uncivil engineers. It's for a 'Strength of Materials' course. You know, concrete, steel … and next is wood.

—Huh.

—Anyway, I'd like to hear you out on that, that, er, issue of yours, cos' I'd rather think about something else, about someone else's shit right now, and….

—Wouldn't you just rather keep it, um, light? said Dr. Ed. Considering the, the circumstances I mean.

—No. Not really. I'm guess I'm kinda in a serious mood, and, well, I think I'd just … rather talk about your troubles, rather than mine.

—I don't have 'troubles' said Dr. Ed, suddenly as defensive as someone on high levels of codeine mixed with alcohol could get.

—I just thought you, you looked like someone who, who wanted, or needed to talk.

—I never talk, said Dr. Ed.

—Not even, said Doug, to your wife?

—Especially not to my wife, and especially not about, about….

—About what?

Dr. Ed couldn't for the life of him fathom just what about.

—About not talking, for instance, he said.

—Why not? said Doug, simply.

—It's complicated, said Dr. Ed. Life gets like that. You'll see.

—But you *do* want to talk to *someone*, right, or....

—Or I wouldn't be sitting here with you? No. Not at all, ever. *I* came here because I wanted a drink, and I guess I wanted a drink because, because, like you, I wanted to escape for a bit. It doesn't happen often, but every now & then, every couple of years anyway, I need to blow off a little steam.

—Here's to blowing off steam, said Doug, raising his glass to clink with Dr. Ed's, both men taking large gulps. And here's to staying safely out of the deep end, he added, and then raised his glass once more to clink his companion's, but Dr. Ed had not reciprocated. Rather, he looked at Doug with a something akin to a pedantic expression on his face.

—Listen, he said, I don't know everything, but if 20 years of psychiatry have taught me one thing, it's that there *is* no deep end, and that psychologists who tell you that there is one are either dupes or liars.

—I, um, said Doug.

—There is no deep, said Dr. Ed. No high or low.

—I'm not, said Doug.

—Hold on. You were just going to say, I bet, exactly what you said before, about G-d: 'I'm not so sure', right? Or 'Maybe, maybe not'.

But 'Deep', 'G-d'? —Christ, those are just words, Doug. *Words.*
Metaphors stabbing out at something that's not there, and never
was. Epiphenomena of the brain.

—Maybe. Like you say I said.

—You like to be sceptical. But *real* sceptics consider the evidence
before them; they certainly aren't romantic dreamers, and they
aren't idle fence-sitters either.

—Hey, hold on, Bud, you sayin' I'm idle?

—Sorry. I, I have to deal with this all the time, at the clinic. It
gets me angrier than I ought to be.

—S'okay. G'won, rant away.

—Where was I? said Dr. Ed.

—Evidence.

—Right. All of the evidence, don't you see, points in one direction, and one direction *only.*

—Yeah, but what about love? Is that just a word, or an 'epiphenomenon' too? Doug smiled here, and leaned back on his chair
so that only the back legs of his chair remained on the ground.
He interlaced his fingers behind his head, elbows pointing out
perpendicularly, and balanced himself there, smiling and waiting for the inevitable.

—Well, I wouldn't want to sound like I'm rubbing your nose in
it, but....

—But you are.

—No, but yes, it *is* just a word, Doug. Love's a noun for some-thing people 'feel', and it's a verb, for something they *do*, or more accurately, for something they *'think'* they do.

—Because....

—Because, just because they 'think' and *'feel'* that it's real, doesn't make it so.

—Doesn't make it not.

—And the evidence, Doug?

—Depends on what you mean by evidence.

—Oh come *on*. You're a kind of scientist, aren't you, I mean you believe in *induction*, right? Experimentation? Measure-ment, *facts*?

—That's funny, said Doug, his chair coming down from its balancing act.

—What?

—You actually think people obey physical laws in the same way *concrete* does!

—And steel, and wood, that's right, fundamentally, essentially, at bottom: yes.

—That's what it all comes down to?

—You got it. Billiard balls, Doug. A complex interplaying of determinants, but still, at bottom, *physical* pathways of causation.

—You know, Ed? For a smart old guy, you're sure pretty young and dumb.

—What?

—Hell, I'm only, what, 21, but you, you remind me of myself when—How old *are* you, anyway?

—44.

Doug laughed again. —Well, then you're a 17 year-old 44 year-old. Or a 44 year-old 17 year-old, whichever.

Dr. Ed forced himself to pretend to see the 'humour' in this, and then expelled a peculiar, emphysemic kind of laugh, which ended in a half-smile. —Both, he then said, after a pause. I guess you could say I'm both.

—Hey, I'll drink to that, said Doug.

Doug's joke had turned Dr. Ed, despite the alcohol & pills, into his naturally serious self once more. —But 17, eh? he said. I suppose I know what you're trying to say, but then again, you don't really know me, do you?

—True, I don't, but s'pose I use your own scientific approach on you.

—How do you mean?

—Your behaviour, tonight, follow the bouncing billiard balls— it's not exactly characteristic of you, I'd bet. I mean, you don't generally hang around in undergraduate pubs, let alone after-hours clubs, do you?

—No.

—What are *you* looking for, Ed?

Dr. Ed was about to say that Doug had it all wrong, that the billiard ball paradigm didn't rightly attempt to deal with such fictions as 'motivation', when, out of the blue (realizing as he spoke that he was being honest for the first time in a very, very long while) he said:

—I don't … know. Then, regaining his balance, he added, after a pause: Oblivion, I suppose.

—No, not really you're not. You could get that on any street corner.

—Not at this time of night.

—I bet that in your house, your liquor and medicine cabinets are fully stocked with oblivion.

—Well, Dr. Ed conceded.

—Hell, and you're a doctor! You could scam pretty well anything you wanted or thought you needed at the hospital. So no, I'd say you're here for a different reason, just like me. We've both succeeded in getting drunk, but instead of being satisfied with that and with chanting with the shovelheads, we're here talking to each other, why's that d'ya think?

—You tell me, you're the *wisenheimer*, said Dr. Ed.

If Dr. Ed had looked (and he did not) he would have noticed that Doug appeared suddenly grave, vulnerable even.

—Ok, Doug said, I'm, I guess I'm talking to you because … I dunno, I s'pose that even though getting drunk took the, the edge off things just now, I, I still want her back….

— Bitch though she is, Dr. Ed interrupted.

— Granted, said Doug. But if I can't have that, I'd like, I'd want … to talk about it, with someone who can empathise, someone who's been there.

— I'm not a particularly empathetic fellow, said Dr. Ed.

— You mean you don't like to be, or want to be. But you want reality too, or part of you does, or you wouldn't be at this table talking to me, like this.

— Huh.

— I think, said Doug, it's time you told me your story.

— What, which story?

— Whatever it was or is that made you come here tonight, and then got you talk to me.

Dr. Ed then looked closely at this boy for the second time that night. Doug did not resemble his 'son' as much as it had seemed to him at first. His nose was a bit of a pug, while Ted's was aquiline, like his own. Doug's ears were also small, while Ted's, again, like his own, stuck out a fair bit, with detached lobes. Doug's mouth was much smaller than either Ted's or Dr. Ed's, and his hair was straight and fair, but his own (or what was left of it), like his 'son's' hair, was black, thick and curly. Wait a minute, then, he thought, then how could, how could he ever have thought that Doug resembled….

Then it struck him: Doug's eyes, like his own, like Ted's, were dark, a bit on the full side, and with something, with a kind of *asceticism* about them. They were the kind of eyes you instinctively avoided, especially in the mirror, because they always made you feel like they *wanted* something from you. Like now: that's just what Doug's eyes were doing, they were asking him to go somewhere that he didn't want to go.

Not only that, but Doug talked like—like a university lecturer for Chrissakes! He reminded Dr. Ed of himself, or worse, of a philosophy or sociology professor, or....

Dr. Ed 'felt' like blood vessels were coming to the surface of his entire body, preparing him, getting him ready for fight and/ or flight, to bolt or bite. He screwed his butt to the chair with all that remained of what 'felt' like his free will: there had already been enough embarrassment in the past 24 hours, he told himself.

—My story, he said.

—Your story.

—I, I have a son, Ed said, for the first time ever without inverted commas. I have a son, and, for the past few nights, I've been having this recurring dream....

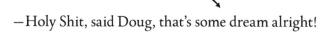

—Holy Shit, said Doug, that's some dream alright!

And it was, and then Ed said nothing, which was only appropriate, and then Doug went to get them some more skunkspiss beer, which was also appropriate, because more beer was required, not to escape reality now, but to aid & abet its soaking in: for Ed was clear now, not at all in the sense of 'free & clear', but clear in the sense of seeing, if no more than this, still, *at least* this: that a father needs to be a father to his son, just as a son needs to be the son of his father.

And this was no mere metaphysical concept or allegory. No, it was entirely practical; it had to do with the tangible here & now, not to mention a very much real, if long unacknowledged, past. It had to do with Ed and Ted. It also had to do with Agnes; that too he would have to clear up. But first things first. First, he must go and see Ted, his son. His own, his only son.

The next tray of beers passed, largely, in silence, and then it was time, and he and Doug parted with a manly, unashamed bearhug. Doug was (like most of the clientele here) still going strong, but Ed 'felt' more than a little bit wobbly as he weebled towards the door.

Dan Shboom was still, faithfully, waiting for him. He had shut the engine off, but was reading by the *Caprice*'s somewhat dim interior light.

—What time is it? Ed asked him through the driver's side window, with a buoyancy not entirely attributable to the anaerobic conversion of maltose (and, in the cheaper brands of ale that filled the trayfuls of glasses at the club, glucose), by certain strains of yeast, into ethyl alcohol.

—Just after 4, said Dan, not a little surprised by the change in his fare's demeanour. Ed opened the rear door and slid his butt, with the aplomb of a national-class curler, across the red vinyl bench seat.

—What are you reading? he asked.

—*The Prison Notebooks*, by Antonio Gramsci, said Dan, pulling the steering column mounted shifter to the right, to 'D', and shifting the car into Drive. Where to now?

—27 Raglan Road, my son's house. Then you're a free man.

—Ok.

—Now who's this Gramshee?

Dan took a good look at the guy. If he'd asked Dan earlier that evening, there would've been no way that Dan would've bothered making the effort, but now, especially after such a generous tip, well, why not? —He founded the Italian Communist party, he said.

—Communist? Ed said in a loud voice, and right then Dan was sure that he'd judged him amiss, but then Ed continued: My son's a communist!

—Is he, said Dan, slightly curious.

—Yup, well, that is, I don't really know, but he did say last week, when I said something particularly nasty about the Catholic Church, and he said that Jesus Christ would've been a socialist, and a socialist's the same as a communist, right?

—Well, said Dan, and he thought: boy, is *he* ever flying.

—You think he was?

—Uh, said Dan, turning from Johnson onto Montreal and crossing Princess and Queen in rapid succession. I … couldn't say, I'm not … religious.

—I hear you, said Ed. So this Gramshee, what's she have to say, then?

—He. Well, it's a bit involved, and we're almost at Raglan, but, have you ever heard of the word 'hegemony'?

This was, he was ashamed to admit, a new one for Ed. He was not a political man, and had always assumed, like the American curmudgeon H.L. Mencken, that those who owned the country ought to, well, run it as they saw fit. Otherwise, he had no real time for politics or politicians of any stripe.

—No, he said truthfully. I haven't.

—Well, said Dan, it's *right* on Raglan?

—I don't know, said Ed.

—You said it was your….

—It's, it's the first time I've, said Ed.

Dan took a right turn anyway, and seconds later applied the brakes. —Well, we're here, he said. To their left stood a small, aluminum-clad cubic bungalow, of the type constructed for the veterans of World War II. Dr. Ed groaned, then shimmied himself out.

—I guess this is where we part, he said through Dan's window. He held another pair of folded 20s between his fingertips, which he motioned towards his driver.

Dan waved them off. —No, really, he said. You've given me plenty already. Ed nodded, dropped the 20s through the open window anyway, and then made to leave.

—Oh, sir? said Dan.

Ed turned back towards him.

—Hegemony, in case you're interested, is, according to Gramsci, how the ruling class maintains power in a democratic state, *without* the use of force.

—You mean brainwashing? said Ed.

—No, not brainwashing. More of an unconsciously agreed-to limitation of what can be discussed; what questions are worth answering, or even asking, and which 'truths' are considered … axiomatic.

—Oh?

—It's, said Dan, it's well maybe it's a bit like how your patients 'naturally' avoid questioning certain things about themselves, because it's precisely by not questioning that they maintain the fiction that their lives are in their control, or at least make sense.

—I'm not, said Ed, a psychologist.

—I thought you said, said Dan.

—Psychiatrist. Different set of axioms. Axia?

—Of course, said Dan.

—More drugs, less talk is our motto, said Ed half-jokingly, patting the roof of the Chev. Thanks for all your help tonight. And for the vocab, of course.

—You have a key?

—No, but I'll be fine, said Ed, and he held his palm up in the air as the cab drove down the street. He watched it turn right, back towards the downtown core, then he turned and faced his son's house.

This was the 2nd time he had stood in front of it, but he had never been inside. 3 months ago, he had sat across the road in his car for a few moments, as part of a little covert investigation; it was a week or so after Ted had first made contact. He was broke, he'd said, and had just moved here from out west, Vancouver Island way, and needed to come up with a security deposit on a small house he was trying to rent. He didn't expect a handout, but were there any vacancies at the hospital, or anything Dr. Blanchette needed doing (unlike Ed, Ted was good with his hands) around the house?

There was only the computer. The CPU fan had just given up the ghost after a month or so of moaning & groaning, and had been down for 10 days. Ed hadn't had the time to deal with it himself, and 'feeling' a bit of pity for the kid, had let him go at it, pulled a string or 2 with the folks at the temp agency, and had advanced him 2 weeks' salary, but on the condition that Ted never, ever call him or make contact by any other means.

And now here he was, standing outside his son's house, wondering what to do next. Uncharacteristically, he hadn't 'thought' any of this through, so he just stood there and stared for some time. The ruined little box of a house had a ruined little white picket fence out front; he'd noticed that before, but what he hadn't noticed before was a little varnished, wood-burned sign just to the left of the front door, which hailed visitors and passers-by with 'The Gosse's' [sic]. Ed 'felt' a strange little tug of some kind inside of him.

'Gosse's'. It wasn't the misuse of the apostrophe, or the unfamiliarity of Ted's last name that disconcerted him, however — for Ted had, quite against Ed's will, informed his birth father of the particulars of the situation of his adoptive family (impecunious yet hard working; neurotically G-d-fearing and Philistine; incredibly close-knit until the passing of the not-yet-40, much beloved father from cancer-of-the-everything; the downward slide into alcohol on the part of the mother, subsequent to the preceding as well as to an unelaborated-upon accident at her place of work; finally, the consequent scattering to the 4 winds of the children, of whom Ted was the youngest).

No, it wasn't that. It was the 's' at the end of that name on the sign: Ted had never told him that … that he was married!

Married? He was only what—26? 27, tops? Did he have children, too? No, he was too immature for … but then again … he wished, he wished he'd known that, if he had known he would have … would have what?

He knew, to be truthful, that he would not have acted, in all probability, any differently than he had done. Well, there was still time to make that, and so much more, up to him. To them, that is, yes, to them both. He felt like Scrooge on the morning after the visit of the 3 Spirits of Xmas. He felt like climbing into a Frank Capra film, like writing a happy ending to a clichéd Canadian novel about broken families and prairies full of wheat….

He moved forward, onto the ruined little front step, looking in vain for a doorbell or knocker. He'd have to rap his knuckles on the—no, wait a minute, it wasn't even 05:00, he couldn't, it wouldn't be right to, not at this time of. He was dressed warmly; he'd wait on the porch for the, what, only 1 or 2 hours or so until the Gosse's, until his son Ted and his beautiful (he supposed) young wife awoke. No pressing need to disturb them now, he'd be fine: it had become overcast since he had gained entry to the after-hours club, and the air had warmed up considerably. His greatcoat was plenty warm (his drink-and-drug-addled brain spuriously reasoned), and there was a plastic bagful of papers put out for recycling in a blue box on the curbside, which he could retrieve and upon which he could rest his behind. No problemo, as the young Doug there would, he speculated, be wont to say. He settled in for the medium haul, his back resting against the black, solid wood front door, and his head on the beveled surface of a bit of door-frame. And (thanks to that potent mixture of alcohol and codeine) as he drifted off into what he imagined would be a blissful, dream-free sleep, Edward Blanchette felt absolutely no pain.

25

FUCKED IN THE HEAD

BY G-D, said Ed, lying on his back, staring at the inside of his eyelids. The partially aspirated phrase was a reference to something one of the generic engineers at the neighbouring table had said at the club: after having obviously eavesdropped on the entirety of Dr. Ed's recounting of the dream that had been shaking him on a nightly basis, the empathetic oaf had nodded sagely to his tablemates and had pronounced, to a radial arc of 5 or 6 tables or so:

—Dreams, you know, shit, they're, like, like getting fucked in the head by G-d.

—G-d sucks, said another engineer.

—G-d rules, church sucks, said a third.

—Church? said the first. Church? Church sucks cock!

Ed had not demurred. But that was hours ago now, and—how was it?—oh yeah, and 'a world away'. It was now late Friday morning, and while some celestial cannon had just blasted him, circus performer style, into consciousness, he was not at all aware of his new surroundings. A nearby, involuntary, feminine gasp, however, followed by the slamming of a door after he uttered the above epithet, granted him the unimpeachable awareness of several things: that he was lying in a strange bedroom; that the room had also been occupied by a strange but definitely female presence; that, moreover, said female had no doubt been shocked and appalled by that which he had just, not entirely voluntarily, said— that which, only 72 hours ago quite frankly, would have shocked and appalled *him* as well.

But this was not 72 hours ago, neither Tuesday morning, nor Wednesday, nor Thursday morning either. This was *Friday*, and he was lying in someone else's bedroom, and through the interference pattern set up by an incipient hangover of erupting, red molten lava and black ash, his ears could still discern with some clarity that there was someone to whom he should immediately apologize. Yet that very someone had, in storming immediately out of the room, made such amends (for the time being at least) impossible to make.

But Ed did not have the strength to move an eyelid, let alone recruit the 'mind'-bogglingly complex chain of requisite motor neurons to bring something approaching recognizable human speech patterns within the realm of current possibility. Instead, he lay on his back, groaning the inward, solipsistic groan of the truly hungover. He had not, as the engineers would have said, worshipped at the porcelain altar; nor had he talked on the big white telephone, or *conduit la grande autobus blanche*. And that was a bit of a pity indeed, for things might have turned out better for him if he had had. How much better? Well, if you asked an engineer, he'd say, most likely, something like this:

—No shit Sherlock, 6.02 times 10 to the 23rd times better if only ya'd done what ya', coulda shoulda woulda.

So, whatever gasping feminine presence the room had contained, it contained it no more. The sound of what could only have been the offended footsteps of one encumbered with the highest of heels could forthwith be traced tap-tapping their way down a short hallway to a most impatiently bruited front door. Henceforth there commenced the firing of an automotive engine, but one so anaemic and unrefined that it could only have belonged to a domestic 4-cylinder with a plentitude of logged miles in her. The engine idled for some minutes, giving Ed more than enough time to discern at least a ring-job if not a full re-bore (or perhaps a loss-limiting disposal) in its future. Then the engine whined off into the distance, and Ed was left momentarily alone with his hangover. Christ, what remained of his 'mind' needed more sleep, required a few hours' escape from the catabolytes of last night's indulgence, from the aldehydes and glucuronides which mercilessly coursed through his veins. His 'mind' had no wish to abrogate the sternly articulated edict that had been issued, by fiat, by his body. The 'mind' would obey, settle in, wherever and whomsoever it was, and hunker down for....

— Ok pal, let's go, coffee's on! A voice echoed from somewhere outside the room where he lay.

Huh?

— Da-aaaaad! It was a young man's voice: playful, lilting, ironic, arch even. It was — oh, sweet Jesus, so *that* was where he was.

— Dr. Blanchette! Calling Dr. Blanchette! Not here yet for his breakfast ban-quette!

His (he quickly recanted, assiduously and guiltily reproaching himself for the almost-reflexive attributions of 'good-for-nothing' and 'alleged'). Son. Came. Up. The. Hall. Singing.

And banging on a metal pot:

> *It's true that all them men were through*
> *with puking up a past they left you to,*
> *while dreaming it was love, or warmth, or shelter...*

— C'mon, Dr. Ed, said Ted, tugging at his bedding. *Up'n'at'm.* Yuvv' got a big day ahead of yas. He then pulled Ed's comforter off with the aplomb of a magician spiriting a tablecloth from beneath a set of fine china.

—How did I get here? asked Ed.

—Well, sir, you were fast asleep against my front door when I got up this morning. When I opened it to go get the paper, you crashed backwards without waking up, and….

You can call me dad, Ted, or Ed, Ed groaned, remembering his drunken 'vow' to himself from the dark hours of the morning.

—No can do *compadre*, said Ted.

Ed shuddered, and then succeeded in unfixing one of his stuck cantilever brakepad eyelids. He conducted, more out of embarrassment than necessity, a rigorous, if extemporaneous, assessment of his current situation, with a 270° cyclopean scan of the bedroom.

—Sorry? he said belatedly.

—My father's dead & buried, Sir. Metastasized cancer of the larynx, Moosejaw, Saskatchewan, 1984.

Ed sat up straight, his other, tardy eye snapping open now without difficulty.

—You never, I didn't, I'm, I'm very sorry, Ted, he said.

—S'alright. There's lots of things I haven't told you. All of which can wait, cos we gotta get you to work, Dr. Bloody Nose.

—Pretty bad, huh?

—Could be worse, Doc, said Ted. There's fresh gauze and tape in the bathroom; I'll get it out, and you go get the rest of you cleaned up.

—Call me Ed, at least.

—Hunky Dory, Ed, he said, picking up a rolled towel of the dresser and lobbing it towards him. Shower up quick, like, and I'll put your brekky in a bag and call you a cab. You're late again.

—What time is it?

—Just after 9.

—Christ. I have no.

Ted lent his birth father a black t-shirt, a white-on-black sweat-shirt (the largest he had, which bore the slogan 'Only Users Lose Drugs') and a bomber-style jacket (Ed's beloved greatcoat was missing, mysteriously, a sleeve) and whisked the still-wet-haired, unshaven travesty out the door, clutching a pom-pommed toque in one hand and his brown-bagged breakfast in the other. He waved a terse wave goodbye to Ed, handed the driver a tenner, and said, before he closed the passenger door behind him:

—How's dinner, 6 o'clock tomorrow sound?

Ed nodded wordlessly. Ted closed the door and patted the trunk of the cab as it began to pull away. Just then, Ed felt compelled to do something quite out of character. He turned around and looked back—out the rear window of the cab. There stood Ted, staring back at him with palm raised chest-high in the air, motion-less on the grey pavement, against the grey western horizon.

The Supplement of Copula

The shock waves passed through him while he was riding up (mercifully, alone) in the hospital's front elevator, and he stumbled backwards against the rear wall of the lift just as it made an abrupt negative acceleration to let him off at his floor. Just like any patriotic footsoldier keen to witness Truth, Justice & The American Way in action at the Los Alamos testing grounds, he:

(i.) saw the flash,

(ii.) ducked & covered beneath the hurricane of shock and heat,

(iii.) heard a blast so terrifying that it relegated those masters of thunderclap and bolt lightning—Zeus, Thor, JHVH—into the books of fable and fairytale.

He knew, however, unlike his conscripted forefathers 50 years previously, that there was more: the deadly silence of the fallout. And he remembered, finally, what he'd so conveniently forgotten the previous evening. He remembered, putting aside the previous day's casuistry, that there would be casualties.

His heart reached apogee somewhere near his Adam's apple, just as his feet manoeuvred this perambulating automaton to the clinic's main door. How could he have. Why didn't he. Nurse Sloggett. Missy. His wife. It could be any of them. But which?

He stood stock-still outside the doors to his clinic, indicting himself. He was a stunned stockjobber, too busy with busy business to feel real guilt, too consumed with the fear of death to live up to life, too—

—Excuse me!

And a short but almost completely round female form, swathed in woolens (scarves & mittens, a poncho and a beret), rolled by him, pulled the door open and went round the corner towards the reception area and nurse's station. He followed her.

—Ec, Ex, Scuse, Me? Ma'am?

She did not turn around, but strode purposefully past the empty nurse's station and towards the door of his office. Still, as if mesmerized, he followed. She knocked on his door, then brazenly turned the handle and let herself inside.

—How can I help you, ma'am? he said finally, after following her into his office. He stopped just past the doorframe, and self-consciously left the door open, for he was of course used to all manner of crazies pulling the whole gamut of crazy stunts on him: several of his more theatrically-inclined patients, for instance, had tried to end it all in his presence, armed with the usual devices (the razor or knife across the wrists, the flamboyant swallowing of a bottle of pills, the ingestion of the full range of household poisons), but never quite succeeding. He had never been taken hostage, but his couch and desk had: both had been defecated and urinated upon, twice each. The culprits, however, couldn't have been more different. The first had been a young

schizophrenic male, whose father was a risk management specialist in the Faculty of Commerce at the university. The young man
had been doing quite well on his medication, and was (prolepti-
cally, as it turned out) preparing to get back to his studies and
write the LSAT when the incident occurred. He never saw the
young man again, but he heard, by the by, that his parents had
sent him to a private residential clinic near Santa Fe.

The second copremic event occurred not long after the first,
but this time the poor unfortunate was an elderly woman named
Violet Starkes, who had become quite nearly catatonic with grief
after having been widowed. Her husband, still a dairy farmer
at 80, had suddenly hung himself during the morning milk-
ing not long after their 60th wedding anniversary. He had left
a note which stated, simply: 'Forgive me, Violet, Rose.' Rose,
Violet's sister, had died of coronary failure in her sleep several
months previously.

Violet's GP, a life-long friend of her children, had referred her to
the Clinic when a standard course of the usual anti-depressants
had failed, and failed utterly, to improve her disposition. She sat
through 9 sessions in Ed's office, uttering nary a word, and then
did the aforementioned deed on his desk one day when he stepped
briefly out to ask Nurse Sloggett for something. She was eventually admitted to the regional residential psychiatric hospital on
the lake, out by the community college.

—Miss? Ed said once more. Madam?

—I'm here to serve you your papers, she said, turning around. She was huge; every limb, every pocket of flesh grotesquely swollen. She looked familiar, he thought at first, but no, he didn't recognize her.

—What papers, he said?

She smiled, waiting him out.

—Who are you, and what right do you have to come barging in here like that?

—I'm the sheriff's deputy, she said, and I'm here to serve you your D-I-V-O-R-C-E papers.

—You don't exactly look like a sheriff's deputy, he said, with a superciliousness that worried him, nevertheless 'feeling' his heart plummet from its perch in his Adam's apple, past his transverse colon, hitting bottom at the south end of his solar plexus.

—I am I am I am too, she said, bobbing up-and-down while shifting her weight from her left to her right foot and back again.

—Let me see your badge, said Ed more casually, humouring her now.

—We don' need no stinkin' badges, she said.

—We?

—We, the, the depu-*tees*, she insisted.

—Who, exactly are you here to see? Who is your doctor?

—You. *You're* my doctor, doctor, she said, clapping her hands in triumph.

—I see, he said. And your name is?

—Birdsall, Moira, not that it's any business of *yours*.

—Just excuse me for a minute, Moira, he said, gently now. I'll be right with you, to sign those papers.

He went out to the nurse's station, which was, worryingly, *still* empty, opened up the *dBase IV* master patient roster file, and typed in 'Birdsall'. And there she was:

Name: Birdsall, Moira
D.O.B.: 15-03-47
Date of Admission: 08-09-89
Consulting Psychiatrist: T.P. Kavanagh
Referring Physician: E. Wisniewski
Reason for Referral: Treatment-resistant exogenous monopolar depression
Notes: Admitted to Alba trial, 9-93

—Christ, said Ed, quickly dialling Dr. Kavanagh's pager and then half-jogging back to his office.

Moira Birdsall sat in his leather desk chair, spinning around and around like a little girl visiting her daddy at work for the first time, gleefully pretending to hold on to the armrests for dear life. Upon sensing Ed's re-entry, however, she ceased her spinning immediately, screwed up her face into a clownish sneer, grabbed her clutch of papers from her lap (which, Ed had previously—and spuriously—intuited as the kind of 'personalized' form letters one receives from solicitous credit-card companies, from magazine subscription managers, or from Ed McMahon) and stood up. He took close notice of these papers for the first time. They were clippings from newspapers, pasted and taped onto 8½x11 sheets of photocopy paper.

—I'll sign the papers, now, if you wish, he said, as submissively as he could. May I? he added, holding out his hands to her.

She turned her disdainful sneer into a triumphant scowl, and then thrust the papers towards him, as though she were not a sheriff's deputy at all, but a star investigative reporter with a massive scoop on her hands, and he was her sceptical, besieged editor, shamed on the one hand into grudgingly accepting her meticulously researched iconoclasms, harassed on the other by turf-protecting higher-ups and controversy-shy advertisers.

He glanced through the clippings, most of which had yellowed significantly with age.

'Local Man Missing' ran one headline, 'Hunting Trip Tragedy' another, 'Day 13: Still No Sign' a third. Ed flipped to one with a picture of the unfortunate man: 'Eugene Birdsall, 1943–1988' the caption said simply. The picture was of a thin, weathered man wearing a MASSEY-FERGUSON ball cap and a sweatshirt that said 'Bassman', and holding onto, a banner in the photo said, the Rice

Lake Derby-winning largemouth bass. Ed quickly scanned the next article:

There's Hope Yet

Missing for 10 days and last seen wearing a reflective orange vest atop a red-and-black checked woolen coat, Eugene Birdsall of Bath may 'still be alive,' authorities say.

Inspector John Wharfrin of the OPP detachment at Golgotha, Ontario, near the Grey Owl Crown Game Preserve, issued a statement earlier today that the search and rescue team has 'not given up hope' of finding the local man alive, and refused to speculate as to when the ongoing search might be called off.

'There is every possibility that he may still be alive,' the Inspector said, adding that 'the Sanctuary is a heck of a big piece of land to get lost in.'

Mr. Birdsall disappeared while on an illegal moose-hunting expedition in the Preserve with three friends, only one of whom has come forward publically. John N. Gore of Enterprise, who alerted the police to his friend's disappearance, was arraigned in provincial court yesterday on charges of illegal trespass and poaching, and has been released on his own recognisance. He is due to reappear in court early next month, and has declined to comment further on the matter. Police authorities say that Mr. Gore has also refused to provide them with the names of his other two companions.

In a brief interview with this newspaper on the day he reported the disappearance of Mr. Birdsall, Mr. Gore described the events of last Saturday night as follows: 'We was all bedded down for the night

and, round, I don't know, 3, maybe 4 a.m., I woke up to hear someone [urinating] against a tree. Then nothing, and I fell back asleep.

Obviously, it was Eugene, but later, when we was sure he was gone, I looked for his footprints, bearprints, anything, cos it had been raining and the ground was soft. But no. It was like Scotty had just beamed him up or something.'

Mrs. Moira Birdsall, wife of the missing man, could not be reached for comment.

Ed frowned. He remembered now. The woman, Moira, had been a friend of his wife's friend Jean. It was a sad story. Just now, as he picked up the phone, Moira was curled up on his couch. He dialled 101, and spoke to an answering machine:

—Dr. Kavanagh, this is Ed Blanchette. One of your, ah, patients is in my office and is quite disturbed. Page me anytime, but I'm going to take her to Emerg for sedation and have her admitted to the Hutch wing....

Which he did. When he returned, however, he found that there was *still* no one in reception. On the floor near the door to his office there was another clipping, much less yellowed than the others, obviously dropped by Moira on her way in or out. It was from yesterday.

Body Identified

The body of a woman discovered on Wednesday in the washroom of a local crematorium has been positively identified, police officials say.

The name of the deceased, who was not carrying any identification at the time of death, is being withheld by police until next of kin can be reached.

The cause of death has not yet been determined, authorities maintain, refusing to confirm or deny rumours that the woman's purse contained empty bottles of prescription medications....

Ed felt his pulse quicken, his blood pressure increase, and his breath become so shallow as to almost disappear, as, he knew, the inexorable fight-or-fight pathway—at the base of the brain, from pituitary precursor, from L- or Levorotatory-dopa to neurotransmitter dopamine, to the ad-renals (quite literally 'near the kidneys') and their eponymous hormone—did its determinist little dance. Then Nurse Sloggett stepped through the doorway, and before either of them could do anything about it, he had his arms around her.

—How *are* you, Agnes? he heard himself say in the upbeat but emotionally receptive tone of voice of a—what?—of a woman eager to reconnect with a girlfriend whom she has not seen for a subjectively overlong period of time.

—Well, she said, taken aback and not at all sure just why he was hugging her. She was positive she had told him about needing yesterday off for poor Ronny's memorial. So why was he...? I was wondering, she said, if you were ... coming in today.

—I was ill this morning, he said, quickly retreating a few paces now himself, and adjusting his tone to align with her more quotidian seriousness. I'm sorry, I should have phoned, obviously, but I, I was completely incapacitated. I'm OK now, though, he added defensively.

—No matter, she said. Lady Luck's on your side today. She paused, and he forced himself to wait for her to continue.

—The 9AM Tri-City board meeting was, of course, cancelled, she said.

—Of course?

She looked at him strangely. —On account of the storm warning?

—Oh yes, of course, he said, pretending to have been merely, absent-mindedly distracted from what was surely common knowledge.

—That left only your 2 forenoon appointments, she continued. The 1st of which was a billable no-show, and you're right on time for your 2nd.

—Super. Who didn't show?

She consulted her clipboard. —Mrs. M. Plumtree, she said.

—Jesus. And the 2nd?

—What is it?

—The 2nd appointment.

—No, I mean the 'Jesus', what did you mean by that?

—Yesterday was a kind of a crazy day, he said, adding, we nearly couldn't cope without—

—Full moon, she quipped, knowing Ed would frown at this, and he did.

He was not at all sympathetic to that tidbit of hospital employee folk wisdom which held that ERs should be supplementally staffed on full moons (days? nights? both?) due to alleged (and never statistically corroborated) case-load surges. Gravitational fields inducing changes in the electromagnetic fields of the brain? Come on. Come off of it.

—Not *exactly*, he said diplomatically. He then gave her a brief, somewhat bowdlerized accounting of Thursday's clinically pertinent events.

—So, he said finally, who's my 2nd appointment?

—I booked in 15 minutes of your time, she said.

He didn't understand. —I don't, understand, he said.

She smiled. —I'm in love, she said.

Oh G-d, he thought, and recoiled a step backwards. She giggled.

He had seen and heard many, many strange things in his psychiatric career, but he had never heard anything quite like that giggle. It was, it sounded like … a cross between (he imagined, as he had never heard either) the 'laugh' of the hyena and the shriek of the vampire bat. But no, it was….

She tried to force eye contact. He tried to force a smile. She noticed. She said:

—Be happy for me.

—What? Why? Wh—?

—I know it's completely the wrong time for me, she continued, I mean it's only been....

She paused, looked at him, smiled the smile of a recently de-fleaed orangutan. She resumed, much more quietly, but only after fixing his unwilling, roving eye with her own:

—But when it's right, it's right, you know?

—Yes, he lied, I know. Of course. *So.* What next, then?

—The reason, she said, for my booking in time with you. I need … if possible, 2 weeks.

Now it dawned on him, and he saw what was coming; he'd forgotten about yesterday. *She* was as bonkers, as moonstruck (and what did his high school Shakespeare say? The poet, lover and madman are of imagination all compact, lunatics all?) as Buddy! Perfect, then. Then they were made for each other. He did not, however, want to *deal* with it—with them, as a couple. An image of Agnes&Buddy on a honeymoon (where? Vegas? The Bahamas? No: DisneyWorld, a real *Alba* honeymoon) briefly, involuntarily and displeasingly preoccupied his own damaged imagination. Agnes plus Buddy equals, A+B = equals what, exactly? =C, evidently; he didn't want to speculate further on just what

'C' might mean or entail, but his literal-minded 'mind' did that for him, as an image of Agnes and Buddy copulating on a tilt-a-whirl surrounded by a torrential team of mouseketeers briefly but thoroughly tormented him.

—2 weeks, that all? he said. No problem, done.

—Done? Really?

—Done. When do you need them?

—This is a bit embarrassing, but.

—Right away? No worries, really.

—Are you sure? What about... ?

—The office will be fine. I'll book my son in; he's an office temp you know.

This shocked her—it was as if a mortician had suddenly morphed into a Jewish mother and had gushed to a stranger about 'my son, the doctor'. She was genuinely moved, and said: —I, I didn't know you had a son, Ed.

—I didn't either, until recently. But that's a long story. Anyway, when do you propose, er, to fly off?

—Tonight.

He was now 110% sure she was illicitly on *Alba*. The question was, though: could all of this impulsiveness, this inhibition of all inhibitions, be quite so common as to be almost universal at the median dosage? The pharmaco-kineticists had not prepared him for this. Could *Alba* induce hypomania (or worse), in *all* non-bipolar patients? He *never* trusted anecdotal evidence, but here was anecdotal evidence, staring him in the face.

—Super, he said. Enjoy yourselves, my best to you both, you'll make a lovely couple.

—Both? But I haven't....

—You and Buddy. You are going off together, aren't you?

—That's absurd!

—You *are* asking for 2 weeks off for your honeymoon, aren't you?

Her expression had turned from one of gratitude and semi-intimacy to that of wounded disbelief.

—No! I....

—It *is* Buddy that you're in love with, isn't it?

—That's, that's *crazy*!

—Who, then, who?

—You don't know her.

—Agnes, he said (not hearing what she had just said and concentrating on trying to choose his words carefully), I, are you, um, self, self-medicating at the moment?

—Not exactly, no.

This hedging and hemming and hawing of hers was making him impatient—why didn't she just come out and say things? What was her *problem*? Ahh, but he knew the answer to that one.

He said, excitedly:

—You can't 'not exactly' be taking pills, Agnes. It's an on-or-off thing, black-or-white, nes-or-yo, I mean yes-or-no.

—I stopped.

—Taking… ?

—*You* know, she said, looking at her feet. A week ago.

—Its half-life is 2 weeks, he said, with cold, clipped, staccato, Germanic precision.

—I know that, Ed, she said, irritation at his pedantry showing in her voice. So?

—So you'll come crashing down in the middle of your little pleasure cruise with whatshisname.

—Pleasure cruise!? She felt hostility rise within her towards this man, this man who had always treated her … more than well: he was a dream employer, really, so, so passionless, so fair-minded and gallant; so thoughtful, so grateful for the work that she did here. Why was he acting like this? It was completely out of character. I'm not going on a *pleasure* cruise. It's a G.D. nature expedition, Ed, not the Love Boat!

—A *what*? he said.

He's all tensed up, irrational, she thought. —Nature, she said. We take pictures (and she mimed the act of looking through a camera's viewfinder) — of *wild*life?

Why was she, he thought, being so evasive? Couldn't she just answer a simple question? —We? Who is this *we*, anyhow? he said.

—What's with the 20 questions? You're my boss, Ed, not my—. She stopped herself short.

—Not my what?

—Never mind. I just need the 2 weeks. Can I have them?

—Not my *what*?

— Ok. You're not my: friend, father, lover, Big Brother, whatever you obsessively want to insert there. Listen, Ed, I've been working for you for how many years now?

—7, 7 or 8.

—8 years and 11 months.

—Right.

—And have I ever once asked you for a favour?

—No.

—Is it because it's such short notice that … ?

—No.

—Then why are you being like this?

—Like what?

She did not elaborate, so he changed tactics, willed himself back to becoming the Dr. Ed she expected him to be, and which, had it not been for last night, he should still have been. But last night's road of excess had led him, if certainly not to the palace of wisdom, at least into (albeit most tenuously and temporarily) something which might (nominally, provisionally) be called the swampland bungalow of his own life: a life seething with Leviathan-sized, long-ignored inconsistencies and irrationalities, to be sure, but a life that was, at least, he hoped, real? A life without a 'switch' he could 'flick'. 'Think' about that for a second, Ed, he thought, 'think' about *that*.

He looked at her. He had never seen her like this before. Her frustration with his frustration, made her look … beautiful. Jesus. He, he….

He 'flicked' his 'switch'.

Nevertheless, at this point his imagination, working in overdrive, was way ahead of him, anticipating that the conversation's resolution would be as satisfying and tidy as a novel destined for cinematic adaptation, that it would leave them both the wiser for having had it, that it would go something like:

—You deserve, he said, in as close to his normal, business-like-yet-diplomatic-as-heck manner as he could muster, *far more* than just 2 weeks. So of course you can. I'm just grateful that you're…

—What? she said, scrutinizing him.

—Nothing. I'll book Ted, that's my son, in. That is, I'll have Ted book himself. We're having dinner tomorrow.

—It's wonderful that the 2 of you are so close, after….

—Close isn't exactly the word, he said, but, but you never know.

—You're OK around here for today, if that's what you're worried about, she said.

—No, I wasn't, but how do you mean?

—Well, when you didn't turn up this morning I called home, got no answer, and since I had no idea where you were I took the liberty of getting Dr. Fraschetti to take your afternoon ward rounds with the residents. I wouldn't normally have done that, obviously, but….

—But what?

—But I sensed you were in some kind of trouble.

—No, not 'trouble', exactly, it's … complicated. We'll talk about it sometime, when you're back. But, I just wanted to say thank you, Agnes, he said sincerely. And you know, it's funny but, I mean, for 9 years now, more, I've thought about nothing else….

He gestured, taking in, in a sweeping arc, the entirety of the clinic.

—And then suddenly … , he added, but then broke off into a kind of bemused, childish state of wonderment.

—I know exactly what you mean, she said. Their eyes met briefly.

—Anyhow, he said, a bit embarrassed and self-conscious now.

—Thank-you, Ed. For everything.

—You're, you're welcome, he said, looking down, and blushing.

Turning away now, towards the front entrance, he raised a significant, salutatory hand.

—Well, she said.

—Well, he said, best be off, business—you know....

—Of course, she said. I know.

As he walked down the corridor 'flicking' his 'switch' back and readying himself to process what Nurse Sloggett had just told him and to calculate how it all might affect Buddy, he met Missy Plumtree at the elevators, his Grinch heart growing almost another half-size upon seeing her alive—and—um, alive, at any rate. She looked terrible; she looked beautiful. And (and this was new to him, to be sure) he saw: he saw that she was caught up in emotions, many powerfully negative, the content and import of which were far beyond his ken. But, he had to admit, here was a young woman who looked ... vibrant wasn't the exact word. She looked, she looked—alive.

—Hello, Dr. Blanchette, she said.

—Miss....

—I'm sorry I missed our appointment this morning.

— ... sus Plumtree, I.

He cut himself short. He wasn't sure what he was about to say, but whatever it was, he didn't say it. He looked at, smiled at, gesticulated at her, meaninglessly. He eventually heard himself say something, something to the effect that it didn't matter, that he had been worried about her, that he was glad that she was....

Pointing at his nose?

—Who did that to you? she said.

—Well, he said, er....

She guessed at it. —I'm so, she said.

—Not your fault, he said.

—No, yes, she said. I've been a guilty bystander in my own life for too long, Doctor. You see, I've come to tell you that I'm quitting.

—The?

—Him, my husband, yes, and school and ... everything.

—You haven't been thinking of... ?

—No, she said, not since I've stopped taking....

—Your medication.

—Sorry. I meant to tell you earlier, but I'm also quitting seeing you. No offence intended.

—None taken, he said. But may I ask why? he said simply.

—May I be honest? she said.

—Naturally.

She frowned, bit her ring fingernail for a second. And then, (and why were people *doing* this so G-ddamn much lately?) she looked him square in the eye.

—No, I don't think we *are* naturally honest, Doctor. I think that we are lying to each other and ourselves, oh, 95% of the time? And that's what sanity amounts to: everyone *agreeing* to believe that our lies are true.

He'd heard this one before, too many times to count, really, but not from Missy of course. He had to admit, however, that there did seem to be some truth to that old hoary psychoanalytic guess-timation that depression usually accompanied repressed anger of some kind, usually *this* kind: the anger of those who had never and most likely could never (without medical assistance, mind you) doff themselves of their biological chains, come out of their personal caves, and adjust, however hypo-plastically, to the harsh light of the only reality that mattered: social reality. Missy, like the unending parade of other misfortunates he had treated, para-doxically needed *Alba* to even begin to entertain the notion that it was precisely *Alba* that she *didn't* need. *Alba* was giving her the confidence to believe that she could make it on her own, that there was a reality to pursue (and here lay the roots of his deep, dark antipathy towards those fraudulent purveyors of the talk-ing cure), a reality *deeper* than that which had been socially and genetically constructed for her. Zealots like Randy Van der Griff and his sidekick little Stuey indulged in hyperbole, to be sure, but they weren't as far off the mark as one might 'think': *Alba* works— of this there could be no question. The only question, of course (and he was ashamed to admit that he *had* gotten a bit unduly paranoid about the matter of late—but then, he'd had a strange, shall we say, last couple of days) concerned tweaking the kinetics of it, to keep the adverse reactions to within a percentile or so of the statistical sweet spot. Oh, *Alba* was working, all right, and that's why she was quitting it. It was all so common, yet none the less pathetic. But he did 'feel' for her, for Missy here. He really did.

— So, he said gently, or as gently as he could, where to now, Missy?

She smiled with nervous confidence.

— G-d knows, she said.

A minor brainwave sent Ed skulking (and why should or would he be 'skulking', anyway? he heard himself ask himself) back inside the clinic and (Lady Luck really *was* on his side today) to reception, to Agnes' desk at the nurse's station. She was not there, good: he quickly rifled through her desk drawers, almost immediately finding what he was looking for, a nearly empty, unlabeled bottle of medication.

He poured the few remaining capsules into the palm of his hand, and picked one with his thumb-and-forefinger. He had to admit: they were, well, *chic* was the word, really. As much R&D cash had gone into the design and marketing as into the initial laboratory research, he said to himself, and this exaggeration, like most, contained, or rather revealed a certain truth, one which in this case made him 'feel' just a tad uncomfortable—although, he knew, he did 'feel' pretty comfortable with *that*.

The pills were white, of course, to go with the etymology of the name, *Alba*, which denotes white, but not just any white. He wondered (briefly) how savvy the young marketing lads at EUMETA really were here—he'd have to ask Randy or Stu the next time either or both of them swung through town—and he wondered just how much homework they had done on this, if it was a less-than-brilliant contrivance or just an uncongenial happenstance. For the 17th century Spanish/Portuguese name for the seabird depicted here (& oh so chummily, in miniature, its tubular snout cleverly, hyperbolically embossed on the off-white ½ of each capsule, the remainder of the bird's head on the remaining, on the 'white-white' portion) connoted, at least to English speakers, something ... other. Perhaps they *had* done their homework after all, and were indulging in a playful, little insider game of irony. *Perhaps*, he thought, with no small measure of superiority, but it was certainly worth taking a bet on: kids these days never looked anything up.

Then, quite suddenly, as if meditating on the blank nullity that the innocuous pill presented itself to be, a thought came thundering down upon him, in the guise of a morbid little joke, the kind one never admits to 'thinking' if one wishes to avoid labels such as 'creep', 'bastard'—or worse. For example: he had once attended the funeral of his cousin Barbara 'Bunny' Corless. The family had had it held off the Island, and (unusually, but, given the circumstances, understandably) closed casket, for 'Bunny' or 'Bun' had quite literally topped herself with a shotgun. It was not known outside the immediate family whether it had been a 10, 12, or 410 gauge though, for the Corless patriarch, Archibald, was known to keep all 3 at the ready.

Bunny had always been her daddy's favourite, the eldest of 6 who had inherited his keen, inquiring 'mind', his love of the outdoors, his weakness for the bottle, and most of all his deep antipathy toward the fiat of any authority other than his own. Bunny had thus made a big, early splash as something of an apostate, leaving the arms of both her pious mother and of Mother Church as soon as she could get her driver's license and get herself the hell off of the Island.

Her funeral had roughly coincided with Ed's own early troubles. Only 6 months before, his and Agnes's families had conspired with the parish priest to whisk the almost-bursting young woman off to a convent in Petropolis, a couple of hours to the north-west. Bunny had been their sole ally & defender, and for her troublesome meddling had been awarded (at the hands of her father) a nose-and-eye as discoloured as Ed's was today.

Nevertheless, black sheep though she undoubtedly was, family *is* family, and young Ed did not help his own still-problematic reputation when he made a decidedly off-colour remark at her not-quite-literal-interment. The parents were pronouncing it as '*intern*ment', and Ed found himself saying to Cousin Jack (an Epsilon-Semi-Moron if ever there was one) that Bunny would have appreciated the irony in all of this. For the wise Bunny's will had explicitly insisted upon an unsanctifiable cremation, and her on-again/off-again lover/executor Hope had bravely stood up to the islanders—to both family & Church.

It was Jack's ugly, inbred *tabula rasa* stare that had made Ed keep going, nervously saying whatever popped next into his head. He pointed out to Jack how strong and dignified Hope looked, how utterly useless the priest's brief sermon and Archie's eulogy had been. He insisted on pouring into Jack's uncomprehending, wax-and-ignorance-plugged ear what Jack already knew, what everybody had already known for days but what Ed himself had only just found out: that she'd done it in her father's [twin] bed.

It was then that he had let slip his little doozey. *Bunny* would have laughed at it anyway, he told himself later. She would also have pointed out to Ed that it referred, in a Freudian slip kind of way, to his own situation.

—Well, Jack, he'd said, I guess the Bun is in the oven now.

But what came crashing in on him at *this* moment, while no less inappropriate than what he'd said to his cousin (and what Jack had—child that he was, with a childishly complete lack of mercy—repeated to all-&-sundry) was for his ears only; only he, Edward Blanchette, was there to think the less of himself for thinking it—neither Missy, nor Nurse Sloggett (er, Agnes), both of whom were, thankfully, still alive, and not his wife either, who was by now only G-d knew where:

—Well, he said, 2 down: 2 down, & 1 to go.

26

WHAT DO NUMBERS MEAN?

What do numbers mean?
I'm About 17.

—Jonathan Richman

H E BEGAN to realise just how worried part of him really was
when he found himself standing stock-still in his wife's
bathroom, the doors to her vanity wide open, his shod feet
surrounded by bottles, vials, tubes, canisters, droppers, boxes &
samples of nearly every product imaginable. How could he have
been content to merely *peruse* the medicine cabinet before? Was
his head even *nominally* screwed on? Now, finally, he had gone the
whole hog: not only had he checked, re-checked & triple-checked
all of the blatantly obvious containers of pharmaceuticals (after
all, she'd been known to hide forbidden amphetamines [good
for her diet, bad for pretty well everything else, including Ed] in
bottles of anti-hypertensives, and had often secreted contraband,

'natural' remedies into prescription bottles for her liver, kidney & thyroid), but he'd checked & re-checked *everything* else too. And he'd turned up nothing—nothing that he'd wanted to turn up, that is, for there *were* revelations aplenty. For starters, there were so many lengtheners, strengtheners, straighteners, toners & clarifiers, exfoliate-, coruscate-, intensificate- & precipitat-ors that, immediately after wondering (rather nastily, he heard a small, unheeded voice say) why these things had not made his wife more beautiful, he immediately felt an intense (if ephemeral) sense of devastation: was he really so remote from her, so … so *Mosaic*, that he could not have noticed this before?

Yes, yes & yes, to be frank—and then it was off to the other containers, in their other hiding places. For example, he found so many of these 'alternative' 'medicines' that it made him wonder just how long he had neglected to bother checking up on her: 1 bottle even came from a homeopathic so-called 'pharmacy', which was aping the style of the orthodox establishments in a pathetic attempt at auto-legitimation.

Anyhow, the label read 'BLANCHETTE, DEWARD' (which itself alone was *very* strange), 29-01-93, LYCOPODIUM 200CH, DOSAGE: 2 PELLETS UNDER TONGUE OR DISSOLVED IN WATER 1X/DAY FOR 3 DAYS. Huh. Another, a herbal absurdity labelled *Masculine Complex*, bore no date but managed to slightly pique his curiosity if not his interest. In all, there were at least 2 dozen packages of such inanities, 1 of which was called (go figure) *MarsAtaxia*. Worse still, there was something, produced by a San-Luis Obispo firm called PHALLOCENTRIUM which actually bore a kosher pharmacy label, made out to a DR. WEDA BLANCHETTE, dated 13-02-93, and which was calling itself *Amor=Us.*

But there was no *Alba* to be found anywhere. He collected everything off the floor, fitted it all into one large green garbage bag (which he put by the door), went to call himself yet another taxi, but on a hunch poked his nose outside. A small, but real sense of vindication brightened his day; it *was* warming up considerably. On another hunch, he rolled his small winnings over and placed a bet on giving the PEUGEOT a go. Payday! It started up. Perfect. He left it to warm the cockles of its internally combusting heart, dashed back inside to get his coat & gloves, and, on impulse, snatched up his *Dictät!* (an inferior grey-market *Dictaphone* knock-off, given out to all department Chairs by the hospital quartermaster) from its charging base.

Soon he was motoring past the city limits, in the general direction of Enterprise. Hills gave way to flat farmland, reclaimed from postglacial swamps by severe, unflinching Ulster Orangemen and their Scottish counterparts. Here, low stratocumulus seemed to have stagnated at the behest of the dull, static landscape. It had been years since he'd been back—27 in fact, but nothing much seemed to have changed.

There is no rolling thunderclap — just one big bang, probably a
sizzle as the lightening leaves the ground. Those most prone to
being struck are isolated people [....]

— Alan Watts, *The Weather Handbook*

In my dream I am always 17 — I'm just on the cusp, and so is the
season, whichever it is. Cold and warm are forever colliding, or is
it the other way around? There is no way to tell — there is a gray-
ing sameness about, the sameness of waning, or at least that's what
the script always has me think as I strut and fret on the ferry, as
it never fails to take me to the mainland (and, I never once pause
to doubt), to you.

And I'm never lacking in confidence; I've got my *savoir-vivre*
working overtime as I self-assuredly navigate my father's truck
to your father's farm. And life's pretty well all — well, 90–95%
all, anyway — sussed out, I figure. And it's not that I'm unaware,
exactly, that those other 5–10 or so 100^{ths} are still out there, around
the next curve somewhere, waiting to make a fool, a rube, a moron
of me. I know this.

But I'm 17, remember, and I don't really know anything, and
that, Agnes, is why I'm on my way to you. I've given you that 5/100^{ths},
to plant, to nurture, to coax into some kind of reality for me, so
we can have & hold it, 'till death do us part, etc. Or, that's what

I'm thinking anyway, those are my plans as, as I drive, as I find, as I make (or so I think) my way to you....

And in the dream you're always waiting for me. And that's always on my 'mind', too, as the truck takes me through the curves just north of town, just as I'm doing now. That's what I'm thinking in the dream, and it's what I'm thinking now: what really matters is that you're always patiently waiting for me, just as I'm always impatient for these curves to straighten out & deliver me onto the straight and thru-way thru the Cavan Swamp, to you — and thus, somehow, to some truer version of me.

It is always (I'm guessing here) 1967, or that's what it feels like. There's no radio in the truck, but I've got 'Baby Please Don't Go', your favourite, 'Down to New Orleans', playing in my head. And I'm remembering how one of your older brothers came back from a trip to England with a suitcase full of what he called R&B bands, with strange names like The Yardbirds, Them, The Animals. Also Chicago bluesmen like Howlin' Wolf and Sonny Boy Williamson. This isn't in the dream now, but it's connected — you'd understand this — because this is always how we talked, wasn't it? I remember. The music made even the Beatles seem tame & timid to us by comparison, and it made us hungry for whatever was over our parents' shrunken horizon; it made us want *more*.

Anyway, in the dream that's what I'm always singing and feeling, and I'm feeling that it's true — what you've always said, 'like

I'm being *let in* on something', something real and important. To both of us. Real Life, capital-R, capital-L. And then the curves suddenly straighten and I begin to see those wetlands and that's how I come to know, in my dream, that this is not just a dream.

You've planted those $5/100^{ths}$ of me in the last patch of good, fertile soil this side of the Canadian Shield, like the sunflower seeds you've planted in that clear window box in the kitchen. And the last thing you always say is always the same, as you trace their pathway of hopeful germination with your forefinger: how they always grow in 2 directions at once — towards the centre, towards uncertainty....

Ed switched off the little recording machine, with its tiny, proprietorially-sized cassette tape. He had arrived in Enterprise. He turned left onto County Road 3, and then right onto the Tapley ¼ Line, towards her family farm, which still bore the title EL-MAR HOLSTEINS, an amalgam of the Christian names of her deceased parents, stout Elmer and stern Martha.

A trio of dappled border collies happily saluted him halfway down the long gravel drive, and herded the PEUGEOT into a little parking area nestled at the centroid of a triangle formed by the large Century tin-roofed brick farmhouse, a haybarn, and a battered, tan trailer home. A childishly hand-painted sign by the trailer read, in black letters on white plywood, Dr. Agnes Hume, dvm.

He got out of the car and made towards the trailer's front (and only) door. One of the Border Collies came sniffing pleasantly around his legs, so he stopped, went down on one knee, and began to rub the dog's neck and back, and scratch the inside of its ears.

—Good boy, he said, *that's* a good boy, yes, you like that, don't you, yessssss.

At this the dog went down on its right side, and lifted its left front leg, so as to offer this obliging stranger access to its scratchable chest.

—Yes, yes you are, you're a *goooood* boy, yes you are! said Ed, in a sentimental tone which he reserved only for domesticated animals.

—She likes you.

Ed spun around, his heart leaping sympathetically to those unexpected, casually uttered words. Agnes' head was poking out of a tiny window at the eastern end of the trailer.

—She isn't keen on most men, she continued, but she likes you.

—That's a good sign, said Ed, not knowing what else to say.

—I'll be right out, said Agnes. Then she whistled loudly, her thumb and index finger in her mouth, and called out: *Maaa-aaaxxxxx!*

And out from the barn scampered his old friend, followed by a goat, and then a rooster. Ed felt like he was in some kind of children's book all of a sudden, and expected that around any corner he might find a lamb lying down with a lion—or pigs discussing, not, as Orwell thought, the extremely relative egalitarianism of life down on the liberated farm, but whether Reddy Fox had been hanging out in the henhouse, and whether Clarabelle Cow had been calving or not.

Max paused, briefly, recognised just who it was that was waiting for him, and then doubletimed it over to his master's side, licking him repeatedly on his stiff upper lip and still-quite-painful nose, all-the-while bashing a nearly hairless tail back-and-forth.

—Ouch, Maxxy-boy, careful with daddy's nose, said Ed, hugging the dog around the neck from the front, and pulling him to his shoulder with the crook of one arm while he used the other to affectionately pat his lower back.

The rooster and the goat had stopped at a respectful distance, and were by this time turning away, no doubt to give Max and his master a moment alone, when suddenly 2 young boys, warmly if a bit raggedly dressed, burst from the trailer and ran together across the barnyard, pausing briefly at the front porch of their house to grab a pair of hockey sticks, then recommencing their sprint, up over a low rise just past the barn.

The trailer door then opened once more. It was Agnes, in overalls, rubber boots and a dirty, ratty brown-on-grey wool sweater. She looked unbearably beautiful.

—Sorry, I was on the phone, she explained. A farmer on the 4th line has had 2 of his pigs die in the last 24 hours.

—What from? asked Dr. Ed.

—Internal haemorrhaging. It happens every so often with the growth hormones, it's not clear why. Though 2 in a day is a bit much … Anyhow, well, how are you, Ed?

—Can't complain, he said, a bit stiffly. Um, Max looks good.

—He's fine. I sent a biopsy on the tumour to the lab not long after your wife dropped him off, but don't worry, it came back yesterday, unequivocally negative.

—That's a relief, he said truthfully. Hey, those are sure 2 cute kids you've got there.

—Thanks. There's 2 more off at school and a little one asleep here in the trailer.

—Wow.

—Yeah, it can get a little crazy at times.

—No doubt, he said. Um, uh, Agnes, there's something or rather someone I need to talk to you about.

—Would you like to come in for a hot drink or something? she said, nodding interrogatively towards the house.

—Um, sure, sure, he said.

—Just let me fetch the little princess, she said, and briefly went back inside the trailer, re-emerging moments later with a plastic, double-handled Moses Basket.

Soon Ed was sitting uncomfortably on the very same settee he had
sat upon 27 years ago. It had been re-covered of course, but it was no
more inviting now than then. Her parents had long since departed
this earth, but he still felt cowed and insignificant in this room,
this room which had borne so little evidence of time and change,
this well-wrought room. The piano was in precisely the same location as it had always been, and the one-dim-bulb overhead light
had stubbornly persisted with (he would not be at all surprised
to hear) the same damn, dim Byronic persistence. The silver tea
service was still in its pride of place, still unused, still shining
like silver.

—Do you take sugar now? Agnes asked.

—Just cream, thank you, he said, his voice as stiff with (internally
and externally) imposed rectitude as his back. He didn't normally
drink coffee in the afternoon, and would pay for it later, but the
available alternatives were either a dandelion-chicory coffee
plagiarism, or herbal tea, so the choice was obvious.

She handed him his mug and he took a sober, careful sip.

—It's about Ted, isn't it? she asked, with much less tension in her
voice than he would have imagined.

—Yes, partly, yes.

—And the other part.

—Nothing important really. Just personal ... things, personal-
slash-professional, he amended. But concerning Ted, have you...?

—We've met a number of times, she said. He looks a lot like you, Ed.

—Hard luck for him, he said, attempting, successfully, to make the both of them laugh and thus relax a little.

—Not at all, she said. But he has a lot of anger, Ed.

Ed went on to relate to her a few recent, pertinent anecdotes concerning the matter, and then the baby started crying. Agnes rose to fetch it a bottle, and he noticed that his feet & underarms were sweating profusely. This is getting to be a bit much, he thought, resolving to pull the parachute here in the next 15 minutes, at the outside.

—Where is your, husband? he asked when Agnes returned.

—At the Winter Fair, with one of our bulls, she said, obviously more comfortable answering this question than he was asking it. Intuiting that Ed thought it was time for 'The Talk', but also sensing that he was too uncomfortable to pursue this line of questioning further, she offered: We met when I was studying to be a Vet. I was an immature Mature Student; Brian was 10 years younger and an Aggie, and very, very serious.

—Kind of like someone we know, he said ruefully.

—I waited a long time for you, Ed, she said, suddenly.

—I know, he lied, feeling pressure in his eye sockets but, engaging his deep reserves of resolve, and displaying, he was certain, nothing.

—It's Ted's wish that the three of us … get together sometime, she said.

Agnes always had had this way, he thought, of taking what seemed at first like great conversational leaps sideways, but which in hindsight always somehow managed to take you to the heart of the matter. It had always unnerved him in the past, this talent of hers, but, back then, becoming unnerved had always felt, so, so very pleasantly tolerable. It had always felt like she was taking him on this perilous but vital journey to—to the centre of the earth.

Now, however, his fight/flight sensors were preparing the countdown to liftoff.

—A dinner or something? That would be good, he said in a tone of voice that made her suddenly silent, which then placed him in the position of having to continue. I've never, he said, felt *able*, at all, to deal with it. So I haven't, I've dealt with it by not dealing with it, for half my life, more, and so … and so I don't really have anything deep to say. Except, and I haven't used these words even in my own head since they sent you away, except that what happened didn't break my heart so much as … negate it. It sent me down an entirely different road, gave me a, completely different set of—priorities—than *we* had.

—Yes, she said, looking at him intently, sadly-but-calmly, now.

—Yes, but, he said, not sure of what he was going to say next. He tried to do an internal scan, to see what it was, if anything, that he was 'feeling', besides a desire to rush away. He wanted more than anything, he thought, just for once in this conversation, to maybe prepare his words and *think* before speaking, but he found, whether inside or merely 'inside', only an inscrutable opacity.

—Ed, she said after a moment, with, he thought, earnest compassion in her voice, don't worry. This isn't, or shouldn't be, about us dredging through the past....

(And oh, how he simultaneously desired, and dreaded, the dredging.)

—But then, she continued, I suppose in a way it kind of has to be. The important thing, I think, is that Ted wants us both to be a part of his life, in whatever capacity life allows us. And that means we have to be, indirectly anyhow, a part of each other's, too.

He rose instinctively.

—Don't worry, Ed, she said, life has a way....

—Of not working out, he said.

—Perhaps. Perhaps you're right. But perhaps not.

A strange feeling of *déjà-vu* came over him.

—Other than that, I've no great insights to offer myself, she said.

—The past is always present, he said, handing her his half-empty coffee mug. *If*, that is, we *choose* to live there.

—That doesn't mean that it makes slaves of us, she said, advancing as he retreated towards the door.

—I don't know about that, he said.

—Well, I'm not so sure either. But when Ted made contact I felt … grateful, some kind of….

—Resolution approaching? What's that charlatan Jon Bradshaw calling it now? 'Closure'? He has the New Age morons eating that up.

—Some kind of opportunity offering itself, to me, to do good somehow, she said.

He wasn't buying any of this, he decided, in a bit of a panic, backing a few steps closer to freedom.

—I've, I've got to go, he said. But, dinner with Ted sometime is fine, really, he added diplomatically. Actually, I'm meeting his wife tomorrow night myself, taking them to dinner.

—That's good, she said.

—We'll see, he said.

—Ed, she said, it really, it has been really, really *good* to see you again.

His back&side-stepping had finally brought his hand to the front doorknob.

—Yes, was all he could say. He opened the door, straddled the front step, felt cool air rushing past him into the house. Or heat escaping.

—Ed? she said, could you hold on just a minute? I forgot….

And she dashed across the yard, into the trailer & out again, put a small blue & white cardboard box into his now-gloved hand as she breezed past him, saying: —Drops for Max. Then she was back inside the kitchen, opening the refrigerator.

—Organic eggs, ours, she said when she returned. And goat's milk. For you and Max, and Dora, of course.

—She, she's gone, he said.

—She'll be back.

—Did she say anything, when she dropped Max off? And how did she find you? Was it through Ted?

Agnes didn't answer, but enfolded both of his hands in her own, and squeezed them. She said, finally:

—She loves you, Ed.

Balls, he thought, but he half-smiled back.

—The baby's crying, he said, a fraction of a second before it began to. This unnerved him more than anything that the preceding 72 hours had yet brought to pass. Just being near her had always made him do/say/think things like that. He shuddered inwardly. Bye, he said.

—Take care, Ed. I'll see you soon.

Sure, I mean, that would be great.

—Maaa-axx! she called, and over the top of the little rise over which the 2 boys had previously disappeared came Ed's dog, tongue hanging and eyes smiling, 3 happy border collies in tow, thinking he must be home.

27

Empty

I N MY DREAM you are not yet 16, and I am never quite there. You are always off alone with your dog, transfigured by sunlight that has broken through the clouds, at the edge of the forest of sugar maples, the forest your grandfather planted. I call to you across a field of alfalfa that's destined for silage, but I'm always too far away.

It's always summer, and when I meet up with your father he always points to the sky, and warns me to warn you. That's when I begin to run. You are always visible, but you never get any closer, and you can never hear me, no matter how much I shout.

The dream never varies; it always lets me get halfway across the field before it lets me in on the joke that's on me, before it tells me that *it* is in charge here, that it isn't even my dream, that it's dreaming you up out of nothing, that it's dreaming me.

And that's when I always give up, stop running, fall to my knees and pray, not to Jesus or to G-d the Father, but to Our Mother, to Mary, for forgiveness. But she can't hear me either.

Then the last thing I always see before I wake is your face in close-up. You're safe inside the house now—I can see that in my mind's eye—safe in your mother's care. But I'm still outside, on my knees in the middle of the field.

Then, from sky to ground and then outward along the ionized path of the leader stroke at 3 times 10 to the 8th metres per second: silence.

Ed stopped the recorder, stopped the car, took the miniature cassette out of the unit and placed it into a prepaid special delivery envelope that he'd brought along and which was sitting on the passenger seat. He found a pen in the glove compartment and set down, in block capitals, the address.

> MRS. DORA BLANCHETTE
> 1216 BOUTELLIERS POINT
> K_____TOWN, ON

He never could remember that damn postal code.

He went downstairs to see what all the barking was about. Max was at the front door, his head and tail both wagging, but to different rhythms, almost as if they were attached to 2 different dogs.

There was no one there, but someone had left a gift bag on the porch, with a short note taped to it:

Your wife asked me to drop this off for you Wednesday. Sorry it's late.
—Anna

Anna. Anna? Dora had been seeing a therapist named Anna, against his wishes, on and off, for a couple of years, but he'd thought she'd stopped all that.

One thing Dora hadn't stopped, apparently, was spending: immediately on returning home he'd anxiously done his best to make sure she was all right, and had reconnected with the good people at COLONIAL CREDIT, with the remote possibility still tugging at the centre of unreason in his brain that she had somehow been the victim of some kind of foul play, and that it was the wrongdoer who was enjoying the New York spending spree, and not Dora. But of course, it couldn't have been; the police would have broken it to him long ago, and an amiable chat with COLONIAL's Jennifer, whose tell-all computerized tracer yielded such predictably reassuring, money-haemorrhaging results (an unfinalized authorization for the WALDORF ASTORIA, hideously large restaurant tabs for such telltale spots as NUIT BLANCHE, MONO/CULTURE, CAFÉ SPLIFF, SPREZZATURAS, NIGHTS OF MALTA AND MYMOMSPLACE, tickets for Andrew Saltpetre's latest bloated spectacle *Down And Out In Paris, London, and Rome*, and a charge for an AIR FRANCE booking so far beyond the pale, so far into the tropopause, that it could only have been for a last minute seat on the Concorde) that Ed felt his body actually *relax*, for the first time in days.

He'd settled in for an evening of 'mind'-less decrepitude on the Tube, something he hadn't done in years, simultaneously watching the current affairs programme *The Medium Is The Massage* and, using the Picture-In-Picture function, the TV movie *Tv Movie*, starring Nina Hagen. It didn't even cross his 'mind' (so intrigued by these programs was he) to wonder why he didn't think too much about that one mysterious credit card charge for 1500 U.S. dollars, at something called the VENCKMAN WOMEN'S CLINIC.

It was just 11 when Max's barking had forced him downstairs, and so Ed missed out on the lead story on the local news: the identity of the body discovered Wednesday was released today by the chief of police—local housewife Mary MacDonwald was found to have taken an overdose of an unidentified narcotic, but her husband is blaming her anti-depressant medication, *Confixxor*, and is launching a civil action against the makers of the medication, pharmaceutical giant NEUTRACEUTICAL. In a prepared statement read by his lawyer, John MacDonwald alleged that *Confixxor* had 'radically altered' his wife's personality and had 'induced bouts of extreme paranoia'. A spokesperson for NEUTRACEUTICAL declined comment at this time. In other news, after several false starts, it appears that winter is finally on the way....

Ed stood for a few moments on the front step, gift bag in hand. Its contents were unusual: a tin of *Chock Full O'Nuts* coffee, decaf, and an unsigned Get Well Soon card, inside of which was a business card, the reverse of which bore a handwritten date and time: Monday, January 3, 1994. 9 a.m. The front of the card read:

LENNOX & ADDINGTON

PRACTICE IN FAMILY COUNSELLING

He looked up into the sodium brightness of the streetlight, and, unmoved, spied a few stray flakes of snow. He went back inside.

He could, he supposed, probably endure a few sessions of marriage counselling without visibly throwing up. Dora had, he conceded to Max as he poured out some kibble into the dog's bowl, some possibly legitimate concerns. Fine. As he stuck the business card to the refrigerator door with a magnetized picture of Edvard Munch's *The Scream,* he resolved to put it out of his 'mind'. But then, hey: it wasn't quite the same as the one reproduced on the notepad holder, was it? He removed the fridge magnet to go and compare, and the business card dropped to the floor.

Huh, whatever. He picked up the gift bag, to throw it in the garbage, and noticed that it was not quite empty: at the bottom of the bag, torn into 8 pink and white pieces, was another greeting card. He pulled one of the torn pieces out of the bag, scratched his noggin over the word 'Expect', and threw the bag away. He then turned to the refrigerator, and opened its door, to put the can of coffee away. What was the devil was with that, anyway? he wondered. Decaf? Why would anyone drink *Decaf?* There was just no point to it, he chuckled.

This reminded him to fill the coffee machine and reset its timer for an hour earlier than usual: he had a lot to catch up on tomorrow, and, it being a Saturday, the clinic would thankfully be deserted. He filled the reservoir with water and retrieved the canister of his usual coffee from the fridge. It felt light, soon to be in need of replenishment with those little El Salvadoran cellopacks.

After he put the first scoop of coffee in the machine's funnel-shaped permanent filter, he felt something strange, something hard in the canister. It was then that he remembered, for some reason, the last name of the therapist that Dora used to see: Anna, Anna Fraser. And then, digging down just a little, into the coffee canister for a second and then a third scoop of the good stuff, he retrieved it: an open plastic prescription bottle. It was empty.

LOVE'S
ALCHEMY

Ça, mon âme, il faut partir

—René Descartes, d. 11 February 1650

1

Horticulture: 1977,

Duxbury, Massachusetts

SHE HAS HER BACK turned to them, and he, he alone (he thinks) remains attentive while she writes on the board. Only he, it seems, sees where she is coming from, where the poet is coming from, where she is trying to take them all:

> *Where, like a pillow on a bed,*
> *A pregnant bank swelled up, to rest*
> *The violet's reclining head,*
> *Sat we two, one another's best;*

Gerald always sits nearest to her desk, at the front of the row beside the window, next to her plants.

The bell rings, and she pretends not to notice that he lingers while everyone else clears out for early dismissal. There is a pep rally in the gym for the upcoming, annual Thanksgiving game against Cohasset, but most of his buddies would be heading elsewhere, to hang out in front of Duxbury Pizza perhaps. One of these, Victor Turnbull, looks him in the eye on his way out of the classroom, clenches his fist and gives it a nearly invisible little pump, something Gerald imagines a real Soldier of Fortune might do—a secret signal exchanged between blood-brothers in the Laotian jungle before setting out to put a sniper's bullet between the eyes of some high-level gooks for the arms-length chicken shits at the Pentagon—all as if just to say, hey, yeah, like, go for it man!

—Did you wish to speak with me, Gerald? she asks, after a rather discomfiting thirty seconds' silence. Turning her back to him, she grabs one of those long, flexible foam chalk brushes. She is purposefully methodical with it, but after several passes the day's lesson is still clearly visible on the board. They were to have anal-ysed a poem by John Donne; God knows how many of them, apart from Gerald here, had even bothered to read it.

> *Our hands were firmly cemented*
> *With a fast balm, which thence did spring,*
> *Our eye-beams twisted, and did thread*
> *Our eyes, upon one double string;*

He had 'read' it (semi-conscious on his bed, on his back, the paperback Anthology man-handled, spine-broken and held aloft towards the shadows of a *Scrooge McDuck N-R-G Sav-R* light bulb), but hadn't understood *any* of the poem until she had led them through it, her sturdy peasant hands circling and underlining words and phrases, confidently, unflaggingly leading them, leading him, to the heart of the matter, to Truth with a capital-T, to….

—Er, yes, Miss Stone. I uh….

—Could you wait here just a minute, dear? I have to run to the rest room.

He stares after her as she whisks herself down the hall. When she is at last out of sight, he notices that his mind suddenly clears, and turns its attention to the other half of the equation: she has divided his loyalties. No, she has *tried* to divide. *Because* he is sensitive as well as unduly receptive, and *although* he has tried (for obvious reasons) to hide this, she has *nevertheless* exploited it. *Furthermore*, he knows that she likes him. *Moreover*, she sure is mean to everyone else, and the fact that she always wears pants made of what he and his friends call 'Pleather' (plastic + leather — they imagine that they have invented the word) — this is the *therefore* in the equation here, the kiss of *death*. As his math teacher always says: 'Q.E.D'.

All that other stuff, *plus* she wears Pleather!? Therefore, she must *pay* — Q.E.D.

He gets Victor's dad's test tubes out of his brown vinyl Adidas bag, thankful they haven't leaked, and makes towards the window. What could he invent needing to talk to her about?

> *So to intergraft our hands, as yet*
> *Was all our means to make us one,*
> *And pictures in our eyes to get*
> *Was all our propagation.*

Oh yeah, the poem. Yeah.

2

THE STORY: 1997, TORONTO

COULD YOU please pass the vinaigrette?

  —Of course. Do you like it?

—It's really, *really* nice. What kind of balsamic do you use?

—Oh I don't know much about these things. It came in a nice blue bottle, shaped like a Bosc pear, from Spain somewhere, I think.

Amē, the hostess, is wearing her favourite velvet dress, which the men at the table notice as she leans over towards Andrea, who had just signalled that she was going to say something discreet:

—I think he likes you! Andrea whispers.

  —Who?

—The Entrepreneur!

—Him? Amē asks, pretending she hasn't much noticed.

—Him.

The Entrepreneur, in a black turtleneck and sports coat, is in a heated debate with another young man, a brushcut-but-not-sporty

type who is way underdressed and who does not really belong
here. Andrea can't tell what the debate is exactly about, but
she can surmise that it is political, and she knows that she
wants to get the Entrepreneur—David, someone she's known,
since oh, like forever!—talking to Amē, and about anything
but politics.

And don't listen to Andrea's kill-joy nemesis, Jill, who bet her
a bottle of Chardonnay because David supposedly kind of has
a thing about not dating women so much taller than him (and
she's *ab*-solutely certain about this, the bitch)—no, and somehow
Andrea just knows, *they'll* click!

> As 'twixt two equal armies,
> Fate suspends uncertain victory,
> Our souls, (which to advance their state,
> Were gone out), hung 'twixt her, and me.

—David, are you inciting controversy again?

She pronounces that word the way the CBC language coach
taught all the Corporation's journalists to (which was, generally speaking, approximately equivalent to the Queen's English)
and which in this particular case places emphasis on the
middle syllable.

—No, well, no. I mean, not exactly. Bill here is educating me on
the increasing problem of homelessness, aren't you Bill?

—You mean you haven't noticed how much the situation has deteriorated in the last ten years? Bill continues, with volume enough to signal to the group that he means to include them all in this: You can't deny that more people are on the streets now than ten years ago!

—Well I'm not so aware of the battle against *home*lessness, Andrea intervenes. But I *do* know that Amē here has a great story about the battle between Mars and *Venus,* so I think we might all profit from a slight, shall we say, metamor-*pho*-sis? In topic?

Amē blushes.

—Andrea! she says, in a stage whisper, her face tightening in embarrassment.

Bill, unwilling to let go, raises his voice still further. —This is all *precisely* about profit — and loss. About having and not having, about the ignorance *in here* of the widening disparity *out there,* he says, gesturing out the east-facing window.

—You're pointing towards Rosedale, where Andrea, Serena and I grew up, David says, anticipating him and smiling. To the others he offers: But of course, *we* wanted for nothing, it's true, maybe Bill's right, maybe we don't — or can't — understand.

He trails off, looks almost wistfully into the imaginary distance, as if he can see with Clarke Kent x-ray vision through the well-crafted plaster and double-brick structure of this Annex-area century home to the increasingly (or so it seems) mean streets beyond. He gives a not-unsympathetic but weary little wave towards the south. Perhaps, he says, perhaps we just cannot understand … the Other.

— Maybe we have an *interest* in not understanding, Bill says.

— Maybe you're full of it, both of you, Serena says. It is Serena's birthday party; this was supposed to be about her, and her voice betrays an increasing level of annoyance.

— Anyhow, Andrea says, surprised that Serena has taken Bill's bait and is, yes, helping to slightly derail Andrea's matchmaking project by furthering this banter. Anyway, everyone knows that the average family income in Canada is what? Fifty thousand?

— Forty thousand, David says.

— What? Bill says.

> And whilst our souls negotiate there,
> We like sepulchral statues lay;
> All day, the same our postures were,
> And we said nothing, all the day.

— Anyone who can't get by on fifty thousand is buying far too many pairs of shoes, I'd say, Andrea adds, knowledgeably.

Sam, a blonde, Afro-ed, wire-rimmed-glasses-wearing Mathematics PHD student says, perfunctorily and almost inaudibly:

— Median income? Standard deviation? Jesus.

—I'd like to hear Amē's story now, Serena says.

—I don't *have* any story!

—Andrea promised us a story, David says, looking first straight-ahead at Amē's chest, then up to try to make eye contact.

—Go on, Amē, Andrea says.

Silence.

—Please? Serena says. For my birthday?

—For her *birth*day? Andrea says. *Please?*

Silence.

—Well if you won't tell it, Amē, I will. You guys know Amē used to live in Japan?

—When did you live there, Amē? David says.

—It's sooooo crowded, why would anyone want to live there? Serena says.

—I'm not sure why Amē moved there, though I have my suspicions. But it was back in '89, wasn't it Amē?

—Andrea!

—Amē, this story is going to be told, whether you tell it or not. David wants to hear it.

> *If any, so by love refined,*
> *That he soul's language understood,*
> *And by good love were grown all mind,*
> *Within convenient distance stood*

—Amē had the hots for this guy, she continues.

—I like the story already, David says.

—I did not!

—Or he had the hots for her, whatever, it doesn't matter. She was hiding out in Tokyo with yet another of her stop-gap boyfriends. She'd spent some time there as a kid; it was a kind of return to a more innocent time, a brief….

—'Interregnum?' Amē interrupts. 'Whilst the soul pauses, taking time to adjust itself to its forthcoming, ineluctable compromises?' Come on, Andrea, spare me the biographical gloss. At least until I've achieved something?

Andrea and Amē have been down this very path before, with other, similar audiences. Some details are added or subtracted, other aspects emphasised or minimised, but the pattern remains. Andrea pretends to affront, and Amē pretends to be affronted. It's a kind of mutual preening, all part and parcel of the perennial renegotiation of their friendship.

—Anyhow, Andrea continues, as if Amē hasn't spoken. He was a Tory speech writer, and he was accompanying some Minister of Something-or-Such-and-Such on a far-east trade junket, and he'd arranged a stopover in Tokyo….

—My kind of fellow, David says, glancing back to Bill before refixing his gaze on Amē. Arranging stopovers….

—*Un vrai homme du monde,* Serena says.

— *Un homme d'affaires*, David counters.

—Who means business, Bill adds.

—Listen, Amē says. If this story is going to be told, I'll do the telling, K-O?

—Do tell! David says.

—That way I don't get ... misrepresented, by a journalist's sensationalising ... interpolations. For starters, I got there in '86; I was gone by '89.

—What was his name? Serena asks.

> *He (though he knew not which soul spake*
> *Because both meant, both spake the same)*
> *Might thence a new concoction take,*
> *And part far purer than he came.*

—They called him The Kid, The Shawinigan Kid, Andrea says. His name was Roger. Roger Scruton.

3

THE INTERREGNUM: 1988, TOKYO

B̲U̲T̲ ̲Y̲O̲U̲ ̲C̲A̲N̲ call me Kid.

—Well, it's nice to meet you, Kid.

—I know what you're thinking, Vic. You're thinking who'd want to be called Kid? Isn't it kind of boyish, a little immature, maybe?

—Well, um.

—But you're wrong. 'Kid' gives you an instant advantage. People feel good around you, you're instantly approachable, and before you even open your mouth you've earned a mountain of goodwill.

—I don't quite see your point, uh, Kid.

—You see, it's a bit like telling people you're colour-blind....

—Are you?

—You bet. Lots of guys are. But *telling* people you're colour-blind earns you some instant empathy, and it lets others relax around you because you're sending them the message: Hey, I'm fallible, I'm limited. I'm not a threat. That kind of thing.

—I'm just a regular guy.

—Correct! How 'bout you? Vic, short for Victor, right, is what nationality?

—Polish, my mom's side. Turnbull's my last name, and that's, I dunno, cos of my dad maybe, just W.A.S.P. American I guess. Anyhow, what's your business in Tokyo?

—Not business. Pleasure. I was over for work last month, to Osaka and Kyoto, but this is my first time to Tokyo.

—How long you here for?

—Well, I have to meet my boss in Singapore in 72 hours, so I guess I'll have to squeeze a helluva lot of fun into the meantime. It'll be short, but hopefully sweet, if you catch my drift. But I'm certainly looking forward to it.

—Sounds great. I wish I could say the same.

—Why? What are you doing here?

—I'm with the State Department. I used to work as an agronomist at NEXCHEM, but now I manage things.

—You look kinda young for that. What kind of things?

—Hey, I'm twenty-five. The higher-ups sent me here to manage a previously botched attempt to prevent a trade war. Basically, I'm here to sell the Japs on American rice.

—Good luck! That's like—

—Yeah I know. Coals to Newcastle.

—Ice to the Eskimos.

—Carrying water to the river. *Porter de l'eau à la rivière.*

—You speak French!

—Some, yes. You?

—Not a bit. I'm from Quebec, though.

—You're Canadian?

—Yeah, Shawinigan is in Quebec.

—I've never been to Quebec.

—Nice. Lotsa nature. Trees, minerals, water....

—Hydro dams. We get our power from you.

—You live where?

—DC. But I'm from south of Boston. Duxbury. Plymouth Plantation country.

—It's nice of you to buy our electricity.

—Nice of you to make it. But I guess you've got rivers to spare!

—You bet. The Indians and the tree-huggers kick up a fuss every time we get a project going, but we've got water up the wazoo.

—Are you afraid of the Separatists?

—It'll never happen.

—How can you be sure?

—You know how it goes: this land is your land, this land is my land, blahblahblah, etc.

—I'm not sure I....

—The frogs could never afford it, see? Money talks, bull-shit walks.

—But how do you....

—Listen, I'm with the government too. The Progressive Conservative Party, actually.

—Wasn't there just an election up there?

—*Mais oui*. That's why I get this mini-break: we just defeated the Liberals, and this is my reward. We sold our voters on Free Trade, so perhaps *you've* got a shot with the Japanese.

—Perhaps. Now, Progressive Conservative, that's kind of like our Republicans?

—Kind of, but better. It's all in the name: we progress, we conserve, it sounds like magic but we can actually do both at the same time, we have a foot in both camps, the future, the past, it's pretty nifty, actually.

—It is! But I still don't see how you keep the French from leaving the ... union, is it?

—Confederation. Listen, I accompanied the Interminable Shadow Minister of Intergovernmental Affairs, when we were still in opposition. I trudged along on all of his ribbon-cutting, glad-handing, pork-barrel-promise-tours and I've seen each-and-every-last shithole town in Quebec, believe me. They talk the big nationalist, sovereignty talk, sure, but like our translator says, underneath it all they just want jobs. Jobs, jobs, jobs. So that's what I write for the Man: jobs, jobs, jobs. They liked what I did

so much, that now we're actually in power I've been promoted
to External Affairs, but that's still what I write: jobs, jobs, jobs.

—Write?

—I'm a speech writer.

—He's a speech writer.

—Who for?

—The Tories.

—Are they like our Tories?

—No one is like your Tories. Not that they don't try....

—So what's he doing here?

—Trying to get Amē.

—Get her?

—Get her to marry him. Sleep with him. Whatever. The former,
I suspect, but I'm sure the latter would suffice, in a pinch.

—How do you know?

—I guess I don't. She's always trolling for something better.
Job-wise, I mean.

—Yeah.

—But something's fishy.

—How d'you know?

—I've met him. He stares. And stares. And not exactly at me.

—You tell her what's what?

—You don't tell her what's what. Not Amē.

—True enough. Fair Enough.

—Not exactly. But then, she's her father's daughter.

—I'll say. Where is she today, anyway?

The two men, Tim and Julian, the first a Canuck from Edmonton and the other an Englishman from Worcester, are standing in the shallow end of a swimming pool in suburban Tokyo, waiting their turn to do a length. There are six people ahead of them, two of whom seem to be resting and socializing, so it will only be a little while now. Not that they mind terribly, because they are both somewhat inebriated. Tim's current concern is that Amē, the girl he lives with, soon won't be.

— Oh, she's working. But they're doing lunch at MONK'S FOODS. Again.

—Brown Rice and Bebop jazz?

—Exactly.

—The place where you two started?

—Precisely. Mind you, it's across from where she works.

—You've met this guy how many…?

— Once. Briefly. He's staying in a suite at the AKASAKA PRINCE.

—Uh-oh.

—We had $20 pancakes there with him.

—A good or a bad thing?

—Well the cakes were a reasonable facsimile of the real McCoy.

—And … what's that phrase you use again?—when you either don't know or don't want to know someone's name?

—Or you're too lazy to say it? Cos that's its most common usage….

—Yeah, so, what d'you call him?

—Buddy Whatsisface.

—And Buddy Whatsisface, how was he?

—A number of adjectives come to mind.

—An unreasonable facsimile?

—That wasn't what I was thinking. But yes.

—What *were* you thinking?

—It's our turn to do a length.

—Besides that. What adjectives? Gimme one.

—Well, to be blunt about it, scabrous.

—How so?

—You know when you're a kid and you fall and you get a scab and you obsess over it? It still hurts and it itches and it's fascinatingly ugly and it's a part of you, and you can't leave it alone?

—You pick at it.

—Completely. Anyhow, he told us a story, just a stupid, pointless macho shithead anecdote, really. But, like an inane, catchy pop song, I can't get it out of my mind. Neither can Amē, and that's what worries me.

—What?

—It's our turn to do a length.

—No, what? Tell me.

—Let's do a length.

—So dad wants to know if you've got all the Japanese women after you.

—Course he does. Tell him that. Tell him: course he does, daddy-o.

—You do? Do you?

—Who's got time for that? C'mon. G'won.

Vic Turnbull and his brother Piotr enter THE SAILOR WHO FELL FROM GRACE WITH THE SEA in fashionable Shibuya, which can be reached by taking the southbound, counterclockwise train from Shinjuku station via the circumnavigating Yamanote Line. Piotr is taking Vic on a pub crawl, and this is their fourth stop. Piotr lives and works here, and now goes by, for the sake of convenience, simply 'Pete'. This means he gets called Pee-tahh-san by his Japanese associates, and Pee-tah Tu-roonn-bu-ru-san by acquaintances. Vic still calls him by his nickname, 'Oater'.

—Women, man, Vic says, grabbing Piotr by the shoulder and giving him a little shake. Women!

Piotr, a three-year expat, had majored in Music and Asian Studies at BERKELEY and had initially come to Tokyo to further his musical education. He'd managed to apprentice himself to one of Japan's National Treasures on the *Samisen*. The National Treasure, a beautiful half-Chinese, half-Japanese grandmother named Imae, had gladly taken him on, and Piotr had found an English Conversation job to make enough money to survive. He had become adept at the many levels of unspoken formality with which the Japanese supplement their own complexly stratified spoken language, and so had become quite popular with both his students and his employer. Now, a mere three years later, he has a lot less time for his avocation than he would like, as he manages a whole chain of English Conversation schools for a woman named Arata. Arata's husband made his fortune in women's cosmetics, and she calls her schools KI-SU ['Kiss'] CONVERSATION, after a line of beautifiers peddled by his company.

—Women? Christ, who's got time for that? Piotr says, his hand betraying a slight tremor, as he points to an advertisement taped to the window of the café: an overlarge, shocking pink pair of lipstick lips superimposed onto the cheek of what appeared to be an affable California surfer-type.

—Huh? That yours? Vic says.

—Yep.

—You're *responsible* for that?

Piotr nods. —Arata likes to keep things in-house, he says. Keeps costs down. Like the model: he's a conversation teacher, works for us right here in Shibuya.

Piotr looks out the window of the café, across the asterisk-like intersection of streets, across the thousands of hurrying pedestrians, each anxious to beat the short-lived crossing signal.

—He teaches in that building over there. Plays jazz on weekends over in Kichijoji. And teaches Yoga. I tried a class or two, but don't have the time. Australian. Real nice guy. Now *he's* got all the women going abso-*lute*-ly….

Vic is only half paying attention; he's scanning the room, which is a mixed bag of Japanese and foreign couples, uniformly dressed in black, a monoculture of hipness—Piotr too, with his black jeans, black turtleneck and sports coat. Vic finds it all a bit unnerving, but it's nothing new: Vic has never felt at ease in his own skin, or in the various skins that conformity has always forced upon him. At college, for example, he'd joined KAPPA IOTA DELTA, a fraternity that didn't seem *too* far above his station, one whose sensibilities and conventions signified 'New-Money-Aspirational'. That is, while certainly elitist, the frat's world-view was also reasonably meritocratic and pragmatic. Above all, though, Vic had found there a culture of rabid jocularity, and it spoke to him, not in spite of his athletic ineptitude, but *because* of it. It was something that touched the soul of each and every would-be pledge: the boys of KAPPA lived for team sports. No one at KAPPA was any good themselves, but everyone was ardent. They loved sports, played sports, and above all watched sports and talked sports. It was a recipe for easy-going togetherness, and Vic liked that. Even 'rush week', the initiation, had been 'friendly' and 'fun', just a series of innumerable drinking games alternating with goofy contests that were designed to get you to 'laugh at yourself', along with everyone else. Vic found that he had made a wise choice, on the whole, for it had given him a leg up in more ways than one. But today, as he looks over the café's sophisticates, he only thinks of his frat nick-name, 'Frumple'. Vic glances from the clientele to himself, and back to the clientele. He knows he could never carry it off, that kind of thing.

Two tables to the left, what appears to be a Scandinavian couple affect a posture of world-class boredom, their eyes assiduously ignoring each other, each as focused on existential nothingness as Narcissus upon his own reflection. On the immediate right, a reclining young Japanese man practices blowing smoke rings for his applauding girlfriend, who has perfect posture and wears a facial expression of acute gratitude. Directly to the front, a set of whiskey-swilling quadruplets scowl over a game of poker. One attempts to fill another's glass, just as the other reaches to take a drink, and the whiskey pours wastefully onto the table.

—So anyway, Vic says, interrupting his brother and changing the subject abruptly, as if a submerged thought he'd been previously obsessing over has just resurfaced. I'm sitting beside this guy on the plane over from Seattle. A Canadian.

—We've got a number of them at KI-SU. Friendly, obedient, eager-to-please—for the most part. Malleable.

—Well this one was a bit of a wacko. Wacko, but not unlikable.

—What was there to like?

—The usual, I dunno, not all that much really. He was funny, upbeat. You know.

—A bit cynical, but in a good way?

—Yeah, but even though his sense of humour was kinda....

—Off the wall?

—I mean *way* off, but ... he was still ... personable....

—Regular.

—Down to earth.

—A Can-Do kinda guy.

—Well ... yeah, essentially, yeah.

The waitress comes to take their order. She has her hair dyed blonde and is dressed like Marilyn Monroe in *Some Like It Hot*. Her friendly attempts at English conversation are politely dismissed by the efficient, business-like fluency of Piotr's Japanese. He orders coffee for his brother and has a half-full bottle of *Suntory Whiskey*—Reserve—brought over for himself.

The whiskey bottle has the name Peter written onto it with a red grease pencil. Puzzled, Vic stares for a moment at the bottle, then at his brother.

—Hey, Piotr says, you like the decor?

The café is done up in an admixture of Japanese right-wing nationalist paraphernalia and *American Graffiti* motifs.

—Wait a minute, Vic says. You a regular here?

Piotr smiles. —If they like you they let you have your own bottle. Same price, but there's something to be said for it.

—Like what?

Piotr raises an eyebrow. —You know, the owner was one of my first students. He's the one behind the bar in the samurai get-up. Owns the gallery next door too, does a Warhol-ish kinda thing himself. Claims to have met Andy a few days after Yukio Mishima died. Said it changed his life, his whole outlook. He was one of the faithful few at the barricades when Mishima committed *seppuku*, but like I said, he's since shifted, from Tragic to Comic slash Ironic.

—I huh, what?

—Nothing. Nevermind.

—You use those a lot, those slashes? They proper English?

—Useful English. Business English. *Our* English, American English, at any rate. It's what they want to learn here, and it's why we don't generally hire Brits. Too anal for the most part, about that kind of thing. The ones you can understand, the ones who elocute well, I mean.

The drinks arrive, delivered by a young man whose getup suggests Jerry Lee Lewis as a Bowling champion. Vic returns to the bee in his bonnet.

—So this guy, this Canadian, he kept telling me to call him Kid.

Piotr pretends to be not at all interested in what his brother is saying, knowing all-too-well how much he dislikes being ignored.

—Uh-huh, he says.

—Listen. He had this ... obsession. That's what you'd have to call it.

—A niceness obsession.

—Not really. It's stupid—I mean, it's *really* stupid. But....

—Or is it compulsion?

—No. *Listen.*

—Cos the two often go together, in my experience.

—Will you just listen, Jesus!

—There is effective medication for the very condition you're describing. DSM-III-R (1987) describes, and prescribes for it, perfectly.

—Christ, I haven't even described it yet, will you let me describe it? At least?

—Would you say that your anger is a ... *problem* in your ... *intimate* relationships?

—Oater, *I'm* gonna pummel you and then I'm gonna start in on your pal Kurosawa over there. You hear me?

—Try starting your sentences with 'I feel'.

—*You* are a dead man, Oater. D-E-D, dead. A. Dead. Man. You.

—Tell me about your mother. Were you close?

—This is a promise I'm making now.

—No, please, really, just kidding, haha. Say haha, Vic, we be friends here. Like brothers be we.

—Haha. We *are* brothers. For the moment anyway. As for the future, who knows, who can—?

—Tell? O-K, Tell me about your little *aero*plane friend, I really want to know, really. Really really.

—Will you be serious for a minute?

—Sure. Scout's honour.

Piotr does the Scout salute, straightens his tie, adjusts his seating position so that he is, if still dishevelled, somewhat erect, and swallows the last of his whiskey.

—He pisses into rivers, said Vic.

—I don't get it.

—What's to not get? He pisses—into rivers.

—Rivers, he pisses into. Into rivers he pisses. He, into rivers … Hey, we could use this in our schools!

—I think that about covers the various permutations.

—Don't misunderestimate the value of rote learning, Vic.

—Very funny stuff.

—No, I just don't get it, Vic. No matter how I rearrange it, I just don't get it.

—He pisses into rivers.

—Now I get it.

—He....

—I got it. I got it.

—No you didn't. Don't patronize me!

—You're right, sorry. I guess I really don't get it.

—He whips it....

—Spare me, please? I *do* in fact have a *mental picture*, Vic-tor, of that which you have only just now chosen to reveal to me, to myself here. Will you let me describe to you just what, in fact, I do *not* get? Will you?

—I will.

—I do not get the *why* here. It is the *why* that I am not getting. *Why* he pisses in rivers. *Why* you mention this, even. *Why?*

—Think about it. It's inherently fascinating. Or don't you think?

—I don't think, I.... And he tried to lick the last of the whiskey from the inside rim of his glass.

—Yeah. That's the ticket.

—... drink. And yet....

—Look, Vic says. It's like this: one day, the guy wakes up, and there's been this *shift* in the cosmos, see, in the *order* of things. The universe presents itself to him thusly.

—Just 'thus' will do. We have classes that can Polish you up. You be good Polack soon!

Ignoring this, Vic says: —Then he looks at himself, and what do you know but there's been another shift, a mirroring of the first one, in the corresponding yet mysterious order of his *psyche*....

—As above, so below....

—That kind of thing. So there's these profound, interlinked shift-ings, and all of a sudden the guy needs, he needs to, the guy has to, piss into every new river that he comes across, big or small, on foot or in a motorcar, regardless.

—No one says motorcar anymore, Vic. It's archaic. We steer our students away from such things, generally.

—I said it for effect. Dramatic effect, cos in my opinion the whole thing is fucking strangely dramatic.

—Strangely bordering on stupidly, more like. Not to mention infantile regression.

—No, just think about it for a sec. He sees a river....

—Are you just relating this, reporting what he told you, here, or are you dressing it up just a tad?

—He sees a Goddamn river.

—I see.

—And he *has* to piss into it. To make his mark.

—Like, like a dog?

—Yup.

—Thanks for sharing, but that's way too deep for me. I don't go in for the profound or the sublime, as a rule. Depths and Vastnesses and such and so forth. Best to live on the surface.

—You're not getting me.

—Wait a minute. You, you're doing this too, now?

—I mean the *Kid*, the Shawinigan Kid, you're not getting me. You're not getting *him*.

—Shawinigan Kid? That's what he calls himself?

—That's what we call him.

—We? Why we? Why do *we* call him that? And which we?

—People. Cos he asks them to. Us. People like us.

Piotr, who had previously been making an effort to stay more or less vertical, now slumps in his seat, so that only his upper thoracic spine touches the seat back.

—Let's recap, he says. He pisses into rivers, for no apparent reason. And you call him Kid, or Shawinigan Kid, depending of course upon whether it's second or third person....

—You little p....

—For no apparent reason.

Vic leaps forward now, and leans across the table so that his nose is almost touching his brother's.

—That's just it, you drunken moron! The reason is not apparent. It is not even presented to us as relevant. The Kid doesn't *care* why he does it. He doesn't even care if *we* care. He just delights in the exalted egoism of the *act*, luxuriates in the opaque infantility—

—Infantilism.

—Infan*tility* of it all. Like you said yourself, best to live on the surface, right, but don't answer me, just shut up, don't even begin to speak here, don't open your lips, cos I'm gonna enlighten your tiny little world just a wee little bit.

—About a bit of wee wee.

—Did I say shut up?

—You did.

—*Will* you?

Piotr nods, restraining, but not restraining, a smile.

—The Kid doesn't know why he does it, but he does it nonetheless. Piotr shrugs his shoulders.

—This is the key, this is the *fulcrum* here. Think Archimedes. The linchpin. The Kid doesn't know, doesn't care to know, doesn't care if we care to know, *any*thing about his motivation. He's no method actor, he's not act*ing*, he's act*ion*. He's not a subject, he's a verb.

—Wow.

—Shut up. You know that old saw, the maxim 'Know Thyself'? Well, the Kid knows that that kind of shit just leads to an exhausting series of vigour-sapping, confidence-draining doubts and questions, forming all manner of negative feedback loops, the superposition principle of which would only turn him into a caricature of who he really is: a man, nothing less, nothing more. The Kid eschews that egghead kind of thing, all that 'rational enquiry' business. Cos the Kid knows what he wants, and action dictates that he enquire no further. The Kid is self-defining. Piss in a river? Hell yeah—it's not 'why?' but 'why not?' The Kid as pioneer, as explorer, as Everest-scaler, as flag-planter.

—Uh.

—What do you think?

—Huh.

—Really? 'Huh'? That's it? Really?

—Sounds good Vic.

—Shut up.

—No, as theories go, it sounds good. Seriously.

—Haha.

—Seriously. One question though.

—Uh-huh?

—You buy it yourself, this theory of yours?

—Not really. Does sound good though.

—He's just a weirdo.

—A bit of a wacko, like I said.

—Like you said. Anyway, how're the sons and heirs apparent?

—Mine? Great.

—And Brenda?

—What did you use to call her? Back in high school?

—Back when you used to throw darts at me from the garage roof?

—Way back when.

—Back when we were just kids, Vic.

—Back when kid spelled backwards was—anyway: tell me. What did you use to call her?

—Aww. C'mon. You know.

—No, I don't know. Remind me. Please.

—G'won.

—No. What did you use to call her?

—I forget. Numerous variations on a theme.

—Forget? Bullshit! That's impossible. Say it.

—Fuck it. Oĸ. 'Splenda'.

—No, the whole nine yards thing. The complete name. Say it like you used to say it. So I can remind you of what a great guy you are.

—It's ancient history. We were kids.

—Say it.

—Make me.

—Say it or else.

—Else what, Vicky?

—Else I'll pummel you, dickhead.

—'Blenda.' 'Blenda Blenda Blenda.' 'Blenda Splenda Rearenda.' There, satisfied?

—What a *guy*.

—Hey.

—Jesus, *what* an absolute g—.

—Hey, we were kids, how was *I* s'posed to know you were gonna up and marry her?

—What *a*.

—How was I *s'posed* to know? Huh? How *wuzz* I?

—What a great, great, fucking great guy. Peckerhead.

—Howwuzz … hey, what the fuck, fuck it Victor Victoria: what can I say?

MONK'S FOODS. They are seated at the bar, half-facing one another, his knee perilously close to hers, almost touching. Zoot Simms is playing on the stereo.

Owner/Chef/Jazzman and lover of all things Native American Hatamura-san is scowling at them this time too. What made her take the Kid back here? What was she thinking about? Hold on, wait a minute, it's just an innocent lunch date, right? Right. So…? So what?

Hatamura-san wordlessly brings the food Amē had ordered for them both: two bowls of *Genmai Oyako Donburi* (a kind of pilaf composed of brown rice, chicken, eggs, onions and peas in a fairly sweet *shoyu* or soya-based sauce). Her childhood favourite, but she decides not to tell him this.

—Wow, that's, um, some story, Roger.

—Don't get all middle-class on me now!

—Middle-class what? All I said was....

—'That was some story.' But we both know what you meant. But I know you don't think the less of me for it. Or you *do* think the less of me, but that's actually why you like me, isn't it?

—You're fairly entertaining, it's true.

—You like to be a little shocked. Just a little. Kind of a catharsis, eh?

—You know, the Japanese have something a lot like our 'eh'. They say '*nē?*' or '*desu-nē?*'

—Don't change the subject.

—It's a way of filling up the spaces, between moments, between people.

—Yup, is all he says.

She says nothing more, begins to force herself to eat. She has no appetite, feels kind of nauseous. He is right, of course, he always is, always has been, ever since they met as undergrads at McGILL, she from Victoria, he from Shawinigan, but both living on St. Viatur and both double-majoring in Poli-Sci and English: she does in fact like him because she doesn't really like him. There's a kind of dangerous power about him, a magnetism that's certainly not based on his looks, such as they are. And just look at him: he appears even dumpier, even more dishevelled and acne-scarred when viewed in juxtaposition to the exceedingly neat and trim and beautiful Japanese. She has never seen a really ugly Japanese person, but you could almost call Roger ugly—almost, and the June humidity is causing him to sweat profligately, even in this air-conditioned restaurant. But still, there is something about him; there is indeed a 'there' there.

—I gots another story for ya, toots, he says.

—Well?

Hatamura-san comes back out from the kitchen, one more bowl in hand. But they hadn't ordered anything else. Of course, the *slippery mountain potato*. Of course. Suspicious, superstitious, Amē knows what their host—and what Life, really—is trying to say to her.

—Here we are! Our compliments, Hatamura-san says, in accent-free English, making a slight honorific bow.

She has always known it, of course, but it only crystallizes at this moment, with the arrival of this complimentary dish: foreigners have a really hard time with the mountain potato.

—Foreigners have a really hard time with the mountain potato, she says. It's too slippery to pick up with chopsticks.

—Yeah, but not this wrangler, Amēkins.

—It's a test, a friendly test, look, Hatamura is smiling at you, Roger, look.

It's a test that both Amē and *Tim* had passed with flying colours, *of course*, last year. He'd been teaching at SOPHIA UNIVERSITY for five years, and she'd lived here as a 'Base Brat' as a pre-teen, for four years while her father was on exchange at the U.S. NAVY base. Amē and Tim had this in common: their attachment to each other was buoyed by a mutually high level of *Gaijin* [foreigner] proficiency. The alienation that they felt here, their separateness from a culture that they loved—but one that could never, would never fully accept them—was much different than that of the run-of-the-mill expat, replete with far more subtleties and nuances than someone like Roger, for example, could ever appreciate. It had been the mainspring of their togetherness, this shared estrangement, this fluent otherness.

Without it, where would they be?

Now, unbidden, a traitorous little thought appears out of the ether and makes its way through her head: if sweaty, crude Roger can eat the mountain potato properly, she'll go along with whatever it is he's here to propose—whatever it is, and regardless of her bloody scruples (which she wished, sometimes, would all just hit the road, Jack, and pack their things and go). If he can't, she won't. It's completely ridiculous, of course, but it's also a safe bet, 99.99% guaranteed to leave things as they now stand, but there you have it. She's thought it. She can't take it back, or won't. Why not? Isn't this just a tad perverse?

She shakes her head a little as if to wonder at herself as she watches Roger look at the bowl. She knows him too well, has analysed her way around all of the contours and fault lines of their 'friendship', to have any doubts as to why he's really visiting her.

He prods one of the potatoes in the bowl, moves it around.

—If you can eat the slippery potato with your chopsticks, they like the hell out of you, I know, he says. They pulled it on us down in Kyoto, last time I was — er, *we* — were there. Amusing. In a stupid kind of way. Like the TV game shows they have, based on the humiliation of the contestant.

—And the degradation of the viewer, as a byproduct.

—Hey, no one *has* to watch. Tvs do have an off button, you know. Anyhow, people seem to like them, to watch them anyway, these shows. They work.

—They *sell*.

—Same thing. Hey, don't be so hoity-toity, missy. Don't affect that anti-capitalist little rich girl pose. Not this late in the day. Or at least not with me, not with your very own Father Confessor.

—Forgive me.

—Come off it, admit it, there's a part of you that likes it too, what I do, what everyone who wants to get along in the world *has* to do. It's just that there's another you that doesn't like that you like it. Or approve, rather. But hey, I like'em both, both the you that desires and aspires, *and* the you that's ashamed of all those oh, not-so-nice things that keep this ol' world spinning round.

—The world.

—The real world, baby.

—Eat your potato, big daddy.

—I shall, no, let me re-phrase that: I will. But first I'm desirous of keeping our nattily beatnik host in a little suspense, if it's OK with you. And I'm gonna let you in on another story, cos I know you likes em, Sam-I-Am.

—Your last one was rather special, it's true.

—This one's not about me. Remember that guy I told you about, the one I was sitting next to on the plane over?

—The one who seemed so shocked about *your* story?

—Correct. Vic was his name. Vic the Oxford button down Sperry Topsider guy.

—Hey you wear those, too!

—But they don't define me, I just wear'em to grease the wheels. He wears'em to escape the trailer trash tag that's dogged him since he was a kid.

—How do you know that?

—Bits and pieces. Interpolations, extrapolations, a few hunches and a couple of blind guesses.

—The usual.

—The usual. It's the late '70s. He is an outsider, not a lot of friends. The friends he does have don't have a lot of friends. Comes into his own at college, later, but we're not concerned with that period in his life.

—No, of course not.

—What fascinates us is his youth, late elementary school—what do they call it there?—middle school, yes, yes, middle school to early high school.

—The interregnum.

—The brief, revolutionary pause. Hormonally, intellectually, physically. The world turned upside down. Roundheads and blackheads.

—And blockheads.

—This is my story, sweetie. Anyway, guys is guys.

—Forgive me.

—Perhaps, but. Nevertheless, there will be penance. Later. Well then, his name is Victor. He's what? Thirteen or fourteen. He lives in a small town, a bedroom community for Boston, on the south shore, where the blood runs as blue and cold as the ocean currents.

—Miles Standish proud, she says, suddenly wistful.

—Correct. Roger looks at her now-otherworldly eyes, decides not to enquire, but she then offers, enigmatically:

—I knew a boy once…, she begins, trailing off into contemplation of a possible, parallel universe.

Two boys. Once upon a time, there were two boys, brothers. One, catalytic Mercury, the other, Polaris, true north, the guide star….

He allows her this moment of transport, watches the rise and fall of her breath. As if unaware of herself, she sighs. A shallow in-breath followed by a deep, collapsing exhalation. He could watch her breathe all day, he thinks, but then the cross-indexing *Rolodex* of his mind autonomically looks for, locates, and retrieves the corresponding, intergraded recipe cards. Breath. Respiration, inspiration. *Inspirare, Inspiratio. Prajna*: 'Avalokitesvara Bodhisattva, doing deep *prajna paramita*, clearly saw the emptiness of all the five conditions….' *The Heart Sutra*. He knows of it, has read about it, has done a little research for that interminable Minister of Whatever, to bone the boneheaded huckster up on the local, ah, culture. Avalokitesvara is a bodhisattva, a would-be, could-be Buddha, who chooses to remain in creation until all sentient beings are guided to enlightenment, past or through the cycle of desire and suffering. Saved. Interesting, in a way. But. But expiration, your soul leaving as you exhale your last breath. Your expiry date, but.

—But Victor, he says. His family does *not* belong to the yacht club.

—Hence his present-day getup. Compensating.

—Affirmative. He is one of the great unwashed.

—The hoi polloi.

—Very quick, grasshopper, you see deeply into the empty mirror. But tell me this: what, what do you think, do you *imagine*, his nickname—among the elect, among his betters, the *Haves*, what his nick-name might, no, *must* be?

—That's a toughie. Uh, um.

—Open wide, your mind: into the void you ride, the black diamond trail, 'like an escaped ski', until to rest you will come, at the mountain's base, where....

—What in the...?

—Where you are not what you are, where motionless you are—but electric. You allow the truth, which is but temporary, which is always arriving, in process, to come and then go. Like the rising and falling of your....

He thinks she thinks he is staring at her breasts, but he isn't, at least not this time.

—Jesus, Roger!

—You're close. Riff on that rhyme!

—Jesus?

—Roger.

—Roger? Lodger, Codger, Dodger.

—Roger Dodger!

—He's called the *dodger*? Victor?

—Over-and-out. Just like his….

—What does he dodge?

—Not him, the *pater familias*, the.

—Dad, what does he?

—And/or did he.

—Dodge? Viet Nam?

—Famously. But more, more that is privy solely to the close relations. Yet, we can imagine, everything, in a word, pretty much.

—Dead-beat dad.

—In the spirit, if not quite the letter of the law, yes, although
the son.

—Let's see, looks up to him?

—Worships this false idol, yes. The truth is, well, what it is:
Victor, just turned fourteen, still *thinks* pa-pahhh is a scient-ist,
white robed, of the priestly class, which the Jews denote 'Cohen'.
Thinks, and therefore is: a horticulturist. From the Latin *hortus*,
garden, and *cultura*, to….

—And dad really does what?

— *Grow* is such an inadequate word here. More of a paying attention to, a, *nurturing*.

—I know, but….

—But there's more to it, my little impatiens, my little jewelweed,
my 'touch-me-not'….

— *Get* on with it!

—Because *cultura*, and *cultus* are intimately *bound up*, inter-twined, deriving themselves as they do from *coelere*....

—Yesyesyes.

—No, little one, you need to understand, this needs to be ruth-lessly underscored, brutally italicized, emphasized with, with....

—Manly emphasis.

—*Naturellement*, a, er, seminal interpretation, ladybug, well parried.

—Murky Buckets.

—Of mercy, but no. No, *my* thanks, yes, but listen: the point being, the connection here, the copula, the equals sign: that there is *bound up* as one and (of course) the same, the concept-ions of growing, *tilling* and devoutly worshipping (in-*habiting*) the land, as intimate with the earth as with the very clothes on our backs....

—And your own habit, of rivers and streams....

—*Moi*? Well, *bien sûr*, I, 'riverrun, past Eve's and Adam's'.

—'All the rivers run into the sea, and yet it is not full.'

—'The snotgreen sea. The scrotumtightening sea.'

There is a pause in the conversation here, and Roger searches out Amē's gaze, to see if she has, to see if she, to see if....

But she looks out the window, at the delivery trucks and motor scooters crawling by on the narrow pavement, at the bustling crowd marching past on the even narrower sidewalk. She glances at her watch.

—Roger, sorry to interrupt, but I'll ... have to be getting back to work soon-ish.

—Yes, of course, I shall condense. Where was I? Yes, in this period of the interregnum, somewheres in the late 70s or thereabouts, and all that late 70s crap is going on....

—*We* survived it, no need to go into it here.

—No, well said, keep to the point, etc., etc., and we shall. Besides, what we have with this tale is something rather more archetypal, if that is not too pretentious a term to employ in mixed company.

—It is, but go on.

She is smiling now, despite herself, despite her schedule, despite her wariness and incredulity. His banter has translated her, only partly against her will, back to MCGILL and those heady classes in Joyce, when she and he would ... when Gerald ... and then Isaac....

—Now, Victor has all the usual teenage male obsessions, but one of them stands out ever so slightly ... and sets him, to this extent only, mind you, momentarily apart from the homogeneous mass of maledom. Apart and yet or therefore, the epitome of.

—Epitomic.

—Yahh.

Roger goes on, and as he does so Amē watches him play with the mountain potato in his bowl, much as a cat will continue to play with a trapped mouse long after it has died, delighting in flinging it about, willfully causing sudden, explosive 'escapes' and subsequent, quite skillful 'recaptures'. A mind-game, in which the imagination gains control of inert matter, gratifies itself by investing the dead object with a life-force, with a kinetic energy, energy that it can never really possess.

She is reminded of her already-forgotten vow of only minutes before, and tells herself not to be an asshole. Of course she won't go to bed with him. Or anywhere else with him, for that matter. She is far too sensible. For that. But why did she think it? What was its meaning? Where is her brain at, these days? she wonders.

—You've lost interest. In my story.

—No I haven't. It's fascinating, go on, continue.

—Let's talk about you.

—Let's not. Your story is more interesting.

—Granted, but.

—And yet.

—Listen, Amē, why are you sweating it out here, so far from the real action?

—Hey, *you're* the one who's sweating, look at yourself. Look, just look why don't you? I mean and this place is air conditioned!

—You've got ambition. Don't waste yourself schlepping around. You've got the right clothes, baby, use'em or lose'em. I mean, how do you say in French? *Get in the game.* Play along, keep the ball bouncing. I can pull some strings for you, get you on a short list.

He stops playing with the potato. She listens.

—The CANADA DEVELOPMENT CORPORATION, he says. You've always dreamed of it, since McGILL anyhow. Overseas do-good-er-ism, the balm or salve your guilty whitebread conscience desperately needs, and a great salary to boot.

—Can't beat that combination.

His chopsticks hover in mid-air. He looks her in the eye.

—Send me your resume.

—Sure.

—Don't put it off. Make hay. While the iron's hot.

—I'll send you my resume.

—Seriously now.

—All kidding aside.

—Cos the universe is expanding, he says.

—Huh?

—Woody Allen.

—Oh.

—In *Annie Hall* Woody's little alter-ego, Alvy Singer, is, oh, twelve? And he becomes precociously aware of the meaningless-ness of existence for the first time, and so he can't just be a normal kid doing normal kidlike things.

—So?

—So this gets his sensible if shrilly worry-worting mom into a stereotypical Jewish Mother tizzy, and she drags his carcass to the good ol' pragmatic, two-feet-on-the-ground family doctor. Little Alvy tells him, he says, with the weariness of one destined to luxuriate further, as his life passes him by, in the roiling but perversely comforting, pessimistic Schopenhauer Jacuzzi, little Alvy says to the doc: 'The universe is expanding.'

—So?

—Exactly: Alvy is depressed, won't do his homework, all because of something *he read in a book*, like his mother says. Little *wisenheimer* Alvy is trapped in his own head: the universe is expanding. The universe will one day rip apart. That will be the end of everything. So, therefore, what's the point of doing homework, what's the point of doing anything? The syllogism is compelling, and it compels Alvy to accept the obvious: that there is no point. *Point finale*, Q.E.D.

—Wow. Bummer.

—Hold on. The wise doctor looks upon him with a knowing, genial, man-to-man kinda gaze. Now Doc is a successful professional in the prime of his life, and from the way he carries himself, he's quite obviously a full-blooded hedonist as well. But he is above all a man, and he too once had his own Dark Night Of The Soul, perhaps back in medical school, who knows, whenever, when his ideals came crashing to the terra firma of blood and sinew, and he got his first truly visceral insight into the essence of reality, into The Impermanence Of All Good Things. So Doc understands Alvy, he really does.

—I'm not sure I do.

—Neither does Frustrated Mom. Uncomfortable with being sent to the sidelines for even a moment, she cuts in on this brief *Tête-à-Tête*, shrieking at Alvy: 'And what's that your business?' And to the doctor, she adds: 'Tell him, what's that his business?' It's difficult for me to reproduce her exact shriek here, but if I say that she howls like a banshee, you get the picture.

—I'm a bit vague on banshees.

—That's not too important for our purposes. What is essential is that you recoil physically, that you have a corporeal sense —a physical knowing, mind you— of a shriek, a wailing, the synchronic sonic summation of your grade five teacher yelling at you as you scrape your fingernails across her blackboard.

—You don't like Mom, then.

—I didn't say that.

—You didn't have to.

—Anyway, I see you're looking at your watch again, so I'll cut this short: taking heed of Mom's interrogative imperatives, Doc counsels Alvy. Mom hectors her son with the obvious: 'You're in Brooklyn, and Brooklyn is *not* expanding.'

—She's right.

—True enough, but she has no empathy for Alvy's predicament. The way she says it, she says it like someone who has never thought a thought beyond the next sale at Macy's, beyond telling us all, over the back fence, over-and-over, that Finklestein's wife has diabetes. She says it like life is about keeping your head down, your nose clean and doing what you're told.

—You think it's not?

—It's about choosing to do what's in your own self-interest. If it's about fitting in, it's only so that you can get what you want out of it. Doc knows this. He's been around. He's seen a lot of life, and he's seen a lot of this kind of mother before. He knows that there's a big ol' world out there, one of which the likes of Alvy's mother hasn't heard so much as a whisper. Doc rocks back and forth on his feet good-humouredly, that is to say: wisely. He doesn't know if young Alvy will take his sage advice. He doesn't know if Mom will let the boy *breathe* a little. But he tries to be as helpful as he can, without letting Mom's hysteria or Alvy's lassitude get to him. He says that Brooklyn 'won't be expanding for a lonnnnnnnggg time yet, Alvy'. And guess what he says next? Heh!

—Beats me.

—It's only polite to guess.

—Sorry.

—'And we've got to en*joy* ourselves,' he says, 'while-we're-here, heh! Heh!'

—Oᴋ, Amē says.

—Seize it with both hands, kiddo.

—And eyes wide open.

He's still looking her in the eye. He's summing her up, that's what he's doing, the prick, and he's succeeding. That's how she feels. She breaks his gaze, watches his chopsticks make a clever, fluent little move. Pretending to casually pick the potato up, pretending to lose interest. The childish delight in the display-ing the fake, the deke, the simulacrum of skill. 'Bangbang, You're Dead!' and other forms of imaginary control. Saying to yourself: 'Hey, *I* could *do* this, I could pick this sucker up *any day* of the week, *if* I wanted to.' If nothing else, Roger is a regular guy, a guy's guy, and (you could make an argument for it, anyhow) there's prob-ably something to be said for that.

—I can get your resume into the swim, he says. Send it.

—Of course. You'll keep in touch?

—I always do.

Rather than picking up the mountain potato with proper chop-stick etiquette, he skewers the gelatinous little tuber kebab-style, and brings it to his mouth. Smiles, shows his teeth.

—You always do.

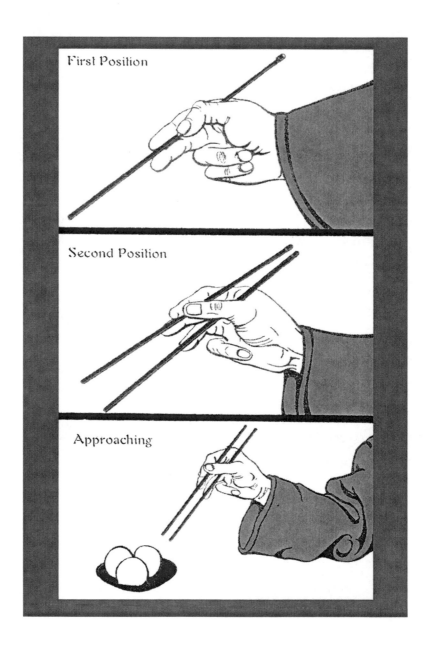

—Whatchew gonna do? Julian says.

—Dunno, Tim Says. Get drunk. Drunker.

The Englishman and the Canadian extract themselves, some-how, from the overstocked fish farm in which they had been tread-ing water, and head for the showers.

—You're that already. You love her?

—Yup.

—Then whatchew gonna do 'bout it?

—What's there *to* do?

—Christ, somethin', anyway! You gotta do somethin', say somethin'.

—I'd say you're doing a bit of a hatchet job on the Canadian accent.

—I'm just taking the piss. But then, you all sound American to me.

—My point exactly. You just don't have the ear for it. For the subtle *variations*. For the, the *frisson*.

—No, you've got the wrong word pal. *My* point was, youse guys is generic, like. Verymuchso. Cookie-cuttered. Franchised. There's just One Standardized, Suburban Accent, from coast to coast. Yer Edmonton is identical to yer Toronto, or yer Ottawa, or Hallyfax.

—That's 'Hal-*if*-fax', chump. But OK, the middle class has its own accent, you want me to deny this? Like it's a scandal or something?

—I'm appalled, Julian says.

—And those with heavy accents don't seem to get ahead much—
is this a conspiracy, or so very different from your neck of
the woods?

—And how do *you* pronounce the name of my, er, neck?

—'War-chester'.

—Try 'Woust-er'.

—'Wuh-ster'. 'Woost-er'. 'Woustershestershistershire'.

—And who has no ear for it?

—Next stop 'Wuss-ter' Shrub Hill, tickets please. All wusses
please disembark Shrubb Hill.

—Anyway, you should say *some*thing.

—Huh?

—You're evading the issue here, Julian says, the issue *at hand*.

—So? Tim says.

—The issue.

—Amē?

—What will you do?

—Drink. Wake up sick, numb. Then, avoid the issue until she
makes a clean break of it. Finally, wallow in maudlin sentimentality and write saccharine verse to her for an indefinite period
of time. Is that OK? Sound about right?

—Sounds like a plan. But Christ you've got to *say* something.

—To her?

Julian does not answer this question. He just stares at Tim, who
is now naked, out of his swimsuit, and edging his way out of

the locker room toward the shower stalls. He won't press it any further. He looks away, moves into a stall next to his friend's.

—What do you make of this sign, Julian?

Beneath the shower head there is a notice, red sans-serif letters on a white plastic background, which reads:

It is prohibited
To use a shampoo

There is also, presumably, a Japanese translation. Weak on their *Kanji*, neither man can tell if it means the same thing.

—I've never figured that one out. You got any?

—Sure. Here.

He hands Julian a bottle of *Body On Tap*, and the two lather up.

—You know what I figure, Julian?

—Uh-uh.

—Neither do I, but I'll say this: it's certainly *Miller* Time, for this cowboy anyway.

—*Miller?* Julian says, affecting an East Enders accent. The archetypal American beer? The beer that tastes like, like nothing? Like a moistened cipher, a wet nullity? Listen you geezer....

—Blahblahblah. You've gone down this road before, buddy. I mean, let's go get blotto. Cos I've got me a *motive*.

—Sing me that *Döppelbrau* song, will yas? Julian says, trying this time for Texas. Cos pardner, I'm fixin' t' git muh hands on one *real* soon. Now there's one—how d'youse Albertans say it?

—Killer diller. It's Texans, actually. It's Texans who say that.

—Now there's one killer diller beer. No more of this *Crapporro* or *Shittory*, no suh. But how's that *Döppelbrau* song go?

Tim doesn't respond for a second. He's closed his eyes. He's thinking.

—Uh, I forget. You know it, you sing it.

Julian clears his throat:

> He shoots, he scores,
> but don't mop the floor
> cos the beer
> keeps on a-pouring
> down,
> when you drink Döppelbrau

—Uh, Julian?

—Hmm?

—I have to urinate.

—'With extreme prejudice?'

—Uh-huh.

—Me too.

The two men, still a bit wobbly on their feet, still ensconced in their shower stalls, begin to relieve themselves, both taking care to aim for the drain.

4

TRUTH TELLING: 1997, TORONTO

I THOUGHT I'd never get you alone, Amy.

   —It's Amē.

—Oh! Sorry!

—Everyone gets it wrong. A-m-ē, actually pronounced 'Ahh-may'.

—'Ahh-may'.

—Perfect. My Japanese mother named me after the rain.

—Spelled with a little hat, a circumflex over the 'a', it means 'soul' in French.

—Now you're flirting. But that 'soul' come-on? I learned that from Leonard Cohen, when I was sitting beside him on a flight to Paris.

—You're joking.

—That's what he said when I introduced myself by my middle name, Suzanne. Then I showed him my driver's license, and ... well, then he looked, into my soul—or so he said. He'd just moved into a Zen Monastery in Los Angeles, and his Roshi was

Japanese. So, then we basically hit it off, and chatted all the way to Charles de Gaulle!

—No way!

—Don't you believe me, David?

—Of course.

—No one else does. But it's 100% true, I swear.

Saying this, Amē crosses her heart with her index finger, then grabs her pint glass and knocks back the rest of her beer. He follows her as she goes in search of more alcohol. She chooses wine because that's what he is drinking. She realizes that she is taller than David, who is only 5 foot 6, and he has a hard time looking her in the eye, it seems. She hears herself telling herself that she would have a hard time dating a man significantly shorter than she, even if he was as handsome and rich as this allegedly capital-E 'Entrepreneur'.

She pushes the thought aside: it wasn't worthy of her to think like that. *That* wasn't Amē, it wasn't like her. Hmm. Of course she *could* date him, but would she? Well, he doesn't seem to mind the height differential, so why does she?

—What do you do, David? What interests you?

—Well, I own a company that owns other companies.

—A holding company.

—Mm-hmm, yes. We're professional holders-on, if not quite hangers-on.

—Describe it for me.

—A lot of paper gets pushed around. We buy low and sell high.

—Of course. You sound like someone I know. Knew. She forced a frown, a furrow to retreat from her face.

—You're smiling. I think these thoughts myself: how puerile, how philistine, right, this snakes-and-ladders game of profit-and-loss? Something so unsubtle and inhumanely rational that it could only interest a seventeen year-old boy?

—Or a forty year-old seventeen year-old.

—*Touché*. No, this racket generates a fair bit of money, but I wouldn't say it *interests* me.

—What does?

—Well I know for a fact that you have an English degree, your friend, er….

—Andrea?

—Yes, Andrea told me. And since I'd very much like to impress you, I'd like to say that my passion was literature, but that would be a bit of a fib.

—I was a double major, actually. Do you think your confession impresses?

—I sense, I … have a hunch, that you value honesty, above all else, and so I am … being honest with you.

—If you sensed that I valued, say, flattery, would you give me that, instead?

—I hardly meant....

—Fair enough. I'm giving you a hard time because I'm a bit drunk—my turn to confess, and I'm afraid I enjoy it.

—Confessing? Or giving people a hard time?

—Uh-huh.

—Oh, but I'm sure you only give a hard time to those who you like!

She doesn't answer. He looks into her eyes, but she averts them, saying:

—So, you haven't answered my first question, what *does* interest you?

—Honestly?

—If you like. That seems to be the game you're playing at the moment.

—Love, he says. Love interests me. It's the only thing that interests me, and it's not a game.

> *This ecstasy doth unperplex*
> *(We said) and tell us what we love,*
> *We see by this, it was not sex,*
> *We see, we saw not what did move:*

—How many times have you said this line before? Honestly, now, remember, honestly!

—Honesty is the best pottery, he says.

—Meaning… ?

—Exactly twice.

—Twice including just now?

—No, I guess three including just now.

> But as all several souls contain
> Mixture of things, they know not what,
> Love, these mixed souls doth mix again,
> And makes both one, each this and that.

—Thrice, in other words, she says.

—Yes.

—Did you love the women you said it to?

—Yes, er, at least I believed I did at the time.

—I see.

—Do you? What do you see?

—I'm not sure. Something, maybe, she says.

—Something? What?

—I couldn't say.

—What could you say?

She takes a drink of wine and says, looking at him steadily now:

—That we, as a society, perhaps, are too jaded to believe that what we see when we connect with someone is anything other than a reflection of our own desires and needs. Agreed?

—It's a theory.

A single violet transplant,
The strength, the colour, and the size,
(All which before was poor, and scant)
Redoubles still, and multiplies.

—It is, she says. Nothing more.

—But we continue to look, regardless.

—Yes, she says. Yes, we do.

—And that's something, at any rate, then, he says.

—Yes.

—But are you saying, as you look into my eyes, that you're not sure that you are *capable* of seeing what is there? Or that there is perhaps nothing *there* to see?

—I'm not sure, she says.

—At least you're the honest type.

—Me, I'm not so sure.

—I'd like to know more about you.

—Join the club.

—I think you enjoy being evasive, he says. It keeps you apart from things. From people.

She doesn't answer, but looks him in the eye again. This guy is quite the package, alright, she thinks. She says:

—You want something from the hip? OK, try this: I'm married.

—But you, too, are looking for love. Any fool can see that.

—But I'm married.

—You say the words, but your heart isn't in them, which makes them merely contractual, not human. Legal terminology, nothing more.

—Nothing less.

—Nothing, really, at all.

—But still.

—Still what? How long have you been separated?

> When love, with one another so
> Interinanimates two souls,
> That abler soul, which thence doth flow,
> Defects of loneliness controls.

—I didn't say I was separated.

—No, you didn't.

—Not long. It's complicated, I don't want to talk about it.

—You really were in love, once, but it was too heavy, too (as you say) complicated, so now you want something … less demanding, emotionally.

—Have you been talking to Andrea? Conspiring, with her?

—The word 'love', the word itself, has become too heavy, almost as heavy as you feel your heart is. Yet you don't want to be alone. You want to be surrounded by people.

—This party is Andrea's idea. A birthday for Serena, a 'coming out' for me.

—And a typical gesture, something good friends do. Gets you back into the swim of things.

—Great phrase that.

—Andrea's great.

—She's swell. No, really, I couldn't have made it through this without her.

—Of course not, he says. But then, you're not through it, are you? Not really I mean.

—No, she says.

—I'm bringing you down.

—You're analysing me to death.

—Forgive me. It's only because, like I said before in different words, I'm a serious person. It keeps me bringing things like this up.

—Right, she says. Have *you* ever been in love?

—You already asked.

—I did, didn't I?

—Let me ask you something: that story you were telling at the table, the one about Japan and the fellow who ... urinated in....

—In moving bodies of water.

—Yes, something still bothers you about it.

—Hardly.

—No, I know, I can see, despite your theory: there's a ghost in there, inside!

He taps on the side of her skull with his index finger, three times, quite casually, and yet with a gentle purposefulness that makes her eyes widen, slightly.

—The elimination habits of men hardly keep me up at night. Remember that Bruce Cockburn song? 'Grey-suited business-men, pissing against the wall?' Well, I've seen it a gazillion times, so, whatever! You guys can be as flaky and boorish as you want to be, piss anywhere you like, I couldn't care less. Really.

—No, that's not what I mean.

—What do you mean?

—I mean—what was your boyfriend's name, the one you were with at the time, in Japan?

—Tim? What about him?

—Were you in love?

—No, not really, no.

 Silence. A piercing stare. Creepy.

—OK, OK, I dunno. No, yes, hey, whatever, we were young. Love?

 More Silence. What's with this guy?

—You think *Tim's* my ghost? Hardly! And why do you just keep staring like that, who are you, I don't even know you!

—I'd like you to.

—I'm not saying I'd mind that, but don't you think you're a bit … *intense*, I mean for a party anyway?

—That's who I am.

—You really have the most … *ascetic* gaze, you know!

—So they tell me.

—Who does?

—Oh, all the girls.

—Ha-ha. I see.

—But tell me something, Amē....

—Semi-seriously?

—At least, yes.

—At most! I'm not in the mood for serious.

—When were you last?

—What?

—Serious.

—About what?

—Anyone, anything.

—Somewhere in the '80s I guess, she says. Why?

—What happened?

> We then, who are this new soul, know,
> Of what we are composed, and made,
> For, th' atomies of which we grow,
> Are souls, whom no change can invade.

—Things happen. You live, you see a lot of things you maybe didn't want to. About the world, about yourself, each other, I dunno. You get tired. You may commit, for a while, but you don't *invest*. You—why am I talking to you?

—Because you like it when someone takes you seriously.

—I like it but I don't like it, she says. Like I said. Want another drink?

—Sure, if you promise to finish your story.

—I did finish!

—I sensed there was more. More in there, he says, tapping lightly at her skull again.

—Less than you'd think. But yeah, there's more to it, the story I mean. But it's kinda sad, I'd rather not, not tonight.

—If you wish.

He stares at her again, intent but, she senses, not without compassion. They're good at this, she thinks, these wealthy ones. Enough time on their hands to learn a trick or two. Good at making you think that they'd like to feel what you feel. But what if you *don't* feel: what then, huh?

—Oh, hell, OK OK, you go grab those chairs by the gas fire and I'll fetch some more wine, OK *desu né?*

5

THE ONE THAT GOT AWAY:

1991, MONTREAL

5:30 a.m., July 15, 1991
St. Swithin's Day, Montreal
Forecast: Rain

My dearest Louise,

Happy Anniversary, my love. I couldn't sleep, got
up early. It's daybreak, but overcast here, seems
more like a winter night than a summer morning. I
miss you.

I know you told me not to call or write, that we
agreed that this was a trial separation, and that
you needed both space and time. I don't expect you
to write back, I just hope that this letter can go
some way towards repairing the damage I may have
done to our relationship, to explain to you where
I'm coming from.

You said, as you left, that you could not respect
a man who kept his past hidden, a secret. You said
that I lied to you, and that the effect was that you
could no longer distinguish fact from fiction, as
far as our life together was concerned: my past (or
my partial accounting of it) bled into our present, tainting it for you, perhaps irreparably.

You said that that was why you were going home to
Boston, for the summer. I respect that. Or, at least,
I'm trying to. But please respect my attempt here
to 'clear the air'. I love you very much — how many
times have I told you that you are my 'America'? If
I have lied to you or withheld the truth from you in
the past, it was only because I loved you so much.
I know that sounds strange, but as Richard Nixon
once said, it also has the merit of being true.

I guess I have always been afraid to lose you,
afraid that if you really got to know me, to know
all of my faults, that you could never love me, that
you would go. When we met, I was seeing a girl that
I did not love; you know this much. But the truth
is, I think, that I was with her because being with
someone helped me get over Ame, whom you read about
when you looked through my journal (which was a
wrong thing to do, you have to admit).

Ame was 'the one that got away', you said, and my
not telling you about her was just one more huge lie
'sitting atop a mountain of other lies'. Yes, I did
love Ame, but she wasn't mine to love. I don't know
if she even loved me back: she never said. In any

event, there was nothing physical between us, and
we were never lovers. I wince as I write that word,
'lovers': you were right about it, and now it makes
me feel the same way. (Can't you see how, how on
many levels, we are of the same mind, almost as if
we had the same mind? Is that why you left? Are you
as afraid of our closeness as I am of losing you?)

I am sending along my attempt to set the matter
straight— my mock heroic origin story, if you will.
Please take the time to read it: I believe that all
that happened to us is connected, somehow, to certain aspects of my childhood and adolescence, but
I also grant that it's possible that I may just be
adding more lies to the top of the mountain here,
lies that I'm telling myself to convince myself (and
you!) of something, of my innocence perhaps.

Perhaps: that may be, but I honestly think otherwise, just as I honestly think we can work this out.

Remember when the old lady at the Smoked Meat
place on St. Laurent thought we were brother and
sister, and then we saw Jonathan Richman in that
tiny club hours later and he looked at us, right in
the eyes, as he sang us a song about exactly the
same thing?

I do.

Love,

Isaac

6

Like Soldiers Do: 1985, Montreal

MY BROTHER has been here since '83, studying at McGill: dismal, most dismal, Economics. Me, I'm the ingénue, I've just arrived, I'm the rookie freshman centre for Concordia, third line, and today I'm having a coffee with my brother's girlfriend. I meet her on the corner of St. Viatur and Parc, as arranged, but she keeps me waiting for twenty minutes, well past the eleventh hour, in a cold, unforgiving Remembrance Day rain. Don't worry, it doesn't matter, I say when she turns up and semi-apologizes, her dark eyes willfully innocent, her small mouth frozen in a half of a half-smile.

She is wearing a yellow rubber raincoat, her long black hair hidden beneath the hood, and she's perched atop one of those Polish foldaway bicycles with the miniature wheels, peddling effortlessly as I jog along St. Viatur beside her in a soaked-through, windbreaker that I once stole from Gerald. The jacket is sky-blue nylon, with a white cotton liner; the arms are way too short and it only hangs down to my belly button, but for some reason I've refused to get myself a new one.

What remains of my lank blonde hair is plastered to my head. I'm not wearing a hat.

—Isaac the twelve year-old, refusing to come in from the rain, she says to me maternally, outside the café where she needlessly locks up her beloved but decrepit bike.

—It hardly ever rained that year, I say simply. She looks at me uncomprehendingly.

—Huh? she says.

—Never mind, Amē, I say.

—Nice coat, she says.

—Huh? I say.

The sleeve of my jacket has gold cursive stitching on it. On the front it says 'Duxbury, Bantam 'A' Hockey.' On the right sleeve: 'Gerald 17 Right Wing', just below an American flag. We're inside now, and I'm shivering uncontrollably. She speaks in a matter-of-fact voice, without enthusiasm, almost as if telling her aunt Rose or her neighbour Mrs. Love what she is 'up to' these days. But my reticence keeps her talking, filling the gaps, until:

—Isaac, I'm going away.

—I … know, I say, with the hesitation of a reluctantly willing accomplice. My teeth chatter.

—Japan. New Year's day. I haven't told Gerald yet.

—Oh?

—I can't, she admits, after a moment's pause, while we both contemplate the Formica table, our coffees, the hip mid-afternoon clientele, the ill-paid but attractive Polish staff, the 1960s French *Nouvelle Vague* cinema posters on the wall, anything.

—You can't...?

—Face up to this.

—No.

—Isaac, tell me a story.

—What do you mean?

—To take my mind off things.

—Off what? I ask, but she doesn't answer. She is crying now. Blood has rushed to my face.

I look down, look away. A woman's voice, but with Billy Bragg's Essex accent, is coming from the loudspeakers, accompanied only by a heavily distorted but quite melodic electric guitar. I recognize the tune immediately: 'Like Soldiers Do', a song that speaks to me about a patrimony—a legacy whispered from one Y-chromosome to another, an inheritance that weighs like a nightmare upon the brains of the living—in which we are given strictly enforced marching orders that conscript us into a Gender War that seems to persist from one unquestioning generation to the next....

She's a good singer, I'll give her that. But she's changed the words:

He landed in a poppy field
He'd caught his own reflection in her shield
Just as love soared past the sun
And turned it black
His father was a soldier
Her son a soldier too
A nuclear family bonds
Like soldiers do

—What kind of story? I ask pointlessly, because I know what kind. And so I tell her. I tell her what I need to tell, and what she needs to hear.

—You know, she says.

—Well, I'm gonna have to read it, then, I say, and I reach into my brother's jacket pocket to pull out what I'd prepared for this day.

7

DEATH AND THE HONOR SYSTEM:

1976, DUXBURY

IT WAS MY BIRTHDAY. The *Hockey Night in Canada* song came on the TV, the most comforting sound in the world. It meant dad was safe in his cave, avidly inert for a few blessed hours.

Gerald pretended to be oblivious. Gerald was on his side of the masking tape dividing line, playing with his crystal radio. It didn't look like much, but he kept it hidden under the bed when he wasn't fiddling with it. He'd grounded it by running a discreet wire through the window, down to a nail that he'd driven into the sod outside. Dad didn't know about this, yet.

It was mid-week, American Thanksgiving was just around the corner, my mom was away, and the Montreal Canadiens were on a road trip. Tonight they were in Boston, only 47 miles north on Highway 3, so dad could've watched them play on the local channel, but that wouldn't've been the same. He needed Danny Gallivan's play-by-play, Dick Irvin's colour, the *Molson Ex* back-to-the-woods commercials, 'Me and the Boys and our *50*'. Dad drank *50*, when he could get it (there was a French-Canadian store in Lowell that imported it with irregularity); I'd kind of grown to like it myself. And although I played the game well, I didn't really like hockey, and I wouldn't have a clear sense of what it meant to my dad until I moved north, years later, as a transfer student. But even then, I was certain that I wanted to be a Canadian too (whatever that meant), like Dad.

Gerald hated hockey. Gerald hated Canada. Gerald hated me. He was 14, I was 12.

Dad had an illegal C-band satellite dish hooked up, the only one in town. We had a couple of acres, and he made a clearing in the woods for it, on a slope that led down to a disused cranberry bog, and strung an illicit wire to the house, knowing that the rich people who were in charge of things wouldn't have given their approbation if they had found out. The rich people spoke in what sounded to us like English accents and hated most anything new. Our town didn't have a MCDONALDS or BURGER KING or anything. All new buildings had to look old. All old buildings had to look good. We were the second or third or fourth oldest town in Massachusetts, two towns north of Plymouth Rock. Pilgrims like Miles Standish had once lived here, and everyone who was anyone claimed to be descended from stock such as his.

— Stock such as his? Isn't that a bit cliché? Amē says.

— Hey, this is *my* story, as bad as it is.

— Yeah but….

— So listen:

Everyone who was anyone's dad drove MASERATIS or ALFA ROMEOS, and every now and then a drunk blonde kid would kill his-or-herself and a few friends by driving off one of our many little bridges into one of our many tidal pools and streams. We had a big bridge, too, a half-mile-long wooden one which went out to our town's six-mile-long beach. You couldn't drive across the bridge and park unless your car had a town sticker on it, so the non-resident riffraff were generally absent. But it was a great beach. We'd go there nearly every day in the summer, eat potato chips and drink soda and lie in the sun.

The beach was a long peninsula, with two sides, the ocean side, where all the sand was, and the bay side, where all the living things were. Dad stepped on a horseshoe crab's tail there once; he nearly had to have his foot amputated because of the infection. They stick them straight up out of the sand, the crabs do, Gerald said while we were in the hospital waiting for Dad. It's to protect themselves, pretty clever, huh?

One day, Gerald came home from his paper route and went to make a hamburger with our new hamburger making machine, the kind that makes grilled sandwiches too. But I'd beaten him to it, as I was hungry after school and I'd used up the last of the hamburger. Gerald was pissed. You're a little shithead, Isaac, he'd said to me, a real little peckerhead. I'll always remember that because it was the first time I'd ever heard him swear. That was around the time when the masking tape dividing line went up. We'd done it before, of course, but always for fun. But it wasn't just the hamburger that was at issue here, I knew that. There was more to it.

Dad worked for a defence contractor, Mr Jones, who lived up the street a ways. His house was *real* big — and so was he, and so was everyone else in his family. He used to be a policeman in Brookline, where Rocky Marciano came from, that's where the plant was too, but somehow he got into making things for the Air Force. That's when he moved to Duxbury and built a house with a tennis court and an indoor pool. There were carp in the pond beside our house because he'd needed to do something with the goldfish which graced that pool for his fat kids' birthday. They were twins, and they rode around on Golf Carts and we used to throw rocks at them, but then they told their dad and he told our dad and our dad put a stop to it.

The fat kids went to Parochial school. We were Catholics, too, but it cost a lot of money, so we didn't. We went to Duxbury High and got our Religious Ed. in different Catholic ladies' basements. We sat in circles a lot, boys and girls together, and had to hold hands when we prayed, which I didn't mind but which Gerald hated, even though he was two years older. He was shy around girls.

We saw lots of filmstrips too. The one that scared me the most was the one about Abraham, whose wife was old and couldn't have kids. Then God gave them one, which was good in a way, but then God told Abraham to sacrifice the kid, which made no sense at all, and turned out to be a bluff anyways, but it was scary nonetheless. I mean, yeah, sure, there's the obvious name thing with the son, but Abraham, who'd seemed so good and righteous and caring, was all of a sudden ready to slit the kid's throat like he was a sheep or calf or some other dumb animal.

Some God, some dad, I said to Mrs. Holiday, our teacher. Her daughter, Elizabeth, was the first girl Gerald ever had a crush on. Elizabeth wore Fair Isle sweaters, bore a striking resemblance to that girl with the 'naturally curly hair' in the Peanuts cartoon, and, even though she herself wasn't blond, dated a blond soccer player who sold Microdots at school. She sailed for the Yacht Club and had no time for Gerald, and I told him so. He stared at me like he didn't know what I was talking about. He looked at me like he was going to say 'Elizabeth who?' or 'Shut up, dickwad'. But he didn't. He just stared.

God was testing Abraham, Mrs. Holiday said. It was a test, to see if Abraham was faithful. People back then did those kinds of things, Isaac, Gerald chimed in, in an ambiguously matter-of-fact voice that made me wonder if he was trying to assuage my concerns or embarrass me. They were barbaric, he said, not civilized like us. We've progressed.

I was called Isaac in honour of dad's brother, and also my great-uncle. Dad had been Jewish before he met my mom, but not the real religious kind. He'd been a communist back in Montreal, too, something which I didn't understand at all, but which I knew had to be bad. You mean he's Russian? I asked after making discreet inquires amongst my friends, all of whom were as clueless as I. Gerald looked like *he* knew, but Gerald wouldn't answer.

I asked my dad about the Abraham thing, which I knew he'd like, because he was sure religious nowadays, going to church weekdays sometimes too, though he wasn't showy or talky about it at all, which both Gerald and I respected. Dad was serious and quiet, when he wasn't in one of his moods, and liked to talk to us about books and things. Gerald read way more than I did, but I still loved to hear my dad talk.

It's a little complicated, my dad said about my Abraham question. But it comes down to trust. God needed to know if Abraham trusted him completely, more than anything or anyone else.

That wasn't really a satisfactory answer, so I asked another question. Dad, are you a communist?

What do you mean by communist?

I don't know, I said. But it's a bad thing, right?

That would depend upon what you meant by the word, he said, pausing to look at me look at him, as if I thought he was playing with me. I was, but he wasn't.

I believe, he said, choosing his words the way we'd choose candy at the store, with a deadly, earnest deliberation, I believe that God is Love. We belong to Him. Everything we have belongs to Him, and He gives us this world because he wants us to be happy. But we, being human, think that *we're* the ones responsible for everything we have or don't have, and that we don't have to share with anyone if we don't want to. And the way we humans have set up the world is so that some have lots of things and others have very little, or even nothing.

That's not right, I said.

No, it's not, he said.

But, are you a communist? I said

What's a communist? he said.

Dad! I don't know! I said. That's why I'm asking! Look it up, son, he said. Look it up.

That was dad on a good day. He had quite a few like that. But there were other, not-so-good days, too. I don't think he liked working for Mr. Jones.

—Why not? Amē asks.

She knows why not. Gerald had gone over much of the same territory with her, but she wants to hear it all again, one last time, from me.

I oblige, and speak as calmly and deliberately as I can, pretending, so I can tell the story as honestly as possible, that we have only recently made acquaintance.

Dad had been a poet, or a writer of some kind anyhow, when he was a student. It had been his dream, I heard him say a couple of times to my mother, that his avocation might one day become his vocation, and when he was young it had felt tangible, palpable. But now it came to him only from time to time, in the occasional nocturnal dream, gossamer shadows flickering on the film screen of the imagination for an hour or two every now and then before the lights came on. And the lights always do come on, and life comes first, real life, and with it the three of us to feed, to care for and worry over.

Life came first for all of us. Gerald got over his crush on Elizabeth Holiday, but then started following around this girl who was at our bus stop. She was small, really skinny, and her hair was like Rapunzel's, but redredred. She was certainly pretty, but she always looked like she wanted to be somewhere else, like riding horses maybe, and she never talked to any of us. I don't think she knew that Gerald existed, and I told him so. He started timing his walks to the bus stop, so they would coincide with hers.

The Religious Ed. filmstrips at this time had to do with martyrs. Many saints, it seemed, had been called upon to give up their lives for what they believed in. The latest filmstrip was on John F. Kennedy. He was from Boston, like the bands The Cars and Aerosmith (and, of course, Boston), and so we all paid attention to this. President Kennedy had done many brave deeds in World War II, in his boat PT109. President Kennedy and his wife Jacqueline had made America into a new Camelot. But more importantly, President Kennedy had sacrificed his life for the Church, and for America. For freedom. Your freedom. My freedom. Freedom from war, freedom from communism. Mrs. Buttons, the parent-teacher for this unit, played Elton John's 'Your Song' afterwards, and talked about where she'd been when the great man was shot and this got us all crying, even the most reserved of the boys, even Gerald. Then Mrs. Buttons gave us all copies of the lyrics. We would be performing it, she informed us, with the Children's folk choir at Thanksgiving.

The year was 1976, and we had a very dry September and October. It didn't even rain once. The leaves fell early, all at the same time, and we made forts out of them. Then Gerald and his friend Victor got a parcel in the mail. Cherry Bombs! Smoke Bombs! Bottle Rockets! It astounded us that the post office would deliver such things, straight to our house, since they were illegal in the Commonwealth of Massachusetts. Anyhow, we could now make real use out of our forts, and so we promptly, efficiently, chose sides.

I'd never liked Victor. We were middle class, and he was working class, but I don't think that was the only reason. There was also the fact that he was even more nerdy, even more of a *naïf* than we were, but there had to be more to it than that. It was probably jealousy.

Jealousy. No, I'd never liked Victor, but I'd always worshipped my brother, had always followed him around. He was two years older, but I went wherever he went, did whatever he did. Watched the same shows, listened to the same music, played the same games. I turned out to be better at sports than him, but he never seemed to mind. When we fought, it was usually on the same Side, against our classmates, or our neighbours, or whomever.

For the draft-picks Gerald, who had invented the Game, made himself General. He knew, of course, that I was the best shot, the fastest runner, had the best arm. But he chose Victor first, and

Gipper Welch, the other General, predictably chose his own best friend (8th grade 'most likely to succeed') Brian Buttons. When Gerald chose one of the Kennedy twins next, Gipper shot him an 'are you retarded?' look, gestured in my direction like he was going to choose me, but then took the other twin—in order, it seemed, to make a point.

—And what point was that? she asks.

—To force the issue. Of why Gerald was not choosing me. Gipper was going to twist Gerald's arm; he was going to *make* Gerald choose me.

—Did he?

He did. He pretty well had to. But in the fourth round. Just before 'ludicrous', but just after 'painfully obvious to all concerned'. So here we had two rather obvious clues that something was up with my brother. I pretended that I didn't notice, but it would have been disingenuous of me to say that I didn't feel hurt: we had always done everything together, and now, here was Gerald, becoming … someone else. Why?

Here's why. Or, here's how I felt about it at the time, because now, I'm not so sure. But in 1976, I thought it was, well, *very* clear, and on the surface. Sure, part of it had to do with dad, with those episodes he always had, every so often. He'd always had them, but they were starting to really piss Gerald off. But part of it also had to do with me.

As for dad's part: Mom had been away for 36 hours, and the place was a mess, he said, shouted actually, while we stood in front of his barber's chair, in the basement, where he sat.

He called her Mom too, never by her name, at least in front of us. But this was not disconcerting to us at the time, because, to Gerald and me, she *was* Mom, not Margaret Mary. Her family called her that, while friends called her Marjie. Letters that came to the house addressed her as Mrs. Harold Tibbs.

Mom was still away, and would stay away for *another* 36 hours too, which was not something that Gerald and I were looking forward to, for it meant listening to dad rant and rave, quite steadily, until her return.

He was not a drunk; he was always quite sober when he delivered his 'lectures', which was generally about once or twice a month, and which *always* took place in Mom's absence. We never complained to her about them, and she never said anything to us, but I was sure, even then, that she knew about them, on some level.

Yes, mom was far away, as he sat in his barber's chair, cracked red leather atop scratched porcelain-on-steel. He'd gotten it from his father's barber shop when we were little, after his father, Theobald, had died. What was the significance of that chair? What did it represent?—the emotional topography of a land that was foreign to us boys, because we never really knew our grandfather, a German-speaking Jew who had brought his own two sons from the Czech Sudetenland in the 1930s, and who had lived near and worked on Rue-St.-Viatur from the day he arrived in Montreal until the day he died. Grandfather somehow had a different surname (Hauer) from ours (Tibbs) — what was up with that?

Dad sat in his barber's chair, and we stood in front of him, listening, taking it in, just taking it: We knew that this was merely one of his Episodes, that he didn't really mean it, but of course there was the distinct, nagging possibility that he did. He was kind, gentle and thoughtful at other times, why did this have to happen?

You'd be forgiven for asking a different question: why did we even put up with it? Necessity, I guess, on a number of levels, but a part of that necessity was also love. In any event, people will put up with a hell of a lot when they feel they don't have a choice.

We had always put up with it, it seemed, ever since we could remember. But *now* Gerald — wait. You have to understand *why* Gerald....

I can't be-*lieve* you two! Dad said. I just can't believe it! The house is a mess, the kitchen a dis-*as*-ter! I take you to play hockey, and this is the thanks I get? Is it? Is this the thanks?

Well, no, in a word, but listen: the whole way back from hockey, the thirty-minute drive from the Pembroke rink, had turned into a compressed, well, all-too-familiar *étude*, but one which, if possible, resembled nothing so much as a neo-Wagnerian operetta, performed *alla breve* and with uncompromising dissonance by a well-rehearsed yet over-enthusiastic trio of Aryan Blackshirts: the recitatives were generally homophonic, the tonal centre always my father's supple, yet daringly accidental, chromatic tenor. Our own grace notes careened back and forth from a *doloroso*, muttered *basso-profundo* to whispered, whimpering *falsetto*. The libretto was reliably melodramatic, replete with staggering alliteration, mixed metaphor and bathetic juxtaposition, while the score was always *fortissimo*, predictably *accelerando*, and, as we neared the Duxbury town limits, mounted to what should have been a climactic, cathartic *agitato*. But then a sudden, *ad libitum* rest led to an interlude performed on the car radio (680 WRKO Boston) by the rock band Queen, while Gerald and I opened our second helpings of Mountain Dew and sipped from the now-warm cans in silence, the considerable levels of caffeine having made us, as Gerald (who was fond of port-manteau words) would put it, 'twired'. The second act would commence when we got home, staged in our concrete-floored and therefore acoustically live basement.

It wasn't (my father began again, once more from the top) it wasn't that we had lost our game against Hull. It wasn't even that the score was 8-0. No. It was that, as a team, we had shown ourselves to be self-centred idlers as well. Our passing, to the extent that there was any, he said, was simply deplorable (the actual word, one of his stock favourites, a word that sings like a dentist's drill in my head to this day, was 'appalling'). Our appalling wingers, excepting, of course, Gerald (who had other issues of his own, with which we were all quite familiar and to which he would be returning in due course), our wingers backchecked with the frequency and orientation of Halley's comet, hanging out whenever possible near centre ice with their backs to the action, but with their heads turned around with an absurd impatience, waiting with unshakeable faith for the defence to complete, on their own, an unlikely breakout from our end. And whenever the puck did manage to randomly bounce into Hull's end, into one of the corners, our wingers had the stick-to-itiveness of Teflon. Moreover, our defensemen for their part were unfailingly polite, Lady Byng nominees all, deferentially removing themselves from in front of the net so that they could look on—admiringly—as Hull's forwards could practice their slapshots in the slot. Etc.

Gerald had gotten knocked around a lot, and it was his own fault. He had three inches and fifteen pounds over dad (who was short, wiry, intense), but dad had never let anyone push him around the way Gerald did, not on the ice anyway. As for me, I was tougher, dad said, but definitely too much of a hothead, and I couldn't argue there. I was quite big for my age, playing up a league, and I didn't take any shit from anybody, especially not those goons from Hull, who were all a good three or four inches taller than most of our players.

Late in the second period, already ahead 5-0, Hull had switched its focus from scoring to maiming, continually stepping over the line and getting awarded penalties so often that, it had seemed, they'd played the rest of the game short-handed. This, however, had gotten in the way of neither their hitting nor their scoring. Finally, with thirty seconds to go in the game, after I had dumped the puck into Hull's end and Gerald had bravely chased it into the corner, a particularly unevolved monster in one of those hemi-spherical Stan Makita helmets had gone after him, charging at him from forty feet out and driving him into the board head-first. His helmet had taken the brunt of the impact, and had fallen to pieces on the ice.

Gerald couldn't get up. He was conscious, all right, but he lay still on the ice, staring at the rafters. I circled slowly 'round and 'round Hull's net. The Neanderthal who'd hit Gerald just stood by the boards, near his team bench, unconcerned, awaiting his penalty the way he might wait for a hamburger at WENDY'S. He rested his gloves on the butt-end of his stick, and his chin on his gloves, his head tilted to the side, and wearing a blank, yet some-how impatient expression. I circled, Gerald moved to his knees, paused, tried to stand up. My circles grew larger. Cro-Magnon man began joking with team-mates, orangutans all, who were now milling about him as Gerald stood, wobbled, fell back to the ice, got up on all fours, collapsed back down, as if under the weight of an invisible force field. One of my team-mates' fathers, a doctor, came down from the stands and onto the ice. I stopped my circling, glided noiselessly over to Gorilla-boy, holding my stick like a baseball bat. He didn't see me coming: I smashed at his ankle with everything I had, dropped my gloves and fell with him to the ice, ripped off his helmet and managed to knock several teeth out of his mouth before the refs could pry me away.

That was the beginning of my role in our family melodrama, as far as I could tell. It was several days before Gerald called me peckerhead, if I remember properly, and the day before the thing with the forts....

This will not do, dad continued, this will just *not* DO. I'd been suspended from the league for the rest of the season. Gerald did not seem to be injured, the doctor had said, which was good, but I'd been suspended, which was bad.

The doctor had eventually managed to get Gerald to his feet and had escorted him off the ice, guiding him by the arm. I followed at a respectful distance, my team-mates patting me on the shoulder-pads and tapping their sticks on my shin-pads and butt, congratulating me in manly voices.

In the dressing room the jocular mood (the kind guys get into after witnessing a good 'scrap') continued, because the coach was still on the ice arguing with the ref about my suspension, and none of the parents had arrived yet. Gerald seemed fine, if a little dazed.

He joked too, with the others, perhaps a bit sheepishly, about the hit—I'm not sure if I'm reading back into this or not—but then one of them yelled out *Que es mas macho?*—which was a gag on *Saturday Night Live* at the time. Then the others all chanted back, in unison, I-*saac!*—meaning, of course, that I was more macho than that puffed-up tarsier from Hull, but Gerald took it differently. I noticed a strange mood come over him, but couldn't say anything because just then the coach came in—and behind him, not advancing through the doorway, our father.

He said nothing, but a nod of his head in the direction of the parking lot meant that he'd be waiting out in the car. Gerald and I quickly undid our skates, grabbed our bags, helmets, gloves and sticks, and hurried out to the parking lot. We were still wearing our sweat-saturated equipment, and it chafed our underarms, elbows, knees and inner thighs as we moved with reluctant speed towards our fate, towards the lecture that awaited us.

We stank, was all he said as we got in. He was saving his best lines for later. And it was true: we did. We smelled to the highest of high heaven. We besmirched, befouled, bedevilled the automotive environment with our meat-eater musk. Pepé le Pieu—that amorous innocent, that suave cartoon skunk hunk who blithely carried pandemonium with him wherever he went—had nothing on us, and our subjective noses, like Pepé's, were blissfully ignorant of our own objective reality. Yet neither Gerald nor I would have cared in the least if we had become aware of it, since as the entire hockey team assessed the matter, smelliness was akin to manliness, and it was esteemed to be a matter of honour and duty to abstain from washing your equipment for the entire season. At any rate, we had no choice but to keep our gear on all through the harangue that followed in the basement, for there could be no question of our showering and changing first. As harangues went, it was typical of its kind, and did not deviate from an all-too-familiar template:

(i.)   Introduce problem as rhetorical question

(ii.) Circumnavigate problem, lingering, as a lover might, indefatigably over each microcosmic detail

(iii.) Pass immediate judgement, assign considerable blame

(iv.) Discover heretofore unnoticed, seemingly trivial facets of problem, without which problem cannot be properly (perhaps even possibly) understood

(v.)   Obsess over said minor details until it becomes undeniably clear that they are, in fact, major—that is, that they are crucial to the penetration of the core, to the essence of problem

(vi.) Elaborate, with lyrical passion, dramatic palpability and epic domain-and-range, upon the who-what-where-when-and-whys of the give-and-take of blame (vii.) Repeat

(viii.) Repeat

(ix.) Repeat

That is, there was no deviation until Gerald said, surprisingly: I think I've heard about enough.

Silence, and the two men (I was only just beginning to realize that Gerald was being drafted into the major leagues) stared at one another. Finally, perhaps a little unnerved by his own new-found nerviness, who knows? Gerald said:

Enough, get it?

And he turned and walked away, moving with a bit too much deliberation, as if he were a drunk trying to evade the gaze of the police, or someone who had just noticed his Ex on the street, and making too much of a show at pretending that he hadn't. He plod-ded up the stairs, each of which protested loudly as he went, and then, I could hear, made his way towards the front of the house. Dad followed him at a fair distance, and I followed dad, each of us speechless and free-will-less, as if in a trance.

When we got to the main floor we saw him standing at the front entrance to the house. He'd opened the main door, but hadn't let go of the knob. He looked back, over his shoulder, smirking as if to say: I'm not really looking over my shoulder, I'm not look-ing at you, and then he shoved his hand through the glass of the storm door.

I knew where he was going, too. He walked down the driveway, his hand bleeding. He was going to Victor's.

Dad never said a word about the window. It got fixed before Mom returned home. And that would prove to have been our final lecture. Things was changin', alright, the wheel was turnin'. Gerald was ascending, Dad descending. But what about me? Where was I going? Where was I?

The game was called *Shot In The Dark*. Before, as kids, we'd played it with cap guns, plastic FISHER-PRICE milk bottles, and a FISHER-PRICE milk truck. It was suitable for three or more people, preferably more. We took it in turns to be the one with the gun, the Outsider, the Vigilante. This individual would have to descend into a pitch-black, basement Rec Room that had been turned into one huge fort of overturned tables, couches, cushions and vinyl bean-bag chairs. The fort was re-arranged after every round, so that the lone gunslinger would have no foreknowledge of where things were or where the others might be hiding. He'd have to descend the stairs and enter a confusing and threatening world where he and he alone was fighting for Truth and Justice. More often than not, of course, evil would triumph, for the Hero's task was an exceedingly difficult one: to navigate blindly through what amounted to a giant labyrinthine mousetrap; to kill, if need be, a corporate enemy (whose name, of course, was Legion), each member of which was vying with the others for the privilege of assassinating the invader with a tossed milk bottle; to re-capture, ultimately, the stolen milk truck; and to re-establish, if only momentarily, a moral universe that had been, and that would again be, overturned—all this, all to earn the right to begin again, to re-enter the trap and to pitch oneself against one's ultimate fate one more time.

As we grew older, the game evolved along with us. We took it outside, expanded its scope, evangelized it to more of our friends, and instinctively proceeded to base it upon what seemed to us to be a more plausible cosmology. Gone was the series of solitary messiahs pitched against an army of vipers (though each real, flesh-and-blood saviour was doomed to fail in the earlier version of the game, it was always understood that the ideal hero, the saviour-at-the-end-of-time, would somehow ultimately prevail). In its place we erected the amoral, Manichean nationalism of the chessboard, in which the forces of light and dark were both opposite and equal, and were locked in perpetual, ineluctable struggle. But we did not impute 'goodness' or 'evil' upon the binary black and white of our game; such terms were empty of meaning within its boundaries. Rather, we simply divided the world into 'Us' and 'Them'.

Gipper pretty well forced my brother to choose me, but I could see the masking-tape dividing-line flash briefly across the surface of Gerald's eyes. Then he dismissed the thought and pressed professionally on to the task at hand, calling his Side to order while the other team went off to their own fort, to their own flag. It was nearly dusk. Both Gerald and Victor were dressed in Camo gear they'd ordered from *Soldier of Fortune* magazine. Victor—distant, formal, rigid—stood by his side, holding on to a green garbage bag-full of equipment, while Gerald addressed us rooks, bishops, knights and pawns.

It is nearly dusk, he said. We 'won' the coin toss, as you know, and Gipper will be expecting us to attack quickly and with full force as soon as it's dark. He thinks we'll be going balls-out on this one, all impatient and hasty, and I'd like him to go on thinking that. That's why I'm going to send two of you out with half our ammunition and all of our smoke bombs, to stage a diversionary invasion. More on that later. Victor, give Bobby the extra Cammo gear. Bobby, you're going to be *The Man* tonight; you're going out behind us to the road, and circle around behind them while they're busy being diverted, and just waltz right in and take their flag, all by your lonesome. They'll have a skeleton crew manning the fort, but they won't be watching their backside. They'll be worrying about holding off our full-bore 'attack', while the rest of them will be coming at us from all sides, expecting there'll be as few of us here as they've got at *their* fort, thinking they can confuse us and overwhelm us & grab our flag before we can grab theirs. But, of course, thinking that, they'll be wrong.

We didn't ask how Gerald knew this. We knew how he knew it. He'd placed a mole inside Gipper's organization, bribing Mike Mullaney with a *gross* of bottle rockets, and had let Gipper choose him for the Other Side. This may or may not have been fair, but it was not yet against the rules. And Mike had reported on Gipper's strategy to his real boss at 1630 hours, at the suppertime break, when the two forts had been readied.

We reassembled at 1743 hours. I was chosen to lead the diversionary invasion, with Bobby's twin brother Jack as my aide-de-camp. *Tora! Tora! Tora!* I said to Jack, who had seen the movie of the same name and understood what I meant by it: the two of us were being sent out as Kamikazes, and would not be expected to return. We would be outnumbered 2.5 to 1, and our only hope of emerging unscathed was our considerable supply of smoke bombs, with which we were to convince Gipper's side that we were a much more potent force than we really were.

Smoke bombs are about two inches long, and $\frac{5}{8}^{\text{ths}}$ of an inch in diameter, the same size as an M-80. We had two dozen of them, which would last us about 9 minutes if we deployed them in judicious one-minute intervals, after an initial volley of six, which needed to be within five to ten seconds of each other in order to create the requisite 'wall-of-smoke' that Gerald had ordered.

Add to that the half-gross of bottle rockets we were to launch, as well as the two-dozen belts of firecracker grenades and the full dozen of M-80 mortar bombs, and we had a lot to deal with, and needed to pay attention. We wouldn't have much chance to watch out for incoming rounds. We've got a fighting chance, anyway, Jack said optimistically. Perhaps, I said, Perhaps.

Gerald called both Sides out into No-Man's Land for a review of the rules. He had typed them, using Mom's ultra-hefty IBM *Selectric* typewriter (pilfered from dad's office at JONESCO) onto the front and back of one of the white cardboard inserts from dad's drycleaned dress shirts. Then he had had them laminated down at the office supply store, so they were pretty much indestructible.

OK, he said, a lot of you already know the rules, but some of you are new. I won't say much about those who know the rules but don't care to keep them, except: watch it! So, anyway, here they are, the rules are as follows:

1. **The Game and Match:**
    a.) The goal of SITD (Shot In The Dark) is to capture the Other Side's *flag*.
    b.) When one Side's flag is captured all hostilities cease and the Game is *over*.

c.) The Side capturing the flag is declared to be the *winner of the Game*.

d.) The first Side to win 4 Games out of 7 is the *winner of the Match*.

e.) There shall be at most one Game contested per night, and no less than one per week.

f.) A tentative schedule will be posted by the Convenor. It will be the General's responsibility to delegate a Communications Officer, who will keep his Side informed of any scheduling changes.

2. Whistles:

a.) Each Side is supplied with a distinctive *whistle*.

b.) Each Side has a designated *whistle-blower*.

c.) *Hostilities* commence at dusk. 'Dusk' is defined by the mutual agreement of both Generals.

d.) Both Generals are said to be in agreement as to the arrival of dusk when one Side sounds its *whistle* and the Other Side sounds a reply.

e.) When a *flag* is captured the losing Side is obliged to sound its whistle a second time, signalling the end to all *hostilities*.

f.) Failure to sound the whistle *immediately* upon the capture of one's flag will result in the suspension of *both* the offending Side's *whistle-blower* AND General for 5 games.

g.) Each Side will make its designated whistle-blower *known to the Other* before the commencement of hostilities.

3. Combatants:

a.) Membership and participation in SITD is a privilege, and is *by invitation only*. No Yacht Club members allowed!

b.) Failure to comply with the Rules & Regulations of SITD may result in forfeiture of membership, at the discretion of the Convenor.

c.) Failure to pay membership dues will result in the forfeiture of the privilege of membership.

4. Death and the Honor System:

a.) If you get hit above the waist (but below the neck) with a bottle rocket, you are officially *Dead*.

b.) If you get hit below the waist with a bottle rocket, you are officially *Paralysed*, from the waist down.

c.) If you get hit in the arm with a bottle rocket, you officially *lose the use* of that arm.

d.) If you hit someone *else* in the head with a bottle rocket, *you* are officially *Dead*, while *they* are officially *Unharmed*.

e.) If you get hit with an exploding belt of firecrackers, you are officially *Dead*.

f.) If an exploding belt of firecrackers lands within one of your *own* stride lengths of any part of your anatomy, you are officially *Paralysed* from the waist down.

g.) If you are hit by, or are caught within 3 stride-lengths of an exploding M-80, you are officially, Unrecognizably, *Dead*. –Dead, Dead, *Dead*, D-E-D Dead.

h.) Failure to own up to, and to clearly (and with sufficient volume) announce your own *Demise*, will result in an immediate 3 game *suspension*.

5. Safety

a.) Protective eyewear is to be worn at all times, upon the commencement of *Hostilities*.

b.) Anyone who goes home crying to Mommy when they get hurt will be *set upon* and severely *beaten*!

c.) Never, ever, under any circumstances, allow ammunition to come into contact with *flammable objects*!

Carpe Diem! Gerald said finally, over much foot shuffling, and the two Sides went off to their respective fortresses. The Other Side blew their whistle shortly thereafter, and Gerald had without hesitation motioned to Victor's brother Piotr to do the same. Victor then electronically ignited the ceremonial ESTES rocket, whose launch heralded the beginning of the Autumn Test Match. The rocket, a yellow two-and-a-half foot-long cardboard-and-balsa stunner, had been built by Gerald and Victor, and sported a clear plastic payload tube near the nose. Gerald had placed three raw eggs in the tube, which would be jettisoned by an explosive charge as the rocket reached apogee, 4 or 5 seconds after the solid fuel ESTES engine ran out. It was unlikely, Victor unnecessarily said, that the eggs would drop anywhere nearby enough to have made it worth it. Jack Kennedy and I put on black woollen caps and crept off into the night, laden with 'goodies', as Jack called them. Hostilities commenced.

I glanced at my watch, which, along with the others', had been synchronized with Gerald's, which had itself been synchronized with the radio signal from the atomic clock in Colorado earlier that afternoon. It was 1757 hours. Gerald had instructed us to wait until 1804 hours. We did.

We hurled our initial volley of 6 smoke bombs, coming at Gipper from a 45° off midline, me on the left and Jack on the right. Jack could throw about 40 yards, and I could manage a good 50 or 55, and we created an elaborate cross-hatching pattern with these first half-dozen. Then Jack began to work the Bottle while I dealt with the various bombs, skillfully alternating the M-80s and the firecrackers with the smokers.

It went quite well, and we obeyed our orders ('Under *no* circumstances are you to get closer than 40 yards of their fort!') to the letter. We deployed our ammunition at such a rate that, it seemed, we were proving successful at concealing the true paucity of our numbers. We worked together so flawlessly, in fact, Jack & I, that it felt not so much like a well-tuned machine as like an organic whole, the organs of a larger body, something truly alive. We slipped into that synergistic groove, that transcendent Zone, for some minutes, disregarding our watches, trusting our instincts. I am certain that we had the defenders both panicked and baffled, that they would have scratched their collective heads if we had given them time to do so. But we didn't. We were uncannily aggressive. I know this for a fact, because barely a round came out of their fort for every five or six of ours that went in.

Then Fortune spun her wheel … and suddenly, I felt hollow, almost nauseous. Then I felt it radiating from my stomach to my nerve-endings, like the kind of lightning that moves from ground to cloud instead of vice versa. Reverse lightning. I felt it, well in advance of any substantive evidence, any merely sensory input could corroborate it. I felt it long before anything actually *happened*.

I glanced down at my watch, for the first time since 1804 hours. It was 1812, eight minutes in.

At 1813 hours we were supposed to deploy our penultimate rounds, and then I was to move 10 yards closer, close enough to put my final 2 smokers just *behind* their fort, on either side. Jack had our team's one signal flare with him (a six-inch, 10-ball cylinder), and he would light it simultaneously with my final volley, which would signal the by-now-ensconced and ready-to-pounce Bobby to ready himself.

I broke silence for the first time, and shouted the codeword, 'Balls', over to Jack. He had anchored the fireworks tube in to the ground, lit it, and I hucked the first of the final 3 smoke bombs. I had two left, and nothing else. The last of my confidence escaped into the ether, and was replaced by that empty, vacant feeling. I was now defenceless, and somewhat afraid. The phosphorous spheres shot up, one after the other at 3 second intervals, each briefly lighting up the sky over our heads. Jack, Bobby and I were all to wait for the last of the charges (and to count to 30 Mississippis, in case of a dud round), and then we were to carry out our Final Orders. After throwing my final two smokers behind their fort, I was to advance with Jack into the rapidly clearing area

25 yards out, and the two of us were to make targets of ourselves, dashing back and forth in front of their fort to distract them while Bobby came at their flag from behind.

The fifth ball of fireworks shot up, exploded like a star, then the sixth, and seventh. This was it. I had my final rounds ready, one in my pocket, the other in my right hand. In my left I held a Bic lighter. My teeth were clenched together.

The eighth ball hadn't yet shot up when I began to feel my right hand getting hot. I looked down. The smoke bomb was already alight, and was starting to burn my hand. I didn't stop to think, let alone wait for the fireworks to finish off. I simply hucked the thing, just to get it out of my hand.

Gipper's fort erupted into flames. The smoke bomb had landed right on top of it, a direct hit. Gipper's guards panicked, scattered. I instinctively wheeled around, to look back for Gerald. Standing right behind me was Victor, tossing and spinning a Bic lighter in the air. He winked at me, and grinned.

—What did he do? Amē asks, somewhat agitated now.

—Guess, I say.

—Did he…?

—What do you think?

—But, what happened with the *fire*?

—Hey, no big deal, Gerald ran to the house and got a fire extinguisher.

—Was it *far*? She says this last word loudly enough to turn heads a few tables over.

—Not very.

—And?

—And, I guess, he somehow managed to put the thing out.

—Jesus! How'd he…?

—Beats me. He only took a minute or two to get back, but by that time the fire was, I dunno, 20 by 20.

—Feet?

—Yards.

—But Victor? What about Vic—*Victor*?

She is surprisingly angry about this, almost as if she were me, the me I used to be.

—What? I say.

—What, she says, just what was that bastard's fucking *deal*?

—He was just a kid, I say. All of us, we were all just kids. You know, boys.

—Yeah, I know. Boys. Yeah.

We got into a predictable amount of trouble over all that. I never told Gerald what had happened out there, just before the fire, and I doubt that Victor would have, either. The upshot, anyhow, was that I didn't speak to my brother for the better part of a week, content to let him silently and mistakenly blame me. Keeping him in the dark and angry gave me something on him, I knew: possessing information that he lacked raised me just a little bit higher in my own estimation. It gave me an edge, an edge that, before, I never knew that I needed.

I felt smug, I felt powerful, I felt as if I had been given a peek into a book of esoteric knowledge of some kind. I had to guard it, I had to keep it to myself, lest it be taken away from me.

Something new, something *given* to me? I wonder, now, if that's the way it was. Or was it, rather, that this edge or power or whatever it was that I now felt I *had* was in fact the result of something having been *already taken* away? Was this new presence, in fact, an absence? Or what?

It was, in any case, a new development. Change of some kind, if not progress or growth. This was a whole new way of thinking about myself and others, and it had just arrived like that, unbidden. It was just a part of the architecture of adolescence that I was entering, I supposed, like pubic hair and body odour. I was, of course, unaware that adolescence was itself merely an opening, a gateway. Looking back, I'm now predisposed to see it in terms of descent, or fall. I know that if I had had a less happy childhood, or if my experiences in 'adult life' had been better, I might see it differently. I might, but I don't.

Here's how I see it. For me, adolescence is an opening into a kind of chute, into which the fuel, our blinking childhood, is poured. There's a furnace in the basement; it's inefficient, and it pollutes. But it produces energy. Energy to keep us going. Energy for other purposes.

—Victor was Gerald's *best friend*, I say (aware that I am being underhanded, that I am as tendentious as they come). I am his *brother*. You are/were, whichever, his *girl*-friend.

This seems to confuse her, is not the answer that she expects, or wants. She gets defensive, gets her back up a bit. *Good.*

—Are you equating us, you and me, with Victor? she says. Because there is no us, Isaac, despite what you might think or desire. You can't make me feel guilty: I haven't done anything.

—Yessss. But you *are* running away.

—Not running—going. Leaving a mess that I didn't make.
 Perfect.

—That's right, it just 'happened'. I agree. You're right. *Point Finale*, case closed, bye-bye.

—Ok, go ahead, mock me, fine. But this, er, 'attraction' between us has showed me that I don't really love him the way I thought I did, that it's time to, to move on I guess, to be blunt and callous and all that crap about it.

—That's it, you got it. Move on. Ease on down the road.

—Funny.

—Keep on keepin' on.

—Ha.

I decide to accelerate the process of this 'facilitation'.

—You don't love him at all, I remind her, as gravely and with as much 'concern' as I can muster.

—I don't love him.

—Me neither.

She turns away now, cups her poor forehead in a support formed by her thumb and forefinger, and I know that the best part is coming. This is what she came for, what I've been preparing her for, and now she's found her place in the script. It should all be downhill from here. Wait for it, now, breathe, take it in, bud:

—I don't love you either, she says, bravely.

—Me neither.

—At least we're clear on this, she says.

—Crystal, I say, adding a jaunty little wink.

—Your problem is … she says, looking skyward now.…

But then she jumps the gun a little, slaps a tenner on the table, stands up, takes two paces away, one back, as if remembering that she'd forgotten to finish her sentence. Her mouth opens, closes. She goes. She misses out on the punch line, on the totalising revelation or epiphany. She doesn't get to hear what happened next.

What happened next was I went to the little red-haired girl at the bus stop, the one Gerald was oh-so-shyly sweet on. Phooey to that, of course. I went and I told her what Victor had said to me

after I'd burned my hand. I told her that Gerald made it a habit
of following her through the hallways at school. I told her that
he timed his arrivals at the bus stop to hers. I told her to check
it out: guaranteed he'd be sitting one table over at lunch, facing
her. She took it all in, mostly blank-faced, but with a tiny movement at the corner of her lip, which I took to be meant for me,
for my concern for her well-being. She started getting rides to
school with her dad.

Advent came (and with it the mandatory trip to the Confessional),
leading up to Christmas and New Year's, which were uneventful. Then big winter storms dumped all over us, and when one
of them caused the State of Emergency to be declared we learned
that Governor Michael Dukakis showed great fortitude and lead-
ership. Spring came and went, and when school got out Mr. Jones
got my dad nominated, seconded and voted in for membership
in the Yacht Squadron two towns over, where all the Newcomers
went. Dad moved us into a bigger house in an older part of town,
about five miles away. We all got new friends. Gerald stopped
going to church, and got an after school job to save up for a stereo
and for college, in case his plans for the AIR FORCE ACADEMY
fell through. Then I blinked and school started up again, and I
discovered I'd somehow made it to Grade 8, and had been thrown
into the BMOC category at the middle school. Then quite suddenly

we'd come full circle, and it was nearly Thanksgiving, and I found myself dating my first girlfriend just before my thirteenth birthday. We met at a pep rally, just before the annual homecoming game against Cohasset. Her name was Liz. She was older, in Gerald's grade.

8

HE GREW OUT OF IT: 1997, TORONTO

THEN, Amē says, blushing and covering her mouth with the
back of her hand, the way an embarrassed Japanese woman
might. Then I simply pedalled off. To Japan and Tim, then to Oz,
and then to Singapore, and then back here and....

—And the 'Kid'? David says. 'Kid River'?

She doesn't say. She says:

—The Shawinigan Kid. Roger Scruton.

—It's a bit odd, isn't it, that he met this Victor fellow on his way ...
to see *you*?

—The Kid's a press secretary now. For the Minister of Finance,
or the Shadow Minister, whatever.

—But this Victor, I don't quite get it, get him, quite. I mean....

She fixes the Entrepreneur in her gaze, stabs her third half-
smoked MARLBORO into the ashtray in front of them, which is
shaped like Elmer Fudd's befuddled head. She assesses the situation for the umpteenth time that evening. No, he doesn't appear

put off. Quite to the contrary: he seems smitten, almost—if one can use that word anymore, nowadays. Yes, smitten, maybe, as if all her indiscretions, her bumblings and stumblings through her own and other people's lives were not pushing him away at all, but drawing him very much 'in'. The fact that she intrigued him intrigued her.

—Victor? she says carelessly. Him? There's nothing to get. He was just a little shithead, that's all. Maybe he grew out of it, who knows?

9

THE EXTASIE: 1977, DUXBURY

THEY ARE BACK at Victor's house, at work on another Project. This one is a 1:18 scale model General Dynamics F-16A Fighting Falcon (affectionately known by its pilots as 'The Viper'), done up in the red, white and blue markings of the original 1973 YF-16 prototype. Gerald watches as Victor tenderly dabs the tip of the needle of the delicate, slender nose of the jet with just a drop of TESTORS MODEL MASTER FS37038 FLAT BLACK from out of one of the dozens of ½ oz. bottles on the counter, while Victor lectures on the jet's chief innovations: its ability to engage in dogfights (unlike the fighters of the 1950s and 60s, which had sacrificed manoeuverability for speed — on account of a spurious Pentagon theory about a permanent historical shift in the nature of air combat), and its afterburner engines, for heretofore unbelievable range in such a compact plane.

Victor, who has better fine motor skills, has done the majority of the assembly and the painting. Gerald is the one with the cash flow, and has procured the paints, which were not inexpensive, and has helped out otherwise where he could. Gerald holds their fragile little baby and proudly dotes on each precious detail, tenderly caressing each & every curve. It looks pretty damn good, he has to admit. Victor pulls out his walkie talkie, and motions for Gerald to do the same. It occurs to Gerald that both he and his friend's last names are represented by the same call sign.

> But O alas, so long, so far
> Our bodies why do we forbear?
> They are ours, though they are not we, we are
> The intelligences, they the spheres.
>
> We owe them thanks, because they thus,
> Did us, to us, at first convey,
> Yielded their forces, sense, to us,
> Nor are dross to us, but allay.
>
> On man heaven's influence works not so,
> But that it first imprints the air,
> So soul into the soul may flow,
> Though it to body first repair.
>
> As our blood labours to beget
> Spirits, as like souls as it can,
> Because such fingers need to knit
> That subtle thought, which makes us man:

—So, then, Victor says, Geronimo Tango, over.

—I read you Victor Tango, over.

—Uh, did *it* go smoothly? Over.

—That's affirmative Victor Tango, over. Putting down the walkie talkie, he continues: It was wicked awesome. Got to tell ya though, I had a friggin' sweatball happening, nearly shit myself thinking she'd come back before I was done.

 Victor puts his walkie talkie down. —Wicked, he says.

—Yeah. You remember *A Bridge Too Far*? We saw it in Hanover?

—With my friggin' *mother*?

—Yeah.

—Uh-huh.

—That scene with Robert Redford, where he's paddling across the river at night, is it Nijmegen or Eindhoven—

—Nijmegen.

—And shells are bursting all around? That was me. I was him, saying Hail Mary's over-and-over, I don't know why, but I did, I kept saying 'em, like a tape loop or somethin' as I crept towards those plants. I don't know why, but those 20 seconds seemed to take hours.

—I know why.

—Why?

—Simple. You were afraid. Afraid she'd catch you with my dad's test tubes, near her precious things. There'd have been no excuse you coulda made that woulda been good enough. You knew it. So you were afraid.

Gerald is embarrassed. He stares at, shuffles his feet.

—You're right, I was, he says.

—There's no shame in being afraid, Gerald. It was a brave thing you did today. Unethical I grant you, but brave nonetheless. And there's no bravery without fear, you know.

—I know.

Silence, as both boys reflect on this thought.

> So must pure lovers' souls descend
> T'affections, and to faculties,
> Which sense may reach and apprehend,
> Else a great prince in prison lies.

—But I kinda feel sorry for her, you know? Gerald says.

—I know. But you had to teach her a lesson. You had to *show* her.

—Miss Stone.

—Her.

—You think so?

—Not really I guess. Nevertheless, the fact remains, you *did* show her.

—I did. I guess I did.

—Let me tell you something, Gerald. The mission you accomplished today was real, it was true, do you follow?

—Yeah, I guess.

—Let me tell you something. My old man? He's been a liar and a coward all his life. He was a draft dodger, Gerald, I'm sure you heard it somewheres, his name, Roger the Dodger. And I'll tell you something else: you know how he used to tell me, us, that he was a scientist, that he worked on inventing these new pesticides and herbicides, the very ones that were in your arsenal today? Well I'll tell you something I've known for a while now, a long while actually, and I'm glad I don't have to keep it to myself anymore. Fuck it, Gerald, my dad was no scientist. He's a technician, a fucking quality control fucking laboratory technician. He does fuck-all for a living, Gerald, and it's not a very good one, I don't have to tell you that.

Gerald says nothing, but looks at him with understanding. He picks up the F-16.

> To our bodies turn we then, that so
> Weak men on love revealed may look;
> Love's mysteries in souls do grow,
> But yet the body is his book.

— She sure is a beaut', he says, with a tentative finger on the fuse-lage. You wanna go test her out?

ROSARIVM

CONIVNCTIO SIVE
Coitus.

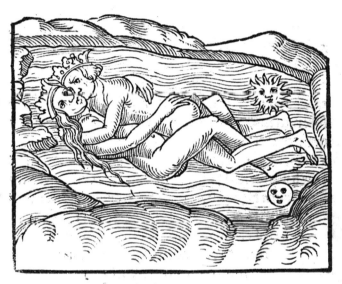

O Luna durch meyn vmbgeben/ vnd suffe mynne/
Wirstu schön/ starck/ vnd gewaltig als ich byn.

O Sol/ du bist vber alle liecht zu erkennen/
So bedarffstu doch mein als der han der hennen.

ARISLEVS IN VISIONE.

Coniunge ergo filium tuum Gabricum dile-
ctiorem tibi in omnibus filijs tuis cum sua sorore
Beya

ACKNOWLEDGEMENTS

The author gratefully acknowledges the following artists for the use of their work in the making of *White Mythology:*

Front Matter — Emblem VIII ("Take the egg and pierce it with a fiery sword"), *Atalanta Fugiens* — Michael Maier (1617).

Pg. 1 — Scrooge Extinguishes The First of Three Spirits, fourth illustration in Charles Dickens's *A Christmas Carol* — John Leech (London: Chapman and Hall, 1843). Courtesy of Philip V. Allingham, Victorianweb.org.

Pg. 117 — Emblem IX ("Putrefactio"), *Philosophia Reformata* — Johann Daniel Mylius (1622).

Pg. 233 — Proserpine (oil on canvas) — Dante Gabriel Rosetti (1874). Courtesy of Art Resource.

Pg. 235 — lithographed by W.E. McFarlane "The wedding-guest sat on a stone...", Plate 2, Coleridge's *Rime of the Ancient Mariner* — J. Noel Paton, (Art Union of London, 1863), Courtesy of Chris Mullen, Fulltable.com.

Pg. 284—Doggerel verse sung by Ted inspired by "The Stranger Song", *Songs of Leonard Cohen* (Copyright 1967 Sony Music Entertainment (Canada) Inc).

Pg. 407—Emblem XXX ("Luna is as requisite to Sol as a Hen is to a Cock"), *Atalanta Fugiens*—Michael Maier (1617).

Pg. 416—Song lyrics inspired by "Like Soldiers Do", *Brewing Up With Billy Bragg*—Billy Bragg (Copyright: Sony/ATV Music Publishing (UK) Limited, 1984).

End Matter—Alchemical Wedding, from *Rosarium Philosophorum* (1550). Also reprinted in *Artis Auriferae* (1593), *Bibliotheca Chemical Curiosa* (1702), *C.G. Jung's Psychology and Alchemy* (1953), and Leonard Cohen's *Death of A Lady's Man* (McClelland And Stewart Ltd., Toronto, 1978).

Capsules image on back cover—Beschreibung: Kapseln *Fotograf: Markus Würfel *Copyright Status: GNU Freie Dokumentationslizenz.

Selections concerning weather forecasting—Quoted verbatim from *The Weather Handbook* (Bloomsbury press, 1994) by Alan Watts.

The author would also like to thank the following for their support and assistance in the making of this book: William and Joan Clarke, Dr. Kenneth Clarke, Karen Christie, Evie Christie, and Dave Bricker.

CPSIA information can be obtained at www.ICGtesting.com
Printed in the USA
LVOW10*0820190616

493159LV00001B/2/P

9 780991 710034